While

Cerberus

Sleeps

A Novel

Leah Noel Sims

November 2016
ATLANTA, GEORGIA

For those who listen, and those who question.

1.

"HESPERIA WATCHES," the caller said. Someone screamed in the background. The call died.

Anxiety ripped through Mila. From her back-row seat in the Hesperia Broadcasting Network newsroom, she stared at her holodesk and prayed the anonymous revolutionary—the Belgae man—would call again.

She glanced around. Everyone else sat ramrod straight, fingers tapping away in a purposeful symphony. They ignored her, the lackey. Overnight shifts passed the slowest—and at three in the morning, she still had five more brutal hours to go.

Ringing erupted from her holodesk's communication panel. She jumped to answer it, tapping the button connecting the call to the berry-sized earpiece she wore.

"HBN, what's your breaking news tip?"

"Here's my tip," the female caller snapped. "Why don't you all start showing the news happening in Hesperia? I don't pay to hear about other countries!"

Mila ended the call. She cradled her head in her hands and groaned. Had she really been an entry-level viewer specialist for almost three years? She had graduated summa cum laude from a prestigious Hesperia university and entertained hopes that her high-powered diploma and diligent work ethic would've propelled her journalism career further forward by now. She had envisioned herself contributing to something meaningful. Instead, her job predominantly called upon her to be a human dumping ground for viewers with irate complaints, psychological fits, and violent threats. Legitimate news tips came few and far between.

The communication panel rang again. The ID read unknown. "HBN, what's your breaking news?"

"It's me," he said.

She puffed out a relieved breath. "Oh—good. I was afraid something terrible had happened." As the words left her lips, she shook her head in disbelief. Her coworkers would ridicule her if they knew she truly cared for this nameless person—the one they hung up on, the one they said was crazy—who had called the tip hotline for months. He'd never even given her a real tip. Not one the network would look into, anyway. Yet she listened—God help her. She always listened.

"Sorry. Things are starting to heat up over here," he said.

"At the Belgae camp in Pacifica?" She was the only person she knew who referred to the revolutionaries by their chosen name. Everyone else—if they even knew about the Belgae—called them extremists, especially HBN. But the network hardly ever covered the story about the Hesperians who, enraged at the government's alleged citizen surveillance program and reports of false imprisonments, claimed to seek secession.

"Yeah. Did you ever look into the Hesperia Domestic Safety Act?" he asked.

"No, sorry."

"But you *have* heard of it."

"Yes, of course."

"Not *of course*. No one knows history anymore. No one knows anything that matters anymore.

That's partly why I trust you, Mila. You know things that actually matter."

Too many things. Her parents had drilled it all—history, literature, philosophy—into her, year after year. Grooming her for a shared destiny: To save society by overthrowing Hesperia. A radical's destiny. It was a future that they never had, that she didn't want.

"Look up the Domestic Safety Act, while I'm on the phone."

Opening a browser in her web panel, Mila searched and found pages of results, but her journalist's training taught her to select the most original document. She chose a result from the Hesperia Ministry of the Interior and scanned the legislation.

"It lets them detain anyone," he explained.

"Really? Anyone?" If her coworkers could hear her, they'd call her gullible.

"Anyone they deem a threat to domestic peace, whether a person is an actual terrorist or associated with domestic terrorism."

"That sounds like necessary legislation."

"Except that they've given no definition for what constitutes an association with domestic terrorism. A professional tie? Casual friendship? Wave on the street? We don't know—"

"Wait." She sighed, pausing at the end of the document. "This was passed over two hundred years ago. The corpse of The Former Nation hadn't even had time to cool."

"So?"

"Everything was different then. The Hesperia Territory was different in the wake of the previous nation's collapse. The Gair Empire in the East had just acquired us. The domestic climate boiled. What do you think the likelihood is that Hesperia still enforces such old, irrelevant legislation?"

"They do, Mila. Trust me. Now more than ever. Our government is abject. Our freedoms are a façade—"

Noise in the background—yelling, pounding—cut him off and silenced him.

"What did you mean when you said Hesperia watches?" she asked.

"Wait—hold on."

She strained to make out what the other revolutionaries shouted in the background.

"Oh my God," he breathed.

"What is it?" She pressed her earpiece deeper into her ear, as if that would clarify the muddy voices. Her palm left a sweaty print on the holodesk's black glass top. "Are you all okay?"

"I have something real for you this time, Mila. I'm emailing a video. You have to get it covered—promise."

"You know I can't promise that. No reporter has ever looked into tips I've given them about these kinds of things. What's going on?"

"I gotta go."

The call died.

In seconds, the video arrived with a note, "Hesperia murdered one of us."

She tapped on the attachment and opened the video. A dead man, clothed darkly from head to toe, lay in a muddy, grassy field. His face, blown apart. The camera moved in, and Mila swallowed to suppress the nausea welling in her gut. She forced herself to witness the shards of his skull, the bloody carrion from his brain matter, and his lower jaw, the lone portion of his head that remained intact.

She clamped her hands over her mouth, then jerked them back to her lap. Glancing around the newsroom, she hoped no one watched her. Unlike the veteran news people surrounding her, she never could get used to the vicious images she encountered in her job, no matter how many she saw. Human suffering tore through her heart like a jagged, rusty spear.

Did blood ever buy real, lasting freedom? She knew what her father would have said. "It's the only acceptable currency, whether we like it or not."

Taking a deep breath, she tamped down her emotions and closed the video. Finally, she had a tip good enough for Alyson Vernon. The senior investigative reporter had won innumerable awards. Mila had admired Alyson for years and had eyed her in the HBN newsroom, but she had never received a tip she considered good enough to bring to her. Until now.

She pulled out a compact and examined her appearance. Smudged mascara bordered her heterochromic eyes—one a dove gray, the other peridot green. She wiped the black blots away, smoothed her auburn hair, and stood. Even at four in the morning, the newsroom buzzed with journalism's special brand of frenzy. Mila walked toward the opposite end where the investigative team sat.

Alyson looked up as she approached. "What do you want?" she snapped.

Painfully aware of her inferior role, she hurried to speak. "My name is Mila Ray with Viewer Services, and a caller gave me a video that I think you'll want to look at."

"Why would I want to look at it?" Alyson didn't roll her eyes, but she might as well have.

"Because it shows the first fatality in the argument between Hesperia and the Belgae," Mila asserted. "I have the contact information for the person who sent it. In his message, he said he's with the Belgae."

"Fine, send it to me."

Mila couldn't tell if Alyson wanted the video or simply saw placation as the most efficient way to dismiss her pest, but she nodded anyway and left, bewildered by the off-camera reality of her role model.

~~~

Eight o'clock couldn't arrive fast enough. By the time it did, a tension migraine wrapped its tentacles around Mila's head, clutching it so tightly she thought she'd vomit. Working overnight shifts had corroded her health, and she had come to expect a migraine on a weekly basis. As she left HBN, she squinted against the searing morning light of the early July sun and stumbled down the busy New England streets, idly wondering what her surroundings had been called before Hesperia renamed them all, consolidating forty-eight states into six regions—New England, Appalachia, Bay, Rocky Mountains, Plains, and Pacifica. More of the many things she'd known once, but forgotten.

Street and city names remained the ghostly bridge between The Former Nation and the current one.

Her bones felt hollow with exhaustion. She boarded the humid subway, collapsed into a seat, and prayed the contents of her stomach would stay put, at least until she arrived home.

Hourly, she thought about quitting HBN. At times, the idea danced and twirled at the forefront of her mind and screamed in her ears. But it wasn't so simple. It wasn't about quintessential success or achievement. It wasn't about what HBN could do for Mila's resume. It was about what she could do for the people of Hesperia. Never mind the opportunities at smaller news outlets, the ones that offered an improved quality of life. At HBN, the largest, most influential news outlet in her country, Mila could hope to make a profound difference eventually.

She gazed at the world and saw stories. Beyond the stories, messages. They played over and over, echoing in her ears. The stories were more than hearsay from faceless viewers. All too often, Mila could dig up a small town article or the minutes from a city council meeting that backed up claims—or at least showed they may not be untrue. Yet no matter how much research she presented to the assignment editors, no matter how often she followed up on the tips she submitted, many stories remained untold.

Hesperian society appeared to her as a choppy, algae-colored ocean scattered with messages in bottles—important ones cast out from hopeful hands. They floated unread, some of them written in the tears and blood of their composers. Mila ardently combed through the bottles, searched their messages deeply for truth, and fought—mostly unsuccessfully—to get the messages heard. The Hesperia Broadcasting Network was to Mila as the looming church doors of Wittenburg were to Martin Luther. She walked toward the doors. If she turned around, traded her purpose for a social life or even her health, the messages would gnaw at her because she saw the ocean, she beheld the bottles, she read the messages, but walked away. And for what reasons—selfish ones?

No. Quitting was not an option.

~~~

"Okay, time to put the qanna away," Mila called to her roommate as she opened their apartment door. The metallic, earthy-scented smoke filled her nostrils and sent fresh stabs of pain through her head. She cringed.

Sam, a stringy-haired, sallow-skinned blonde rolled her eyes. "Screw you," she responded lackadaisically, a twisted grin on her pallid face. She rocked forward off their sunken, black couch in the living room and slithered down the hall and into her room on the right, looking so thin she might as well have had an exoskeleton. Sam wasn't the type of roommate Mila had in mind when she found herself in need of a new one, but provided that Sam hid her affinity for psychoactive drugs from the Hesperia Amity officers and paid her rent on time, she could ignore her quirks.

Mila flung her purse and keys onto the rickety entryway table and followed Sam's path down the hall, but turned left into her own bedroom and flung the door shut to prevent the nauseating smell of qanna from filling her room any more. The room was small, with mustard yellow fabric draped around the top perimeter to hide cracks in the drywall. Scuffs and stains from previous residents scarred the tan walls. Mila closed her curtains for optimum darkness and undressed quickly, eager to get into her bed, but the picture on her nightstand caught her eye. Within its simple black frame was a photo of a bald man with a salt-and-pepper mustache, his gray eyes crinkled in happiness as he hugged a ginger-haired woman with soulful green eyes and a faraway, dreamy smile. Mila sat on her bed and gazed at the photo. Her phone screeched and broke her reverie.

"Hello?"

"Mila, it's Mark," her real estate agent replied. "Just wanted to let you know the house is selling today. The buyers are scheduled for the contract signing at ten this morning. Congratulations."

"Great, thanks for all your help, Mark."

Relief and sadness peppered her voice. Her childhood home in Clearwater-Florida, Bay Region, had been her burden to bear since the mysterious gas explosion had robbed her of her parents and their Old Tampa Bay inn a year and a half ago, but it felt like burying them all over again to see it gone forever. This final piece of Fredrick and Anne Ray's estate was now taken care of, yet Mila found no peace, no closure. Amity officers had never pinpointed the cause of the explosion. Had it truly been an unfortunate accident? Or had her parents—the dormant revolutionaries—roused for another fight, not knowing it would be their last? That option didn't make sense, either. They'd always been so careful. Paranoid, even. How many times had her father cautioned her about timing and vigilance? How often had he rattled off the names of their ancestors who'd been caught by Hesperia, and worse? If the pieces had fallen into place—if the Rays had found the right movement ready to act at the right time, with the right tools— they surely would have told their daughter, even if she had refused to join them. But they'd said nothing. Now, they never could.

2.

THE LITTLE BRASS BELL over the door of Eddie's Rummage Shop jingled when Mila entered. The shop's cool air clashed with the clammy July heat outside. Tugging on her blazer, she glanced at the clock hanging above Eddie's counter. Just enough time to see if he had any good books, and then maybe a cup of coffee before her next overnight shift.

As usual, she was the only one in the book section at the very back corner of the cluttered store. Eddie never had a good selection, but his was the only store in all of New Cockaigne-New England that sold books, at least to her knowledge. After all, Hesperians didn't read much, and if they did they read on screens, not paper. Paper books had become collectors' items and decorations long ago.

Sighing, she brushed her finger over the dim spines of several hardbacks. What did she expect to find? Hesperia had halted the availability of any written works that mattered. "Lack of demand" was their official reason, but she knew better. "Dull minds are easy to rule," her mother used to say.

Shuffling footsteps interrupted her thoughts. Mila turned toward a teetering tower of old crates, figurines, and cracked dolls just in time to see Eddie, a short, stocky man with circular glasses, peek out from behind it.

"We close in fifteen. Help you find anything?"

"No—well—I don't know. You don't have a copy of *Areopagitica*, do you?" She bit her lip, unable to believe she'd actually asked the question. John Milton's essay on free speech and expression was probably one of the first on Hesperia's literary hit list.

Eddie's thin eyebrows knitted together. "Doll, I can't say I've ever heard the word before. But there's some pretty ones in that stack, right there." He pointed before disappearing again.

Mila shook her head. Like the eyeless dolls and scraped up horse figurines next to her, books were just more junk to Eddie, meaningless except for the minuscule profit they might deliver. God, what she wouldn't give to have her family's books again.

The Ray books—her family library—held titles collected by her father and his ancestors, their lone, small victory against the government they'd tried to change, expose, and overthrow throughout generations. With works spanning literature, philosophy, history, psychology, sociology, anthropology, and even essays, most of the library had been considered contraband since Hesperia's inception. Like centurions preserving knowledge, they had lined the shelves of her parents' living room, creating the best kind of wallpaper from their navy, hunter green, black, and burgundy bindings, their gold-leaf titles shimmering even in dim light.

A deep ache for the books, even if only to feel their weight in her hands, filled her. But even if she could retrieve them without Hesperia catching her, she had no space for them in her apartment. They'd have to stay hidden in their dark Florida storage shed, like a nobleman tossed into a pauper's grave.

Turning, Mila glanced at the pile Eddie had pointed toward, stuffed under a rickety, scratched end table. She knelt and her eyes drifted over the titles, locking on a thin, yellowed pamphlet wedged underneath a hardback, third from the bottom. Carefully, she slipped it out from the stack. It flopped, flimsy with age, perhaps as many as fifty years old.

Antidote to Apathy: A Plea to the Hesperian People.

The crooked, blotchy text looked as though it had been composed on some kind of archaic machine—distributed illegally, to avoid detection by Amity officers. No author's name sat proudly underneath. Biting her lip, Mila flipped it over, then began searching the inner first pages for any clue to the writer's identity.

In the bottom center of each page, she spotted a symbol, bleached into the paper. Squinting, she brought the paper closer, her heart tripping over itself as she discerned the swirling, circular emblem.

Tyrannis Letum? The fringe revolutionary group had been slaughtered by Hesperian forces more than seventy-five years ago, the night before they'd planned to go to battle. Theirs was one of many uprisings that had been erased from Hesperian history, but not the Ray family's long memory. Mila's great-great grandfather had been a member. The Ray books contained a copy.

How had this one gotten into Eddie's Rummage Shop? Had a Belgae member placed it, or had it gotten thrown in a pile of donations? The forbidden, familiar work burned in Mila's hands. But if she bought it, Hesperia would know.

"Sir?" she called out. It was a risk, asking like this. But it made no sense for him to carry the book. Would he be suspicious?

"Yeah?" Eddie answered, his voice coming from the store's front.

"You don't happen to have anything called *Antidote to Apathy*, do you?"

"That's a medical suspense, right?"

"Um, I'm not sure."

"Let me check my database."

Mila held her breath and waited until Eddie finally called, "Nope, sorry." Opening her blazer, she slipped the pamphlet inside its lining. Guilt gripped her. She'd never stolen before. Scanning the remaining books, she grabbed an old, gold-colored hardback from a stack and brought it to the front desk to purchase.

"Good choice," Eddie said, processing her payment. "You know, some people rip out pages and muss them up, maybe paint something over them, toss them in a frame. Looks classy."

"Good idea," she said.

On the sidewalk, Mila hugged her blazer tightly around her and headed toward The Phonograph, a coffee shop near HBN. The city lights blared in the dark like a galaxy fallen to earth. She turned her gaze upward at the skyscrapers, a musing habit that had resulted in more than her fair share of trips, bumps, and hasty apologies. So many of their windows were dark, and had been for scores. Things had changed much and not so much since Hesperia's inception. Mila's teachers said it was all for the best. Technology hadn't stagnated, they insisted, it had simply reached its peak. Jobs were plentiful, but the workplace culture had morphed—no one needed the excessive office space anymore. The empty skyscrapers loomed as unlit monuments to progress.

Mila sniffed at the memory of her teacher's explanations. Like a sweater assailed by moths, her formal education was thin in some areas and had holes in so many others. Yet Hesperia made it virtually impossible to pursue any other form of education, recognizing only public education for admittance to college, which was why her parents had elected to supplement her public education with their own: the Ray books. She'd resented it, at first—forcing her to attend their own school as well as Hesperia's. But as she read, the books had seemed to change in her grasp, transforming from mere ink on paper to irreplaceable treasures. Her heart, too, had melted toward her parents. Instead of seeing them as educational drill sergeants, she had regarded them and her ancestors as curators of knowledge who would guard the truth and fight for it, no matter the cost. Even if she eventually came to disagree with *how* they wanted to do it.

She pushed open the wooden door of The Phonograph, shoving aside the memories of her dead parents, the Ray books, and the images of the hauntingly empty skyscrapers. In the coffee shop—with its cozy seating and rustic stone walls—she could forget the holes in her world, the loved ones gone too soon, and her inferior job, and lose herself in the way hot coffee warmed her neglected insides. Cradling her mug, she curled into one of two large, plum-colored chairs tucked into a corner near a window.

From her seat, she watched. A couple snuggled on one side of a brown couch as an elderly man read on the other. A group of well-coiffed young women chattered wildly over the cover article for a tabloid magazine they shared. Students studied. Baristas whispered behind the pastry case.

As she absorbed the vignettes unfolding around her in comforting normalcy, her thoughts drifted back to the Belgae, then to Hesperia's Domestic Safety Act. Could it be that as everyone gathered and sashayed through their seemingly stable world, something stirred beneath? Could it be that this stirring was made possible—and the groaning of the imprisoned kept silent—by the mere perception of security by the majority? Mila shook her head, dispelling the thought. Attempting to anchor herself in the world of the seen instead of what might lie beneath, she glanced around The Phonograph, locking eyes with a girl in a green, long-sleeved shirt sitting in the chair next to her. Had she been there the whole time?

Mila smiled, but the girl looked away and began tracing patterns in the velvet chair.

She scrutinized the girl. Her full lips pressed together like a dam holding emotions at bay. Mila noticed her pants, tattered and wet at the bottom for being too long, and watched the girl attempt to fade into the background of her environment, molding to the curves of the chair. Her desire to remain unnoticed emanated around her.

Not wanting to cause embarrassment, Mila leaned close. "Do you need anything?"

"No, thank you," she said softly. "My ride should be here soon." She looked back to her lap, and Mila followed her sightline.

Fresh bruises and raised scars covered her palms and fingers. How many more hid under her sweater? She withdrew a scratched-up phone from her pocket and pressed the buttons but the screen stubbornly remained dark.

She inhaled deeply and met Mila's gaze once more. Her eyes shimmered with brewing tears. "Could I possibly use your phone, if you have one?"

"Of course." Mila retrieved hers from her purse and gave it to the girl, who walked outside. She watched out the window as the girl paced on the dark sidewalk. Soon, her hand flew up to cover her face. Her chest heaved as though she gasped for breath. Finally, she pulled the phone away from her cheek and looked at it bitterly.

A few minutes later, the girl walked back in with a confident smile, but redness colored her cheeks and the whites of her eyes. "Thank you," she said, a catch in her voice as she returned the phone. "I really appreciate it."

Mila searched the girl's face. "Do you need a ride somewhere?" Mila didn't need a vehicle in a city with a vast public transit system, but she kept her parents' magnecar if ever she needed to venture farther than the metropolis. A short subway ride back to her apartment building to get the car, that's all it would take.

"Um..." She fumbled in her pocket, producing a crumpled piece of paper, so flimsy from wear it flopped around like fabric. "Maybe you could drive me... to this address, if it's not too much?

Mila examined the address—an hour outside of New Cockaigne-New England. She'd be drastically late to work. But the girl was utterly alone and abandoned, not unlike herself, and all those bruises and scabs.... What if she was in danger?

If Mila didn't help her, who would?

"Of course," she answered.

~~~

Mila drove along precarious, two-lane roads, some unpaved and none lit. Roadways had been magnetized long ago in order to cooperate with the development of hovering, self-driving vehicles. Paved roads interacted with magnecars like a dance, propelling them according to the destination set by the driver via the autodrive system. For more rural, unpaved areas—like this one—the magnecar reverted to four-wheel drive. Mila focused hard on the road, clenching the steering wheel. It had been years since she'd been a driver, not a pilot.

The girl—Haley, she'd said—stiffened as their destination grew nearer.

"This place we're going," Haley began, "I don't exactly know what it is."

"That's okay."

"I just... needed to leave. For good."

"I know," Mila said softly.

People spoke of this place, this bucolic vicinity away from the city, as being quite the place for repose in its day, before the land became Hesperia. Mila supposed it still held some of that appeal, but the charming Cape Cod-style homes bore chipped paint, their lawns marred by fallen fences. Beauty with a twinge of eeriness. Especially now, when the magnecar's headlights illuminated only a sliver of the dark.

As the paper instructed, Mila turned onto the driveway at the split-rail fence. The dirt road rolled and roved through an expansive, grassy property dotted with generous oak trees and an oblong lake. Beyond the lake, the driveway meandered through a dense forest and, following it, they arrived in front of a Victorian-style home. Porch lights illuminated a wood sign carved with ornate script, labeling the place Haven House.

As if on cue, a tall woman stepped onto the porch, into the path of the magnecar's high beams. She wiped a plate dry repetitively, as if making sense of the situation before her. Finally, she walked forward. Her sable hair twirled in a braid like a snake draped over one shoulder, her caramel skin was vibrant against the peach, billowing blouse she wore. When she bent and craned her neck to peer into the windshield, her lips spread into a wide smile.

"Well, I'll be damned," she said, crossing to the passenger's side window as Mila cut the engine.

"Hi," Haley said, stepping out of the car. Mila followed suit.

"Go on in, honey," the woman said. "There's a pitcher of lemonade in the kitchen." Turning to Mila, "Would you believe I wrote this address on a receipt for that young thing six months ago?" She shook her head and brushed a strand behind her ear. "You staying too?"

"Oh, no. Thank you. I just drove her here." She extended her hand. "I'm Mila."

"Helen," she said. "It's so kind of you to bring her. I don't know if you know—"

"I don't. Well, she hasn't told me, but I suspect—her home life isn't so good."

"Honey, that doesn't begin to touch the surface of her situation. That girl's father beat the living daylights out of her as though she were a dusty rug."

Mila grimaced. "How do you know all of this?"

"I saw her in a coffee shop in the city and she opened up to me. People often do. I gave her my address and told her there was a place for her whenever she was ready to make a change." She slung the dishcloth onto her shoulder.

"With all due respect," Mila began carefully, "why didn't you take her then?"

Helen smiled as though she expected the question. "You can't make people do things they aren't ready for. Even if their whole world is poisonous, you can't force them to leave. You can only make the choice available to them." The welcoming sparkle in her eyes snuffed out, and she looked toward the house. "The reality is that too many of these women don't stay. I hope they will. I do my best. But too many just... don't." She turned back to Mila, her smile tempered. "But I'm so glad you brought the girl here. Why don't you come in for some lemonade and help Haley get settled?"

"I wish I could, but unfortunately I'm late for work. It was nice to meet you."

Helen nodded and started toward the home.

As Mila climbed into her magnecar, she mulled over the woman's words. Haley was misled. Exploited. How could she be held responsible for removing the cloth that blinded her? For saving herself?

Turning the car around, she pulled up the driveway and back onto the dark dirt road. She squinted, straining to examine the landscape beyond the tunnel of her headlights.

A man darted across the road. Mila jerked the steering wheel, but a loud thud echoed on the side of her car. She screamed and slammed it into park, killing the engine without turning off the headlights. Scrambling outside, she raced around the front of the vehicle. The man lay in a ditch, his dark clothing powdered with dirt.

She fell to her knees beside him. "Are you okay? Oh my God..." she muttered, fumbling to pull her phone out of her blazer pocket.

"Don't," the man said. "Don't call anyone."

Mila's skin prickled. His tone struck too authoritative a note for an injured person. He sat up. She opened her mouth to yell—but his firm hand atop hers stopped the sound in her throat.

"I came here to speak with you."

She clambered backward, clawing the dirt in a frenzied attempt to escape.

"I'm a friend of your father's."

She froze. "What did you say?"

Standing, he dusted himself off and offered his hand.

She stared at it, then him. He was tall, dressed well, as though he'd recently left an office where he held a top-tier job, his dark hair shiny and wildly tousled from his lurch across the road. His hawkish dark eyes cut straight into her. The honesty shining in them allayed some of her fears.

She clasped his hand. As he pulled her to her feet, she whispered, "Are you—?"

"No." He shook his head. "I'm not your anonymous caller. Away from the magnecar. We can talk far away from the magnecar. And I understand this sounds strange, but you must leave your phone behind as well."

She pulled her hand from his. "Why should I trust you?"

For a moment, he watched her. "You don't really need a reason to trust me. You just know." He arched an eyebrow. "But you can take the pepper spray you store in your center console, if it makes you feel better."

She stammered, shocked, but he turned. He walked ahead, where the road curved around a hill to the right, and dipped down to a lonely pasture on the left. Mila glanced into the windshield of her car. Rushing to the driver's seat, she leaned in, cut off the headlights, locked the doors, and reached for her phone, but left it on the seat. She stashed the keys in her pocket before hurrying toward the stranger ahead.

They strode in silence to the curve. He touched her elbow and whispered, "This way," before heading down the hill.

Her eyes adjusted to the darkness as she followed. The treeless pasture ahead of them met the boundary of the sky in a swaying line, like water under oil. The stranger stopped suddenly, turning to face her.

"Here?" she asked.

"Far from anything that can be used."

Her gaze darted over her surroundings. "It's been years since I've been this far from the city, away from technology." She winced. "I'm so late to work."

"I know. Yet another overnight shift, where the hours plod by and no one listens to you. You, however, listen to everyone. It's part of why I picked you."

"Picked me for what? How do you know all of this?" Chills traveled down her back like an army of beetles. She shivered and folded her arms.

"Hesperia watches, remember?" Closing the distance between them, he said, "I helped design the data facility—the Walden—that massively expands their power. Something like this hasn't been seen in centuries, not since The Former Nation. It's a vampire everyone thought was dead—but they didn't drive the stake deep enough." His eyes narrowed. "Power lust is never killed forever. Eventually, it rises again. Always."

"Who are you?"

"My name is Carlo DaVanti. I wish I'd never lent myself to the aims of Hesperia."

Closing her eyes tight, she could only manage, "Hesperia watches?"

"Everything, in real-time. Video conversations. Audio conversations. Through the phone, the holodesk, the *magnecar*—list any kind of technological device, and there's a damn good probability that Hesperia can turn it into a bug. This is a world, Mila"—her heart stumbled at his first use of the name she never gave him—"where, if you want real privacy, you need to live in a cave underground. Now, take that information and combine it with the legislation your Belgae friend gave you last night, the Domestic Safety Act. Unlimited access to citizens' lives plus carefully designed loopholes to arrest and detain them without charge, indefinitely. It's toxic."

Hadn't her parents taught her all of this? Her memory flailed and roved, but she'd buried so much of what they'd told her when she'd buried them. "How long?"

"The facility began functioning five years ago. But Hesperia's watched for much, much longer than that. Thousands of wrongful arrests—billed as *missing persons*—for scores. Generations. It's gone on too long. They have to be stopped." He pursed his lips so they formed a wrinkled, whitened line.

His words acted as a match, striking and striking against the surface of her heart. Smoke billowed—the flame flickered—but something within her snuffed him out. "You're speaking of overthrow. Violent overthrow."

Carlo watched her gravely.

Stepping back, she crossed her arms. "Brutality to buy freedom? Blood to purchase peace? I refuse to stoop to the same level as my government. The problem, Mister DaVanti, is lies—centuries of lies, aided and abetted by people like you. That is what enslaves the Hesperian people. The first step to all of this is releasing *the truth*—and that's what I'm trying to do, by—"

"They killed your parents."

She recoiled from the blow of his claim. *No—he has to be manipulating me.* "My parents had done *nothing* for Hesperia to kill them," she growled through gritted teeth.

"You're right. They didn't. But Hesperia didn't need them to."

Mila watched him, daring his lie to crumble.

His gaze fell with a deep, burdened sigh. "From what I could tell, Fredrick studied and learned a way to sneak into the Walden's center, to see how far the beast sprawled. He wanted to know the extent of their searchlight so he could make his moves in the shadows, no matter how thin they were. But"—he lifted his eyes—"he tripped up. Just barely. Like a little toe falling over the line. And they got him. And they got your mother." His voice cracked when he spoke again. "You're right, Mila, your parents had done nothing. But ask Hesperia, and they'll tell you your father knew too much, and they could only assume the same for your mother."

"You said you were my father's *friend.*" The word came out in a frothy burst.

"When I made up my mind to undo Hesperia, I began searching. See, I know how to do that without them knowing. I studied the failures of Tyrranis Letum, of Agito. And I found a common thread in every group—"

"Besides failure?"

"A branch of the Ray family tree."

Mila huffed. "You'd think we'd have learned. Fiery hearts, hard heads. My family."

"I found him. Through a scrupulous courier, I made contact. We conversed a few times before I received his final note. *Are there more like you?* That's all it said." He shrugged. "Maybe he thought the time had come—his chance to strike a blow at Hesperia and win. I think he could be right. The explosion happened a week later.

"That is our enemy. An enemy who can only be defeated fire for fire. I laid low for a while, but I searched and I thought—I *hoped*—I had found an ally in his daughter, the only remaining Ray, continuing her family's mission through her work in the news media. The woman who listens." Footsteps crunched under the parched grass of summer as he stepped toward her. "So Mila, my question is, are there more like me? Are there more like him?"

Urgency, regret, and hope billowed from Carlo's countenance like a determined storm cloud. The truth he bore crushed her. She'd suspected for so long, but the knowing sapped her of breath. Hesperia had caused the gas explosion, blowing her parents into such small pieces that she couldn't even kiss them goodbye as they lay in their coffins.

She forced herself to inhale, to stabilize. Planting her feet, she said, "No."

He jerked. "No?"

"I'm not like you. I'm not like my father. I won't listen."

Carlo's hand shook as he raked his fingers through his hair. "Do you know how much I've risked to come to you? Do you know how much your parents risked and sacrificed for you? They gave you their everything. And you—you have knowledge and resources that *no* one, not even the Belgae, has had access to for generations. And you're telling me—"

"No."

The word hung suspended, creating distance between them like the opposing ends of two magnets.

"I never *asked* you to come to me, Mister Da-Vanti," she said. "My parents chose to educate me the way they did of their own accord. And by the way, they chose to do the things they did because they wanted me to think for myself. And I have.

"Hesperia is evil. But they're evil in a devious, underhanded way that leaves plenty of loopholes and plenty of excuses. They're evil and subversive in a way that few have the information, the evidence, or the clout, to pin back on them. But if the Belgae—or *you*—overthrow Hesperia, not only are you stooping to the same level of immorality as our insidious rulers, you are stealing from the people the chance to choose their own future. You are enslaving them, forcing them to bend to your whims and rush along in your tide. I *will not* be a part of

any mission that steals open discourse or with-
holds the truth from the people."

The fire in her words spread through her limbs.
Spinning, she marched away from him.

"Mila."

She kept walking, challenging him to shout with
every step that took her farther.

"You're right. Please, stop."

She stopped but kept her back to him. "You're
lying."

"No." Footfalls pounded as he jogged until he
stood in front of her once more. "No." He blustered
a sigh. "Truth for the people."

"A foreign concept?"

"Truth before revolution."

"Truth, before everything," she emphasized.

"And how?"

"Through my work. Through reporting—I'll get
the truth to the people."

Carlo sniffed. "*Alyson Vernon* is not going to
cover the Belgae video."

"She will! She has to. I won't stop until she
does."

"Mila." He rubbed his temples. "You know better. You were taught better. *This*"—he jabbed his
finger at her—"this is denial at its finest. Journalism turned a blind eye to the people a long time

ago. Another master feeds them. They won't bite the hand that feeds them."

She couldn't stand the look in his eyes—the insistence, the grief... the truth. Gazing desperately upward, she combed the night sky, as if the response she needed could be found in a constellation.

"Mila."

She forced her eyes on his.

"Do you truly doubt what I say? Or do you *need* to doubt what I say?"

She didn't know. Didn't those committed to truth—whether in the public or private sectors—hold the corrupt ones accountable? Journalism was a safeguard that still abided by its original purpose. It guarded society against injustice as Cerberus guarded the world against the souls of Hades.

Didn't it?

If what Carlo said was true, Cerberus slept.

He'd shot an arrow into her perceptions of the industry she respected—her life's calling—and hit bull's-eye. "I have to try," she said.

"And if you bring them truth, and they pursue violent revolution?"

"Not my ideal, but at least the people made the choice together."

Nodding, he reached into his pocket and with-drew a small square of black.

"What's that?"

"Some of the truth. Footage. Disconnect your personal phone from all networks before you watch it and *don't* give it to anyone at HBN. There are other ways to get the truth to the people." He held it out to her. "In twenty-four hours, I'm going to the Belgae."

"But the Belgae want to secede, not fight."

"Not for long. Not once they see this, on the heels of the murder of one of their men. If you come with me, together we can persuade them to do things our way—we can have the upper hand. We can bring the truth to the people, and show them a way to change Hesperia."

He thrust the chip toward her, but she didn't take it. "Why me? All I have is book knowledge, theoretical training—"

"Because you *listen*. You don't shut down, you don't close up. You took a strange girl all the way out to the country, late at night, to find her a safe place to stay. You care—not about bottom lines, not about cost versus benefit, but about people. I couldn't trust this crucial information with some-one whose biggest concern is themselves. I needed someone who loves the people, like..." he swallowed, "like I wish I did, before."

In the swelling pause after his words, she read his face. His dark skin bore the lines of a man wracked with purpose perverted, with love that had arrived too late—with hope that time remained, that the knots might still be untangled before the noose strangled them all.

She thought of bottles bobbing in the ocean. If Carlo couldn't trust her, whom could he trust? Without her, would his bottle fill with tainted water, then spin, dive, and sink to the bottom of the ocean floor?

The shaking in her hands and arms diminished and determination pulsed in its place. "I'll go with you to the Belgae," she said, taking the chip. "Find me tomorrow, and I'll go."

3.

ILA PULLED INTO HBN at one o'clock—two hours late for her shift. She rushed into the newsroom, but skidded to a stop. Her boss sat at her holodesk.

"Terrance." She hadn't expected him to be covering the gap between shifts.

"You're finally here," Terrance snipped. "It's been ridiculous for an overnight shift. I've hardly had a minute to go to the bathroom." He stood and kicked the rolling chair over to her.

Mila blinked furiously as she digested the situation and lowered herself into her desk chair.

"I trust everything is okay?" he challenged.

She cast furtive glances over both shoulders, desperately hoping other newsroom staff weren't eavesdropping. "Yes—yes."

"Okay, good then. Because I need to talk to you about your performance," he said tersely.

"My... performance? Now?" It made no sense. At her last evaluation, Terrance had talked on and on about a possible promotion.

"I was going to do it in the morning when I got in, but, well—this works better." He leaned against her desk. "There have been complaints from the newsroom regarding tips you've sent down—"

"Complaints?"

"—and, quite honestly, I agree with them. You know we do occasional checks in order to make sure the team is providing good service. You spend too much time talking with people who... let's just say their sanity is obviously questionable."

"Anything I've ever passed along to the newsroom I have researched and found proof for. I would never waste their time with anything I couldn't back up."

"See, that's the thing." He sighed and adopted a condescending smile. "Alyson Vernon personally called me to complain about a baseless tip you gave her."

Mila's jaw dropped. "Baseless?"

"You gave her a video, yes?"

"Yes."

"You couldn't back it up, no?"

"I could," Mila said a little too loudly. Quieter, she added, "I gave her some contact information."

"Of the person who took the video?"

"No, of—"

"Baseless." Terrance straightened and let the word hang. "Baseless as far as Alyson Vernon is concerned—and her concerns mean a lot. You wasted her time."

"I don't think I did, Terrance. It was important information regarding the Belgae."

"What you think doesn't matter, *Mila*," he said. "An important newsroom member believes someone on our team wasted her time, and it affects our reputation—a reputation we've fought hard for. That can't happen."

Mila stared staunchly at her boss for a moment before relinquishing. "I'm sorry," she said flatly.

"Don't be sorry." He stood. "Make it right. And stop researching ridiculous, so-called tips. I don't— won't pay you for that."

Terrance left before Mila could counter him. She turned, dumbfounded, toward her holodesk, signed into her account, and shoved her earpiece into her ear. Her disbelief sharpened into fury—

pointed directly at Alyson Vernon. With feet moving before her mind could catch up, she strode across the newsroom to Alyson's desk.

"Miss Vernon," she said.

"I'm busy." Alyson didn't look away from her holodesk.

"I'm here to follow up on the information I gave you last night."

"What information?"

Her insides boiled. *She's screwing with me.* She focused all her willpower into keeping her voice calm. "I gave you a video showing the first death in the Belgae-Hesperia conflict. It's a startling escalation to the situation, especially since the man killed was Belgae. Our government killed one of its own citizens."

"Oh, that." Alyson sighed and finally made eye contact, her eyebrows arched in spiritless disdain. "Yeah. I deleted it."

"You—you—" Mila tripped over her words, her eyes wide and angry.

"I didn't call the number you gave me, either." One side of Alyson's mouth turned up in a contemptuous smile.

Mila placed a hand on Alyson's holodesk and leaned close. "You complained to my boss. You said I gave you baseless information. And you didn't even *check* on it?"

"I also didn't watch the video," she bragged.

"And why the hell not?"

"Lack of editorial interest." Alyson turned back to her workspace and gave her attention to one of the four screens perched above her holodesk. The whole setup screamed of her importance.

Mila straightened and crossed her arms tightly. "Lack of editorial interest? You truly think our viewers wouldn't care to know about this story?" She teetered on the brink of shouting, and she didn't care.

Alyson slammed a hand on her desk. "Look, Mila," she said. "I don't have to explain my decisions to a pathetic peon. Rather than spending your shifts arguing with the network's senior investigative reporter—which really works against your career aspirations, by the way—why don't you concentrate your efforts on getting the hell out of your worthless job."

Every finger stopped typing. Every mouth quit speaking. Every eye trained on the scene, a rapt audience to watch Alyson scrape excrement from the bottom of her shoe.

Mila froze. Steeling herself from any response, she spun and returned to her desk, holding her chin high but clenching her jaw.

The Belgae man didn't call. No one called, save the occasional irate insomniac, hurling insults like fireballs. The clock ticked slowly, but finally Mila signed out of her HBN account and left the newsroom, pretending some of the staff didn't watch her as she did. As the door shut behind her, her phone rang.

"Hello?"

"It's Terrance. Your shift ended?"

"Yes."

"Good. So has your job." *Click.*

4.

MILA TRUDGED UP the stairs into her apartment building. She stood directly in front of her door, yet still felt lost. She smeared her palms down her cheeks, lazily wiping tears away. What would she do now? Terrance had ripped her job away from her as quickly as a magician pulling a tablecloth from under fine china.

Where would she go now? If her situation didn't change in ninety days, she knew where she'd go: The Hesperia Office for Worker Aid, where her name would enter a database to be matched with the first available opportunity, no matter where it was in the Territory. She knew no one who was forced to resort to that option. To grace the doors of the OWA would be more humiliating than Alyson's shredding a few hours before.

Shoving her hand into the inner lining of her blazer, she fumbled for her apartment key, brushing against the *Antidote to Apathy*—and another loose item.

The chip.

Terrance and Alyson had commanded so much of her attention, she'd nearly forgotten. A fresh current of hope coursed through her. "There are other ways to get the truth to the people," Carlo had said.

Tonight, he would come for her.

She entered her apartment, the chip poised in her grasp—but she stopped at the sight of couch cushions, picture frames, pots, and pans strewn about the place. Cabinets and drawers laid bare, thrown open with such force they were ripped from their hinges and tracks.

"Sam! What the hell did you do?" Mila stepped through the entryway, over kitchen utensils and cutlery, and stood in the living room. "Look, I told you I was fine with qanna, but if you started doing other stuff, I can't deal with it! Do you hear me? Oh my *God*..."

One step forward and something crunched beneath her foot. The picture of her parents. She bent to pick it up. The sight of their smiling faces, crumpled and scratched by broken glass, sent her crumbling to the floor. She held the photo to her face, glass shards and all, and bawled.

"Mila Ray."

The deep voice startled her. It came from the end of the hall, near her bedroom. She looked up and locked eyes with a man in navy uniform. A Hesperia Amity officer.

"Yes," Mila whispered.

Another Amity officer stepped out of Sam's room. "You're under arrest for violation of the Hesperia Domestic Safety Act."

"What?" Mila hurried to her feet. "Why?"

The men approached her but didn't answer. She gasped to let out a scream, but one of the men grabbed her and plunged a syringe into her neck. They wrested her arms behind her back. Cold metal enveloped her wrists. Blackness swallowed her consciousness.

5.

THE DARK HOOD OVER HER HEAD concealed everything. Warm air from her quick, shallow breaths pulsated against her cheeks—breathing it in made her dizzy. Her heart thundered inside her chest. The blood slowly flooded away from her head and the sounds of her environment crescendoed. Her head lolled helplessly to one side, and she moaned. Footsteps—three pairs?—came closer in response to her sound.

"Please—please, I didn't do anything." Her words rushed out in breathless, weak succession.

"Tell us what you know about the opposition." His voice was like a brewing storm.

"Opposition?"

"The Belgae."

Thoughts reeled. Had they spied on her conversation with the revolutionary at HBN? Did the video she shared trigger their suspicions? Did they somehow know about her meeting with Carlo—how? She still wore her blazer—had they searched it while she was unconscious and taken the chip?

"I want—a lawyer. What did I do?"

Someone ripped the hood off her head—a clump of her hair came with it. Mila screamed and cowered into the chair they shackled her to. Her teeth began to chatter as uncontrollable shaking overwhelmed her body. She tried to open her eyes, but the accusing brightness of interrogation lamps stung.

"Pl-pl-please," she stuttered, clenching her jaw to stay the rattling in her mouth. She squinted into the light.

A tall figure materialized amidst the glare. A man with harsh, dark eyes stared gravely at her from a tanned face, his arms crossed over his broad chest. His black uniform and peaked cap fired new terror within Mila—she'd never seen a Hesperian official dressed like that. *Where am I?*

"The Belgae," he said.

"I did nothing," she whispered, shaking her head. "I want a lawyer." But her words were dry and brittle. If Hesperia had watched, no plea, no promise, no lawyer could save her.

"You'll have no lawyer here." The official looked to a man on her left. "Take her."

The hood sounded like a pair of heavy wings as the man whipped it over her head. A piercing sensation in her neck again. Blackness.

~~~

Spidery eyelashes swayed and fluttered until the substance coursing through Mila's veins subsided. Foggy-minded and fatigued, her every eye movement seemed to pull, tug, nearly split the muscles and tissues in her head, but she forced her eyes open.

Her fingers ran down the coarse, thin cloth mattress she lay on, then patted down the thin sheet covering her. Pulling it off, she sat up, grimacing and clutching her forehead as the migraine battered her skull like an iron bar. She dared open her eyes, forcing her gaze to travel over the stone floor... stone walls trapping her on three sides... a door of steel bars locking her in. A cell.

My cell.

She hung her head and noticed they'd taken her clothes. Now she wore a tan jumpsuit. A bold, black patch on the chest branded her with the number thirty-four. Fear engulfed her. She felt as though her lungs, heart, and stomach all tried to trade places. Levying all of her focus, she made herself take slow, measured breaths—but soft cries drew Mila's attention to the cell across from her.

"Won't s-someone help me," a woman lamented.

The white hall lights shined only a couple of feet beyond the bars, as though even they themselves wouldn't dare encroach on the misery within the cell.

"Find me, please... p-p-please-s-s-s..." The last word trembled, sputtered, and degenerated into whispering, hissing sobs.

Silently slipping off her bed, Mila crept on all fours toward the front of her cell. She strained her eyes, barely able to discern the figure of a tiny woman sitting on the ground in the darkness, her back toward Mila. She hugged her knees to her chest and rocked back and forth. Then she spun, flinging herself so she lay prostrate at the cell bars. She covered her face with her hands and whisper-screamed. Tendrils of silky black hair reached like desperate fingers toward the hallway.

Mila timidly curled her fingers around her own cell bars and knelt down. "It'll be okay," she began softly, to herself as much as to the prisoner. "Try not to worry. It's all a mistake. They'll let us go. It's a mistake."

The woman panted and clawed at her scalp.

"It will be okay."

"*No!*" the woman shrieked. Her head snapped up as she sprung at the bars and clutched them.

Mila staggered back, horrified. The border of bright light revealed the prisoner and the black, green-yellow, blue, and purple bruises that clouded the woman's face, rendering her ivory skin barely visible. Her coffee-brown irises stared, wide and terrified, from bloodied eye sockets.

Mila recoiled—then two stormy gray pant legs stepped into her vision and blocked the revolting sight.

"Prisoner Thirty-Four."

The prisoner whimpered and scurried back into the darkness as Mila slowly met the gaze of a prison guard. His icy, relentless stare matched his uniform and peaked cap. Dutifully, she stood.

"Stand against the wall with your hands in front of you."

She obeyed, backing against the far wall. The guard pressed his hand against something beside her cell and the door opened with a shrieking *clang* that seemed to embody all of the human cries ever to occur behind its bars.

Mila's heart picked up pace, but sank when he cuffed her.

"Come with me."

She followed him to the right, down a seemingly endless hallway with cells on both sides. No signs. No clocks. No posted notices. Only gray stone and steel bars. A few times, she dared to look into a cell and meet the hollow, resigned gaze of another prisoner. Solid steel doors populated the final portion of the hallway. The guard opened one of them—labeled Receiving & Discharge—by pressing his hand against a panel in the wall.

The guard held the door and Mila entered. From the floors to the walls to the ceiling, the windowless room might have been a shade of bleached white, but it had been dulled by time into a sickly ochre. It held only a metal cabinet and a holodesk with a metal chair on each side. Behind the holodesk sat a bald man, fifty-ish, in a gray suit similar to the guard's but more decorated.

"Sit down," he commanded.

Mila shuffled across the room. She sat across from the man and shivered against the cold metal of the chair.

"You have been booked at Flint Hill Detention Facility on suspicion of association with those involved in activities of a terroristic nature," he said sternly.

The words snaked inside Mila, rooting around her bones and gripping her.

"You will remain booked here until you comply with our investigation or your innocence is determined." He squinted at her and tightened his lips, then tapped on his holodesk.

"Sir, I promise, I swear to you, I'm innocent." She craned her neck, willing him to look at her.

He ignored her. As if by rote, he verified her basic and background information, then took her fingerprints by pressing them down onto one of the holodesk panels. She answered all of his questions, her throat drying out with every word, her mind in a whorl.

The man withdrew a handbook and two stacks of clothes, one white and one brown. He slid the handbook across the table to her. "Everything you need to know is in this document. Read it. Especially the count times. If you miss a count, disciplinary action will be taken."

The yellow paperback cover featured the seal of Hesperia—a rearing white horse with scales of justice in its mouth—and below it, the motto FAIR. JUST. HUMANE. She opened the front cover to see a blurry, black-and-white photo of the man across from her, Warden James Gregory.

Warden Gregory pushed a meager toiletry kit and the folded white clothes toward her. "This is your kitchen smock, worn only during kitchen detail. At all other times, you will be in your tan Ward A jumpsuit. The black shoes you're wearing are the only pair you'll get. We took the liberty of conducting a strip search while you were still unconscious." The slightest uptick of the warden's mouth followed his last statement.

The chip. If they'd found the chip—and she was certain they had—she faced a mountainous battle to convince them to let her go. And what of Carlo—would they find him because of her? She opened her mouth to speak, but the warden said, "You may go."

Everything inside her flailed and bucked like a tortured horse. "Warden—please, this is a mistake!"

"Thirty-Four"—her chest burned at the name— "discussions regarding your case will be handled by the investigator assigned. You may go."

"Please, Warden," she begged, her voice cracking, "let me talk to him now. I can explain—"

"You. May. Go."

A scream rose in her throat, but she swallowed it back—histrionics would not help her. Her eyes locked on her feet as the guard carried Mila's items and escorted her back down the Ward A hall to the last cell on the left, labeled in thick black paint as Cell 1.

With each footstep, her disillusionment and fear coagulated into a rickety blend of resolve. As soon as the investigator assigned to her case approached her, she'd tell him everything—almost. She'd find a way to explain the chip, without endangering Carlo... if it wasn't too late. She fell to her bed.

"No," said the guard.

Mila hurried back to her feet.

"Prisoners make their beds at the wake-up call. They don't touch them again until after evening count. Read your handbook." He walked away.

The prisoner across from Mila hadn't moved. She no longer cried. Mila weakly walked to the front of her cell and crumbled by the door, resting her forehead on the cold steel bars. When despair ballooned within her chest, she stifled it with a clench of her jaw. She had a plan.

6.

SPECIAL AGENT VICTOR FALK reclined in his burgundy wingback chair and sipped scotch to the tune of the angry July thunderstorm. His quarters far outpaced the other guard quarters at Flint Hill Detention Facility, not only in cleanliness but aesthetics. Ink-blue curtains hung heavily over the window of the one-bedroom flat—distracting the eye from those despicable wood-paneled walls. Claw-footed mahogany furniture filled his bedroom and living area. In one corner stood an antique brass serving tray, crowned with jewel-toned glass decanters filled with the finest liquors.

The guards hated him for being able to afford such hedonistic luxury. But at thirty-six years old, with eighteen years of law enforcement experience under his belt—plus a claim to fame as the youngest person in Hesperia history to make special agent—he'd more than earned it. When he left his Challis-Idaho, Rocky Mountains Region home at eighteen, he had taken nothing but his ambition with him, his sights laser-focused on joining Hesperia Defense's Domestic Terrorism Section. And if it weren't for the imbeciles who had tripped him up, he'd still be there—not banished to Flint Hill Detention Facility in Kanawha-West Virginia, Appalachia, to serve as a guard as punishment. He had paid his penance for a year, then finally charmed and cajoled his former supervisor Forsythe Marlowe, the Domestic Terrorism Section's Special Agent-In-Charge, to force Warden Gregory to give him a unique role which allowed him to function as both interrogator at Flint Hill and investigator for the Domestic Terrorism Section. He'd done that for two years now, reporting to both Marlowe and Warden Gregory. Marlowe had been hesitant about the situation, but when Falk's ferocity as an investigator and unsurpassed interrogation abilities led to the capture of Dale Trent, the most notable domestic terrorist in a century, he had won almost unquestioning support from his supervisor.

Falk swirled the scotch in his glass and thought about Trent's arrest seven months before. Satisfying, but not enough. He wanted out of Flint Hill. He snarled at his drink and swung his feet onto his desk, but yanked them back down—taking a stack of papers with them—when someone knocked on his door. He looked at the clock. Almost nine. He had already changed out of his uniform. Smoothing his longish brown hair into some semblance of order, he stood to his full, six-foot-five height, and said, "Come in."

Forsythe Marlowe opened the door. Decades of counterterrorism work had carved deep grooves in his pasty forehead. His gray hair was slicked back and oily, and he glowered at Falk through deep-set brown eyes over baggy eyelids, a bulbous nose, and a long, thin mouth set in a perpetual state of contempt.

"Agent Marlowe," greeted Falk.

"Agent Falk," Marlowe started, but wrinkled his forehead. "What are you wearing?"

"I wasn't expecting company."

Marlowe shook his head and leaned against the doorframe. "Dale Trent's sentencing was today, I'm sure you knew. And partially due to your thorough investigative techniques, Trent's headed to death row. You did excellent work, Falk. You should be proud."

"Thank you, sir."

"The Domestic Terrorism Section rewards work like yours." He stepped into the room.

Falk nodded stoically, but held an expectant breath. *I've finally bought my way out of this damned prison.* Marlowe produced a rectangular, brown paper package he held behind his back. He handed it to Falk without expression.

Falk opened it and pulled out a glossy, wooden plaque with a brass plate that read, The Hesperia Department of Defense recognizes Special Agent Victor A. Falk as a recipient of the Quality Counterterrorism Award. His lips curled up at the shoddily-made award—a fill-in-the-blank, mass-produced plaque. He looked at Marlowe.

"You deserve it." Marlowe smirked. He smacked the doorframe twice and exited down the residential hallway, leaving Falk's door open.

Falk gently shut the door, then flung the plaque onto his chair. Turning to his mahogany desk, he lifted the wooden top to reveal the holodesk underneath. Reviving it, he opened the prison's personnel system and used the password he stole earlier that day, then scrolled through the list of names until he found Forsythe H. Marlowe. He clicked on the medical category. High blood pressure, prediabetes, numerous prescriptions, and benign but foreboding tumors... Falk stopped to read the doctor's additional notes. *I recommended that Mr. Marlowe retire as soon as he is eligible at age fifty-seven, or take a medical leave of absence ASAP.*

He scrolled back up to the general information. Marlowe's birthday was in August, five intolerable weeks away. Falk's frustration cooled to coal-hard determination. He would be the next special agent-in-charge. Turning off the holodesk, he stood.

The moon's rays provided the only light in his quarters. They glimmered through the single, bulletproof window and cast themselves in streaks across the room. Tonight, one of them sliced down a bookshelf, illuminating a flat, metal tool, twelve inches in length, with a hook at the end. He walked to the shelf and picked the item up, turning it over in his hand.

The skull chisel.

~~~

Edwin Falk was a coroner with a drinking problem. The sun beat down on the Falk family home back in Challis-Idaho, and when Edwin staggered through the lopsided front door, slurring and yelling and shoving Ingrid Falk against the wall, young Victor Falk and the even-younger Edgar charged into the tall, tall grass to hide.

"Slow down, Vic, I can't keep up!" panted nine-year-old Edgar.

Victor kept running, but cast a look over his shoulder. His brother shoved grass away from his face and spat a piece out of his mouth. "You got no other legs but your own, Ed. Better learn to run with 'em!" Victor charged ahead. The house was getting smaller now, but they could still hear the sound of glass shattering against its pine walls.

"You come back here, Ingrid! Dammit!" their father screamed at their mother.

The boys winced and bolted farther into the field. The space between Victor and Edgar grew.

"Victor, please!" Edgar's high-pitched boy's voice cracked in desperation. "Wait!"

Victor kept running. He ran until he reached the edge of the woods, and ran farther still. Edgar's cries grew fainter and fainter, until Victor lost his brother and lost himself in the forest. His pace slowed to a walk as he spotted a break in the trees. He had never been this far before—Mama wouldn't let them. "I best never catch y'all tryin' to go past the tree line," she said. Victor's gangly arms throbbed with newfound power. He was deep in the forest and almost out the other side. He kept going, until he emerged at the outskirts of a farm.

A farm! All this time, he had thought they were alone. Pop got to go to town, but he never let them go. Not even to school—Pop told Mama she had to handle schooling all by herself. He never let them leave. Victor ambled onto the farmer's property and stopped at the sight of a large building. Metal! He must be so rich, Victor thought. He looked left, then right and—taking a deep breath—walked slowly toward it.

It was taller than he ever thought buildings could be, with big rolling doors. He heard something. His forearms, green with finger-shaped bruises, prickled. Were those screams? Closer, closer, closer... louder, louder, louder... but Victor walked until he came right up near a window on the building's back side. He blew his shaggy, nut-brown hair out of his eyes and tilted his head to peer inside.

Pigs. Screaming, wailing pigs moving slowly somehow—he didn't know how—up the left border of the building. Their legs dangled and kicked. He followed one with his eyes as it lifted its flat nose into the air and screeched in terror, inching closer and closer to something... bad. It disappeared for a moment, behind something metal, and Victor barely heard a pop amid the screeching of the animals. Then it appeared on the other side, hanging upside down. Motionless. Soundless. Mouth and eyes still open.

A man waited on the other end of that metal thing. He had a long, bloody knife and sliced its neck, releasing a thick stream of blood into a bucket. Victor laughed one quick, exhilarated laugh—then clapped his hand over his mouth. The man was so powerful! He had never seen someone with so much power. Not even Pop.

He watched ten more pigs and laughed quietly behind his hand.

The house was quiet when he got home. No more yelling or screaming, breaking or beating. No Mama, no Pop, no Edgar. Furniture was tipped over, a wicker chair in pieces, beer ran down a wall and pooled around a broken growler. It took Victor fifteen minutes to find Mama—her head through the second floor window, the skull chisel through her eye. He stole it that day.

~~~

Falk returned the skull chisel to the bookshelf. He rubbed the tattoo on his wrist and poured a glass of whiskey. His father had never been very smart. If it'd been him, he'd have handled Mama so the Amity officers would never have found out.

~~~

Morning came sooner than he wanted. Falk fastened the last button on his uniform and studied his appearance. Guards needed no reminder of his superiority when he strode the halls in his perfectly pressed uniform, with squared shoulders, zero stubble, and an unassailable glint in his dark eyes. Tugging on his black peaked cap, he left his quarters at the far end of Ward A.

Walking the halls proved good exercise. Falk roamed the horseshoe-shaped prison numerous times each day, making his way from Ward A on the left border to Ward B at the base, then to Ward C. When his long day ended, he returned to his quarters, tucked at the bottom end of Ward A, wedged between quiet guards' quarters and oft-empty offices like Receiving & Discharge. Such a prime location offered him a good night's rest. After all, Ward A held the tamest detainees—Level 1 prisoners—the ones who complied with the rules and were held on suspicion of lesser offenses. Ward B housed Level 2 prisoners, significantly more dangerous criminals with serious or repeated infractions. The most wicked, violent detainees—those charged with acts of domestic terrorism or those who tried to attack or kill others at the facility—were held in Ward C. Every single Ward C prisoner remained captive individually, in cells behind three doors made of steel, metal, and iron bars. And they deserved it—most of them, anyway. If inmates—even the most brutal ones in the facility—complied with interrogation procedures, they could get bumped down, even to Ward A.

The opposite was true, too.

He continued down the interminable main hall of Ward A. The walls of the other wards reverberated with damning screams and threats. This one, home to the tamest, most compliant detainees, sounded with sobs, sighs, and supplications. To Falk's right, a man of fifty-something with a scraggly, seaweed beard clung to the bars of his cell.

"Please, Investigator, my side hurts," he moaned.

Falk shot him a smile, baring his full delight at the man's pain. The prisoner fell back from the bars, eyes taut with fear as his hand clutched his right side. Next to his cell, a thin, translucent hand reached through the prison bars and pawed at Falk. He smacked it away. It cracked like a winter branch. The woman shrieked and collapsed to the floor. The weak ones weren't any fun. He preferred Ward C.

Falk smiled as he approached Cell 1. The last time he'd seen this one—less than twenty-four hours ago—she had cowered and hyperventilated under the hood they'd wrangled over her head. Certainly, her terror had primed her. Looking in, he saw Thirty-Four sitting with her knees hugged to her chest, facing the back wall. A thick auburn braid fell down her tan jumpsuit to her mid-back. Falk rapped his knuckles on a prison bar. Thirty-Four stayed seated but turned to him on her hands and knees. Even as recognition flitted across her large gray and green eyes, her gaze remained detached but determined, not desperate. Hollow, tinged with hope. Not sad.

Interesting.

~~~

Mila's heart skittered as she met the cold, brown stare of the man in the black uniform, the one who'd questioned her as she wore the canvas hood. No one—not even a guard—had paid her any attention since she was interrogated the night before. All night, she had clung to her cell bars and watched, waiting for someone, anyone to so much as look at her. No one did, not even the sobbing prisoner across the hall. Not even the guard who had shoved a meager serving of food through her cell door with a tiny cup of water that morning. Though her stomach churned and growled—when had she last had a meal, before even going to The Phonograph?—she couldn't make herself eat or drink. Despair had gnarled around her. Her parents were dead, her life revolved around work. If she couldn't earn her own escape, who would ever care enough to look for her?

She eyed the official standing at her cell door. Maybe she had a chance. This man didn't dress like the guards in gray—he seemed superior, even to the warden. Her muscles twinged, prepared to leap at the opportunity to declare her case and plight. Instead she resisted, quietly meeting his gaze.

"Come with me." He unlocked her cell.

She stood. The elastic band of her jumpsuit forfeited its rightful place at her waist and sagged down to her hipbones. A dizzying fuzz whooshed into her ears and overtook her vision. She leaned against the stone wall for a breath.

Finally, she stepped forward and offered her wrists for him to cuff, pressing her lips together to stifle the stream of questions she'd harbored all night.

The tall official—FALK, his badge read in commanding capital letters—took her to an unmarked room near her cell. A man with greasy, mushroom-gray hair, in a highly-decorated, black uniform waited within, next to a simple metal table and three metal chairs. A guard stood beside him.

"Thirty-Four." His voice was deep. Cavernous. "Sit."

Mila obeyed.

The official clasped his hands behind his back. "By now you know why you're here—"

"No, sir, I don't."

"The Domestic Terrorism Section knows of your association with groups and individuals who are a threat to domestic peace. We expect you will comply with our requests for information."

The official moved close to her. Mila forced herself to prove her confidence, raise her head, and make eye contact. She noticed the man's badge, MARLOWE, and resisted the urge to look away once she met his eyes, obstructed by sagging, reptilian skin.

"I'll tell you everything I can," she replied hoarsely. *I have to stick to my plan.*

Marlowe rocked back on his heels and cast a look over at Falk, who stood near the door. "What do you know about the Belgae?"

Her interrogators would be watching every twitch of a muscle to discern her truthfulness. She took a breath and willed herself to keep her body language in check, to keep her voice low and even. "I know they've wanted to secede from Hesperia for a little while..." She paused, unsure of how much to share. "The conflict may—be turning violent." She shifted her eyes to Falk then back to Marlowe. They gave nothing away.

"Tell me about the violence." Marlowe took one step closer.

She shoved the image of the bloodied, faceless man out of her mind and stated as steadily as she could, "There hasn't been much."

"What has there been?"

"One death." She swallowed. "Only one person has died, that I know of."

"Who died?"

"A Belgae man. They said Hesperia killed him."

"Do you think Hesperia killed him?" Marlowe challenged. "Do *you* think your own government killed the Belgae man?"

"I don't know. I turned the video over to an investigative reporter, so she could find out."

Marlowe folded his arms. "Who provided you with the video?"

"I never knew his name." *Thank God, I never knew his name.* A little current of relief cycled in her.

"Were you ever provided with any other videos or material?"

It had been part of her plan all along, to tell the truth. But her pulse surged as she said, "Yes. I had a small chip that I assume your men took from me when they strip-searched me."

"What was on the chip?"

Straightening, she answered, "I never got the chance to watch it."

"Who gave it to you?"

"It was taped to my car's rearview mirror the night of my arrest. I don't know who gave it to me."

Marlowe narrowed his eyes. Mila looked back, harnessing all her will to keep her face blank. Carlo's safety depended on it. The success of their plan depended on him.

He wheezed a breath. "Have you been in possession of any other anti-government materials?"

Automatically, she replied, "I have not."

At her answer, Falk stepped into her vision and slid a document across the table. When he lifted his palm to reveal it, a pit formed in her gut. How could she have forgotten?

Antidote to Apathy: A Plea to the Hesperian People.

"An ongoing communication with a Belgae member in an attempt to help the anti-government group win public support. A microchip containing stolen, classified information regarding Hesperia Defense's domestic security activities. And a stolen, illegal pamphlet that was the magnum opus of a terrorist organization seeking to overthrow your government. What aren't you telling us, Thirty-Four?"

Her cheeks burned with incriminating red heat. Her tongue stuck to the roof of her mouth like a mouse to a glue board. "I didn't... didn't realize... what it was."

"Didn't realize?" Marlowe scoffed a laugh.

The chip, the pamphlet, the video, the Belgae—all of it together was too much. Her mind reeled for an explanation, but nerves and desperation fractured her composure, and the terror she felt at losing control made it teeter and tumble.

"A final question, Thirty-Four. Why was your magnecar left unattended in a rural area late at night, for more than an hour?"

Carlo's voice pounded in her mind. "Hesperia watches, remember?" Searing pain cut through her head, and the emotional hemlock sent her heart palpitating. Dizziness swallowed her whole. Her stomach contracted. She fell out of her chair, heaving bile onto Marlowe's shoes. She gasped for air but got stomach acid instead. Marlowe stepped out of her vision.

"That's all we need to know." He spoke in a disgusted gurgle. "In time she'll be more truthful, no doubt. Take her back to her cell."

A pair of gray-sleeved arms hooked under her armpits and pulled her up from the ground, but she fell back down, choking. An arm snaked around her waist and dragged her out the door as she stumbled and heaved.

She'd ruined it. Lost her chance.

~~~

Falk slammed the door shut behind the guard who lugged Thirty-Four's limp body into the hall.

"Watch yourself, Agent," Marlowe warned.

Turning, he crossed to his superior's desk and thumped a palm onto the metal table. It rang and vibrated against his blow. "If you want to kill this mess with the Belgae, you have to get it at the root, Marlowe—"

"Agent!"

He reined himself in. If Marlowe's position—if Marlowe's glory—was to be his, he had to convince his boss not to take action. Not yet. Coming on too strong would only cause the man to push back more. He spoke firmly but evenly. "You get people in there without full understanding, you'll draw out the process and the situation will get big enough to catch public interest, attention, then outrage. Is that what you want? Shut it down, shut it down fast—to do that, you need all the facts and an iron-clad plan. Then you walk in, get it done once, get it done right. Get it done for good."

Forsythe Marlowe stood and stepped back from the table, crossed his arms, and lowered his voice into a deep, hollow growl. "I will remind you, Agent Falk, that your inclusion in the effort to extinguish the Belgae is a favor to you. If you value it, you will watch yourself. Otherwise there's a gray uniform hanging in your quarters, quite literally with your name on it."

Falk suppressed the urge to scoff. Lies. Marlowe needed him more than any of his other agents and they both knew it. He leveled his gaze with the steely gray one of his supervisor. "Sir, I don't think it's time for Operation Charcoal yet."

Marlowe pinched the bridge of his nose, then lifted the glass of water from his holodesk and slurped loudly. "The push comes down from the National Security Bureau Director, Agent Falk. Just because the crux of the Belgae incursion is happening in the Rocky Mountains region doesn't mean it's not the concern of all of Hesperia. The director wants it stomped out before it explodes."

"It *will* explode if it's not done with complete precision, sir. And as much as we know about the Belgae's objectives, I'd want more information before any more action is taken, if it were up to me."

"You have Twenty-Nine. What more do you want?" Marlowe snapped.

His thoughts fired for a strong rebuttal. "Twenty-Nine wasn't on the inside—not on *their* inside. Everything we've extracted from him so far tells us he never got to the Belgae, never learned their strategies. He's not as useful in Operation Charcoal as you'd think."

The men stared at each other. Tension twisted between them like a well-wrought rope. Marlowe's eyes narrowed, but his shoulders sagged—one more good shove and the old tree would topple. But what? He dropped his gaze in order not to seem too aggressive. A drying streak of Thirty-Four's bile caught his eye.

"Thirty-Four knows much more." He lifted his chin. "I'm convinced. Her communication with the Belgae caller at HBN, her attempt to get their plight covered, the materials we confiscated from her—not to mention what I learned of her family background just last night, after you left."

Marlowe shifted. "Family background?"

"She comes from a long line of insurgents, including her dead parents." Falk waited, then dared to push further. "I have not been able to verify who her accomplice was," he lied. "The microchip may have been hers from the beginning—supplied by the Belgae, to plant at HBN. I'm telling you, she knows more. And if you hold off on Operation Charcoal until I can get it out of her, your success against the Belgae will be certain."

Marlowe released a slow, steamy breath. "I swear to God, Falk. You want me to argue with a chain of superiors all the way to the director. If I didn't know your capabilities..." His globular nostrils flared. He spun and clasped his hands behind his back.

Falk could taste his advantage. "It will be a bigger accolade than the Trent case I got for you," he pressed.

Marlowe turned and pressed his lips into a deadly serious line. "What more do you need to do before we're ready to launch?"

Falk's eyes smoldered. "Give me three weeks."

7.

THE FLINT HILL KITCHEN appeared spacious to Mila until all of Ward A crammed inside it for kitchen detail. She trembled as the room filled with her ward mates, terrified at being in such close contact with other prisoners. The women eyed her with distrust and disdain. The men—who weren't housed in separate quarters, as reported by the government—leered and ogled. Mila backed against the wall by the door and watched as the captives shuffled and lumbered like automatons to various stations around the kitchen. Some unloaded ladles and spatulas and wide frying pans spotted with rust and crust. Others retrieved grossly large plastic containers from the refrigerator and freezer labeled with peeling old tape and names like EGG SUBSTITUTE, GRAVY, and BIS-CUITS.

A hand grabbed her backside and jiggled it. Mila jolted, swatting at the hairy arm.

"If you're too good to work with your hands, pretty princess," muttered a man with pocked cheeks, "I've got another job for you."

Flinching, Mila stepped away.

The man's laugh degenerated into a smoky cough. "No fight? No fun. Thin skins don't last long around here, pretty princess." He walked away.

"Come."

The quiet, insistent word came from her other side. Turning, Mila eyed her almost-cellmate, her bruises bright and face swollen, her brown irises surrounded by a red sea of ruptured blood vessels, her tan jumpsuit labeling her #102. She took Mila by the wrist and led her to the large counter facing the mess hall, where Ward B prisoners, clad in yellow jumpsuits, had begun to file in, awaiting their six o'clock breakfast. The petite woman handed her a rusted metal casserole dish and poured a huge tub of grayish scrambled egg substitute into a bent frying pan. The mixture sizzled and smelled of aluminum.

"I'll cook. You serve," she lisped through swollen lips, handing Mila a ladle. "I'm Lu."

"Mila."

Lu turned back to her work. Mila picked up the ladle and stared at it, wishing she could become invisible to the rest of the prisoners. The previous day and night—after her interrogation with Falk and Marlowe—had crept by. Once she'd recovered from her panic attack, she crawled to her cell bars, her head throbbing, and pressed her face between them, desperate for a second chance to convince her captors of her innocence. Instead she fell asleep at the base of her cell door.

They *had* to come back. Maybe after kitchen detail. Maybe —

Brown liquid splatted her breasts and dripped in curdles down her smock. Mila jumped, then shrieked as a rotting stench filled her nostrils. Cackling erupted across the counter from her. Looking up, she met the cruel smile of a Ward B inmate, his hand dripping with feces. Snatching a ladle, she gripped it tight, her arms shaking with rage. She scraped a ladleful of eggs and pulled it back, ready to launch—but Lu snatched her wrist.

"Do you want to start an all-out ward fight?" she hissed. "Leave him be. Leave him be. Leave him be."

The inmate shoved his tray with an empty plate toward her and smiled wide. Seething, Mila splatted runny eggs onto his plate, then glanced around frantically for a guard.

"You think they care to clean you up?" Lu spoke without looking at her. "Get used to the stench. You'll wear it all morning. Leave it by your cell door later. They'll clean it —- if, if, *if* they remember."

Sickened, Mila trained her eyes on the casserole dish and took shallow breaths through her mouth. Lu didn't speak to her for the rest of kitchen detail, but she never left her side, either.

Generators hummed ominously that night, the only sound in Ward A. The evening count had ended at nine. Lights remained on until midnight. Air stung Mila's eyes but she couldn't seem to close them, her gaze senselessly locked on the stone ceiling. Her hands found the sleeves of her jumpsuit and she mindlessly fingered the tan cloth, a childhood habit. When she was eight, Mila had received a nightgown from her mother, as soft as butterfly wings, the luminescent pink-purple color of heliotrope flowers. The fabric's comforting silkiness against her skin wasn't enough. She couldn't help but grasp it in her fingers. Seventeen years later, she continued the habit with her coarse, tan jail clothes. Something stiff stopped the exploration of her fingers—the little patch at the cuff of her sleeve.

Thirty-Four.

Her captors couldn't just ignore her here—they'd return. Wouldn't they? Or was she so inconsequential that they could toss her away and forget about her, satisfied by the mere fact that they'd cleaned Hesperia of a woman who had stolen a book and talked to people she shouldn't have talked to about things that shouldn't be spoken of? She pressed her eyes shut as a sinking sensation engulfed her, and in the hopeless quiet, on a hard bed in Ward A, Cell 1 of Flint Hill Detention Facility—the very bowels of Hesperia—she had nothing left to focus on, not even the ticking of a clock to count the seconds' passing. She traced the numbers three and four... over, and over, and over, until a loud *clack* reverberated through the Ward.

The generators stopped humming. The lights went out.

"Thy soul shall find itself alone." Lu's voice floated across the hall like an eerie pianissimo. "'Mid dark thoughts of the gray tombstone."

Mila shivered and tore her gaze from the ceiling. She barely perceived Lu's figure, back to the bars, blue-black tresses falling and blending into the darkness. "Poe," Mila said quietly.

"Yes. You know of him."

"My parents owned a collection of his works."

"Such quaintness. Rarely does a person read books nowadays, even rarer do they own them."

Mila heard the brittle sound of cloth scraping against dirty floors. Straining, her eyes yet unadjusted to the darkness, she barely saw Lu turn and crawl toward the bars, her black-coffee eyes glittering out of their swollen sockets. "Poe might've found much inspiration here, don't you think?" Lu cocked her head.

Mila only managed to twitch her lips.

"Why are you here, Thirty-Four? I'm sorry I've forgotten your name."

"They said the Domestic Safety Act, but it's all wrong." Mila left her bed, tiptoed to the edge of her cell, and knelt by her prison bars. The darkness settled in her vision and Lu's face became clear.

"Isn't it for many of us?" Lu thoughtfully brushed a finger down a steel bar, producing a metallic hiss.

"This happens often?" Mila whispered.

"Oh, Thirty-Four. You've deemed yourself an anomaly, have you? You're not, you're not, you're not. Accept it from one who knows, knows, knows."

She smiled bitterly, placed her finger to her full lips and gave the tiniest shake of her head. "At times, the innocent are recognized, released. At times, you're still assumed to be helpful to an investigation. At times... well, bureaucracy just loses you. You're only a number, after all."

"I'll get out. I'll get out and make sure Hesperia knows about these horrible mistakes."

Lu leaned her head on the stone bordering her cell door. "Hesperia." She drew out the word in a long, scornful whisper. "Great, plentiful land of freedom, choices, and luxuries. Yes, they know. They know, Thirty-Four. The information is out there, recorded and reported in places they access daily. It's there, right there." She punched at a speck on the prison bar with her forefinger as if the story were so tangible, so close. "They do not care. Their stomachs grumble and growl for the delectable tales served up by the lowest common denominator. Stories—mine, and yours now—are there, but buried deep, deep, deep because the beloved simple is what keeps business a-flowing. It must be highly accessible, supremely digestible, and deliciously spreadable. We are not those things, are we? Oh, no, we are not. Our cases are complicated, obscure, and unpalatable. They take too much time and thought. Hesperians do not want to think about fellow citizens being imprisoned and forgotten—much less what it all reveals about their government, the best, best, best in the world, part of the Gair Empire."

"The Belgae do. The Belgae are going to fight—"

"*Shhhhhh!*" Lu leapt and clung to her bars, a petrified spark in her eyes. "That name must never come from your mouth. Never! Stop. Listen."

They remained silent, waiting for any clue to a roused guard.

Lu sat back on her heels. "I do not know who *they* are. Neither do I know their plans. But I've seen things happen to prisoners who mentioned them."

Mila swallowed. "How long have you been here?"

"Count with me," Lu murmured. She tapped a finger on a steel prison bar to make a light, metallic ring. *One.* Again. *Two. Three, four, five...* With every tap, dread inched over Mila. Finally, Lu stopped.

"Fourteen... months?"

"Years, Thirty-Four. Fourteen *years.*"

A shiver sprouted at the base of Mila's neck and bloomed like vines down her spine. "Do you think you'll get out?"

"No." She said it with whispering finality. "But if I did, what then? The mistake means nothing to society—the mark is there on my record. 'How did you accidentally get placed in a detention facility?' they'll ask. Innocence, innocence, innocence... it matters so very little compared to the mark. They'll figure I had to have been leading a murky life anyway, to wrongly perk the ears of the government. 'Yes, yes, that must be it,' they'll think. 'It's she, not our governors. Not our leaders. Not our home. It doesn't happen here. Not unless you deserved it somehow.' How would I work and live? I've ceased trying to think I can."

The silence swooped in and hovered heavily over them. Mila shrank from the bars.

"They think I know them," Mila said. "They think I know—*them*."

A long, deep breath across the hall. Lu leaned her head against a cell bar. It covered half of her face so only one dark eye peered out. She blinked slowly.

"Oh, Thirty-Four," she breathed. "How I pity you."

8.

MILA'S BODY TREMBLED with anxiety and exhaustion. She'd laid awake all night, with Lu's words coiling around her like snakes, and had only begun to drift off when the loud-speaker announced the morning count. Now she stood on shaky legs at her door, waiting to be released for kitchen duty by the guards who dotted the halls, prepared to escort. The cell doors simultaneously unlocked with a jarring *crack*. Her breath quickened and she watched and waited as prisoner after prisoner exited cell after cell, relieved she was at the very end of the hall and the very end of the line. A blank-faced guard pulled open Lu's door, then Mila's. Lu shuffled out with her head down and Mila followed suit, but a hand grabbed her arm from behind. She turned. Agent Falk towered over her.

"Back in your cell," he ordered. She obeyed, and he followed her inside and pulled the cell door shut. Her thoughts flashed like oil in a hot pan as she fought to remember everything she told herself she'd say—and not say. The prisoners' dragging footsteps faded down the hall, and Falk watched her.

A door at the other end of the hall shut. Silence overtook the ward.

"You and I have some talking to do." Falk spoke calmly, but the glint in his eyes was fierce. Mila began to protest, but he lifted a hand. "Not now. I want to make sure you're in the best frame of mind to be completely honest with me. No sense in wasting our time on games. I prefer to get to the bottom line."

He stepped toward her, advancing until she was forced to move backward.

"That's right. To the wall."

Her skin crawled, her extremities pulsating with racing blood. She scuffed back, back, back, until she was almost to the wall and the back of her knee joint bumped something. She looked down. A simple metal ring jutted from the stone wall. Frantic, she met the gaze of her interrogator, raising her palms in a promise. "Please, I had no intent—"

Falk snatched her wrists and encircled them in a pair of handcuffs.

"No—listen—"

But he jerked her down as though she were a disobedient dog, pulling her until her she bent at the waist. Reaching between her legs, he opened the metal ring with a small key—then pushed the chain of her handcuffs inside it and locked the ring closed once more. Stuck with her hands chained between her bent knees, she could neither sit nor straighten her legs. Blood rushed to her head.

"I'm innocent!" she cried, her voice nasal as fluids rushed upward to her head. "Believe me, please—"

Falk's mouth pressed against her hair and ear. "Think about your accomplice for awhile." His hot breath burned. "We'll talk again later."

He straightened and his boots stepped out of her vision. The cell door clanged open, then shut.

Her muscles screamed in agony. She panted and cried, her throat dry and her stomach roiling with hunger and sending acid into the back of her throat. She longed for—and dreaded—Falk's return. Confusion and misery whipped her thoughts into a tangled mess until one desire blared over every other—*I have to get out. I have to get out. I have to get* out. Her thighs burned and shook until she thought she'd collapse over them and snap her forearms like twigs. Lu's cell door screeched open and slammed shut—kitchen duty had just ended. Mila wailed. It had only been two hours since Falk left.

Lu muttered things to her across the hall but Mila couldn't make out the words over the pounding of blood in her ears. It beat in her skull when the prisoners left for grounds duty. It made her eyes bulge through every single count.

After the evening count, her cell door squeaked open.

Dizzy and nearly delusional with pain, Mila lacked the strength even to look up. Over her desperate, mucous-filled breaths, she didn't hear his footsteps until his boots once again entered her vision.

"How do you feel now, Thirty-Four?" Falk asked. "Pliable?"

She released a short, sharp cry. "I'll tell you everything, Agent Falk, please," she begged, "just let me lie down." *I have to get out of this place.*

"Confessions first. Comfort later. What do you know of the Belgae's plans?"

"Dear God, nothing," she wheezed. *I have to get out. I have to get out.*

"Who gave you the microchip?"

I have to get out. But Carlo's insistent eyes appeared and implored in her memory. "I don't know!"

Falk grabbed her hair and jerked upward. She broke into a shriek. He bent his face close to hers. "Let me *ease* your struggle, Thirty-Four. Your accomplice gave you up. We have him in another facility, and he. Gave. You. Up." Spittle from his final syllable littered her nose and cheeks.

Mila grasped for breath and searched Falk's serious glare. He lied. He had to be lying. Carlo had risked too much only to break down. But the pain—oh God, the pain was almost enough to cause her to say his name, to compromise him, if he wasn't already compromised. Could they have pushed him too far after all? But if Falk lied—if Carlo hadn't given her up, or if he was still out there, working toward their goal to deliver truth to the people—she would sabotage him, sabotage all of it if she said his name now. She couldn't bear that responsibility. Sagging under Falk's grip, she closed her eyes tight. Her legs quivered. Every sinew stung.

"I don't know him." Her voice broke over the last word. She looked at Falk just as he bashed her stomach with his knee. Her breath catapulted from her. She drew it back and screamed, leveraging all her little strength against collapsing over her arms.

"You do know him," Falk said.

"No—no," she wheezed, "he knew mine—he taped the chip—but I—I never—"

Her voice dissolved into desperate rasps. She wanted her own freedom more than food, more than water—but not more than another human's well-being. Not more than Carlo's life.

Her breathing hitched when Falk's hands reached into her vision and between her knees. He unlocked her, un-cuffed her, and shoved her to the floor.

"Pity, Thirty-Four. If you won't cooperate with us, we'll just have to—*ask*—your partner again."

Unable to move from her crumpled position on the floor, Mila watched as Falk left, slamming her cell door like the lid on a casket. Certainty ebbed over her. There may not be an escape for her, whether she complied with Falk or not. But did truth for the people still matter? Her body rang with pain, but the determined whisper in her soul spoke louder.

"Truth, before everything," she had told Carlo. If there was any chance that his footsteps fell outside the walls of Hesperia's damned prisons, she had to protect him. She had to protect the truth.

9.

MILA YANKED A VINE from the electric, barbed-wire fence surrounding Flint Hill. It released its grip and she tumbled to the ground with a grunt. Wiping rivulets of sweat from her face, she looked up. The mid-morning sky had deepened to a dishwater gray.

"Rain coming," she said.

"Hurry, hurry, hurry," said Lu, crouched by the fence where she pulled weeds.

Mila dragged the vine over to the burn pit with the other refuse. The guards would burn it after the evening count to make sure no prisoners took advantage of things on fire. She hefted the thick vine into the pit and trudged toward Lu, her only semblance of a friend. She looked back over her shoulder at the inmates, all in tan, working the grounds. Three men and a middle-aged woman hoisted huge bags of gravel to pour around the sidewalks. A skinny man with a scraggly goatee and shaved head knelt beside a shovel and wiped his eyes with his wrist, his hand covered in russet dirt. He coughed. A guard broke up a fight between another two inmates.

Anger screwed into Mila's chest. She knew not all—probably most—of the Flint Hill prisoners weren't like her and Lu. Of course some deserved to be there. But some didn't. Not her. Not Lu. How many others at Flint Hill? How many others at detention facilities throughout Hesperia? She, and Lu, and all of them—crumpled messages inside glass bottles, lost at sea.

Falk hadn't returned to her cell since he'd fixed her to the wall days—how many, five?—before. He was leaving her to stew, no doubt, to wonder incessantly what they were doing to her unnamed accomplice, and if it was his fault that she was imprisoned in the first place... and it had worked. She clenched her jaw. Every night, Carlo's dark, insistent eyes haunted her, filling her with fear—of whether they'd captured him, and what they were doing to him if they did. Fear of what Falk would do to her when he returned once again, and if she'd crumble under his pressure. Fantasies of escape—especially what she'd do, what she'd demand of Hesperia if she ever had a voice again—were her only distraction. *I'll accept nothing less than the release of prisoners whose only crime is questioning their government, and the complete end of citizen surveillance.*

A howl shook her back to reality. The prisoner with the scraggly beard lay moaning on the ground. A guard stood next to him with one foot planted on his rib cage. He spat on the prisoner, shouted something, and kicked him away.

"He talks much too much," Lu muttered.

Mila joined her at the fence and began tugging and untangling another burly vine. "What's going on?" she whispered. As long as they both remained consistently active in their chores and didn't look at each other too much, the guards' interest might not be aroused. Plenty else demanded their attention near the concentrated group of prisoners closer to the facility.

"Did you hear me? I said he talks too much. Now you ask me to talk."

"I don't know why he would've gotten kicked. He was doing his work."

Lu stopped weeding for a moment and chewed on her bottom lip, keeping her face to the ground. "Unrelated to his chores," she finally said.

Mila wrenched a portion of the vine from the fence and tossed it aside, resisting the urge to press Lu further.

"I overheard... overheard he was on his way out. Out... somewhere. Stowing away on a magnetrain. A train near an old, old, old water tower. They caught him before he got to it. Acted suspicious— wouldn't say where he came from or where he was going. Questions, questions, questions, none he would answer. They took him. They think he has information about *them*."

Mila bit her lip.

"But I've heard whispers about the train before." Lu looked intently at Mila. "Only a few. The prisoners died in their cells, refusing to give the information to the guards. All said the train went to a place"—she dropped her voice to a barely audible whisper—"where not even Hesperia can find you."

"Thirty-Four!"

Mila's head snapped up to a see a guard striding across the grounds toward them.

"Are you hearing me?" Lu whispered insistently. "There's another one. A third organization. A secret organization."

The guard closed the gap between them. "Follow me."

Mila followed the guard across the grounds and toward the Ward A entrance, but her mind traveled elsewhere. A third organization? For what? Were they helping the Belgae or the government? Did they have their own agenda? How could Hesperia not know about an organization when they knew nearly everything else?

The guard stopped. Mila blinked furiously, forcing herself out of her head and into her surroundings. He'd led her back to her cell.

Agent Falk stood in the center of it.

Tremors sprouted in her midsection and spread down her limbs. "I had no accomplice," she said, her nerves causing her words to stick in her throat. "I had—n-no—anti-government—intentions."

Falk looked at the guard and jerked his head toward the door. The guard left. Crossing his arms, Falk said, "Then how do you explain your entire upbringing, brought up in a household with two would-have-been enemies of state?"

His question crept over her like a hundred tiny scorpions crawling up her ribcage and burrowing into her spine. She said nothing.

"You say you're innocent," he said, "that you had no plans for the microchip other than to turn it over to an investigative reporter, that you didn't know what the pamphlet you stole was about. And yet you spent your entire life being groomed for government overthrow."

As he spoke, she felt her measly hope for freedom drain away like blood from her face. Her mind started and jerked but couldn't form a response.

"Imagine what Forsythe Marlowe would do if he knew. No, Thirty-Four, I haven't told him. But if and when I do, you can be certain that you'll be calling Flint Hill home for much, much longer. Talk now, talk to me, and I might be able to help you. Remain silent and Marlowe alone decides your fate." He crossed his arms. "Which will it be?"

The still-unhealed bruise on her midsection and the cuff-shaped rawness in her wrists throbbed, insisting that Falk was lying. He wouldn't help her. Yet the fantasy of release dangled in her imagination like meat before a starved dog. If she got out of Flint Hill, she could tell the people the truth of what their government did to its citizens. Together, they could unite and demand change...

But how much did she have to say to satisfy the ultimatum without endangering Carlo? Falk still refused to name her accomplice. If they hadn't captured Carlo, they certainly hunted him. What should she say?

"I—didn't want violence." Her voice creaked like a rusted gate.

"No?"

She shook her head and swallowed. "I didn't want—my parents' way." A kernel of regret beaded in her gut. Though they were dead, she felt as though she betrayed them even by acknowledging their mission to the Hesperian official. "I only wanted—truth. For the people. I don't believe in violence."

"And yet you had ongoing communication with a member of a dangerous extremist group."

"Communication isn't endorsement."

"It doesn't work in your favor."

She shook her head.

"And your accomplice?"

The kernel metastasized into hard pit. Her pulse quickened. "I don't know who gave me the chip."

Falk's lips curled. He reached to a sheath at his waist and clasped the handle protruding from it. "Thirty-Four, you should know that I'm here for more than just the results. I enjoy the journey as much as the destination."

Ice-cold fear shot through her veins. She stiffened.

"I'll make a deal with you," he continued. "A name for a name. Theo Wilkes. The dead Belgae man you spoke about was Theo Wilkes. I know the agent who shot him. He's a good shot." An amused glint appeared in his eyes.

The pit in her stomach exploded into molten rage that melted every trace of fear. She latched onto it and for the first time since she entered her ransacked apartment, she felt stronger instead of weaker. "You're sick," she spat.

"You owe me information," he said.

"I owe you nothing."

He stepped closer and folded his arms. As he did, she noticed the name in ink on his left wrist. "Who's Edgar?"

Falk's eyebrows flicked up. "Brother. Institutionalized. Ten years ago. Schizophrenia. A dog bit his finger off." He cocked his head. One side of his mouth ticked outward, nearly imperceptibly.

Mila didn't miss it. The anger screwing within her turned to dust, blown away by sheer terror at the wickedness gleaming in Falk's eyes. "Oh my God," she said. "You're the dog."

A wide smile spread over his face. "Congratulations, Thirty-Four. You're the only individual who knows, besides Edgar. Now I've humored you. Tell me about your accomplice."

"There's nothing to tell."

"You're lying."

She glared and gathered the shards of her confidence. "I can tell you Theo Wilkes was nobler than any Hesperia officials have ever b—"

Falk's hands closed around her neck. He slammed her against the stone wall.

Pain clattered through her shoulder blades. Her lungs clenched with lost breath.

"Exactly what I expected to hear from you."

Mila grasped for his hands, fighting for air.

Keeping his fingers around her throat and his eyes locked on hers, he called to the nearby guard, "Prepare a cell in Ward B!"

She kicked at him savagely, clutching and clawing at his fingers, trying to pry them from her throat. He released her with a brutal shove that sent her flying across the room. She smacked against the metal bed and collapsed to the floor, gasping.

"You sick monster!" she screamed. "I'm innocent! Do you hear me? I'm not supposed to be here! You said you'd help me!" She screamed it so her ears rung, so her neck strained, her blood vessels inflamed, and her throat burned.

Falk marched up to her and pressed his lips to her ears. "Be thankful, Thirty-Four. Ward B *is* me helping you." He shoved her again before standing and exiting her cell, slamming the cell door behind him.

The walls of Ward A vibrated with her screams.

~~~

Falk strode into his quarters and flung the door closed. Swiping a decanter from the serving tray, he poured a generous glass of scotch, sank into the chair at his holodesk and turned it on, dialing Forsythe Marlowe's number into the communication panel. The video call connected right away. "Victor," Marlowe said. "Scotch in the middle of the day?"

Falk took a swig. "It's never impacted my performance before, has it?"

Marlowe shrugged and reclined in his chair, a wall of windows behind him. Marlowe's office in the Hesperia Defense Department's Erie bureau perched high and powerful and boasted a panoramic view of the city. Jealousy fermented inside Falk. The office should—would—be his.

"Give me what you've got," Marlowe said.

"I'm close, sir, but need more—"

Marlowe straightened and raised a stiff hand. "Unacceptable. Here's the deal, Falk—I just left a meeting with the director. Operation Charcoal *will* be launching in *seven days.* You're on our timetable, not the other way around."

"Sir, if the operation is launched without full knowledge—"

"You're not hearing me, Falk. We *will* have full knowledge. If we don't, my deal with you is over. You'll remain in Flint Hill as a guard—and nothing but a guard—for the rest of your career. Get. The. Information."

The screen blackened. Falk glared at it, then downed the rest of his liquor and pitched the glass against the wall. *All these years of watching me play people like marionettes, and you still believe you're in control, Marlowe. Foolish mistake.*

He'd had enough gratuitous fun with Thirty-Four. It was time to break her, corner her, and make her useful.

10.

SHE WAS ONLY DOWN THE HALL, but it felt like a world away. Nights in Ward A hung with a heavy, humid hush—the sort of silence dense with despair. But the stillness floating throughout Ward B was a pensive, planning, predatory one. The quietness of the vindictive, not the plaintive. A noiseless growl.

Ward B inmates saved their voices for the counts, when guards patrolled the hall. As they stood with their faces visible in their small, rectangular cell windows—as demanded by count protocol—they shouted threats that emanated clearly, even through the solid metal doors enclosing them in their quarters.

"If I get out, I'll come for you first!" one detainee had yelled to a guard outside his window that morning.

"You come for him, I'll come for his wife!" returned another, spawning a crazed cackling from some of the cells. Since her transfer the afternoon before, Mila had remained silent through all of the counts, not wanting to attract the other inmates' attention.

Her yellow Ward B jumpsuit flagged her as more dangerous than her Ward A counterparts, demanding extra vigilance from the guards whether she required it or not. Today, as the hot summer sun beat down on her, the jumpsuit clung to her in sticky, salty despondency.

Mila clenched and released her fists. Her dry hands seemed to crinkle as she moved, the skin fissuring like mudcracks in the desert. Soreness radiated throughout her wrists and palms, but she gripped the handles of the post hole digger anyway. Hoisting it as high as she could, she shoved it into the ground with a grunt, twisting to deepen her puncture wound in the earth. Pulling the handles outward, she grasped the loose clay, lifting and releasing it into a pile next to the hole. Struggling to extract a breath from the humid air, she wiped sweat and sticky auburn tendrils away from her face with her wrist and rested her chin on the tip of her tool.

The first time she had seen Ward B prisoners wielding heavy, sharp yard tools for grounds duty, she had been a new member of Ward A. She couldn't believe the guards entrusted potential weapons to detainees. It took a moment before she noticed the shackles around the inmates' ankles. In Ward A, such restraints weren't used, and grounds detail involved chores that could be done by hand. But now the tops of her feet and backs of her heels ached under the pressure of the heavy iron that had cuffed her all morning.

"Hey!" a guard called from his watch point on the nearby sidewalk. "No rests! Two more hours of work left."

Mila lifted her tool under her arm—ignoring the soreness in her muscles—and shuffled a couple of yards to make the next hole, kicking the iron links between her feet out of the way. She'd dug eight holes already. The guards had better be satisfied with the fence she and the other Ward B prisoners were building for them. It would border the walkway extending from the facility's main entrance in the middle of Ward B. As if they truly needed it—they just needed a new way to make the prisoners sweat.

She raised the post hole digger but paused at the sound of footsteps on the walkway. Setting the tool down, she turned to see Agent Falk marching behind Warden Gregory. Falk clenched his lips into a grim line, his eyes squinting at the man in front of him. When he caught Mila watching him, his face split into a dark smile.

She slammed the post hole digger into the ground, firing all her fury into the blow. Her parents were right—she never should have gone to HBN. Their debate about her choice swirled in her memory. "You can't fight an immoral opponent on a battlefield of morality, Mila." Her mother had sighed, folded her arms and looked to her father for backup. He had nodded. "You are so far removed from the real conflict. For you, it's all in your mind. But when you're face-to-face with freedom or enslavement, life or death, you fight with all you have—means don't matter anymore. Only the ends. That is what we're down to."

Now, she could see it. Too late. Rage drilled inside her chest. The new hole she'd made was big enough, but she jammed the tool into it again and again, until her bones reverberated with spent strength and her anger caved into exhausted despair.

"Thirty-Four!" shouted a guard. "Restrain yourself. Move on!"

She shot a glare to the guard but he looked past her now—toward the entrance gate. Mila craned her neck and saw a group of guards, tense and alert, escorting a new inmate down the walkway. He wore an orange jumpsuit—perhaps he'd been transferred from another facility—and the guards made him bend at the waist and walk with his face downward, pinning his arms behind his back. The number on the back of his jumpsuit labeled him twenty-nine. Glossy, dark curls swayed as he shuffled down the sidewalk.

"Bend down!" one of the guards ordered.

"I am!" The inmate turned his head, attempting to call over his shoulder to the guard.

"Keep your eyes *down!*" The guard walking behind the group kneed the inmate in his tailbone. The inmate tripped and fell face-first into the concrete. They bullied him back to his feet. In the midst of the struggle, the inmate lifted his face, glanced around—and met Mila's gaze.

Chills blasted over her body like lightning bolts. In the hopeless glaze over those dark eyes, she saw the death of her hope and mission—everything that had kept her going despite a future without freedom.

"*No!*" she screamed instinctively, tossing her tool aside and lunging toward him, forgetting the shackles around her ankles. But even before they could trip her, a guard jerked her back by her waist. He wrangled her arms behind her, grabbed her neck as though she were a wild animal, and shoved her head down.

"Stop!" Carlo shouted the warning. "Don't!"

But she couldn't stop. She screamed over and over, flailing with all of her might against the guard's grip. Her sweaty hair fell into her face, but through the swinging strands she saw the other guards pushing Carlo forward and beating him.

The guard holding Mila shoved her into the dirt. She heard a snap in her nose. A throbbing pain thrummed over her cheekbones, sending warm blood down her face to the rhythm of her fervent pulse. She rolled onto her back and a bloody, dirty mix ran over her lips and into her mouth, choking her curses.

"You better cooperate, you little bitch," the guard spat.

When he grabbed her arms again, she cocked her foot back and sent a swift kick to his face. He howled and toppled backward, swearing.

"Back up!" he roared, scrambling to stand. Seemingly from nowhere, guards ran to his aid, yanking Mila to her feet, pushing her downward and cuffing her wrists behind her back.

"I hope you got what you wanted from that little trick," one of them growled into her ear. They forced her forward, toward her cell.

"Get 'im, girl!" one prisoner called.

"It's always the quiet ones, huh?" called another.

"Yeah, little missy's got some fight in her!"

"Oh, let her in my cell. We can fight all night long," a throaty voice chuckled.

"That's right, guard—keep her bent over! Just how we like it!" The other inmates responded with low whistles, catcalls, and clapping, as a guard called for order.

The guard pushed her though the Ward B door and slammed it shut. Blood dripped from Mila's face, leaving a trail of thick red droplets on the stone floor. They stopped in front of her cell while one of the guards opened the door. Another thrust her forward so violently she tripped over her shackles and banged her head on the floor. She rolled to her back. He stood over her, glaring. The other two guards stepped into her vision.

"Wanna put up a fight now?" one of them challenged, kicking her in the side. She moaned and drew her knees to her chest.

"Not so gutsy when it's three against one, are you?" said another.

The third gripped her upper arm so tightly she thought his fingers would break into her muscles. He tore her from the floor and thumped two fingers on her nose. She bit back a cry. The drying blood crunched on her skin. "How's that feel?" he snapped.

"I told you you'd pay for this." The guard she'd kicked moved dangerously close to her, until her back touched the wall. His nose had already begun to swell. The streaks of blood he'd wiped looked like war paint. "I wanna know what it's like to do a girl with two different-colored eyes," he threatened, pressing his pelvis against her.

"We've never had an inmate this pretty before," said the second guard, his voice thick as oil. "Gotta take advantage of that."

Mila's heart raced. A hand grabbed one of her breasts with hostile insistence. She cried out.

"You'll behave, won't you?" the original guard asked with mock gentleness. He leaned in to put his mouth to her neck.

A monstrous hand clamped around his throat and pulled him away from her.

"*You'll* behave, won't you?" Falk thundered, pinning the guard against the wall.

The guards scattered. Falk towered over them all. His lips, just inches from the guard's face, curled into a deadly, derisive grimace.

"Out," he bellowed, tossing the guard from his grasp. "All of you."

The guards left, but puffed their chests as if they only obeyed out of their own free will.

Falk crossed the cell and shut the door. He turned toward her and folded his arms over his chest. "You lied to me."

Mila's head drooped in exhaustion. She lifted one hand to scrape blood from her face—and Falk snatched her by the wrist, gripping the collar of her jumpsuit with his other hand.

"You lied. To *me*." His lips curled back so his teeth showed, savage and angry. Her heart hammered, prepared for violent punishment, but he tossed her to the floor. "You could have had a deal. Why protect him at harm to yourself?"

Licking blood from her lips, she peered up at Falk. Her breaths came heavy and painful. "I never—believed you. I'd rather—protect a stranger—than aid a lying—monster." She kept her eyes on him, convinced that he'd lash out at her, but instead he smirked bitterly.

"Forsythe Marlowe never tolerates inmates who attack guards. He told the warden to put you in Ward C."

She shifted her focus to the floor, determined not to let him see the fear in her eyes.

"You could have had a deal. There's no one to blame but yourself." His footsteps scraped toward her cell door, but stopped. His expression was dark as soot when Mila looked up at him. "This thing that almost happened here," he said, "I saved you. You owe me."

~~~

Falk marched through Ward B toward the facility's main entrance, where Warden Gregory's office sat. The metal door was shut, but he knew the code. He cracked the door and leaned in. Warden Gregory hunched over his holodesk entering information into one of the panels. He tapped his temple.

"Warden, a moment?"

The warden looked up. "Ah, Agent Falk. How can I be of service?" He offered a weak smile.

"There was an incident with prisoner thirty-four moments ago, I'm sure you heard."

"Yes. We'll be sure to keep her from crossing paths with inmate twenty-nine ever again, to avoid a repeat situation."

"A judicious decision, sir. But Agent Marlowe and I have discussed the ordeal. Her relationship with this highly dangerous individual and her out-burst today have revealed her to be much more of a threat than we realized. We agreed she must be escalated."

The warden propped his elbow on the holodesk and leaned into his fingers, rubbing his stubbly head. His eyebrows knitted together. "Really?" he asked. "Now, I don't know about that."

"Marlowe insisted. She's continued to hold out information and is becoming increasingly irascible. He believes escalating Thirty-Four to Ward C would speed up our investigation and inform our handling of the opposition."

The warden looked down and puffed out a breath. When he again made eye contact, he shrugged. "If Agent Marlowe wants it done, it will be done. I'll have her escorted after this evening's count."

"Thank you, sir." Falk exited the warden's office.

Back at his quarters, he opened the communica-tion panel on his holodesk, pressed his hand to it for a moment, and then lifted his palm, opening the holographic video capability. He phoned For-sythe Marlowe at his Erie Bureau office. The holo-graph purred and flashed a mix of gray, blue, and green before Marlowe answered and his image replaced the fuzz.

"You're late," Marlowe snapped.

"I know."

"You were supposed to update me on the transfer of Twenty-Nine an hour ago."

"Yes, sir. It was successful, but we had an incident. Thirty-Four saw him enter the facility during grounds duty and tried to reach him. She attacked a guard."

The saggy skin around Marlowe's eyes tightened in concern. "Why would you bring him in when she was right there?" he exclaimed. "That's idiocy!"

Falk prickled at the insult but he buried his frustration and refused to react. "The guards handled it quickly and effectively. No harm done."

"I hope to God you made sure they're never in each other's sight again."

"I did, sir. I also told Warden Gregory to move Thirty-Four to Ward C."

"You think that will help?"

"I think it will motivate her to talk."

Marlowe seethed. "It better. The Operation launches in six days, Agent—with or without you."

"I understand, sir. It will be done."

Nodding, Marlowe ended the call. Falk huffed a laugh. *Six days. You'd make them wait six months for me if I wanted you to.* Falk had spent his entire career proving his keen judgment again and again. Now, he'd entrenched himself in Marlowe's mind, causing the man to consider him his eyes and ears. Whether Marlowe realized it consciously or not, the special agent-in-charge wouldn't act without the go-ahead from Falk, no matter how much pressure he received from his higher-ups. He believed he'd be flying blind. Soon enough, Marlowe wouldn't be flying at all.

11.

FLAT ON HER BACK on a Ward C cot—a thin mattress on the floor—Mila stared at the ceiling in a daze. It felt like an eternity, but only hours had passed since the guard—the same one who had tried to rape her—entered her Ward B cell, jerked her from her cot, cuffed her wrists behind her back, and then pulled them up toward her head, forcing her to bend at the waist and walk with her head down all the way to Ward C. She was locked in a cell behind three separate doors. The first two, closest to the hall, were made of some kind of metal. The last was of bars.

"You have no privileges in Ward C," the guard had said. "No duties. You'll never leave your cell." He slammed the doors when he left, and the only other noise she'd heard since then had been the sound signaling the hourly suicide checks.

She'd spent her time at Flint Hill fantasizing about her release—and if not her release, then Carlo's success. *If I ever get out...*

If she ever got out, she would devote herself to unveiling truth. If she ever got out, she would take it upon her own shoulders—alone—to tell her fellow citizens what really happened underneath the surface of their privileged, cushy world. How it wasn't so privileged for some. How their appetites for the simple and the salacious compromised the very well-being of their nation, freeing corrupt opportunists to pull puppet strings because hardly anyone watched them. She knew. Carlo knew. She may never escape Flint Hill, but she imagined Carlo carrying their banner, making the people know. If the people knew, surely they would act. If they really knew, things would change. She knew it.

But they'd taken Carlo.

The possibility of his freedom was all that had propelled her—the thought that maybe because she hadn't compromised him, he could give truth to the people and return hope to Hesperia. How could she continue on, with no hope for her own release and no hope for her country? Would the remainder of her existence echo Lu's—trapped, forgotten, dead and alive at once? She could not resign herself to a life like Lu's. Only two options remained: To escape in body or spirit. Of course the idea of death by her own hand had occurred to her. Yet she couldn't take that road even if it were available to her. There had to be another way.

At the very least, Falk would return at some point. She rolled to her side and faced the wall, determined to wait and grab the first opportunity.

Clanging echoed in her cell. Someone unlocked the first door.

"Suicide check," a voice said. Guards performed them every thirty minutes in Ward C with a simple glance. He reached the second door and peered through its small window. She had fifteen seconds to respond—with words or by movement—or else the guard would break into her cell. She waited.

"Thirty-Four, respond."

Her pulse skirred like a roach across a cold floor. She willed herself still and counted five, four, three, two...

The doors clanged as the guard began to unbolt them. If he called for backup, she'd have no chance. But what guard's ego could take calling for backup to enter the cell of a female who stood five-foot-four on her tiptoes?

Adrenaline tangled with a thread of relief when the guard called for no one and his heavy footsteps grew closer. She hadn't thought anything through. Her mind raced. When the guard's warm hand clapped down onto her shoulder and he pulled her to face him, she wrapped one arm around his neck, pulled herself up, and pressed her mouth to his in a long, seductive kiss.

The guard held her tight—then pulled away. Confusion glinted in his eyes, but his lips curled in satisfaction.

Her heart beat like a war drum. "Let me speak with Agent Falk..." She let her eyes make the promise she couldn't speak.

The guard smiled like a panther. "Payment before product," he whispered, straddling her. He kissed her again—savagely. She hid her panic by wrapping her arms around him, pulling him close even as her eyes remained open. *What have I done?* She scanned his frame as best she could while she let her hands explore his torso, but he wore no gun, no asp. Writhing, she pushed and struggled against him, pulling her mouth from his.

"Let me speak to Agent Falk," she repeated.

He shoved her to the cot with such speed, her head smacked the floor. "You think I don't see through this? You're an idiot. You asked for this." He snatched her collar with both hands and yanked, ripping it open.

Swallowed by feral terror, she reached up with both hands and grabbed his head, digging her nails into his flesh and clawing his eyes. He yelled and pulled back. She sat up and shoved him off of her, frantically kicking his crotch and abdomen.

"Back up!" he shouted.

~~~

Falk stood idly outside Flint Hill's primary entrance. He desperately wanted to drench his throat in the glistening amber liquid decanting in his quarters, but his workday was hardly half over. He leaned against the stone, twirling his cap on his index finger. The canopy of trees, which stood for miles between Flint Hill and any sign of civilization, swayed like the pendulum of an old clock—ticking, ticking, counting down until the gray skies relinquished their rain.

The storm rolled in. Tugging his cap over his head, Falk turned to go inside, but a whirring sound stopped him. He turned.

A sleek, black magnecar whisked over the road and purred to a floating stop at the Flint Hill gate. The back passenger door burst open. Forsythe Marlowe stomped out and slammed it behind him. Falk ambled toward him, but when he saw his supervisor angrily jab a finger on the panel to open the towering, wrought iron entrance, he sped to a jog.

"Agent Marlowe," he said, meeting him at the gate.

Marlowe flung the gate open. Falk barely dodged it.

"Where are they?" Marlowe demanded, blazing past him.

"Where are who, sir?"

Marlowe spun and put his face inches from Falk's. "Twenty-Nine and Thirty-Four! The opposition disappeared and took one of our men with them. I'm not waiting anymore. Damn it!" He strode toward the main entrance with Falk hurrying behind.

Suddenly a click, squeak, and *thrap* emanated from the intercom system as someone turned it on. "Medical emergency," a fervent voice called. "Medical emergency— Ward C, cell eighty-three."

Marlowe shot a glare over his shoulder. "Damn you, Falk," he said, stomping to the entrance door.

Tightening his jaw to stay his fury, Falk matched his supervisor's pace. Marlowe threw open the door. It smacked against the wall. The men turned right, through the second half of Ward B, then into Ward C, toward cell eighty-three.

"Fill me in, Marlowe," Falk said. "What's happened with the opposition?"

Marlowe kept his stare ahead.

A gurney suddenly wheeled out from a cell, nearly plowing into the men. It bore a body underneath a white sheet. The men skidded to a stop.

"What the hell is going on here?" Marlowe demanded.

The guard navigating the gurney cast a hesitant glance to the bespectacled coroner standing beside him.

"Suicide," the coroner said. "Hung himself with his mattress cover. He'd been chewing it until he could rip it into a noose. Probably hung himself while there was so much distraction over the guard attack."

"Guard attack?" Marlowe's voice was incredulous.

The coroner jerked his head in the direction of an-other cell. "Inmate thirty-four ambushed a guard during a suicide check. Had to call in back-up and medical personnel. That's all I know."

Falk growled and looked at the sheet-covered corpse on the gurney. "Which detainee's that?"

The coroner adjusted his glasses and looked at his clipboard. "Number twenty-nine. Carlo DaVanti."

~~~

Falk opened the door to his quarters and made a beeline to his antique serving tray. He snatched the decanter of brandy and lifted it in Marlowe's direction. Marlowe nodded. Flipping two brandy snifters, Falk poured two fingers of the sap-colored liquid into each glass and served one to his supervisor. He took a seat in the burgundy wingback, leaving Marlowe to the button-tufted black leather chair on the other side of the holodesk. Rain slithered down the windowpane like millipedes on wet ground.

Marlowe threw back the brandy snifter and gulped the entirety of its contents. Falk raised his eyebrows.

"Operation Charcoal's suspended," said Marlowe. "I'll talk to Thirty-Four myself."

Falk leaned back and cupped his drink with both hands. "What's happened?"

"The Belgae have been in a standoff ever since the first fatality. The Counterterrorism Division anticipated the situation blowing up after that, like most movements do when they get their martyrs. Everyone in the Division was prepared for it—to quash them when they reacted rashly to the death of a comrade. But—" as if suddenly realizing his stress level, he abruptly stood and refilled his glass. He took a hasty sip, leaving droplets of brandy above his upper lip. "They didn't. No—instead they retreated. It is inexplicable." Brandy splattered from his face when he made the "P" sound. He wiped his lips. "So we sent a spy. He infiltrated the Belgae faction in lower Appalachia, regularly contacting us with updates. Then it all went cold. The Belgae scattered." He took a deep breath and exhaled impatiently. "Now, we can't find our man. We don't know what they're planning. We can't launch our attack until we know more." He propped an elbow on the arm of the chair and leaned into his palm, squishing the skin near his eyelids, then downed the rest of his brandy.

Falk knitted his brows. "Sir, I don't understand how Thirty-Four could have been of help. She was imprisoned shortly after the fatality. She couldn't tell you why the opposition reacted the way they did."

"But Twenty-Nine *was* in touch with the opposition—it was recently confirmed," he said, his voice firm. "He was also in touch with Thirty-Four." He drummed his fingers on his glass and pursed his lips into a wrinkled dot on his face. Falk sensed his boss's anger bubbling as he recounted all of the details. "His employment history at Hesperia Defense, helping to create the Walden Data Facility, gave him the know-how to communicate in ways that we couldn't detect. And now we'll never detect."

Falk peered into his glass, swirling the brandy inside. When he looked up, he consciously molded his face into a thoughtful expression, pausing for a moment before he nurtured the seed growing within his supervisor's mind. "Unless he told Thirty-Four what he knew."

"Exactly." Marlowe stood and moved toward the door, stopping beside the bookshelf. "I'm interrogating her tonight."

Falk hesitated—pretending to consider—before he nodded.

Marlowe picked up the skull chisel on the bookshelf and examined it. "What the hell is this?"

"A reminder of where I came from," Falk said.

"That's right. Victor Falk, the backwoods boy from Challis-Idaho." Marlowe plunked the chisel back to its place.

Falk feigned a smile.

Marlowe walked to the doorway and pointed at Falk. "I'll get what I want. You watch and see."

When his supervisor shut the door, Falk rose and moved to the window. He drew the last, long sip of brandy, letting it wash over his tongue, relishing its burn down his throat. The descending night displayed only the essence of lightning, flickering in sheets through the thick, heavy rainclouds.

Carlo DaVanti, the coward. The quitter. Falk had no use for cowards and quitters. No, the hopeful, the relentless—*those* he could use. Thirty-Four, he could use.

Whether propelled by hope or by hate, she'd give him what he sought. She'd run under the flag she waved for the people—all he had to do was show her the way. Whip her—startle the mare—and watch her run

12.

MILA'S BREATH WHIRLED hot and thick on her cheeks. The heavy, black hood over her head barely allowed oxygen in. She wriggled, trying to straighten so she could inhale deeply, but she couldn't. Not with her arms stretched high and tight above her head, her wrists cuffed to the wall. Every breath sent her head throbbing and her thoughts swirling, stumbling. Their voices couldn't be real, and yet she found herself talking—mumbling—back.

"You had a chance," her mother said. "You had *our* chance. Wasted it."

"Peace," her father spat. "I tried to tell you, Mila. Evil destroys peace. Look at you."

"You're not real," Mila murmured. "You'd never... speak... to me that way. You're—you're not..." She strained, grasping for air. "Revolution steals—"

"Revolution *reclaims*." Her father's voice emanated around her head, a ghostly basso profundo.

"You failed!" she cried. "You failed, just—like—everyone before."

"No, Mila," he said solemnly. "I tried. *You* failed."

All of her arguments crumbled. Her head pounded, her muscles and the bruises on her torso and legs wailed, and everything within her groaned of her failure. Truth and peace seemed flimsy weapons against evil. Who could stand up to Hesperia and win?

If I ever get out. What a foolish thing to hope for.

Creaking. Clanging. "Suicide check."

Sucking in humid, spent air, she wheezed and whimpered.

Laughter. "Confirmed."

She sagged. The handcuffs dug into her wrists. Eleven? Twelve? How many suicide checks had passed since the guards had beat her and shackled her here that afternoon? The last number she remembered was nine. Everything got so foggy after that.

Banging and thudding at her cell again. But instead of stopping at the window, someone opened the final door. Her heavy breathing nearly covered the sound of his footsteps, but her skin crawled as his presence advanced. He ripped the hood off her head. Its bottom hem caught under her chin and jerked her head with it.

"Thirty-Four," Forsythe Marlowe sneered. His eyebrows slanted in oblique contempt, his lumpy, clay-like skin sallow and sickly. "Agent Falk hasn't succeeded in getting from you what we need. It's unusual for him to fail. So I stepped in. I hope you'll be compliant."

Marlowe's presence and intention put every inch of Mila's body on edge. She glanced at the door. He'd left it open.

"We have somewhere to be." He flashed a smile that teetered on the border between self-satisfaction and infuriation. He wrangled the hood back over her head and she felt his clammy hands fiddle with her handcuffs and release her. She cried out, bending her stiff, sore arms like rusted hinges, when Marlowe shoved her forward, snatched her wrists once more, and cuffed them again—this time behind her back. Grabbing her wrists, he forced them as far up as they would go, so she had no choice but to bend over. Clasping her hands, he pushed her forward like a wheelbarrow.

"Walk!" he yelled.

~~~

They marched the halls and came to a door. They exited the building. Her rubber shoes gritted and skidded on concrete, then found bare earth—and still he made her walk. Crickets fiddled a frightful tune and the night air blew warm and sticky against her skin. Soon, she heard nothing but the crickets—no hum of generators, no faint buzzing of fluorescent security beams. Marlowe forced her far from the building. But where, and why? With every pound of her pulse, her weakened body throbbed in pain.

Suddenly, he gripped her hands tighter and pulled back, as if she were his horse. He stopped her and removed her handcuffs. A domineering hand clasped her shoulder and shoved her. Tumbling, she landed on the side of her ankle, sending shoots of pain up from her foot, into her shin. Crying out, she pulled her knee to her chest.

"You dug this grave," Marlowe hissed.

Her arms flailed, hands patting the boundaries of where she'd landed—she couldn't even straighten her arms before she hit dirt and roots. Realization blazed within her. She broke into a sweat and frantically reached for the hood.

"Leave it!" Marlowe ordered. She heard him fumble with something. A metallic click, whirr, and then the sound of something being lodged against the metal. "I'm going to ask you a question." He spoke quietly, like a hunter taking aim. "If you answer wrongly, I'll pull the trigger."

She wheezed and scrambled, clawing the sides of her pit. Dirt crumbled under her grasp and clogged her fingernails. Suddenly, she froze in the feeling of earth—not stone—under her palms. Mere hours ago, she'd seen no way out. But now, with the scent of dirt and open air filling her nostrils, fresh hope pumped in her veins.

If I ever get out. Her mind scrambled for her next move.

"What have you been told about the data facility?"

Thoughts swirling, she allowed answers to burst from her. "It's new. Five years old. Watches everything."

"And?"

"Hesperia's always—always watched." *Think. This could be my chance!* "But not like this. This goes further—"

"And?" Marlowe prodded. The gun's hammer clicked.

Her pulse soared—time slipped through her fingers like the crumbles of dirt in her grasp, but she had nothing. No solution. "That's all." She gasped. "That's all I know!"

An explosion pierced her eardrums as Marlowe fired the gun. Mila jerked—then stilled.

"Wrong answer," Marlowe said steadily. "You're lucky that one was a blank. Let me ask again. How much did Carlo DaVanti tell the Belgae about the data facility?"

Tiny legs prickled and skittered along her injured foot, then something bit her ankle. She kicked at it, whimpering and gasping for a moment to buy herself time. Finally, she willed herself to go limp in the pit. She swallowed—the idea could backfire, but it was all she had. "You're a fool." She spoke low, and lied. "I *wanted* death. You're offering it. Shoot me. Take your questions to DaVanti."

She heard the grass crunch under Marlowe's heavy footsteps, coming closer to her pit. "Thanks to your stunt, I can't ask Carlo DaVanti," he said. "While everyone was distracted by you, he hung himself in his cell. If it wasn't for you, he'd still be alive."

Something stung her again. She hardly noticed. In the tense silence following Marlowe's words, all of Mila's panic and desperation evaporated into the sticky night air. *If it wasn't for me...*

Marlowe fired the gun. She felt the heat as the bullet whizzed past her face and lodged into the side of the pit. Dirt sprayed her sharply.

"Ah," he breathed. "Phase two."

Mila strained with all her senses. Heavy footsteps moved in their direction and stopped near Marlowe. A *zip*. Rustling of cloth. The sound of dragging on the grass.

"Go ahead, Thirty-Four," taunted Marlowe. "Remove your hood."

She reached up and pulled off the cloth, but kept her eyes down. The grave was small—barely enough depth and length for one person under a shallow mound of dirt. She fought back a cry.

"Oh, you didn't think it was *your* grave, did you?"

She looked up. Marlowe hoisted the corpse and dropped it into the pit. Its head smacked against hers, its torso crushing her to the ground with arms splayed out in a deathly embrace. She screamed like a wraith and closed her eyes, but the body—with its putrid stench crawling over her skin—still laid on top of her, matched perfectly against her body so its lips pressed on her cheek in a limp, lifeless kiss.

"You'll have all night," Marlowe said. "You can tell him how you tried to turn him over to me."

Her heart thudded. Her eyes flew open as if she had no choice. Staring back at her, through the cloudy film of death and decay, were the bulging brown eyes of Carlo DaVanti. He was naked, his face and entire body marbleized by pooled blood. She jerked her head away and vomited. It ran down the ground and pooled, warm against her neck and hair. Marlowe laughed and began walking away.

"If she tries to escape," she heard him say, "shoot, but don't kill."

~~~

The moon rose higher, advancing to its throne. Mila did everything in her power to keep her eyes on the moon, but Carlo's face was next to hers. His body continued the decaying process. Every few minutes, he'd gurgle and sputter, emitting gases that sent Mila dry-heaving into the dirt. She squeezed her eyes tighter and tighter, until her forehead felt dizzy, and tried to hold back her sobs—sobs that forced her to take sharp inhales through her mouth, that made her taste his stench, too. Through gritted teeth and tight lips, she cried underneath the corpse.

"Mila," a hoarse male voice whispered.

She opened her eyes to meet Carlo's unblinking stare.

"You're not going to let them finish you off, are you?" The smell of his breath was nearly enough to asphyxiate her. She could swear she felt his heart beating against hers. She looked into the clouded, glassy eyes.

"You can't let them get you, Mila. They're not worth it, not even in this terrible, nasty grave of a place."

"You did." She spoke through clenched jaw, tight lips.

"Ah, but I passed everything on. To the Belgae. They have the knowledge now, and no one can take that from them." He smiled a yellow, decaying smile and winked.

Mila came to, and stared into his dry, open eyes. He was dead.

~~~

The moon began its descent into the navy night. She heard the sound of footsteps trudging toward her, until Forsythe Marlowe towered over the pit. He sent the guard who had been watching her back inside, and extended a hand to her. The narrow pit forced her to lift Carlo's tepid corpse and hug him close as she struggled to stand, then push him aside and let him crumple to the ground. She balanced gently on her injured ankle and grasped Marlowe's hand. He pulled her out of the grave.

"Turn around. Put your hands behind your back." He clutched her wrists and cuffed them, then led her in that same humiliating posture even farther from the facility, toward the tall electric fence with the dense forest on the other side.

"He had such a promising future with Hesperia. No one thought he'd end up here. You know he helped design the data facility?"

Mila remained silent and tried not to stumble as she limped through the darkness, squinting and scanning for any opportunity to escape.

"Well, he did. It was ingenious. No one had formulated such a thing since the days of The Former Nation. But he got cold feet, began worrying about ridiculousness like freedom of speech and privacy... things that any realistic person knows have long been dead. He left." Marlowe paused. "His name was immediately put on the watch list. I hope your night with Carlo has prepared you for today."

"It has," Mila whispered.

"Good. Because I have collateral if it hadn't." They stopped. He let go of her wrists and surprised her by removing her handcuffs and dropping them to the ground. "Straighten up."

Mila straightened. A few feet ahead of her, just in front of the electrical fence, Lu lay unconscious, bound at the wrists and ankles. And though darkness shrouded her face, Mila could make out the shadows and bulges of fresh bruises.

"So, tell me—the Belgae. Everything you know they know about averting our systems."

She took a deep, shaky breath. "I know nothing."

Marlowe stepped closer, so his heat radiated against her back. "Nothing?" he drew out the question in a brandy-infused breath.

"Nothing," Mila said.

He leaned into her, extended his arm out in front of them, and pointed the gun at Lu. Pressing his lips against her ear, he whispered, "Wouldn't you like to reconsider?" He flipped back the hammer.

"No—!"

The gunshot shattered the silent night. Mila jumped and shrieked. Dirt and grass exploded like fireworks in front of Lu—but she wasn't hit.

"Thirty-Four, there is a bullet in every... single... cartridge of this weapon," he said. "Would you like to reconsider your answer?"

Trembles wracked her body. She had made it possible for one friend to die—she couldn't be responsible for Lu's murder too. Frantically, she tried to think of something—anything—she could tell

Marlowe. Anything to make him to put the gun down, or even fire it at her.

"I—helped them... the Belgae—" the sentence began despite her not having an ending for it. She faltered, but footsteps hurrying from behind them interrupted.

Marlowe kept the gun aimed at Lu but stepped away from Mila. "I told you I'd handle it," he growled.

Instantly—the sound of a blow. Marlowe's head smacked into Mila's. The gun dropped to the ground, followed by Marlowe.

Mila spun and dropped to her hands and knees, patting the grass for the gun, but a shiny black shoe stepped on her hand. Her gaze traveled up to meet the eyes of its wearer. "Agent Falk?"

Falk stood over her, his brown eyes fierce under his black cap. He dropped the metal bar he held. "Mila Ray, if you value your life and your free-dom"—he reached into one of the pockets of his uniform and withdrew a rusted, flat metal object with a hook at the end—"kill him."

Everything within her froze. She studied his face for any clue, any giveaway, any sign of deception, but his eyes reflected nothing but pure, dead-ly seriousness.

"Kill Forsythe Marlowe," he repeated in a measured snarl, "and you will be free of this place." He extended his hand, holding the hooked object out to her. It had streaks and spots of an aged, rusty color. It had been used before.

"No." Her voice broke over the word.

Falk didn't blink. "Use it on Marlowe, or use it on her. You will live," he threatened. "Which decision can you live with?"

Her mind whirled. Who was she, Mila Ray, in the roots of her being?

She hurt for the hurting. Carried the burdens of the burdened. Her convictions offered no room for taking a life, no matter how *evil* that life was. She could never murder. She was not a murderer.

But her father's voice shouted in her memory. "Blood is the only acceptable currency to buy true freedom. If we won't pay the price—with ours or theirs—we'll never be free." She'd argued with him, rejected his ideas. But hadn't her time in Flint Hill proved him to be right? None of her other attempts to earn her way out had worked. Her eyes traveled to Marlowe. Freedom, true freedom—held hostage by men like Marlowe—it couldn't be asked for, argued for, begged for, bargained for. It had to be wrested from their vile, vise grip.

They *forced my hand.* They *brought me here, to this point of desperation.* They *cornered me. They gave me no other choice.*

She'd have her freedom. Lu could live—she wouldn't be responsible for her murder. Marlowe was the problem. He would be gone. Maybe she, Lu, the Belgae... maybe their world could have hope with Marlowe eliminated. How many other lives would be spared if his existence were obliterated from Hesperia? If she took his life, tonight in the darkness... it would be her resurrection. She would devote the rest of her days to saving society from others like Marlowe. She'd appease the tombstones, the silent grave markers that challenged her to matter, to make things right. She could trade Forsythe Marlowe's life for her meaning—for the world's good. But only if she could shed his blood like a snake shedding old skin.

Falk and the full moon—the only witnesses.

She reached out, her hand quivering... then pulled it back. Kill, and then stand for peace and truth? How could she dare? How could she live with herself? She couldn't.

"You don't have much time," Falk pressed.

Marlowe's life, or Lu's—Falk's ultimatum. But there was another option. She took the object. Its coarse coldness shocked her with resolve. Her body trembled. The metal object bobbled in her hand, but she tightened her grip. One good blow and he'd fall like Marlowe, robbed of consciousness so she could run.

She swung, aiming the hook for Falk's temple. He snatched her wrist and jerked so she thought her arm would snap like a toothpick, and he twisted her around, pushing her to the ground next to Marlowe's head.

A tidal wave of adrenaline rolled over her as Falk forced her hand forward and plunged the blunt hook into Marlowe's jugular. The act was over in seconds, but before Mila's horrified eyes it passed slowly—as though someone had grasped the dishrag of time and wrung it, wanting to savor each drop. The unconscious man's skin gave under the force of the metal. His vein buckled under the weight of the weapon, and then succumbed, broke, and burst open. Blood spewed from the puncture wound. It covered her hand, hot in accusation—sticky, as though it may never wash off. It ran down his chest.

Horrified, she watched the life leave her torturer's body, hardly feeling Falk release his grip on her. She lifted her head, eyes wild, and met Falk's unaffected gaze.

"Go."

She dropped the murder weapon.

"Go."

Shaking, her legs threatened to collapse under her as she stood, leaning her weight on her right foot. She whipped her head around in search of her exit.

"Climb the fence. I turned it off for you."

She lumbered as fast as she could with an injured ankle, bracing for electrocution when she grabbed the fence. But it was off—Falk hadn't lied. She climbed, with both feet, and clenched her jaw to fight back cries of pain. Finally, she was at the top, then over the side. Once she touched the ground, Falk walked toward her.

"Fair warning," Falk said quietly. "I said you'd be free of this place. Don't think you're free of me."

She froze.

"Go!"

The full moon streaked through tree limbs and leaves and lit her way. She staggered into the dense Kanawha-West Virginia forest.

~~~

Falk watched Mila limp into the woods until the sound of her uneven gait faded, faded, and disappeared. He turned around and stepped toward the body of his supervisor, the special agent-in-charge. Eroded and rusty with age, it had been years since the skull chisel glinted. But thick with Marlowe's blood it gleamed, reflecting the subtle glint of the moon.

"A promising leader, murdered by Belgae scum," he eulogized in a throaty whisper. *They'll worship me when she's caught, you're avenged, and the Belgae is crushed under my foot.*

13.

THE FOREST, with its looming trees both guarding her and blocking her way, acted as a protective barrier and a blindfold. She forced herself deeper and deeper into the trees, straining and squinting into the shadows, unsure how much time she had before Flint Hill roused and launched into action. The crickets' song served as a ticking clock. She hobbled and wiped her hand on her scummy jumpsuit, plastered with dirt and vomit, smeared with Carlo's stench and fluids, and streaked with Marlowe's blood.

She panted and flicked her tongue inside her mouth, trying to coat her scratchy throat with any moisture, but it was dry as sand. How long had it been? How far had she gone? She paused and glanced over her shoulder, in the direction she assumed she had come from but couldn't quite remember. No sign of the facility seeped through the trees in any direction, as far as she could see. She had to have hobbled far, maybe for an hour, but she lurched forward and pressed on.

A whooping sounded in the distance. An alarm. Her skin prickled. *They know he's dead! They know I'm gone!* She picked up her pace and pushed forward. Would this be her life now, forever on the run? How free was she, really? She shoved the questions aside, buried them. She refused to think of the pain in her ankle, the grime on her jumpsuit, the blood drying on her hand. Only one thing mattered. Escape.

Her gaze flitted around the forest. The guards would disperse in every direction. She had to choose a path. The woods were wild with summertime and thicker, harder to navigate with every limping step Mila took. Soon she was clawing her way through undergrowth, forcing herself through briars.

In the world of the woods, pine, beech, and sweetgum trees served as the guards, their watchful legions ever present. The warm night wind sent them swaying and rocking, as if urging her, warning her to move onward. Their incredible height made them a haven for the birds, but not for her. Her injured foot snagged on a vine—she pitched forward, landing on a dense bed of thorns. Whimpering, she scrambled up and fought through the underbrush, plucking nature's teeth from her clothing and exposed arm.

There, ahead—a thicket of foliage-dense trees. She rushed forward, relief and desperation drowning out her ankle's protests, closing the distance between herself and her safety. Finally, she reached the coppice. Cedar, oak, black walnut—hardwoods with thick waists and branches low enough to climb. She paused and held her breath. The entire forest stilled.

The howls of search dogs percolated through the branches. Her pursuers were on their way.

"Psssst! Psssst!" came a sound from far above.

Mila peered high into the canopy. On the branch of a large oak tree, its haunting black eyes boring into her against its glowing white face, perched a barn owl.

"Psssst! Psssst!" it insisted.

Mila wobbled toward the oak tree. The first branch grew far out of reach, but knots and holes riddled the oak's trunk. She curled the fingers of both hands around one large knot and steadied the ball of her right foot on another. Lifting herself, she began to stand on her right foot and stretch her injured foot toward a hole, to lodge it inside.

The bark creaked and snapped off. Her back smacked to the ground so hard it knocked the wind out of her. As she frantically tried to refill her lungs, the pain crested and paralyzed her—but the dogs' barks grew louder. Bucking against the pain, she forced herself up. Clutched the knob. Hoisted herself up on the knot and rode her momentum, swinging her right arm to grasp the nearest branch—calluses earned through grounds duty helped her cling to it. She flung her left hand over. With both hands holding the limb, she squirmed up the tree. Her ankle screamed.

The others were easily within reach now. She perched for a moment. The barn owl lurked another fifteen feet above her, the light color of its flight feathers, back, and head made it appear to be wearing a graceful cape. It bounced eagerly next to a large hole in the oak tree, screeched, and flew into the darkness.

Mila fought her way up the tree until she reached the bird's former spot. She peered ahead, but the oak's dense foliage shrouded her and blocked her sight. She allowed herself a pause for breath, thankful for summer's cloak of protection instead of winter's harsh exposure. But her rest fluttered away as quickly as the barn owl. In a forest filled with tall pines and other trees whose lowest shoots were still nearly fifty feet from the ground, her thicket would be the most obvious place to shine a light.

Resisting the exhaustion that threatened to steal her drive, she turned around, hugged the oak's trunk, and stood.

Her jumpsuit. Red as an ambulance. The perfect opposite of nature's green. No matter how high she climbed, she'd stand out. Her fingers fumbled with the jumpsuit's zipper as she eyed the hollow in the oak. She'd climb naked if she had to, and stash the jumpsuit in the hole. She reached inside—wetness. She dipped her hand farther, until her arm was up to her elbow in gathered rain, then yanked it out. Dirty water drenched her sleeve.

Clinging to the tree for balance, she shimmied the jumpsuit off her shoulders and down her hips. Hissing and choking back a cry, she removed her shoes—stacked them on a branch—and tugged the jumpsuit off at her feet. Her heart lilted at the sound of voices in the distance. Wadding the material into a ball, she pounded it inside the hole. Fought it under the water. Rubbed it against the insides of the tree to loosen the decaying bark, scrubbing Marlowe's blood off her palm and out from under her fingernails as she did. She could endure any grime and filth, but not that.

She tugged the dripping jumpsuit out. Splotches of dirt, fungus, and owl feces covered it. The water darkened it. She scrunched it up and hurried it over her body, finally zipping it and putting on her shoes. The water cooled her and made the fabric stick.

Despite all the muck she wore, she felt cleaner.

Up, up, up she climbed, until she neared the top—about fifty feet. Young, thin limbs dominated. She looked down—a long, long way to fall, but still not high enough. She had to climb higher—higher than the guards would ever cast their beams. The oak tree wasn't enough. Leaning onto her stomach, she flattened herself against a stocky branch and hugged it. It extended nearly ten more feet from where she was. It tickled the trunk and branches of one of the precarious, skinny beech trees.

Eyeing the beech tree, Mila inched her way across the oak's thin arm. It creaked, swayed, and wavered, but she kept going. At the point where the oak and beech branches crossed, she timidly lifted into a straddle, then tugged on the new limb. Solid. She reached above to grasp it, then scooted forward—distributing her weight evenly between the two branches—aiming for a portion of the beech limb that seemed just thick enough to rest on. She seized it, swinging her feet from their dangled position on the oak and curling them around her new branch. She hugged herself against it. Holding her breath, she carefully twisted herself to the other side.

For the first time since she reached the thicket, she looked for her pursuers. In the distance, beams of flashlights darted through the woods. The crunch of trudging footsteps followed. *Higher—I have to go higher.* Hurtling herself against the dangerously thin tree trunk, she began climbing again. The tree swayed as if to warn her away, but she moved higher and higher, until she guessed she was seventy-five feet above the ground. She curled tight against the tree's trunk, masked by its leaves, and sucked in a breath.

Dogs bayed. A light beam darted in the direction of the thicket.

"There," she heard a man say. Three beams zeroed in on the oak tree she'd vacated. The dogs barked incessantly.

A strong, steady breeze whipped through the forest, rocking Mila's tree like a pendulum. Her stomach lurched. Three beams panned around below her. The men shouted. The dogs silenced.

"Look in the trees," she heard a guard say.

A beam strayed in her direction. The forest hushed in anticipation. Her heartbeat seemed to echo everywhere.

"That tree is more than a hundred feet tall, idiot. How the hell do you think she'd get up there?"

"Something moved."

Mila held her breath as the beam crept up the trunk of the beech tree, perusing every branch.

"*Scraaaaaaaaaaw!*" The barn owl launched from the beech tree and swooped toward the ground before flying into the dark forest. The dogs went wild.

"Samson, Scout—heel!"

"Stupid dogs distracted by a barn owl. Keep moving."

Mila watched as the lights retreated farther into the forest and faded from view. She leaned into the beech tree and rested her head against its trunk, so flaccid with relief she thought she'd drop to the earth. Supported by branches and encased in a cocoon of fluttering leaves, the tree sheltered her. Safety had eluded her for so long. Now she balanced in this refuge, disconnected from the ground but not quite in the sky, nearly unnoticeable yet able to notice, as free and safe as she could hope to be without possessing a pair of wings.

She imagined trees to be humanity's secret keepers, sure-footed centurions of the forest. Aged and wise and silently ever-watching, they had witnessed human triumph and treachery, love and loss, freedom and oppression. They bore the sharp blade of the axe, allowing humans to consume them—often gluttonously—and yet, still, they watched. They watched from their places in cabins and homes, benches and barns, at times as caskets and guardians of the dead. On this night they guarded her, the fleeing convict, the innocent prisoner, the cornered killer. She had wiped a man's blood on the oak tree's trunk and washed it away in its hole, yet the oak wouldn't tell a soul. The beech concealed her from the guards, kept her high and out of reach. All the timber in the forest watched her run, and they would never say where.

The torment and chaos of the past few hours threatened to engulf her. Every millisecond of the horrifying scene etched her memory forever—salivating with a wide mouth, ready to swallow her whole. She had been forced to kill a man. No, not a man—she wouldn't allow him that. She had killed a monster. And she hated Falk for it. She hated Forsythe Marlowe and Agent Falk, Flint Hill, and Hesperia itself for what they had forced her to do. Why should she carry blood on her hands when it was they who had dragged her to that wretched point?

She had to kill. She had no choice. Anger blazed inside her—then cooled to rot.

~~~

The moon and sun began trading places, until the navy night diluted into a cerulean morning. The hours had been free of footsteps, flashlights, and murmuring voices. She hoped it meant the guards had searched all of the forest in her area and determined it clear. As the sun yawned, she noticed the forest's end—not far, perhaps a couple hundred yards ahead. The tree line broke into a golden, grassy field. As quietly as possible, she inched down the beech tree and climbed down the oak.

She could no longer ignore her ankle. Every bit of pressure she placed on her left foot sent waves of excruciating pain radiating up her foot and shin. She lumbered a few steps before noticing a hearty fallen branch. Picking it up, she broke off the tapered end to give it a thicker tip, then wedged the other end under her armpit to use as a makeshift crutch. A slower way to move, but it kept pressure off her injury. She broke free of the woods, into the field.

The grass stood inches taller than her diminutive frame. It offered her a reed-like shield as she limped farther from the forest. She watched for broken twigs and flattened or bent areas in the grass to indicate lurking guards, but saw none. *Maybe I've truly escaped.* The thought lightened her dragging steps. But then what? Her stomach roared and railed against its emptiness. Her body begged for water. She needed clothes, and something to wrap her ankle. She needed somewhere to go. But where? She was nestled deep in a field of grass that covered her vision and had no perceptible end, away from Flint Hill but not far enough, and per-haps nowhere close to society of any kind.

Despite her undefined destination, she trudged forward. The sun ascended higher and beat down harder, and Mila's clammy, damp jumpsuit trapped in the heat. Her shoulder and armpit ached from using the stick. Her ankle was swollen and tender.

If she had been smarter, she'd have taken Falk's object and jammed it into her own neck instead.

After what felt like an eternity of hobbling, she spotted a rusted water tower standing high above the field. Not much amid miles of untamed grass, but maybe it meant a road—or human life of some kind—wasn't far. She plodded until the tall grass abruptly ended and became a recently-cut field, then continued until she stood underneath the wa-ter tower.

Beyond it were magnerails, which used a precise mixture of electromagnetic forces to propel magnetrains forward by binding them to the tracks, yet keep them floating ever so slightly above, resulting in the fastest, quietest transportation option in the freight rail industry. The field continued on the other side of the magnerails, with no end in sight.

Mila limped to the tracks and followed them until she saw the black engine and boxcars stopped on top. Next to it stood a modest concrete train stop, marbleized by mold and mildew. She hesitated. She smelled worse than a garbage bag and looked like a nightmare. In her red jumpsuit, blotched and stained with God knows what, any self-preserving Hesperian would march her straight back to Flint Hill. She looked over her shoulder, back in the direction from where she'd come. She had escaped, dodged the guards. She was two stops from freedom. Even the water tower looked smaller, for how far she had followed the magnerails...

She glanced back at the train, then again at the water tower. Lu's words floated back to her mind.

"All said the train went to a place where not even Hesperia can find you."

She dropped her walking stick.

14.

THE TRAIN STOP lacked loading platforms, and the small concrete building stood humbly on the ground with one open door. It seemed to be more of a break area for the conductor than a train station or destination of any kind. Mila inched closer.

A complicated, metallic melody floated from the dingy concrete building. She recognized it—a hammered dulcimer. A bygone instrument hardly anyone knew, but her mother loved. Hopeful, she forced her dragging, damaged body forward, limping closer until she neared the cement platform. The dulcimer music stopped, and Mila paused. She heard the unidentified musician rummage around inside, and then...

Chutck chutck.

A stocky middle-aged woman stepped through the door. She leveled a shotgun at Mila's face. "Step back, missy." She puffed her windswept, mouse-brown hair out of her eyes. "I'd hate to blow them pretty eyes clean toward the north and south poles."

Her arms shook as she raised them in surrender.

The woman stomped forward, her heavy leather boots smacking against the slab. "I said step back."

Mila obeyed.

"Now what do you want?"

"I—heard your music," she faltered.

The woman cocked an eyebrow. She snaked her fingers around the barrel of the gun. "Girl, you gather yourself and tell me why you're standing at my station looking like the Devil himself just had his way with ya, or you'll have a front-row seat to my other hidden talent—taxidermy."

"I need help—"

"Clearly. Flint Hill?"

"Yes. I escaped. Last night. I was innocent."

She snorted. "Isn't everyone?"

The woman's retort stung. Was she a fool to think she'd be able to have any sort of life outside of Flint Hill? The words she planned to say clogged in her throat. But movement drew her eye—the woman's finger slid away from the gun's trigger.

"Guards already came and went. Asked me if I'd noticed anything. Told me to alert them right away if I saw you. Tell me this instant why I shouldn't put a round in your leg and drag you back to prison."

Mila swallowed, then let her thought rush out before she could regret it. "Because if you thought you should, you already would have."

The woman's face stayed still as steel.

"They had me for... a couple of weeks, I think," Mila continued. "They thought I knew things I didn't know—shouldn't know. Please." She let her arms drop slowly back to her sides. "My ankle's hurt and I haven't had anything to eat or drink. Help me with those three things, and I'll leave. I won't tell anyone about you. Please." She bit her lip—she had forgotten a key request. The most important request. If this woman conducted the train Lu spoke of, she *had* to board it.

Speak up—speak up! But her lips locked tight. *This woman barely gave me—an escaped convict—the time of day. I can't ask now. Not yet.*

Keeping her shotgun raised, the woman squinted. She glanced around, then lowered the gun.
Jerking her head toward the door, she said, "Get in
here."

~~~

Thirty minutes later, Mila sat on a wicker rocking
chair with her ankle wrapped, iced, and elevated,
and a hot bowl of soup in her hands. The soup
overflowed with earthy goodness—sausage, carrots,
celery, sweet potatoes, spinach, and beans, all swirling in a spicy broth. It took all her restraint to keep
from devouring the delicious meal like a starved
bear. Only after she finished—her stomach bal-
looning out with satisfaction—did she examine her
surroundings.

The small stop's main room appeared to double
as a living room and bedroom. She rocked over a
braided old rug while her hostess—Ada, she'd
said—sat in an identical chair across from her,
plaid-clad arms crossed over her chest, a dulcimer
next to the seat. From her spot, Mila could see a
meager kitchen through a doorway on one side of
the main room. In the opposite direction was a tiny
bathroom. The sun towered in the sky outside, but
the stop's windowless interior was dark as midnight, except for the lone kerosene lamp sitting on
the floor next to Ada.

"You don't have electricity?" Mila asked.

Ada lifted the lamp and stood. "I do—the freight station furnished this place. But I hardly use it, 'cept in important situations." She nodded toward Mila's ankle.

"Thank you for the ice. And—everything. Really."

Ada only walked to the propped-open metal door, kicked away the stop, and let the door slam shut. She barred it.

An unexpected surge of anxiety sent prickles of sweat over Mila. Being shut in a small, stone room with a metal door had been her life for too long.

Ada stared at her with lips pursed and bushy eyebrows knitted. Her eyes—piercing as blue flames—glinted with analytical detachment and genuine concern. "They're tracking you."

Mila started. "What?"

"Flint Hill injects some of their prisoners with devices, and my gut's tellin' me you're one of them. Do you remember any injections of any kind? Vaccines, sedations, medications?"

"Injections? Only when they first—first captured me. They put a hood over my head, asked me questions, and"—she swallowed against the terror budding within her at the memory—"there was an injection. It knocked me unconscious."

"That ain't all it did." Ada stalked into the kitchen, out of sight, and Mila heard clicks and clangs as she rummaged.

Falk is tracking me. Tracking me like I'm his dog. Her stomach clenched as though she'd eaten rancid meat.

Ada returned, a small device—a scanner, perhaps—in her hand. "Stand up, girl, and hold up your hair."

Mila struggled to her feet, her head swimming. "What is that?"

"It'll locate ninety-five percent of the trackers Hesperia uses and disable them without more than electromagnetic waves. No needles, no nothing."

"But you don't use electricity."

"I don't use *Hesperia's* electricity."

Who was this woman, and why did she have such a remarkable device? How did she get it in the first place? Stifling her curiosity—and her growing desire to board Ada's train—she turned around and piled her matted hair atop her head.

Ada's footsteps closed in from behind her. A beep sounded, and Mila's skin prickled in response to the device's nearness. It whirred quietly as Ada scanned her, beginning with her head. At the nape of her neck, it emitted a series of beeps, then a buzz. Mila tensed.

"It's not activated," Ada whispered.

"What?"

"You've got a tracker, but whoever planted it inside you never turned it on—or turned it off at some point."

Falk... Falk framed me, then let me escape. He turned the electric fence off so I could climb it... The guards. The guards couldn't find me because he didn't want them to find me. Knowing crept over her like a storm over the sea. Falk's words echoed in her mind. "I said you'd be free of this place. Don't think you're free of me."

A click and a short, high-pitched ringing sound interrupted her thoughts. The tiniest locus of heat bloomed at the base of her hairline. Mila turned, her heart racing.

"Let's see 'em chase you now." Ada stared at her through narrowed eyes. "What'd they think you knew, girl?"

"Um," Mila tried to keep the flood of traumatic memories at bay as she answered the question. "They thought I was helping... the opposition. And a person they thought was a terrorist."

"You don't have to call 'em the opposition here, girl. And, really, whether you've got a people opposing a government gone nuts, or if you've got a government opposing the people's desires for transparency and stuff, either one could be the opposition. Depends on how you look at it."

"How do you look at it?"

"The way I see it"—Ada lumbered toward the kitchen—"you and me aren't friends, and I don't share personal information with strangers." She returned, having traded the scanner for her own bowl of soup. "But I'll tell ya this much. I didn't kick your ass back to Flint Hill, did I?" She pointed her spoon in the direction of the facility.

"No," she blustered with a sigh. *No, I can't possibly ask for even a tablespoon more of kindness from this woman.*

Ada smiled and her rigid posture softened. "I don't know what your plans are after you leave here, but I'm guessing you'll have a hard time getting it done if you're traipsing around in a bright red prison jumpsuit. Am I right?"

Mila nodded.

"Okay then." She balanced her bowl on the seat of her chair. "Go on in the bathroom and take you a shower. I'll find something for you to change into." She shuffled over to her makeshift bedroom and rummaged in a box, pulling out a plaid shirt and a length of rope.

An old brown towel sat on the tiny bathroom counter. Ada set the clothing and braided rope by the sink. "If you wear my jeans, you'll be tripping all over yourself," she said. "This was my late husband's. Figured it should go down about to your knees and you can use it as a dress." Stabbing a finger in the direction of the shirt, she spoke through tight lips, "If anyone asks you where you got it, tell 'em you bought it, stole it, or tell 'em you shaved a bunch a squirrels and weaved it yourself. I don't care what tale you spin, long as you don't tell anyone you got it from me. Got it?"

Mila nodded.

"Good. Now enjoy your shower." Ada walked off, mumbling, "Lord knows you need it."

Mila hadn't had a shower since her arrest. She tore her prison clothes off of her body as though hornets swarmed inside the cloth, unwrapped her tender ankle, and stepped into the streams of water. The hot water trickled over her body, the steam enveloped and purified her. She closed her eyes, letting it permeate her matted hair and wash away the dried vomit and corpse fluid.

A brown glass bottle, with scrawled handwriting labeling it shampoo, stood on the shower shelf. Mila poured a dollop into her palm. It was scratchy as sand and smelled like metal and minerals, but even the rough, pungent stuff was like a potion crafted by Panacea herself. Mila scrubbed it into her scalp, sighing in deep contentment as she ran her fingers through her long, soft, wonderfully clean hair. A half-melted square of black, home-made soap stuck to the ledge. Mila pried it off and slid it over her skin. The grit of pulverized pumice scraped her clean, and she relished it.

When she stepped out of the shower, she re-wrapped her ankle and tugged the flannel shirt over her body. The plaid shirt swallowed Mila like a sack but the well-worn fabric comforted her. Securing the braided rope around her waist, she towel-dried her hair and finger-combed it, letting it fall in loose waves around her shoulders. Barefoot, she returned to the living room to put on her prison slip-ons.

"That's more like it," Ada said. "Now go get me your old stuff."

When Mila returned with her jumpsuit wadded into a ball, Ada stood in the living room with a huge metal pot hugged in one arm and a stick lighter and small, unlabeled bottle in her free hand. Tipping her head toward the pot, she said, "Put that in here."

Mila did. Ada set the pot on the floor, dribbled clear liquid from the bottle into the pot, clicked the stick lighter, and ignited the clothing.

"I'll dump the ashes on one of my stops when I head out tomorrow morning," promised Ada.

"I can't thank you enough." For the first time since before her arrest, Mila smiled. "When I heard about a magnetrain near an old water tower from another inmate, I didn't think about it. But then when I saw it here, I hoped—"

Ada froze with one hand poised to put the lid on the pot. Her eyes smoldered like the contents inside it.

"What?" Mila whispered.

"Say that again."

"I—said—"

"They're talking about my train at Flint Hill?" With her chin-length, wild tresses framing her intense stare, the older woman looked feral.

"Yes."

Ada slammed the lid on the pot and rushed to her bed, falling to her knees beside it. Reaching underneath, she snatched a large cloth bag and began to throw belongings into it.

"What's wrong?"

Ada jumped to her feet and whipped around. "Talk doesn't happen just among prisoners! Don't you see? Prisoners find out, guards find out. What've they been saying? Spit it out!"

"That if you find—if you find the train near the old water tower, it'll take you..." Mila checked herself in Ada's stare. The woman jutted her chin as if to push the words out. She finished in a whisper, "Take you where not even Hesperia can find you."

Ada stumbled back. Her eyes glazed over. "Hell," she breathed. "Those devils found my footsteps." Her gaze snapped back to her bed. Dropping to the floor, she snatched and hurled items into her sack.

Mila took a tentative step forward. "It's true, then?"

"'Course it's true. I take this freight train all the way north to New England region and all the way south to Bay, and steel ain't all I carry." Hustling around the building, she pitched clothes, food, and her gun into the pack. "It's true. I take people where Hesperia will never find them. Not ever. Unless prisoners run their mouths and the guards beat the information out of 'em." Yanking the zipper up the bag, she straightened and crossed her arms. "I can't stay here. And I can't let you wander off and get captured again, now that you know. I don't know where you thought you'd go after you escaped from Flint Hill, but you're not going there anymore." She walked to the living room, stopping by the smoldering pot. "Make yourself useful. Put out your arms."

Mila extended her arms, expecting to receive the pot, but Ada packed up her instrument. She shoved it at Mila.

"Over my dead body will they take my dulcimer," she spat. Slinging her sack over one shoulder and hoisting the metal pot in her other arm, she charged to the door and flung it open. "Now come with me and say your goodbyes to Hesperia."

15.

JULIAN MERRICK shielded his eyes against the bold afternoon sun. Even Savannah-Georgia's powerful live oak trees couldn't block the strong rays of ripened summer. Adjusting his grip on the two grocery bags in his other hand, he picked up his pace, rushing to prep his pub for opening.

He hurried down Abercorn Street, past stately, centuries-old homes built to last with Bath Stone, brownstone, and red brick. The essence of the nearby Savannah River permeated the Spanish moss-scented air. He tasted its salty tang as he turned, panting, down McDonough Street, ahead to Chippewa Square, which fluttered with artists, picnickers, and pedestrians. The historic city straddled the line between small town and metropolis. It deserved big attention for all it offered, but didn't quite attract it—precisely why he had moved there three years before with his mother, Natalie.

He hustled to a four-story Victorian-era home, regally clad in clay-colored brick and topped with a black roof supported by a matching corbel. He climbed the steps to the second-floor main entrance—the first floor, partly underground, remained sealed off—and ducked under the oval oak sign that labeled the place in carved, black cursive. VOLTAIRE'S.

What a wreck the place had been when he'd discovered and bought it. But he had nurtured the nineteenth-century building, taking it from battered to beautiful. He pressed four of his fingertips into the security panel—pinky, thumb, middle, index. The door clicked. Pushing it open, he strode across the gleaming black walnut floors, from the foyer to the main area. The crook of his arm throbbed, anxious to be rid of the weight of the grocery bag. Swinging the bag from his arm, he allowed limes, lemons, and every other cocktail garnish to slide free across the counter. He rubbed the sore skin at his elbow.

A nearby booth creaked. He jumped at the sight of a figure, but relaxed. "Mama! What are you doing down here?"

The middle-aged woman, ash brown hair twirled loosely atop her head, shook as she gripped her walker and nudged her way toward him. "Hieu helped me down the stairs," she said, a glint of mischief in her warm cocoa eyes. "I don't *have* to stay in our apartment. Staying on the fourth floor makes me feel like an old bell-ringer."

"Oh," Julian sighed. "You know perfectly well we have no bells."

His mother reached the counter of the massive, oval mahogany bar. "I can help you. I want to help you."

As if it were a piece on a chessboard, Julian slid a lime across the counter. "Slice a lime?" He waggled a paring knife.

"Of course." She shrugged. "You've put your entire life on hold to provide for me and support me. Slicing one lime is the least I can do. Literally."

"The list of what you accomplished is much longer."

Married at eighteen, single mother at nineteen, Natalie Merrick had worked multiple jobs just to put a roof over their heads. He still remembered the exhausted but beaming smile on her face when she finally brought him to their very own home for the first time, when he was eight. That dilapidated, mint green bungalow. A bucket as a dinner guest on rainy nights, the roof adding to the conversation with its constant drip. The tattle-tale thin walls, always getting him into trouble for writing on his archaic, heirloom typewriter well past bedtime.

A passionate breeze could've blown the place down. But it had everything on Voltaire's.

He passed his mother the paring knife. "How are you doing on medicine?"

"Okay." She pursed her lips.

"Mama."

"I have four pills left."

He stopped his preparations, leaning—arms rigid—against the counter. "I feared as much." If she didn't have more soon, she'd get really bad. He gritted his jaw, remembering her last close call—the uncontrollable shaking, the frightening stumbles as her muscles lost control. He pursed his lips, fighting off the images by forcing himself to focus on his pub prep.

"Don't worry, Julian. We've never been without before."

"There's a first time for everything," he said. "Hieu promised he'd come by tonight. I'll get the medicine then."

~~~

Voltaire's blazed with business most nights and this one was no different. Julian and his four employees hustled around the pub, pouring beers, mixing drinks, and taking payments. Chatter reverberated throughout the rooms. Julian worked so quickly he hardly had time to notice who asked for what.

"Mint julep?" a young woman asked. Julian nodded and tossed a sprig of mint into a highball glass as a reminder of what to make, and looked to the next customer.

"Emerson's Belgian Ale, please!" the elderly man called. Julian nodded to Damien, who promptly tugged on the tap, spewing golden, bubbly liquid into a beer mug.

"Gin and tonic, light on the tonic."

"Can you make a Brandy Alexander?" a woman asked.

"Oh, you're testing me tonight!" Julian joked. "You're gonna make me have to dig out my book for that one." He winked and the woman bubbled with laughter. Sprinkling nutmeg to top the drink, he looked up to see Hieu approach the counter, shiny black hair and silvery dress shirt reflecting the warm lights in Voltaire's. Pouring a glass of brandy, he slipped it across the counter for his friend.

Hieu lifted the glass in silent thanks, tilting his head toward the back of Voltaire's.

Julian nodded and returned to taking orders. Hieu's chiseled features appeared even more stony tonight. Now was not the time to wonder why. He turned his attention to his customers, ignoring the clenching knot within his chest.

Hours later, he leaned against the counter and guzzled water, letting his glance dart to the large clock over the bar. Twelve forty-five a.m. Only fifteen minutes until last call, but a final stream of orders would bombard him once more before he could close up shop, no doubt. As he sipped the final drops of water, a group approached the bar.

"Cabernet?"

Julian looked to Damien.

"Got it." Damien spun and reached for a red wine glass and uncorked a bottle of Cab.

"Vodka cranberry."

"Can you do a rum and root beer?"

"Can I!" he exclaimed.

"Do you have any pale ales on tap?"

Julian pointed to Damien, who waved the customer over to talk him through the options. Julian began mixing his final two beverages, thankful the recipes didn't require much. He sensed one more patron approach the bar.

"What can I get you?" he asked, keeping his eyes on the shot of rum he was pouring.

"A place to stay," an unfamiliar female voice asked quietly.

Julian's head snapped up. He was certain he'd never served the young woman standing in front of him. She might have been beautiful once, but she was thin—troublingly so, with a complexion that might've been rosy, a face that might've been heart-shaped if it weren't for her drained color and sunken cheeks. Long, wavy hair the color of cherry wood fell wildly around her shoulders. She looked at him tiredly but earnestly through large, heterochromic eyes, rimmed by dark circles. He'd never encountered someone with irises so purely green or silvery gray.

Startled by her question, he stuttered, "I'm sorry, what?"

Her gaze darted around nervously. She toyed with the sleeve hem of the plaid dress she wore. "I was told to find Voltaire's... Is this an inn and tavern or something? I don't have any money."

Julian chuckled. "It's not an inn." He leaned across the counter. "Who led you here?"

"Ada."

"Okay," he said, pouring gin, amaro, orange liqueur, and bitters into a lowball glass. "This one's on the house. My own invention." Adding an orange peel, he slid the drink across the counter to her. "A Zetetic."

"What's a Zetetic?"

"One who questions everything." Extending his hand, "I'm Julian."

She took it. "Mila."

"Nice to meet you, Mila. I'll be closing up soon. Wait anywhere you like and someone will be with you. I'll join you the minute I get a lull."

He watched as she wandered—with a slight limp—across the pub to an open seat. Ada hadn't brought them a new one in such a long time. This one must have quite the story to tell.

~~~

Ada had told Mila nothing about this place, only how to get there and what to say to the "Adonis of a bartender". Mila had been so thankful for Ada's help, she didn't press for any other details about the mysterious destination, not throughout the entire two-day trip. But now that Ada was gone—"going underground, mole-style," as she'd said—

and Mila was here, in this beautiful building in the middle of a city where customers came and went non-stop, she wondered how safe she truly was. The nervous vibrating in her hands threatened to turn into full-on tremors. Clasping her glass, she sipped her drink. It singed her tongue with an herbal, citrus flavor. Resisting the desire to down it all, she took frequent, small gulps until someone approached her booth. A striking man in a silver shirt looked at her intently with onyx eyes.

"May I sit?" he asked in a robust baritone.

Her nerves bunched in her throat. She managed a nod.

"I'm a friend of Julian's. Hieu. And you are?"

"Mila Ray. Ada brought me."

Hieu nodded once. "Ada is very selective about who she brings to us." He slid into the seat across from her. "Tell me how you earned your ticket."

She took a few deep breaths. Should she tell the man everything? If they sent her away, she'd have no other options. She might as well be dead. But the call of truth pressed heavy on her. Could she run under the flag of verity, be a champion for openness, if she wasn't willing to live in truth herself? If she wasn't willing to die for it?

Julian approached and slid into the booth, and the response clogged in Mila's throat.

"Good timing," Hieu said. "Mila is going to tell us how she got a seat on Ada's train." He eyed her, insisting.

She nodded. Another sip of her drink, and she told them. Through stutters and chokes, pausing every so often to gather herself, she recounted it all. How she would have killed herself before anyone else. Her night in the grave with a dead man. How Marlowe wrapped her fingers around the gun and aimed it at Lu, and would force her to pull the trigger if she didn't give him the information she didn't have. How Falk intervened—and the heavy strings attached to his offer. His tight, cold grip as he forced her hand.

"I could see no other choice in that moment," she said. "I still can't see another choice. There isn't a word to express how I feel about Hesperia making me a murderer." She pressed her eyes shut. She'd rather pour vinegar on an open wound than see how the men looked at her now. Surely, they'd send her away, to fight her battle alone, until Falk finished her off. When silence became too much to bear, she dared to look again.

Julian's eyebrows narrowed—in horror, definitely. In anger, certainly—but whether at her or Hesperia, she couldn't tell. But the concern on his face caught her off guard. She blinked, unable to look at him for fear of shriveling in shame.

Hieu crossed his arms and leaned back in the booth. For a moment, he only watched her, eyes dark and grim. Then he leaned forward, propping his elbows on the table. "Do you think your story scares us? That you're a risk? We are not afraid of Hesperia. Let that statement alone tell you how fortified we are against their *watching*. You came here because you need a place where Hesperia—where Agent Falk—cannot find you. This is that place—if you abide by our rules. It is a rare place, and a fiercely protected one. Ours is the kind of place that, once tainted, once compromised, can never be recreated in Hesperia again. It would be gone. Forever."

He waited. Mila shifted uncomfortably.

"Ada checked you for tracking devices?"

"She found one, and deactivated it."

Hieu nodded. "We take it with the utmost seriousness when someone new comes along, and newcomers should take the decision seriously as well. Take a few days and think about whether or not this is a step you should take. I will continue considering your case as well. Then, I may tell you more about who we are." He patted the table in finality.

What now? Where can I go in the meantime? She opened her mouth to ask, but Julian spoke first.

"I live upstairs," he said. "You look like you could use some good rest."

"You're—inviting me to stay? After everything I just told you, you are willing to let me stay with you?"

He shrugged, his mouth cocking to the side in a small smile. "All of us here are fugitives from Hesperia in one way or another. We all have each other's backs—and I know you'll be safe here. C'mon. There's a bed and plenty of room for you."

A bed. A real bed. Deep exhaustion sacked her. "Thank you." She struggled to stand on her tender ankle. Julian extended his hand to help her up. Taking it, she nodded to Hieu.

Mila walked with Julian to the foyer, then he led her up one flight of stairs to the third floor. A simple chain blocked the rest of the stairway, with a sign alerting customers of the private residence beyond. Julian unhooked the chain, moved the sign, and helped Mila up the rest of the way.

A couple of floor lamps cast a cozy glow around the main area of the apartment. Two tattered leather couches faced each other in the middle of the room, a coffee table between them.

"Make yourself comfortable," Julian said, gesturing. Mila took a seat on the couch to the left, and Julian sat on the one opposite her.

Silence hung between them until Mila finally said, "Your bar is beautiful. I've never been to another place like it." Such a trivial thing to say in light of their discussion downstairs, yet it was all she could muster.

"Thank you." Julian's blue-green eyes sparkled when he smiled. Mila already enjoyed his company and his magnetic, yet authentic, spirit.

"You must be incredibly proud, to accomplish such a dream so soon in life."

"Well, it was first runner-up." He shrugged.

"Really?"

"Yeah, I kind of developed the entrepreneurial spirit out of necessity."

The decisive tolling of a grandfather clock alerted them to the hour.

"I became a night owl out of necessity, too," Julian grinned. "But you're probably exhausted. You'll sleep in my room and I'll take the couch."

Mila started to protest but Julian stood and folded his arms. "Tell me how long it's been since you've slept well." He cocked an eyebrow. "Thought so. Stay here."

He disappeared into a doorway located behind the couch she sat on, and she heard him rummaging. She scanned the apartment, but there wasn't much to look at. A simple bookshelf stood against the opposite wall, filled with books stacked every which way. To its left, an arched opening led to a small kitchen. Against the wall to her left, next to a sliding door leading to a small patio, stood an old, scratched grandfather clock. She looked at the side table next to her seat. It held one framed photo, faded and crinkled, of a beautiful young woman with a big smile and wide-set eyes sitting on porch steps, beaming as her arms wrapped around a curly-headed boy of about eight years. Turning around to the direction Julian had gone, she saw the doorway to another room. A walker stood next to it. Mila knitted her eyebrows, wondering about its owner.

Julian returned. "Your room is all set," he said, continuing past her and toward the stairs. "It's not much, but I'm fairly confident it's better than Flint Hill. I have to go back downstairs and get something. You're welcome to look around if you like."

"Maybe tomorrow." Mila stood. "Thank you."

Julian smiled and descended the stairs.

Mila limped into Julian's room and turned on the light. A mattress lay on the floor, surrounded by stacks of paperback notebooks hand-labeled "Prototypes and Codes", "Observations", "Voltaire's", "Finances" and "Thoughts". It appeared to be Julian's brand of controlled chaos—like stepping into his mind. Starkly different from the class and opulence of the pub downstairs. The only piece of furniture in the room was a chest of drawers, which stood next to a closet door. Untying the rope around her waist, she removed her flannel shirt-dress and crouched to fall into bed. The mattress gave against her weight, molding around her. She pulled the sheets up to her chin, relishing the way their clean coolness soothed her skin.

For a moment, she stared at the ceiling. *What have I walked into? Where am I, really—is this the destination, or just another stop?*

Sleep hushed her rushing thoughts, its susurrations lulling her from worry. She surrendered to it, deciding she didn't care where she was as long as Falk couldn't reach her.

~~~

Julian plodded down the final steps and returned to Voltaire's. Hieu waited for him at the bar.

"I hope you brought it," Julian called as he crossed the room.

Hieu produced a bag filled with white capsules.

"Thanks." Julian sighed, taking the bag and seating himself at the stool next to his friend. "Every time we need more, we're getting closer and closer to running out. You're starting to scare me, Hieu."

Hieu ran his fingers through his hair. "I know."

"You know how dangerous it is for her not to have it in her system. What's going on?"

"The Squire we get the xianepam from is..." Hieu took a deep breath. He let it out slowly. "He's having a tough time."

"How so?"

"On one side he's got Hesperia—they're holding a magnifying glass to his pharmaceutical practice, wanting to know everything he's selling, everything he's getting. He thinks they suspect he's creating his own drugs on the sly, which puts everyone in a dangerous spot—your mother and you, him, and everyone else who shares her condition. He has a hard time obtaining the ingredients he needs to make the meds without the government knowing. And if they found out he was creating and supplying a med that they weren't making any money on..." He shook his head, dismay carving deeper lines into his golden skin. "He might as well be dealing qanna or harder drugs, for the repercussions he'd face. And then Hesperia would take his creation, make it completely unavailable, and put it through all kinds of red tape for who knows how many years. And once they made it available—*if* they ever made it available—do you think anyone could get it for the price Don gives us now?" Hieu tightened his fist. "All of that is to say, Hesperia's got their eyes on Don, and he's having a really tough time staying under their radar and still providing us with xianepam without putting himself or us at risk. And..." Hieu clenched his jaw.

"And what?" Julian said. "Hieu. Tell me."

"As if that weren't enough," Hieu closed his eyes and rubbed his forehead. "Don has reason to believe the Belgae are monitoring his books—who he's providing to. They're..." Hieu locked eyes with Julian, his expression grim. "They're looking for you, Julian. They need you back. Ever since Hesperia took Dale Trent from them, they've been struggling. Seriously. I think they saw some hope when Carlo DaVanti did his data drop and wanted to help them, but—Hesperia took him, too."

Julian bit his lip and released a slow, steamy breath. "How dare they. I warned DaVanti, damn it... I told him it wasn't worth it." He pounded a fist on the bar. "Damn it!" His voice echoed off the walls, repeated, and faded.

"He knew what he was getting into, Julian."

"I know, I..." His voice fizzled out and he retreated into his thoughts for a moment, absent-mindedly tapping his fingers on an imaginary holodesk. "I can..." He looked at Hieu. "Tell him I can encrypt his systems."

"If either the Belgae or Hesperia are already in his systems, you can't kick them out and encrypt the systems without risking us all."

Julian held up the bag of pills and counted them, mouthing the numbers. "Eight days' worth. I can work with that. I can come up with something between now and then, Hieu. And then maybe Don can quit squiring and go completely underground, so we'll never have to worry about this again."

"One step at a time," Hieu cautioned.

"No. It will happen. I'll make sure of it." Julian clutched the pills. "Thanks for these." They both left their bar stools and began walking toward the foyer.

"I'm sorry it took so long."

"Not your fault." Julian drummed his fingers on the security panel and unlocked the door for Hieu. He held it while his friend exited, then shut and re-locked it.

Leaning against the door, he slid down to the floor and pressed his palms to his eyes. No matter how far he went, how hard he'd worked, he'd always feared the walls of the life he'd built for his mother and himself would crumble down. Tonight, the first rocks toppled. His breath rattled—he must keep them safe. He couldn't waste time if his mother was to have a fighting chance. Jumping to his feet, he ran toward the back of Voltaire's.

16.

COFFEE'S PERSUASIVE, nutty wafts woke Mila from a sleep deeper than she'd had in years. Rousing, her muscles stung and throbbed—had she not moved all night long? She opened her eyes, jolting a little before remembering where she'd come. Crawling off the mattress, she tugged on her shirt-dress—wrinkling her nose at the pungent scent of body odor and Ada's musty train car—and moved with shrinking steps to the kitchen.

Bacon sizzled, its inviting, salty scent making her stomach grumble. She peeked through the doorway to see Julian at the stove, flipping the strips with a pair of tongs. A woman in a yellow bathrobe sat at a round glass breakfast table, mug of coffee in hand. The woman in the photo on the side table—a couple of decades older.

The woman looked up from her coffee, her eyes brightening. "This must be our new guest!"

Julian cast a smile over his shoulder.

"Mila, I'm Natalie Merrick, Julian's mother. We're so glad to have you stay with us. I'd get up, but..." She tipped her head toward the walker parked next to the table. "Come sit! Julian will pour you some coffee. Do you like coffee? Would you like some eggs and bacon?"

"Please." Mila joined Natalie at the table. "I can't thank you both enough for taking me in."

"The pleasure is all ours. We love having company."

Julian snatched a mug from a cabinet above the stove and filled it. He held up a carton of cream and looked at Mila, raising his eyebrows in a wordless question.

"Yes, thank you," she answered. He dribbled some cream into the mug and set it in front of her. For a moment, she only cradled it in her hands, enjoying how it heated her palms and fingers.

"Julian," Natalie began. "I woke up around five o'clock and you weren't on the couch. Did you stay up all night?"

Julian stopped stirring the eggs. "Yeah—Hieu needs me to develop something. It's kind of a short notice project, so I had to get started right away."

"Oh." Natalie knitted her eyebrows. "Don't push yourself too hard."

Julian set a plate of bacon and eggs in front of his mother. The two of them stared at each other for a moment in a silent standoff. "Don't worry about me," Julian said as he moved back to the stove. Natalie flashed Mila a grin and shook her head in mock surrender. Even in their brief moment of tension, Mila sensed the deep, abiding devotion between the mother and her son. Their warmth stung the raw wound left by the deaths of her own parents.

After breakfast, she helped Julian clean the kitchen while Natalie searched her closet for extra clothing Mila might be able to wear. With dishes done and counters cleaned, Mila walked into the living room and perused the bookshelf. Julian had many of the same titles she used to own. Classics like Dickens, Hugo, Dumas, Fitzgerald, and Hemingway stacked on top of poetry by Tennyson and Plath, plays by Shakespeare, and philosophy from every angle, from Sartre, Nietzsche, and Rand, to C.S. Lewis, Kant, and Kierkegaard. He even had some of Jung's writings on dream interpretation.

As though starved, she devoured the sight of the tomes, their gold titles faded and burnished. Mila ran her fingers over the lettering, as though their delicate, engraved edges could connect her with the loving life that once was hers. Pausing over a worn paperback copy of Jean-Jacque Rousseau's *The Social Contract*, she pulled it off the shelf. This one, with its ideas of a world bursting with harmonious synergy between the person and the populace, was a favorite of hers from long ago.

"Read anything you like."

Mila started and turned to see Julian standing behind her. "I've read many of them. This is a good one." She held up Rousseau's essay.

"Really?" Julian cocked his head. "What do you like about it?"

"Well…" Mila flipped through the thin book, running her finger down a page. "If we enquire wherein lies precisely the greatest good of all, which ought to be the goal of every system of law, we shall find that it comes down to two main objects, freedom and equality. Freedom, because any individual dependence means that much strength withdrawn from the body of the state, and equality because freedom cannot survive without it.'"

Julian shrugged.

"What, you don't like it?" Mila asked.

"I like it fine." He scratched his head. "I think his analysis of where the individual will ends and the general will begins is interesting and scrupulous, and I think he covers important what-if scenarios, particularly his acknowledgement that time, population, and specific incidents will change the political needs of a given state. Government systems aren't one-size-fits-all."

"But...?"

"*But* I think he makes some assumptions about human behavior that fatally undermine his ideal political system. For all the tedious details he works out and plans for, the one thing he doesn't have a plan for is humans *not* acting logically."

"How so?" Book still in hand, Mila folded her arms, but she smiled slightly. Even though Julian's position surprised her, she found the philosophical sparring match invigorating.

"Give me that." Julian smirked and put out his hand. She handed the book to him and he cleared his throat dramatically. "'It follows from what I have argued that the general will is always rightful and always tends to the public good; but it does not follow that the deliberations of the people are always equally right. We always want what is advantageous to us but we do not always discern it. The people is never corrupted, but it is often misled; and only then does it seem to will what is bad.'" He cocked his head at her and lifted his eyebrows, as if to say, "See?"

"That is entirely accurate," Mila argued. "In every government gone bad, the people are misled—they didn't know the truth, and in some cases didn't even have access to it. That's how it was for The Former Nation, or the Soviets and Germans from hundreds of years ago—pick any society in decay, and I'll show you the common thread. When the people are deceived, there is nowhere to go but downhill. What issue do you take with that?"

Julian snorted. "In short, Rousseau's faith in humanity! People tend toward the good of *themselves*, not the good of all. Give them two choices, both of which are beneficial, one of which is slightly more beneficial *to them* specifically, and they will choose the latter. That tendency alone makes them easy to manipulate. And even *if* we assume that the people is never corrupt, but only misled—which is not true, but I'll wait to argue that point with you until you've had more sleep—how do you prevent societal deception? Or, even more difficult, how do you un-deceive an entire populace? The ideal society, as outlined by Rousseau, must meet all kinds of requirements, from population size all the way to geographical makeup." He tapped on his fingers as if to count off the list. "It was an unrealistic model even during his day, and it is downright impossible now. But the one thing that his entire political philosophy hinged upon was that Man is reasonable and logical. But Man is not."

He smiled jovially, but everything he said twisted within her like a corkscrew. Pretending the conversation was as lighthearted as he apparently thought it was, Mila smiled and put out her hand. "That book should be given to someone who appreciates and understands it."

"One day in and you're already confiscating my books. We'll see how long this lasts." Julian handed the book to her.

At that moment, Natalie entered the room with a bag of clothing swinging from her walker handle. "They may not fit just right, but most of them are dresses and skirts, so it hopefully shouldn't matter too much," she said. "It's times like these I'm glad I rarely clean out my closets."

They agreed it safest for Mila to remain within the building for the time being. Julian left to prepare to open Voltaire's. Mila washed away her journey in the guest shower, then dressed in a beryl blue cotton dress—which hung from her undernourished frame like clothes on a scarecrow—and a pair of delicate black flats before retreating to the back porch, the only safe place for her beyond the building's walls.

On the patio, potted herbs and flowers shivered under the tickle of the spring breeze. Scents of mint, sage, lavender, basil, and delicate flowers circulated in the air. Though it overlooked a cramped, dirty alley, the little porch offered a flirtatious view of the top of a beautiful church with an old clock on its steeple. Looking left, Mila spotted Natalie rocking in one of two chairs, watching a brilliant cardinal hop around the edges of a bird feeder hanging from the porch.

Natalie turned. "Isn't he beautiful? I adore cardinals. I see them all the time, even when I'm not looking. They're nature's reminder that you can still have passion and beauty when times are gray."

Mila smiled, taking the empty seat beside her. "There used to be a great blue heron that would walk onto the porch of my parents' inn in Clearwater-Florida. Even if I was sitting there on the swing, he'd stay and let me feed him."

"Your parents ran an inn? That must've been very nice."

Mila nodded. "It was their dream," she lied.

"*You* are their dream," Natalie corrected. "For all the aspirations and plans I may have had, it's my son who's the fulfillment of my life. It's the same for your parents. Nothing is more meaningful and fulfilling than family."

A stinging, hard knot balled within Mila. Certain it'd show in her eyes, she jerked her gaze to the bannister, spotting a pair of scissors. "Would you like me to trim anything?"

"Please. Julian uses the mint and lavender for drinks."

Mila clipped the herbs and handed them to Natalie, who secured them into bunches. The afternoon progressed easy as a meandering creek, with conversation flowing just as naturally as silence.

Julian's mother personified gentleness. It shined in her eyes, trickled through her voice, and by the end of the afternoon, Mila was convinced Natalie's spirit even nourished the plants on the patio. But the woman exuded quiet strength as well. Like an oak tree that gives protection in its delicate leaves, support in its branches, and rest in its shade, Natalie had strong, deep roots. Though confined to the top floor of the building due to her condition, she extracted a life's worth of joy in her prayers, her son, and the nature that alighted upon her back porch.

"My prayers fill up my spirit, my son fills up my heart, and I believe the plants and animals are the purest of God's creations," she reflected.

At times, Natalie talked in a stream-of-consciousness fashion, and when she spoke this way Mila sensed she wasn't speaking to her but rather to an unseen entity, simply allowing Mila into their intimate conversation. She spoke unabashedly of her past, of the whirlwind romance she had with Julian's father. "He was a true Renaissance man, excellent at everything he tried—except commitment," she remembered. "And of course, I was young and wistful and believed in the best, in weathering the odds. *C'est la vie.*"

She continued, recounting the story of her eighteen-year-old self, whisked off of her feet by the rapturous young man in his twenties, led by passion's impulsivity to the altar of a tiny church to be wed with no one else in attendance but the pastor. Eight weeks later, he disappeared for six months. She served him divorce papers. He signed them willingly, but not until after he lured her into bed one last time. He vanished again, his signature barely dry, then she learned she was pregnant. Julian's father never knew he existed.

Mila twisted a snipping of lavender in her fingers. "It must have been so difficult," she tried, unsure of what to say.

"It was," Natalie admitted. "But I knew my purpose, and I couldn't let anger or bitterness pervert my purpose. I think my life's journey has been about learning to love and not judge—and sometimes, not even to understand. Pure love sets you free." She rocked in her chair. "We cannot stop or prevent pain. The only thing we can do is choose what we'll do with the experience."

Natalie's words and presence swirled within Mila, as though trying to untie the gnarls in her tortured heart. But the screwing—that deep, burrowing sensation that began in Flint Hill—coiled tighter inside. Her purpose and her anger fueled each other now. The anger solidified her, made her relentless, determined to tell the people the truth, to save them. In fulfilling her purpose, she'd free the people, pull the mask off Hesperia, avenge herself, and cleanse her hands of Marlowe's blood. She couldn't let go.

Footsteps clacked across the apartment's wooden floors, breaking her thoughts. The glass door slid open, and Julian peeked out, saving Mila from having to reply to his mother.

"What do you have for me?" he asked.

Mila held up one bunch of herbs.

"Excellent." He disappeared through the doorway.

She rocked forward, out of her chair and followed Julian inside, herbs in hand. He retreated into the kitchen, snatched a coffee mug, and filled his cup with coffee from the pot. Mila's nose wrinkled. The brew had to be at least nine hours old by now.

"Ah," he sighed, returning to the living room. "I'm exhausted. I'd drink sewer sludge if it'd get me through this afternoon slump." He gulped from the mug.

Mila grimaced. "What is it you're working on for Hieu?"

Julian halted mid-sip. He brought the mug down to chest level. "Just a, uh—it's a security-related project."

"Oh." She shifted uncomfortably. "Do you need help with anything?"

He pointed at the herbs in her hand. "Lots of mint today, I hope. A good many customers want mint juleps."

Mila passed the herbs to him—but held on a second too long.

Julian tipped his head, eyeing her. "Something on your mind?"

"Where am I, Julian?"

He pursed his lips. Dropping his eyes to the coffee in his mug, he said, "I can't tell you yet."

~~~

Four days passed this way, in fabricated normalcy. Mila remained with Natalie in the mornings and helped Julian in the afternoons. Hours overflowed with conversation, often carefree, often deep. The comforting ebb and flow of the days brought to mind the years she had spent working alongside her parents at their inn, and the reminder was a simultaneous salve and sting. Living with Julian and Natalie became the closest thing to family she had known since her mother and father had been alive. Yet questions simmered underneath the comfort she longed to embrace. Where was she? Could she call this new place home, and these new people her own? Did they have a mission, and did it dovetail with hers? Julian seemed to sense her ruminating, often breaking her thoughts by whispering, "I promise we'll fill you in soon."

But another, deeper concern crept in the corners of her mind—one for which Julian couldn't provide reassurance. She couldn't possibly be safe from her ever-watching government, not in the middle of a bustling town, living above a thriving business. Every footstep, every creak, every hair-raising breeze was Falk right behind her. Each night, she slept less than the one before, her muscles tense with an overwhelming urge to run.

17.

THE FAINTEST CRACKING sound outside Mila's door shattered the silence like a thunderbolt. Her eyes flew open. She sat up in bed, struggled to quiet her ragged breathing, and strained to listen. Drawing her knees to her chest, she backed against the bedroom wall.

The mattress underneath her liquefied and melted away. The wooden floor swirled and the dove-gray walls accumulated cracks—until both turned into stone. The closet door morphed and thickened until it bore bars.

Ward C.

She looked down at the nightgown Natalie had given her, but it transformed into the bloodied, charred, and torn red jumpsuit. When she looked up, Forsythe Marlowe's blood-drained, bluish face lurked inches from her own.

"Hello, Thirty-Four."

His voice—cavernous in life, abyssal in death. He knelt in front of her, the gaping wound in his neck still leaking blood. His gray eyes bulged as death purged him of gases and fluids. A wet burp escaped his mouth and filled the room with the scent of worms. He smiled, and three crawled out of his mouth and slipped down his oozing neck. Mila's stomach clenched.

"Thirty-Four, Thirty-Four, you're better off dead," a haunting sing-song rang through the room.

Mila tore her gaze away from Marlowe to see Lu hanging from the cell door, a sheet wrapped around her neck, her face colorless and eye sockets empty. She spoke slowly. "You didn't save me."

"Lu, I tried..." she wheezed, barely able to form words in her horror.

She extended her arm, her hand limp. "They buried me, buried me, buried me... right next to your friend Carlo. And how much happier we are,

Thirty-Four. Yes! Believe it. We smile beneath the dirt."

Forsythe Marlowe stuck a long finger into his neck and searched the cavity within until he withdrew a bloodied skeleton key. "Stray from your cell, Thirty-Four. Stray far away. I still hold the key."

"Oh, Thirty-Four..." Lu wailed, her voice echoing and ringing against the walls. "How I pity you."

~~~

Mila jerked awake. Sweat covered her body. She shivered, willing herself not to close her eyes—not even to blink, to keep the terrible images from flooding her mind again. She glanced around the room. It was Julian's. The walls were gray, the mattress was beneath her. She wore the ivory silk nightgown. The clock read two. She couldn't stay here, in this room that so effortlessly mutated into her jail cell while she slept. Hurrying to her feet, she wrapped the nightgown's matching bathrobe around her and tied it at the waist as she hurried down the quiet stairwell toward Voltaire's.

The shiny floors felt cool underfoot as she padded toward the bar, softly lit by faux hurricane lamps after hours. Julian wouldn't mind if she had a glass of wine, even two. She'd never sleep without it now. Tiptoeing behind the bar, she snatched an open bottle of Merlot, uncorked it, and dumped it into a glass until the red liquid nearly reached the brim. She brought it to her lips and took a long draw.

Voices echoed in the adjacent room. She froze with the glass to her lips.

"It's. Too. Risky," a male voice argued.

"Think about it, Hieu." It was Julian. "Put yourself in that position. There was no other choice!"

"That's not what I'm talking about." Hieu sounded exasperated. "You know what the real issue is."

"I think we should make an exception. I've spent time..." His voice trailed off, then grew louder. "And I can tell you she's different."

"That kind of passion runs deep—"

"My passions changed, didn't they?"

Footsteps clipped on the wooden floors. Hieu and Julian appeared in the doorway, engrossed in heated debate.

"Julian! She—"

"Mila," Julian announced. Hieu started, but then composed himself. Julian still wore his bartending clothes, the top few buttons of his white dress shirt undone to reveal a V-neck undershirt. His brassy curls stuck out haphazardly. "Can't sleep?"

She shook her head.

"Me neither. Though truth be told, I wasn't trying." He took a seat at the bar. Hieu joined him.

Mila tightened the robe she wore. "What's keeping you awake?" Julian asked.

"Nightmares," was all she could say.

Julian squinted in concern.

"I hoped to speak with you over the next day or so," Hieu began.

Julian turned and raised his eyebrows, but Hieu continued. "I asked you to do some serious thinking. But the past few days haven't just been for your benefit, they've been for ours as well. Of course we wouldn't extend an invitation without vetting someone fully." Hieu tilted his chin down and gave her a knowing look. "You are a Ray."

Mila's jaw slackened. She stared into her glass. *Is this their concern? My lineage? Would they reject me because of my family?*

In her mind, Forsythe Marlowe smiled and held a key.

"I don't understand," she said.

"We can protect you from Hesperia. We can hide you from Falk. But we can't protect you from yourself. And most importantly, if we let you become one of us, we can't protect ourselves from you." Shaking his head ever so slightly, he said, "So much zeal in the Ray line. Fatal zeal. That's not how we work here. If you join us, you're one of *us*—you don't charge ahead and fight your family's battle."

"I think you misunderstand my family."

"You do?"

"Yes." She straightened. "My ancestors weren't bloodthirsty. My parents didn't *want* to have to kill for freedom, to die for freedom. But all of them were working with the tools available to them—they were using everything they had at their disposal, and still they saw no way around the spilling of blood. And honestly, neither do I. I fought them on it. I tried another way. And look what happened. Blood is the only reason I'm here now." Her shoulders slumped under murder's massive weight. "If there's *another* way—a bloodless way—by God, I want it." She looked at him and let desperation seep into her voice. "Show me the way."

Hieu stood. "Come." He and Julian began walking toward the back of Voltaire's. Mila set her glass on the counter and followed them.

Embedded in the far back wall of the main pub area was a large wood-burning fireplace constructed of stacked stone, with cozy seating arranged in a floret of intimate semi-circles around it. Charcoal tinged the fireplace's interior. Julian walked to the fireplace and knelt at the hearth. Running his fingers over the stone slabs, he paused at one and tugged it outward, revealing a security panel. Mila gaped.

Julian thrummed his fingertips on the panel in quick succession, then slid the stone back into place. A whirring erupted from within the hearth before the bottom jerked out of place, descended, and retreated underground and out of sight. Julian bent and sat, his feet appearing to dangle into the opening. He climbed below the fireplace. Hieu followed, and Mila approached the opening. An iron spiral staircase disappeared into the darkness below. She began her descent, her bare feet against the rough, icy iron steps.

Immersed in darkness, Julian flipped a switch that closed the fireplace and triggered the lights. A warm, low glow emanated from a hurricane lamp below and filled the large, stone-floored room.

Mila's feet met the floor. Red brick walls surrounded the room, dotted in areas with bright, new patches and old, faded ones—some so ancient the bricks melded into each other. In the center of the room stood a circle of ten wooden chairs gathered around an expansive, wooden circular table.

Dazed, she walked farther into the room. Framed paintings of historic figures hung from the walls, along with sketches depicting notable rebellions from around the world and throughout the ages, true to the artistic styles of their times.

Against the wall, directly across from the staircase, stood an easel and sketchpad. She glanced to Julian. He nodded, and she approached the easel. On the sketchpad was an unfinished drawing of five people—three men and two women—standing in the middle of a city street, holding hands and raising them high above their heads. The man in the middle waved a flag inscribed with the phrase, "*Vivre libre ou mourir!*". In the buildings flanking the street, people leaned out of windows, and some of them whispered to each other. Mila moved closer to examine the drawing.

The citizens had no eyes. The revolutionaries' wrists were all cuffed by the same chain—a chain they didn't seem to notice. The signature on the sketch attributed the creation to J. Merrick.

She turned. "You're an artist?"

"I dabble." He shrugged.

Mila didn't know what she expected to see after descending a secret staircase hidden under a decoy fireplace, but she was confused to see that the lair appeared to be nothing more than an extension of Voltaire's, albeit a beautiful one. "What is this place?"

"A basement," Julian answered, lips twisting into a wry smirk.

"It's a gathering place," Hieu said. "We are the Zetetics, an organization that can best be described as, in a word, underground. The gathering place where we stand tonight is only one of many throughout Hesperia, and one of many within our hub. I, Hieu Kien, am the director of this one, the Croatoan Hub, which extends from this part of Bay into Appalachia.

"Do not confuse us with the Belgae. We have remarkably different philosophies, but you will learn that in time. We are indisputably separate from the Belgae. In fact, they don't even know who we are. Neither does Hesperia, and neither do the Hesperian people. We are silent. We are individuals who seek true freedom, and we seek no one's permission for that.

"Many newcomers ask how we began. The broad answer is that zetetics have always been. They may not have always existed in name, but they have always existed. They are born from the success or failure of revolutions." He gestured to the artwork around the lair. "And they are children of oppression. Zetetics have seen and experienced humankind's darkest sides on levels ranging from the individual to the institutional, and they recognize that such darkness has always existed, and will always exist.

"History documents this entropy. Centuries of corruption, of oppression, of crimes against humanity that went unchecked—all have occurred repeatedly, and no system is immune. It is entropy, the inevitable movement of order into disorder. It is inescapable. As the pattern has repeated, so zetetics have become. However, the collaborative group has been christened as the Zetetics for only two hundred years."

"Two hundred years?" Mila said.

"In the span of humanity, set against the ancient tapestry of human pain and sabotage, two hundred years is but a blink. Who are Zetetics? In one word, skeptics. We are even skeptical of ourselves, but particularly skeptical of humanity at large. Two hundred years of planning, structuring, and execution, all with the utmost precision and care, and with the witting or unwitting assistance of people and groups of history."

He walked toward her. "You see, now, why I asked you so many questions at our first meeting. This is not a simple hiding place. This is a life-encompassing choice. To choose it haphazardly is to compromise two centuries of work. I've told you everything, and yet I've told you nothing. This,

Mila Ray, is where you've come. If you become a Zetetic, you will take on a role that keeps you completely out of sight. Every measure that can lessen your chances of being found by Hesperia will be taken, but you will have an active role in our organization. If you walk away now, we lose nothing."

Struck silent, she felt as though Hieu had handed her an ancient treasure and asked her what she would like to do with it. Another drawing caught her eye, this one of multitudes of people on horseback, riding through the wilderness. Men and women and children, some hunched over and wrapped in thick blankets, some walking with weary expressions on their faces. Interspersed in the group were men in uniform, holding weapons. In the clouds, the artist had sketched a quote attributed to Alexis de Tocqueville.

In the whole scene there was an air of ruin and destruction, something which betrayed a final and irrevocable adieu; one couldn't watch without feeling one's heart wrung. The Indians were tranquil, but sombre and taciturn. There was one who could speak English and of whom I asked why the Chactas were leaving their country. "To be free," he answered. I could never get any other reason out of him.

She twisted her hands and looked at Julian. Could she commit to these people, this way of living? What other option did she have? Falk was hunting her. She hadn't come this far just to stay within his reach. She couldn't defeat him alone, she couldn't enlighten the people on her own. Through the Zetetics, the burden of violent revolution would be lifted—so they said—and yet their mission could still be accomplished. Freedom. If her parents had had this choice, she knew they would have taken it. Freedom.

Eyeing Hieu, she said, "The Zetetics' aim is freedom for Hesperia."

"*From* Hesperia," Hieu corrected.

"Not unbridled zealotry, but a careful, calculated mission."

"Correct."

She straightened. "I believe we share an aim."

"Is that so?" asked Hieu.

"Yes." She walked to the table. "I want to become a Zetetic. What do I have to do?"

"There's more for you to know." He nodded to Julian, who moved back toward the iron staircase and then behind it. Mila followed him, standing beside him as he knelt.

He looked up at her. "Take three steps back."

Mila obeyed. Julian reached under the bottom step. He seemed to press something, and a quiet buzzing sounded below the floor. The plank of stone underneath the final stair step shook—then plummeted downward and disappeared.

Julian raised his eyebrows. "Are you sure you want to do this without shoes?"

"Yes."

Again, Julian descended first. Hieu motioned for Mila to go next. She sat at the edge of the opening and dangled her legs until her bare toes curled around the first rounded step of a ladder. She stepped into the cavern below.

She was doubly underground. Voltaire's secret basement extended partially underground, and yet this pitch-black cavern trenched farther below, submerged, like another world beneath the streets of Savannah. A world that coveted complete silence. It came so very close to it, but sounds of dripping water and ambient humming filtered through the cracks. The cold, clammy air tickled her skin and sent goose bumps down her arms. It smelled mostly of nothingness, with the faintest hints of old, stagnant water. But there was something else there, too... something beyond her senses, something that whispered through time. She shivered.

Fifty steps down, she counted, until Julian placed his hand on her back to let her know she had reached the ground. She took the last step and stood on cold, slippery brick floors, thick darkness filling her vision. She forced herself to blink, to make sure her eyes were truly open. Shapes appeared in the blackness as her vision adjusted and Hieu reached the ground.

One hasty scratching sound against the wall behind her. A feeble flicker of light emanated from the match in Julian's hand. He lifted an old gas lamp from beside the ladder and lit its wick, and the faint flame blossomed into a heaving, breathing flare that danced in his peacock-blue eyes. His pupils constricted in the light. He dipped his head toward hers.

"Welcome to the tunnels of Savannah," he whispered. His echoing voice assumed a life of its own, whorling down the passageways.

Old brick archways formed a tunnel system so large that Mila could neither discern an entrance nor exit, a beginning nor end.

"The city certainly is a fine Southern Belle," Julian said. "A damn near perfect one, actually. She has beauty, grace, finesse, and a respectable lineage. And as any good Southern woman knows to do, she hides her dark side oh, so well." He offered his arm to Mila, and she linked her own around it. He ticked his head to signal their direction and began walking, the crunching and splashing sounds of

wet, crumbling brick floors mixed with mud echoing as they went. It squished between Mila's toes,
caking the sides of her feet as they walked. "Savannah's made plenty of mistakes in her many centuries of life. But this... this may be her darkest one.
The tunnels of the city are where this Southern
Belle got her skirts real dirty. It's the mark on her
record, the secret everyone knows but no one
speaks of—the only aspect of her history that isn't
inscribed in markers on the squares." He stopped
her with a light squeeze of her arm. "Be still now."

They stopped in the worn brick tunnel.

"Do you feel it?" Julian asked. "Savannah hid her
slaves down here. The ships docked in the river,
full of sick humans, half-dead from treacherous sea
voyages. Of course they wouldn't sell in that condition. So the traders waited. Then, in the middle of
the night, they funneled and forced them into these tunnels. People from Africa and even Ireland,
side by side in desperation, side by side in oppression—trapped under society's feet until they could
be shined up and sold on Wright Square. Everyone
knows it happened, but—in true Southern fashion—for all the markers commemorating historic
people and events in Savannah, a marker was never
placed for this one. Do you feel it?"

She did, poignantly. The fabric of time seemed thinner—even fraying—in this spot. In her mind, she saw their hollow eyes. A shiver slithered over her. For a moment, they stood still, the ethereal calling washing over them once more.

"How did you... how did you find this?"

Julian locked eyes with her, his smile simmering with the excitement of a long-held secret. "Hesperia may have sealed off the tunnels over a century ago, but they can't erase the knowledge of their existence. Hieu knew of them. I knew of them. Zetetics knew of them and made use of them beginning two centuries ago. I bought Voltaire's for more than just its historic beauty—it's a strategic location."

"What do you mean?"

"I told you the Zetetics are underground," Hieu said. "They're underground both figuratively and literally. Julian and I have particular roles that keep us straddling this line. We are Squires, which means we live with one foot in society and one foot out of it. In this position, we can help Hesperians transition out of society and into the Zetetics, as well as monitor what happens aboveground that may impact us. But many other Zetetics are purely off the radar. These individuals need a means to move, transport, and meet without being seen.

Considering your past, it is most advantageous for you to become one of the underground. Quite frankly, it's your only option."

Mila's heart fluttered. She jerked away from Julian, her body twisting like a coil ready to spring. "Are you saying I'll have to stay here, in these tunnels?"

"No, no, no," Julian said, placing his hands on her shoulders. "You'll continue to stay in Voltaire's for the time being, as you have for the last few days. But in order to keep Hesperia from hunting you—and consequently, finding us—we have to take certain measures."

She narrowed her eyes. "What do you mean?"

But instead of answering, Julian again linked his arm through hers and led her down the tunnel, the pulsating circular light offering them just a peek at the path ahead. She clung to him as she slipped and slid in her bare feet, clabbered with mud, her long hair curling in the dank underground.

"It's not the only time humans have been forced underground, whether due to oppression or to escape it," Julian said as the trio trekked farther into the tunnels. "Remember the catacombs in Rome? Those cramped passageways had veritable bunk beds carved into them, stuffed with the corpses of Christians. But they weren't only secret burial grounds used to defy Roman burial laws. They were secret gathering places. They ran through those tiny passageways, which led into chambers where they could hide and worship in secret. Roman soldiers found the Christians and massacred them in their own graves.

"The old city of Nottingham had the City of Caves, man-made sandstone caves that functioned as disease-ridden refuges for the poor in the nineteenth century, as well as shelters during the Second World War in the twentieth. From Cappadocia to the Holocaust, the most horrific times of history have perpetually pushed humans beneath the earth.

"Of course nowadays, many governments don't immediately need overt oppression to control the people. They've learned that the most efficient way to enslave a population and keep them cooperative is to create the illusion of freedom. The easiest way to do that is to dull their minds, and make the process of mental erosion as pleasant as possible. In a term? Dopamine dependency. Humans can't get enough of it."

They approached a split in the tunnels and stayed to the right. Julian was right. She had witnessed it herself in her three years at HBN. Without fail, the stories that sparked the most viewer response were sexy, inflammatory, or pure gossip. Her mother always quoted, "Great minds discuss ideas. Average minds discuss events. Small minds discuss people." Invariably, HBN ignored the issues in favor of gossip about the people—and the viewers liked it that way. A mutually superficial relationship between the news outlet and its customers. It was one of the many things Mila had wanted to change, had her career—and life—gone the way she had planned.

Now, with the help of the Zetetics, things could change...

Julian stopped at an inset portion of the tunnel. Another ladder crawled up the brick like an iron vine. Next to it, a brick had been removed in an apparent attempt to insert a tiny dumbwaiter. A concave metal plate sat inside the opening, and the tunnel appeared to be of circular metal. Hieu stepped to the opening, rummaged in his pockets, and produced three silver balls, which he placed in the plate. He swirled them, producing a faint metallic ring which traveled up the tunnel.

"Now we wait," Hieu said.

"For what?" asked Mila.

"For the Squire at this location," Hieu answered.

"I don't understand."

"You understand that Squires straddle the line between society and the Zetetics' underground," Julian said. "Some are small business proprietors, like myself and Hieu. Some are pharmacists, or other professionals. The Squire we're meeting tonight is a coroner." He lowered his head as he looked at her as if she was supposed to immediately grasp his insinuation.

"And..." Mila prompted.

Julian opened his mouth to respond, but the ladder began rattling with the weight of a new arrival. "You'll see."

A woman, wrapped in a blue bathrobe, descended the ladder, her blonde hair pulled back into a ponytail. Behind her black-framed glasses, she appeared to be in her thirties. She stepped to the ground, adjusted her bathrobe, and nodded to the men.

"Julian. Hieu," she said. "Been a long time since you've called me this late."

"Samantha. We apologize for waking you," Hieu said, bowing slightly. "We need to get something taken care of as soon as possible. Mila Ray comes to us from Flint Hill Detention Facility. She escaped and is highly wanted."

Samantha adjusted her glasses and looked at Mila. "I'm thinking suicide," she said plainly as she pulled a small notebook and pen from the pocket of her robe.

"Agreed," said Hieu.

"What's going on?" Mila asked.

"Your family will—" Samantha began.

"I don't have family," Mila said curtly.

"Oh. I'm sorry." She flipped open the notebook. "It does make it less complicated, though."

"What is going on?"

Samantha looked questioningly to Hieu, then Julian.

"I hadn't gotten that far yet," Julian said to Samantha.

The coroner put her notebook away. "We have to fake your death."

Mila blinked. "What?"

"It's the best way we can ensure your safety without compromising the secrecy of the organization," she continued. "We can't just hide you from Hesperia. We have to make sure they don't even look for you anymore. The best way to do that is to convince them you're dead." She fumbled in her pocket before retrieving the notebook again. She scribbled furiously. "The paper trail may lure some attention, but not for long. I can forge all the necessary documents from the coroner's office. I'll probably go with drowning. Suicide by jumping from the Fifth Street Bridge after midnight. One witness saw you—she found your note taped to the bridge, reported the death, but remained anonymous and left the scene. No need find the body. You're a transient, no one knows you. And of course we have the medical examiner at Candler Hospital should we need anything further." She tapped the pen on the paper in finality and looked up at the group. "Good?"

"Good," Hieu confirmed.

"I'll put it through immediately." She turned back toward the ladder, then stopped. "As always, I recommend doing everything within reason to change her appearance, if there's any doubt that she'll remain underground."

"There's no doubt. Thank you, Samantha," said Hieu.

Samantha nodded to each of them and climbed back up the ladder.

Julian offered Mila a hopeful smile. She feigned one in return and took his arm as the group of three made their way back toward Voltaire's.

She'd be safe. Falk would stop looking for her. For all of it, she was deeply grateful. But Samantha's words repeated in her head. "No need to find the body. You're a transient, no one knows you."

If she ever did return aboveground, she truly had nothing to lose.

18.

CLIMBING THE STAIRCASE toward his new office in the Domestic Terrorism Section's Erie Bureau, Falk paused to survey his new work environment. Crisp, sleek, and clean, the place bustled with workers who would take their orders from him—a glorious difference from his dank purgatory at Flint Hill. Instead of that horrible peaked cap, he donned a suit and tie, or—if he traveled to Flint Hill—a black, double-breasted uniform shimmering with ribbons, insignias, medals, and badges. Ascending the final step, he strode toward his new office, stopping to glare at a janitorial staff member outside his door. He cleared his throat.

"Oh—I'm sorry, sir," stuttered a pudgy, forty-something man. He wore a gray jumpsuit, not so different from the guards' uniforms at Flint Hill. Hopping back from the door, screwdriver in hand, he stammered, "I was just—attending to one final thing for your office." His eyes flitted toward the closed door.

Falk followed the man's gaze. The door still had the old plaque, which read, FORSYTHE H. MAR-LOWE, SPECIAL AGENT-IN-CHARGE.

"Well?" he snapped. "*I've* been in charge three days now. Take care of it!"

The man jerked forward and pried the plaque from the door. "I'll have your new one on it by the end of the day, sir. Sorry, sir." He hung his head and pushed his custodial cart down the hall.

Falk flung the door open and slammed it behind him. Marlowe's body had barely been cold by the time Falk secured the title of special agent-in-charge. He had packed up his quarters at Flint Hill and arrived at the Erie Bureau one day later, and had been as patient as possible as the administrative and janitorial staffs cleared out Marlowe's old office to make it personal for Falk. He sauntered to the window, lips twitching in smug satisfaction at his new daily view.

Thank you, Thirty-Four.

But irritation scraped over him. She'd served his purpose—he had Marlowe's job now, and Marlowe was dead. Why did thoughts of her seize his mind? Of all the inmates and criminals he'd had the pleasure of torturing, why did she remain his obsession? He had no reason to think of her, no reason to follow or use her.

And yet...

He crossed his office and sat at the holodesk. After a few minutes of delving through databases, he leaned back into his chair and roared with laughter.

His door creaked open. The janitor peeked into the office. "Everything okay, sir?"

Falk waved him away.

The door shut, but bounced back open. The janitor curled his chin around it. "I fixed your name plate, sir."

"Go."

The janitor scrambled to exit. Falk ran his fingers through his hair and chuckled. Mila Ray's certificate of death filled his screen. He examined the report. Suicide by drowning in the Savannah River in Savannah-Georgia, Bay Region, Hesperia on July 21—only the night before.

"You didn't." Falk smirked as he skimmed further. Her body had not been located.

19.

ENTERING THEIR QUIET QUARTERS, Julian crossed the living area and collapsed onto the sofa. He pressed the heels of his hands against his eyes, his body aching with exhaustion. Between taking Mila to Samantha the night before, a full day of Voltaire's preparations, an evening of work, and then more hours devoted to the security project for Don and Hieu, he'd hardly slept at all.

The grandfather clock chimed three times. The late nights weren't as bothersome as the seeming futility of it all. By the time he had been able to encrypt all of Don's systems, he couldn't be sure how much had already been compromised—either to Hesperia or the Belgae. By now, all of his efforts could be too little, too late.

Damn the Belgae! To use my vulnerability—my sick mother, my need to obtain her medication—to track me? Disgusting! He punched the side of the couch. If they believed the only reason he deserted their group was to care for his mother, they were delusional. Even if his mother hadn't been sick, he'd have left them.

Hard to believe it'd been six years since he'd been a twenty-two-year-old with an activist's spirit and an ideologue's mind, inspired to his depths by the revolutions of yesterday and the books that had been his training ground. When he found the Belgae, they were the external embodiment of his own internal state.

Even in its first days, the group had impressive numbers and plans. And with leaders like Rigo Laslo, Dale Trent, and Emory McFallon, they certainly had the brains to pull it all off.

Julian shook his head, remembering the magnetic pull of purpose and belonging. Stronger than the earth's two poles. Emory had pinpointed his technological skills, training him until he surpassed even her. When they had assigned him his primary duty—to secure the Belgae's systems and penetrate Hesperia's—they had stoked the fires of his ego. Brotherhood, blandishment, and belonging. What more could a young man want? But within a year, he had begun second-guessing the movement.

Then strange things started happening to Julian's mother, beginning with lapses in her motor skills, and culminating in a dangerous fall. It had been time to take a hard look at his priorities—and family won out. Julian abandoned the Belgae, covering his tracks just as they'd trained him to. Then Hesperia got Dale. Called him the most dangerous domestic terrorist in a century.

Of course Mama was his main reason for leaving. But the ideological fallout he'd had with Rigo and Emory had placed at a close second. Had they forgotten about that? He was on his way out, even if his mother were healthy. And still they had the gall to step between him and life-saving medication, in order to locate him—as if that would win him back. Idiots.

The squeaking of his mother's walker pulled him from the storm cloud enveloping his thoughts. He sat up. His mother stood in the doorway, eyes barely open, wiping disheveled hair from her face. "Julian?"

"It's me, Mama. Go back to bed. I didn't mean to wake you."

"You'll sleep, won't you? All these late nights aren't good for you. You're pushing yourself too hard. It's not worth it."

"It's completely worth it," he countered. "Please trust me."

Leaning on her walker, she wobbled over to him and eased herself onto the couch. Brushing her fingers through his hair, she smiled. "You know you're doing a wonderful job taking care of us, don't you? Always my helper. Now my supporter." Her voice rasped with sleepiness.

Julian leaned over his knees and rested his forehead in his palms. "I don't know if I can protect Don," he said. "He might have to stop making the xianepam for a while, so Hesperia doesn't catch him. We might be without meds. Indefinitely."

Her delicate hand rested between his shoulder blades. "I'm happy, Julian," she said. "My happiness doesn't depend on the condition of my body, or if I am in pain. So don't let this burden you. My spirit is full. I'm content."

An ache rooted deep inside him. She had that voice, the voice that radiated courage, hope, and confidence, and defied normal human understanding. The same voice she had when he was younger, when they faced financial setbacks, when he learned the story of his father and launched into an indignant rage. When she received her diagnosis.

He straightened, meeting her gaze with a skeptical slant of his eyebrows.

"I'm serious," she said.

"I know you are. But none of that will stop me from doing everything I can to keep you as healthy as possible. I've promised to take care of you, one hundred and fifty percent. It's my privilege to do it. And I will."

She leaned forward and planted a gentle kiss on his forehead. Cupping his cheek, she said, "Just don't forget to live your own life, too. Don't use me as your hiding place." With a grunt, she pulled herself off the couch and, leaning on her walker, went back to bed.

Live my own life? I am. What does she think I'm doing?

~~~

The next morning came much too soon. Julian bumbled out of bed, slogged into the kitchen, dumped some coffee grounds into the brew basket, and bent over the counter, burying his face in his arms as it brewed.

This morning, even for just an hour, he would allow himself to escape, in hopes that a little reprieve would cleanse any stress and mental blocks, permitting him to see any other solutions to Don's problems—and therefore, his own.

The timer beeped, and the coffee sounded like it whispered when he poured it into his mug. He sniffed it, relishing the way its nutty scent invigorated him.

"Got any leftovers?"

Julian turned. Mila stood in the kitchen doorway. With some color returning to her skin and messy auburn waves cascading around her shoulders, against the luminescent ivory nightgown, she looked like a sleepy angel. He couldn't help but smile. "Grab a mug."

She walked to a cupboard, standing on tiptoe to reach the mugs on the higher shelf, the draping nightgown just barely hugging her slender curves, hinting at the shape beneath. She held out her mug to him and inhaled loudly as he poured.

He had intended to spend the morning in solitude, but soon found himself inviting Mila to join him. After they each dressed, he led her through the fireplace and into the basement, he with his sketch pencils, she with one of his books. She collapsed onto the long couch against the far back wall, near the sealed former entrance, and opened her book, while he returned to his unfinished sketch of the chained revolutionaries. He didn't know how long they stayed in silence, only that the time was even more restorative since he shared it with her.

"So, you sketched all of these?" Mila asked.

"I did."

"They're incredible."

"Thank you. I started as soon as I could hold a pencil. Sketching is one of the cheapest hobbies for a kid, so Mama encouraged it. That, and writing. All you need is a pencil and paper."

Silence filled the space in their conversation, and Julian sensed a deeper question brewing.

Finally, Mila asked, "What does it mean to be a Zetetic? And I'm not asking philosophically. I'm asking practically. I'm thankful to be here, but I'm still confused about what is going on."

He furrowed his brow. "I'd say being a Zetetic means something different to each person, so it depends on who you ask." He glanced over to her, but she dipped her chin in dissatisfaction. "For me, it means being self-sufficient. It means rejecting the current standard of living in modern society, and living my own way, without having to make an unproductive scene of it. It means that instead of protesting and begging Hesperia to change its ways to work for me, I simply leave and work for my-self—make my own way. It means I have hope, because I can make my own destiny and I'm not at the mercy of politicians whose only real concern is their own reelections. I think that's what it is for most of us—true independence from an unredeemable system."

He watched her press her lips together, her eyes laser-focused on a spot on the ceiling. He could practically see the gears turning in her mind as she decided whether or not his answer was satisfactory.

Her eyes darted up. "How?"

"How what?"

"How—all this? If you're so disconnected, what about money—loans for your business? Food? Communications? How?"

Julian smirked and twirled his pencil behind his ear. "I forget how little you've seen." Crossing to the couch, he collapsed next to her. "Much of it was an unwitting gift from history. The tunnels under Savannah, the caves in Appalachia—they've been here for centuries. Forgotten for centuries. We make use of them. But I don't think you realize —the Zetetics has been around for nearly two hundred years. Since shortly after Hesperia passed the Domestic Safety Act. That's a lot of time to perfect systems.

"As for getting by, we help each other, as you've seen. Squires live with one foot in Hesperia and one foot in the Zetetics, so they can help members receive goods and services they'd have no access to otherwise. But the members who are exclusively underground, like you, are vastly gifted. We have agricultural specialists, healthcare providers trained in a number of disciplines and philosophies, security gurus, financiers, even military professionals. You've only met an iota."

"And the objective is?"

Julian shrugged. "Live freely."

"What about everyone else?"

"What about everyone else?"

"Hieu said the Zetetics' mission is freedom from Hesperia. Is this an exclusive offer, or is it available to everyone?"

"Everyone who wants it."

"But no one knows who you are." She huffed out a breath and leaned back into the arm of the couch, running fingers through her hair. "They're just stuck with the way things are, with no one to fight for change?"

Julian grinned at her exasperation, at the uncanny familiarity of her perspective. "Aren't you the humanitarian..."

"I witnessed unlimited suffering in my job, Julian," she snapped. "And I experienced it firsthand, unjustly. Forgive me for wanting to try to help people escape from such things."

"Hey, I didn't say humanitarianism is a bad thing. I'm a humanitarian too. I'm just a selective humanitarian." He grinned wider.

"So...?"

"Can they not fight for change if they want to? Can they not find us if they want to? It's called taking responsibility for your way of life. It's called being proactive. Trust me, Mila, in my three years of being a Zetetic, the people who want to find us, find us."

"My parents spent their entire lives searching, and they never found you." Crossing her arms, she continued, "You have to know what I stand for, Julian—what I want. I want the people to have truth. I want freedom for everyone. And I want Falk—Hesperia—to be stopped."

He sobered. "There's still so much I can't divulge, Mila. But we *do* have a mission—and I think you'll be an important part of it."

Sighing, she jumped up from the couch and stalked over to one of his drawings. "What are you trying to say in all of your drawings?"

Laughing, he rocked forward from the couch and moved to where Mila stood. "Oh, come on now! I'm an artist—the whole point of my work is *not* to have to spell things out. If I wanted to do that, I'd be an essayist. You have to work for my message —if you can't find it, it wasn't for you."

"You're evasive." She turned to him and glared. "It's irritating."

He pulled the pencil from behind his ear. "How about this. I'll sketch something specifically for you, and you'll get the message right away." He brushed the pencil down the length of her nose, leaving a black streak.

"Fine," she said, smirking and wiping the charcoal from her skin. "But if I don't, you have to give me an essay. Five hundred words, minimum." She rubbed her nose again and checked her hand for streaks. "You're a pest."

"Why, thank you." He puffed out his chest in mock pride. She smiled but rolled her eyes and returned to the couch and reopened the book she had borrowed.

Julian watched her for a moment. She lived for her mission, and nothing else. No doubt Flint Hill's horrors had deepened her determination. He could see the hatred that had taken root in her heart. It brewed in her eyes when she recounted her trauma.

He understood. He knew what it was like to feel passionate about a cause, and willing—no, hungry—to fight for its realization. Some things could only be learned from experience. No one could have dissuaded him in those early days. He had to fight. No one could dissuade Mila now. She would fight.

But the Zetetics was the wrong place for fighters. And yet he couldn't bring himself to tell her. Lose her. The hair on the back of his neck prickled.

~~~

Placing a lime wedge onto the rim of a glass, Julian slid the icy mojito across the countertop to the busty brunette who had ordered it. Her lips spread into a seductive, burgundy smile as she lifted it to her lips. Julian spun back to his spot and continued crafting the long string of orders he'd accumulated.

Truth be told, he'd grown accustomed to hungry smiles from women in his bar, as vain as it sounded to admit it to himself. Usually, he flashed them a wink or a "Thanks, beautiful," for their attentions, but not lately. The titian-haired, elfish beauty borrowing his bedroom preoccupied his thoughts, increasingly so. Despite his impression that Mila enjoyed his company, Julian sensed he needed to proceed with caution. For everything about her that lured him closer, something about her seemed precarious. She was alone in the world, fueled by both her mission and her bitterness. Vulnerable. Yet he couldn't shake her from his mind.

"Julian?"

Damien stood next to him, a stein in one hand, a red wine glass in the other, a perplexed expression on his face. "Hey," he said. "I said your name three times, man."

"D, whatcha need?"

"Nothin', but this gentleman does." He gestured to a man on the left side of the oval bar. "He couldn't get your attention."

"Wow, thanks. Sorry I got foggy for a second." Julian patted Damien on the shoulder and walked to the new patron, a debonair man dressed impeccably in a black dress shirt, with glossy, sculpted brown hair. "My apologies for the wait, what can I get you?"

"Your best whiskey," he said.

"You got it." In seconds, the customer had his whiskey—and the seductive brunette from the other side of the bar, too.

Fumbling with a bar cloth, Julian surveyed Voltaire's. Everyone seated at the bar had been served, and customers tucked away in booths engaged in fervent, flirtatious conversation, with no sign of refills needed in the next few minutes, at least. He looked toward the front door. No one. At ten o'clock on a Tuesday night, he couldn't hope for a better time to break for it. Tossing the bar cloth down, he turned to Damien, who stood on tiptoe, reaching for a fresh bottle of Bordeaux.

"Think you can handle things? I'm gonna step away for a few minutes." Julian blurted the words, as if someone might come through the door and snag his opportunity to steal away.

Damien twisted the bottle in his hand. "Uh, sure. Yeah, go ahead."

"Great, thanks." He snatched a bottle of Cabernet.

Damien scratched his head and shot him a look. "You going to visit the girl?"

Julian shrugged and smiled. "Gimme a break, man." He strode through the main seating area and into the lobby. Once he approached the stairs, he bounded, taking them in twos, all the way up. She was where he figured she'd be—curled on the couch with a book. Her head snapped up.

"Hey," he breathed.

"Hi." A question gamboled in her eyes. "What are you doing?"

"Uh, taking a break. I get those sometimes." He sauntered to her.

"I see."

In the low light, her thick tresses glowed. He couldn't help but grin when he noticed she had traded in the fancy silken nightgown for one of his black T-shirts. Somehow, he liked that even better. As if she could read his mind, she looked down, twisting the fabric in her fingers. "I needed to wash the nightgown but I didn't have anything else... sorry."

"No worries, have it."

"Thanks. What do you have there?"

He held out the bottle for her inspection. "I thought you might like a glass of wine with your literature."

Her eyebrows shot up. "Think it'll make the Dostoevsky go down smoother?"

Julian chuckled and began walking toward the kitchen. "I don't know, that's a tall order and this is only the house red." Prying the cork from the bottle, he grabbed two wine glasses and filled both with the garnet liquid. Returning to the living room, he joined Mila on the couch and passed her the drink. She lifted it to her lips and closed her eyes with the first sip, releasing a satis-fied sigh.

"Like I said... it's only the house wine," he teased.

She grinned. "I'm not picky."

He took a draw from his own glass, then jerked, re-membering. Digging into his back pocket, he removed a small, folded square of sketch paper. "I kept my promise," he said, extending the paper to her.

She looked at him curiously, eyes glinting in the lamplight, appearing as two different planets, a physical expression of psychological duality. He studied her as she took the paper and unfolded the eight-inch square, laying it between them. Perched on a branch against a dark backdrop during snowfall, he'd drawn a barn owl with its head turned fully downward, eyes closed.

Mila lifted the picture, looking closer. "It's beautiful," she breathed. "Sad."

"Or poetic. What do you think? Do I need to write an essay?"

She met his gaze, but her own appeared vacant, as though she was still lost in the picture. "Oh—no. It's in-credible." She ran a fingertip down each of the features as she spoke. "The winter hibernation, the downward posture of the owl, its eyes are closed. Wisdom turned inward. Or even turned blind. Wisdom without direc-tion. It's—it's truly beautiful, Julian."

When she finally looked at him again, there was something pained in her countenance, as though she knew something tragic but couldn't remember what it was or how long ago it had happened. Julian reached for her hand and laced his fingers into hers. "I'm glad you appreciate it."

Her lips parted, but she paused, as if changing the course of her thoughts. "Can you be away from the bar this long?"

He exhaled pent-up anticipation—for what, he didn't know—and sniffed a laugh. "Probably not, no. I guess I better get back."

Crossing to the stairwell, he stopped for one more glance at her. Mila held the sketch up in the light, peering into it deeply, as if it had an answer it wouldn't reveal. Feeling like an eavesdropper, he hurried down the steps. When he rounded the sharp turn before the third-floor landing, he almost slammed into a customer.

"Whoa!" Julian grabbed the railing to keep from plowing into the man.

"Excuse me." The man in the black shirt hardly seemed rattled.

"Sir, the area beyond this floor is a private residence," Julian said, placing his hand on the man's shoulder. If he hadn't been standing two steps above the man, surely the customer would trump him in height by a good four inches.

"I apologize, there was no sign."

They descended the final steps to the third floor landing. Glancing around, Julian spotted the chained sign reading, PRIVATE RESIDENCE. It was unhooked, dangling against the wall—but the text faced outward, clearly visible. Had he forgotten to put it back into place when he rushed up to see Mila? He couldn't remember. Lifting the sign, he showed it to the customer before hooking it back into place.

"Must've forgotten to replace it." Gesturing for the man to continue down the stairs in front of him, he asked, "How was the whiskey?"

"Just fine, thank you. I could certainly go for another one."

The man had no trace of an accent—no biting "r" from Appalachia, or drawl from Plains. Almost as though it'd been weeded out of him. Julian's skin prickled. "Of course. Is this your first time visiting Voltaire's?"

"Yes. It's quite an establishment you have here."

"We certainly take pride in it."

They crossed through the foyer and toward the bar. The man returned to the stool he had occupied before, minus the company of the voluptuous brunette. Julian strode behind the bar and served the man another whiskey.

"You sound like an out-of-towner," he said, passing the man his glass. "What brings you here?"

"Ah, work." The man sighed. "New job. They didn't tell me how much travel was involved, otherwise I might not have taken it."

"I hear ya."

The customer smiled and lifted the glass to his lips.

"So what kind of business do you do? Sales, corporate training?"

"Law enforcement."

"Ah." Julian's heartbeat cantered. He wiped a spot on the counter to distract himself. *God—was I too late? Did Hesperia find me through Don's databases?* He shot a desperate look at the clock—ten forty-five. Still two hours and fifteen minutes before he could close up shop and breathe easy—if the man wasn't here for him. Gathering himself, he managed a perfectly congenial, "Well, let me know if there's anything else I can get for you," before returning to his spot at the front of the curved bar. But no matter how busy he got, his skin heated under the laser-like stare of the man, always watching him from a few stools away. The Belgae, or the government—who would he prefer to be found by? A close call, but he'd take his chances with the Belgae. At least then, he could still take care of his mother. Maybe.

Time passed in a slow, torturous drip. Relieved by strings of new orders, he crafted three margaritas, an Old Fashioned, a peach Bellini, two mojitos, and four Cosmopolitans. He plucked a maraschino cherry and mint leaves, sliced limes—and then slit his finger instead of the orange for the last Cosmo.

Cursing, he hurried to the sink and retrieved the small kit to bandage the cut. The stinging of his wound was nothing compared to the sensation of dark eyes boring into him. Unable to take it a minute longer, he snatched a bottle of scotch and poured a shot, downing it. The burn warmed his throat, then his chest, then his mind. But it didn't slow his heart rate.

"Gin and tonic, please."

Julian jumped and spun at the sound of the smooth baritone voice.

Hieu stood by the counter. "Everything all right?"

"Of course." Julian splashed two ounces of gin into a highball glass and dumped tonic water over it. It frothed and bubbled over the edge. He snatched a pile of napkins and wiped up the mess, then slid it to Hieu, sans lime wedge.

"Jesus, Julian," Hieu whispered, "what is going on?"

He took a deep breath, then let it explode from his lungs. "The man in all black is from out of town. Here on business. I caught him trying to go to the fourth floor. Said he works in law enforcement. And I—I don't know if he's here because—"

"Don." Hieu's jaw ticked.

"Yeah. He—" Julian looked over his shoulder, where the man had been seated, but it was empty. "Good Lord." He snapped straight.

"What?"

"He's gone again." His glance pinged around the bar, but he forced himself to look at Hieu. "I can't follow him around. It won't look right. Can you—?"

Hieu gave a stiff nod and slipped away. Julian chugged another shot of scotch. The risks of being a Squire ratcheted up every day. It wasn't worth risking his mother's health and safety, or the group's secrecy.

One more close call and I'll go completely underground. Hieu can run the business.

Finally, Hieu emerged from the left side room and raised his glass ever so slightly as an all-clear. Minutes later, the man approached from the back of Voltaire's and returned to the bar, where he perched along with a handful of patrons until twelve forty-five. At last call, he ordered a third whiskey.

Julian wiped the counters, refrigerated garnishes, and gathered sticky, empty glasses, willing the clock's minute hand to reach one o'clock. He glanced toward the door, prepared to whisk away any last-minute visitors. A shadow loped in the stairwell near the front lobby. Knitting his brow, he checked the bar—the man in black still sat on his stool. He looked toward the foyer again.

In the lobby doorway, two wine glasses in hand, stood Mila, eyes wide in a terror that made the hair on the back of Julian's neck stand rigid. Slowly, he looked over his shoulder, following her sightline all the way to the man in black. When he looked back, Mila was gone.

Bolstered by a protective instinct and flooded with confidence that the man's presence had nothing to do with him, Julian strode over to the mysterious customer. Flashing a wide smile, he said, "It's about time for me to lock the doors. But you're welcome to decompress from work as long as you're in town." He extended his empty hand. "I'm Julian."

The man grasped his hand in a powerful shake. A snakelike energy slithered through the cold, hard hand.

"Victor," he said.

~~~

Julian bounded up the stairs, leaving Hieu to his book-work at the closed bar.

Mila sat frozen on the couch, a half-empty glass of wine in her hand and the empty bottle on the table. He rushed to her and took her hand. She was shivering.

"Mila."

She stared past him, at some nebulous point.

"Mila, was that...?"

Her eyes widened further, a fresh spark of fear crossing them. Her lips parted and formed an "F" sound. She slurped wine. "Falk," she said, finally. Her eyes jerked from their focal point in the doorway, meeting his. "He's found me."

"He didn't find you."

"He didn't see me?"

"No. But he's looking."

Mila jumped from the couch and downed the rest of the wine. Pacing, she muttered, "He'll find me..."

Julian rose and stood in front of her, clasping her shoulders. "Hey—Mila. Stop. Falk will not find you." He paused, tried to think. "You'll leave."

"Leave?"

"Not us, but here. Away from the Croatoan hub..." He released her. "I have to get Hieu."

"Julian—"

"You'll be safe," he promised.

~~~

Everything swirled around her. Julian ran to get Hieu. Somehow, they all—Natalie included—ended up around the breakfast table. Mila sat, dazed, as the men's voices ran together like watercolors. Their conversation darted in a passionate back-and-forth, only a swirling fuzz of nonsense to her ears, until —

"I agree," Hieu said. "She can't stay in Savannah, or the Croatoan Hub at all."

"What?" Mila asked, but no one acknowledged her.

"We have to get her out," Hieu continued. "Kairos will have a place for her. I'll contact him first thing in the morning, but you"—he gave a pointed look to Mila—"need to pack and leave tonight. Julian will escort you."

Mila stiffened. "What? How? Isn't it too risky to be on the roads?"

"You won't be on the roads," Hieu said. "Not for most of the way."

Julian's warm hand on her shoulder allowed her breath to even. "I told you Croatoan was bigger than Hieu, Samantha, and I," he began. "The tunnels below the city don't just wind around under the town. Zetetics expanded them in the last century or so, into Cooper

Marl under Charleston-South Carolina. The riskiest portion of our trip comes when we go aboveground just out of Charleston, and we have half a day's trip to the safe house in Roanoke. Ada will take you the rest of the way."

"Just me?"

"I can only take you that far, then I have to come back." He flashed an impish grin. "But you know Ada can handle anything."

His levity didn't lighten her concerns. "Where will she take me?"

"To the main Zetetics' hub. Once you're there, as far as Falk and Hesperia will be able to tell, you'll be nonexistent."

Her thoughts blurred. She sank into her chair.

"Drink your coffee." Natalie's healing voice broke through Mila's confusion. "You'll need all the energy you can get."

Absentmindedly, she sipped, barely noticing that Hieu and Julian retreated into the living room.

Falk came tonight. To the same city, to the very building. Two floors below my bed. He knew it too—he has to be sending a message. That he's keeping his promise to follow me. Find me. Use me. Messing with my brain like he always has. Why? How? The question crawled over her like a cluster of spiders. Her fear mixed with the anger she hoped she'd repressed, the hatred that screwed itself into her chest. It was still there.

Falk was still there.

"Sanctuary," Natalie chimed, covering Mila's hand with her own. "You have sanctuary. Don't let him take up residence in your mind."

She broke her gaze from her coffee mug to look at Natalie, who peered back at her through tired but peaceful eyes.

"Don't let him have your mind."

Nodding, Mila rose from her chair and wandered into the living room. Hieu stood in the doorway, poised to leave.

"One hour," he said, and descended into the dark stairwell.

20.

MILA PLAITED HER HAIR into a hasty French braid and traded Julian's black tee for a long-sleeved navy shirt, a pair of slender, dark denim pants, and a sturdy pair of old work boots, all from Natalie. By the time she tossed all of her borrowed belongings into a pillowcase, it was time to go. She hoisted the sack over her shoulder, stumbling from the lingering effect of the wine.

Julian's sketch. She couldn't leave it behind. Lifting it from the couch, she folded it into a small square and tucked it into her pocket.

The chirring of Natalie's walker came from the kitchen doorway. "Safe travels, dear Mila," she said.

Mila met Natalie in the doorway and embraced her. "I wish I didn't have to leave." Her words stung even truer as she spoke them. Natalie's healing soul had brought more comfort than she'd experienced since her own mother lived. And Julian didn't just make her laugh, he guarded and protected her. Though her time with the Merricks had been brief, something in her heart fastened to them, yearned for them as for her own family. But she had to leave. Break the budding connection.

Natalie's reedy arms clutched her with surprising strength. Mila pulled back, and Natalie opened her mouth to speak, but Julian trudged up the stairwell's final steps.

"Shall we?" Julian stood in the stairwell in a black zippered jacket, worn denim, and sturdy shoes, a backpack slung over his shoulders.

Mila flung her makeshift luggage over her shoulder and followed Julian down the stairs, through the fireplace, and deep into the tunnels.

~~~

Wisps from Mila's braid clung to her neck in the tunnel's humidity. She breathed in the scents of fetid water, senescent stone, and forgotten earth. In night's deepest hours, the disconnect between Savannah's subterranean and the streets above it seemed to gape further.

Her feet trudged farther from Voltaire's, splashing muddy wetness with every step, but her mind stayed behind. Falk wasn't supposed to be able to find her—Ada and Hieu and Julian had promised. How was he doing it? With her thoughts commandeering her focus, she didn't realize Julian had stopped walking. She plowed into his back.

He turned and clasped her, steadying them both. "Sidetracked?"

"Sorry. Yeah." She stared at her mud-caked boots. "He wasn't supposed to be able to find me. The death certificate..."

His lips pressed into a tight, concerned line. "He didn't buy it. We expected he might show up in Savannah, start poking around. Then it'd only be a matter of time before he made his way into Voltaire's. That's why you had to stay out of sight. Now, we're taking it a step further—moving you out of Savannah and underground. Hieu and I will throw him off, don't worry." A sudden smile flashed to his face. "Let's keep your mind off all of that. Come on." He turned and continued walking. "Twenty questions."

"I doubt that will work."

"Tell me your favorite color."

"Um—heliotrope."

He shot her a look. "What the—what kind of obscure favorite color is that? *I* don't even know what that means."

"It's a purple-pink," she sighed. "You have a better one?"

"Yeah. Sketch-pencil gray."

Through the tunnels they twisted and veered for miles, tossing questions at each other. She preferred daylight. He liked moonlight. Her first pet was a teddy bear-faced Wheaton terrier named Hans. He had an honorary pet, a stray, three-legged mutt named Long John Silver.

"What are your favorite memories from growing up?" Julian asked her as they crossed into a new section of the tunnels.

"Christmas time," she said. "Each year, we observed the traditions of a different culture. Mom always let me pick, and my childhood best friend would come over too. We'd cook or bake a traditional Christmas meal or snack and share with the neighbors. And every night leading up to Christmas, we'd take turns reading *A Christmas Carol* aloud, next to our Christmas tree with colored lights. I'd always have gingersnaps and hot chocolate. I never felt more warm or safe than at Christmas time. For a little while, we all could forget we lived in Hesperia." She sighed. She'd spent recent

Christmases at work or in her dim apartment, the smell of qanna seeping out from under Sam's room. Would holidays ever be as bright as they were when she was smaller, when she had a family? Shaking her head, she turned the question around on Julian. "What about you?"

"Oh!" He looked over his shoulder, flashing her a conspiratorial smile. "Well, when we first got our house, we were poorer than ever. Mama couldn't afford field trips through school, so we'd walk through the city with popsicles and she'd take me to the historic places. Of course we couldn't go in, but we'd sit on benches nearby and she'd tell me the stories. But I think my favorite time of all was when this brilliant play was being performed at a tiny theater. I was twelve or thirteen and desperately wanted to go, but ticket prices were outrageous and we were saving up to fix some leaks in our roof.

"The night of the play, we went on a walk instead. Mama walked us to the theater. Next thing I know, she's taking me up the fire escape to the top floor, jimmying open the back door—"

"What?"

"—and we're watching the play from the catwalk above the stage. Thank goodness it was a low tech show, so no stagehands were up there. That was fun."

"Your sweet, moral mother did that?" she laughed.

"Don't you ever tell her I told you."

They traded question after question, a natural pause growing between each inquiry and answer until they fell into easy silence. Mila soaked in the sounds of their journey, their footsteps creating a syncopated rhythm in the soundtrack of drips and discarnate whispers. Against the backdrop of old brick, in response to the flickering flames from Julian's gas light, their shadows shrank and grew and jerked in a phantasmagorical dance.

Another hour, and Mila's legs fought movement, stiff like an old folding chair. The soles of her feet ached. Her body chastised her for staying awake all night. "Where do you think we are now?"

Julian sighed heavily. "Still got hours to go before we surface in Charleston. You feeling drained, too?"

"I can go on if you can." But the tired, tinny sound in her voice gave her away.

"Nah. Let's find a dry spot to sleep for a few hours."

A few yards away, a recess in the wall offered just enough room for both of them. Opening the backpack, Julian withdrew a plastic tarp and spread it on the ground. He set his backpack and her pillowcase down as makeshift pillows and lay down with a grunt. Mila followed suit, her legs and back protesting as she bent. As she lay still, the cool, damp air descended upon her. She shivered and hugged herself. Next to her, Julian shifted until his shoulder pressed against hers. Mila's body immediately relaxed in his warmth.

Julian blew out the gaslight. As blackness engulfed her vision, Mila listened to the near-nothingness in between the occasional plunk of a water droplet. Sleep eluded her, despite her exhaustion.

"Julian?" she whispered.

"Hm?"

"What are you most afraid of?"

"Still on the twenty questions game, are we? Hm." He sighed, and Mila sensed his reluctance to answer. Finally, he said, "Failing my mother. Losing her. Being alone, without a family."

Her stomach sank. His worst fear, her reality. Time hadn't made it any easier, either. Frequently, and often when she didn't expect it, mourning pulled her down like quicksand. The thought of Julian experiencing such relentless grief filled her with dread.

He folded his hands behind his head. "You?"

"Besides the psychopathic government official hunting me, you mean?"

"Right."

She bit her lip and thought for a moment. "Getting to the end of life and finding that I wasted it—that I didn't do anything of importance. Meaninglessness, I guess. That's what it was before everything happened, and it's still there."

"Hm."

Mila turned her head to look at him. "What?"

"That sounds vague."

"You're... are you actually criticizing my fear?"

"No." He shifted, propping himself on his elbow as he looked at her. "I just mean—meaninglessness. How will you know when you've done something of worth? How will you know when you can check that box off your list? Achieve meaning in what area? All areas? That's a tall order. It's a pretty vague thing to be afraid of, and—without specifying—you kind of set yourself up for failure."

She stared at him for a moment, mouth open in her loss for words. "I want... I want to bring truth to Hesperia. That goal is what gives me meaning."

Julian nodded carefully.

"What now?"

His eyes widened. "Nothing."

"Nothing?"

"I think that's a really noble calling."

"You do," she said flatly.

"Just know that..." He trailed off. Even in the darkness, his eyes swirled with unshared thoughts. "Just know—if Hesperia doesn't listen, it's not your fault." For a moment, he watched her, unmoving, as though he might say more. But he lay back down.

She stayed awake long after Julian's breathing evened. How could he be so certain that Hesperians wouldn't listen? The only way to know was to give them a chance. As long as the lies prevailed, those like Falk reigned.

~~~

Hours later, Mila forced herself back to her swollen, aching feet. She and Julian resumed their journey once again, minds rested and muscles sore, stomachs filled just enough by the fare Julian had packed. They trudged for hours, took another rest, and pressed on farther. Just as Mila wondered if they'd ever leave the underground labyrinth, the tunnel veered and they stopped in front of a gate.

Wrought of iron into the form of a tree, the trunk sprouted strong in the center, its delicate, rusted branches curling and winding outward, stretching to each side of the tunnel. In the middle of the trunk was a tarnished, bronze Z.

Julian walked to the gate and tugged on the letter Z. It opened to reveal a touchscreen security panel. He dabbed his fingers on the screen, inputting the code. The gate released its lock with a rusty *clang* that rolled through the tunnels. He leveraged his weight against the gate. It creaked in protest and seemed to fight back, but finally it opened.

"The tunnels in Cooper Marl," he said. "Welcome to Charleston."

Mila approached the entrance. On the other side of the gate, the brick and stone that lined the Savannah tunnels abruptly vanished, leaving the Charleston tunnel to continue in a substance that looked like raw sediment.

She followed Julian with hesitant steps. "Is this... structurally sound?"

"We'll find out, won't we?"

"When was the last time anyone used these?"

Julian cast a grin at her over his shoulder and laughed. "Seriously, it's fine," he said. "We've used these tunnels since the gate was installed two centuries ago. Cooper Marl doesn't need much structural reinforcement. It's all fossilized limestone, which dried once it was exposed to air when the people hollowed out the tunnels in the early nineteen hundreds. Geologically, it's pretty rare, but completely safe. Come on." He waved her over.

Footsteps became yards and yards became miles, until they stopped at a simple metal ladder attached to the side of the limestone tunnel. He handed Mila her pillowcase and approached the ladder. She watched as it swayed with his weight, but still he climbed with the gaslight in one hand. He pushed on a portion of limestone as if it were a ceiling tile, and slid it out of the way to reveal a security panel.

"Don't worry, she's expecting us," he said as he typed in the code. The remainder of the limestone jerked up and out of the way. Julian ascended a second ladder, his broad shoulders and backpack barely slipping through the small opening.

Mila took a breath and stepped up to the ladder. Threading the tail of the pillowcase through her belt loop and into the waist of her pants, she grabbed a cold, clammy rung and pulled herself onto it. Its sway made her stomach flip, but she steeled her focus on one step at a time. Once she crossed into the tiny passageway, every muscle in her body flickered like an ungrounded wire, ready to surge. She steadied her nerves with deep breaths and counted steps. Five, six, and seven became fifty-five, fifty-six, and fifty-seven, until the coffin-like quarters of the tunnel, the packed pillowcase pressing tightly against her, and Julian's big, dirty shoes above her head grated on her composure. "How much longer?"

"We were about a hundred and twenty feet underground in Cooper Marl, so I'd say we're a little more than halfway there."

She forced herself to keep counting, and did her best to ignore the rattles that followed each of their steps. Finally, Julian stopped. Somehow, staying still in the long, tiny tunnel was more unnerving than climbing through it.

Above her, Julian tinkered. *Another* panel. Wood creaked. A sliver of light bloomed into a large shaft as Julian pushed open a wooden cellar door and ascended the final steps of the shaky ladder.

Relieved, she hurried up the ladder's last rungs, crawled onto the floor, and entered a small room. A cramped room. Floor, walls, ceiling—all made of stone. Stone like a prison. Stone like a cell. Stone like...

She froze. Her legs wobbled like thin, green twigs. Her heart thudded, pounding blood into her head like a mallet. The room spun around her. Collapsing to the floor, she lay prostrate, cupping her forehead in her palms as her breath raced.

Flint Hill.

"Mila?"

His voice echoed, and sounded so far. So terribly, despairingly far. She gasped, but couldn't respond. His footsteps neared her, but swirled.

"Mila, where are you?"

His warm breath puffed against her ear, firing tremors down her body. "D-don't touch me... F-Falk..."

"It's Julian."

A hand touched the back of her head. She thrashed and screamed.

"I'm Julian. Mila, you're with me, you're not in Flint Hill. Can you look at me?"

She whimpered and curled into a crouch with her head on her knees.

"Look at me, okay? It's Julian."

I have to. I have to. She forced herself to open her eyes, raise her head.

Julian watched her, his eyes squinting in concern. She stared back. But his brass-colored hair straightened and became stiff like hay. Sea-colored eyes grew dirty until brown ones stared back at her. Falk took over. Their forms fought, each breaking through and superimposing onto the other. She clenched her jaw and bared her teeth, fighting against her building terror.

Hands grasped hers and lifted them until their palms pressed together. He interlaced his fingers with hers. Falk's face faded.

Julian won out. "You're with me, Mila. You're with me," he repeated, gently using his thumbs to stroke the palms of her hands. Without breaking contact, he moved his hands to her forearms, then her upper arms. He cupped her face, searching her eyes. "Are you with me?"

She hissed through her teeth, trying to allay her flailing pulse. "Where are we?" she demanded in a tense whisper.

"Sidney's storm cellar. It's just a storm cellar. She'll be down here soon, okay?"

Mila nodded and allowed Julian to lead her in a crawl to the back wall, near two black tables that appeared to be a type of holodesk she'd never seen before. When he encircled her in his arms, her rigid muscles intuitively released. She leaned into his chest, allowing the feel of his heartbeat on her cheekbone to soothe her. When he put a finger under her chin and tipped her face up to meet his gaze, she lost her breath at the closeness of their lips.

"Are you feeling better?" he asked, but metallic scrapes and clinks interrupted her reply. She looked across the room, to the source of the sound—a storm door embedded in the ceiling at the stop of cinder block steps. The large metal door lifted and folded backward to reveal the area above.

"Merrick, come on up," a female voice called from beyond the opening.

"You ready to go, or do you need a minute?" Julian asked Mila.

"I can go."

The storm door led straight into the living room of a small home. She blinked to take in the shocking contrast to the prison-like storm cellar. Deep indigo walls intersected with heart of pine floors dotted with colorful floor cushions. A holodesk stood to her right, and a curved, gray couch beckoned from one corner, with abstract canvases in all sizes haloing it on the wall above. The eccentric decor grabbed her attention so Mila didn't notice the tall woman standing next to them until she laughed. Sand-colored locks fell to her hips in gentle waves. Her hazel eyes brightened as she flashed Julian a wide, precocious smile.

"I feel used when you only visit me during emergencies, Merrick," she teased, bringing him in for a hug. "You're just in time for dinner though." Lowering the door back into place, she set the code in the security panel and slid a section of the wooden floor over it. The door to the cellar blended perfectly with the rest of the hardwood, but she gestured for Julian and Mila to step aside and rolled a large, over-dyed magenta rug over the spot. After Julian made introductions, Sidney waved them into the kitchen behind them, insisting that they help eat the batch of vegetable stew on the stove.

Designed with cabinetry in the same golden heart of pine as the living room, the kitchen offered a cozy warmth further enhanced by the smell of tomatoes, sausage, and spices wafting through the air. Mila's stomach growled.

Two more people, a man and a woman who appeared to be between Mila's and Julian's ages, perched at an L-shaped counter topped with black tile.

"Julian, you know Quinn and Cauley," Sidney began, gesturing to the woman and then the man. "Quinn, Cauley—Mila." Sidney pulled two bowls from a stack by the stove, ladled a generous amount of steaming stew into each, and grabbed two spoons. "Quinn's cover is as a freelance writer," she said, pointing the spoons at Quinn. "Cauley's a research associate for a company under contract with Hesperia." She plunked the spoons into the bowls and set them at the short end of the L. Mila and Julian took their seats. Sidney served them glasses of water and took the open seat at the corner beside Cauley.

"Covers?" Mila asked, blowing on a spoonful of stew.

"We're not underground, so we have to make our livings somehow," Cauley said.

"Our day jobs dovetail pretty nicely with our work for the society," Quinn added.

"What do you do?" asked Mila.

"We're part of ARAT," Cauley replied.

Mila furrowed her brow. Julian jumped in. "The Zetetics' Aboveground Risk Assessment Team. They watch developments in society and assess the risk level for Squires in case there might be an incident that requires us all to go underground."

"How do you do that?"

"I do media monitoring," Sidney began. "So basically, I prowl various outlets to see what types of stories are central to their coverage and what the messages and themes are. Quinn does—"

"*Social* media monitoring," Quinn said. "I watch top platforms and message boards to see not only what stories the public is latching onto, but what their response is to those stories. Fear? Anger? Also, Sidney will uncover stories that should be getting public attention, but aren't, and we'll monitor developments on those to see if Zetetics need to concern themselves with it, even if the Hesperian people aren't."

Quinn inhaled a spoonful of her dinner and looked at Cauley. Cauley adjusted his thick, black-framed glasses, fogged with steam from the stew, and turned to Mila. "And I measure outcomes by keeping tabs on new research, surveys, and statistics that are relevant to the things we're seeing, that way we can measure whether or not the public is actually *taking action* based on a story, message or theme. Are they blowing hot air, or are they rallying? I can get a pretty good feel for what the deal is by seeing if political groups have seen a surge in memberships, purchases of protective items spike, economic data, et cetera.

"At the end of every week, the three of us compile our data into a report that we send to all arms of Zetetics. If an issue arises in between reports, we create a one-off report and monitor those developments to see if it resolves itself or may require action on our part."

"Fascinating," Mila said.

"Yeah," Cauley agreed. "Way more than some Squires, who only have to mix drinks."

Julian grinned. "Hey, Hieu keeps me plenty busy on the side. And how many of you know how to make a kick-ass Toronto to take the edge off a long work day? I *thought* so."

Sidney slapped her palms on the counter. "Good idea! Why don't you get started on those?"

"Great," he groaned.

"*You* suggested it, not us." She winked and stood. "We'll be in the living room, bartender."

Mila watched the trio shuffle into the living room and cast a glance at Julian as she prepared to follow. "See you in there?"

He saluted.

Sidney and Cauley collapsed on floor cushions and Quinn sat at the holodesk.

"I've never seen holodesks like the two in the storm cellar," Mila said, seating herself on the couch. "Are they new models?"

"No..." Quinn answered with a quizzical squint. "Those aren't holodesks."

"Oh."

"You really haven't been here long, have you?" Cauley teased.

"No, not really."

"We just call them sleektops," Quinn explained. "They function similarly to holodesks, but they're the Zetetics' own development. No Zetetic can use any Hesperian technology—it's crazy dangerous. We use holodesks for our day jobs, but all of our monitoring work and communications with the rest of the society are done on underground inventions."

"That's impressive."

"Oh, you don't even know the half of it," Cauley smiled. "You'll see when you get where you're going."

Julian strode from the kitchen, balancing four glasses in his hands. "Torontos," he called, passing them out.

"Strong, I hope," Quinn said.

"Only way I know how." He plopped next to Mila.

Taking the ice-cold rocks glass, Mila sampled the drink—blinking against the burn of whiskey. But it went down smooth. Turning to Sidney, she said, "So, what's your cover? You never said."

Sidney took a hasty sip of her drink before answering. "Public relations account manager."

"And what's that like?"

Sidney offered a playful, tight-lipped smile. "It's like being a magician. My clients hire my agency to put on a show for their audiences, and with charisma, costumes, the right tools, and sleight of hand, we can get the audience to stop thinking and just believe my show is real. Or maybe it's like being a mathematician and the public is the formula.

We know exactly what to plug into the equation to make it spit out what my client needs, whether it's a response or a distraction. I can also appeal to a reporter's need for content and deadline pressures to get them to run nearly exactly what I tell them to. When you have the eye for it, you can read an article or see a broadcast story and know it reeks of press release."

Mila bit her lip. "You must have a mind built for strategy. But does it ever bother you to tamper with reality—to feel complicit in deceit?"

"It's my cover job." Sidney shrugged. "So I don't let it keep me up at night. It's not like the machine would shut down if I stopped doing it. And honestly, it works because we have the implicit consent of our audiences. They don't have to buy our messages—they want to. That's not on me, that's on them. So... nah, it doesn't bother me. Just a day job."

Talking about life above ground sent a craving for information through Mila. "Can you tell me what the most recent of your reports are talking about?" she asked Quinn. "I have no idea what normal Hesperia life is like lately."

Quinn cast a glance to the ceiling. "Hm... nothing unexpected. The most popular national headlines revolve around the death of a much-loved celebrity, a defamatory remark a political candidate allegedly said during his college years, and how to get the best deals on some new tech devices. Oh!"—she straightened—"but we've noticed chatter on message boards that a string of purported Belgae members have turned up dead throughout Hesperia."

She thought of her anonymous caller back at HBN—eons ago. Was he one of the dead? She sipped her drink, hoping the alcohol would calm the curdling in her stomach. Tightening her grip around her glass, Mila maintained a measured tone. "Really?"

"Yeah. Just in the last few days. Seven dead in Plains, New England, and Pacifica. Seven deaths isn't much, but their roles were of decent importance, and it can't have been coincidence."

"You think it's Hesperia?" Mila asked.

"It has to be," Quinn said. "We think Hesperia's tactics have changed. We think they want to pluck off the important Belgae members so the movement is handicapped and ultimately snuffs out from sheer weakness. A stealth approach like that appeals—it isn't likely to result in mass chaos, or even attract attention from the Hesperian public. Though whether or not they ever had the public's attention is debatable."

Julian huffed. "That's not going to work."

"You don't think so?" Quinn asked.

"Course not. The Belgae might not be as good as we are at staying out of Hesperia's sight, but they're damn good. The seven dead—God rest 'em—are not as important as Hesperia thinks they are."

"Maybe not."

Sidney leaned back on her arms. "But why now? That's the part that still doesn't make sense. What's changed in the last week or so on Hesperia Defense's end that wasn't there before?"

Quinn shook her head, but Mila knew. *Falk. Falk is in charge now. And he used me to get that power.* Anger, hot as white flame and cold as ice, flooded her veins.

"So," Cauley began, "I heard you came from Flint Hill."

"Cauley," Julian said.

Cauley raised his hands and shrugged. "No, I just mean—you seem pretty docile. I can't imagine why they'd need you."

Mila shifted. "Yeah, well..."

"So what's up with that?"

"Cauley!" said Sidney.

"It's fine," Mila said. "Because of some things I did at my job before, I guess they thought I was aiding the Belgae. I had a conversation with a former government official who talked about things he shouldn't have talked about, so I got pulled in. They didn't believe me when I said I had nothing to tell them."

"Figures," Quinn muttered at her holodesk screen.

"Yeah, you shouldn't have met with that official if you didn't want to get sucked in," Cauley said flippantly.

Mila shot him a pointed look. "Thanks."

Cauley kept prodding. "Who was the official?"

Sidney smacked the back of his head. "God, Cauley, are you writing a gossip column?"

"I'm just saying—I could do some recon on him. See if he can help us out."

"No, you can't," Mila said, her tone a little too sharp. "He's dead." Standing, she stalked into the kitchen, hearing Sidney's scolding whispers to Cauley. Burying her face in her hands, she took deep breaths and massaged her scalp. The torment of Carlo's death would never fade.

A warm hand settled between her shoulder blades. "Hey, sorry about Cauley," Julian said.

She looked at him and shook her head. "It was because of me."

"Nah. Cauley's always like that."

"No—Carlo DaVanti. He killed himself because of me."

Julian's eyes darkened. "Don't put that on yourself. Carlo was a razor-sharp guy. If he saw no other options—"

"You knew him?" When she'd recounted her story to Julian and Hieu back at Voltaire's, Julian hadn't reacted at the mention of Carlo's name.

"Yeah. I talked with him once. He, uh—he came to me when I was... when I was with the Belgae."

She straightened. "You were Belgae?"

He pulled up a stool and sat down. "Right after its inception. Left about three years later."

"Why did Carlo come to you?"

"He was working for Hesperia Defense at the time and was—quite frankly—enraged and terrified about what they were doing, especially with the Walden Data Facility. I was on my way out of the Belgae, and he wanted to talk to me about the group. He was putting out feelers, but I guess he didn't leave his government position for a while longer."

"And?" Mila pressed.

"And... I told him not to get involved with the Belgae."

"Why?"

"For the same reasons I'm no longer involved."

"Which are..."

"The Belgae are an incredibly bright but volatile group. I saw the trajectory they were moving on, and it wasn't going to end well—for them or Hesperia."

Julian's concerns sounded all too familiar—the same reasons her parents were reluctant to commit to the group.

"Carlo said he'd think about it," he said. "I guess he decided the risk was worth taking."

"He took one risk too many when he came to me, then," she muttered, studying a spot on the tiled counter. A risk worth taking. Was it? Carlo was dead now, never to know whether it was worth it or not. And no matter how brief her encounter with him was, his death rested partially upon her shoulders. Could she keep his death from being in vain, through whatever work she could do with the Zetetics? She had to try.

Sidney entered the kitchen, an apologetic twinge in her eyes. "Hey. Sorry about Cauley. He can be, uh... well, an ass. Let's not sugarcoat it."

Mila dismissed her words with a wave. "I'm just tired. What time is it, anyway?"

"After ten. I can take you to your bed if you want."

"That'd be good, thanks."

"Your stuff is still in the storm cellar," Julian said.

"That's okay," Mila stood. "I was going to sleep in these clothes anyway."

She followed Sidney back through the kitchen and into the living room, up the stairs to the second floor, which opened into a landing with two doors on each side. Sidney opened the first one on the right, revealing a bedroom with two twin beds and a window on the far wall between them.

"The other three bedrooms are mine, Quinn's, and Cauley's, so you'll have to share with Julian. Take the bed on the left," she added in a playful whisper. "It's the most comfortable."

Mila thanked her hostess. Shutting the door, she curled into the bed on the right.

~~~

Barely excusing himself, Julian wandered into the kitchen. For a moment, he stood frozen at the counter, unable to go upstairs to bed and unwilling to go downstairs and face whatever messages might await him on the sleektop communication panel. What if Falk had returned to Voltaire's, or Mama took a fall—or a turn for the worse? He winced—his imagination only made it all worse. Returning to the empty living room, he pulled up the rug, unlocked the little door, and descended into the storm cellar.

He sat at the sleektop, pursed his lips, cracked his knuckles, and determined to get it over with. Turning the device on, he signed in with his credentials and opened the communication panel. Of course, a message from Hieu topped the list. He swallowed his nerves and stuffed them down as he opened the message.

Julian, I'm sure you and Mila have found yourselves safe at Sidney's by now. I have full confidence that you will arrive safely at the Talbott's home by tomorrow evening.

A nonchalant beginning. A good sign. Julian read on.

There's no point in ambling around the matter: Don MUST go underground. In fact, he already is. Hesperia shut him down. His pharmaceutical practice is gone now. He has to start completely from scratch, and though I have the fullest confidence that he'll get the materials he needs from other Zetetics around Hesperia, the timing of when he'll be able to do so and deliver your mother more medication remains ambiguous. However, I'll remind you that we are fortunate to have members whose expertise lies in coping mechanisms and alternative therapies, and I encourage you to find consolation in that until Don can come through for us once more, as I'm sure he will.

As for what the Belgae knows... that remains dubious. I've kept a sharp eye on the clientele around here, though, and have seen no familiar faces or shady sorts, so as far as I can discern, you are safe for now. Your mother is doing just fine, a beam of sunshine captured in a person if there ever was one.

There have been no more sightings of Victor Falk. Whether this is good news or bad news for our new member, however, I don't know. Stay alert. Don't let her compromise us.

Julian closed the message and the communication panel, then exited the system and turned off the sleektop. Pressing the palms of his hands into his eyes, he released a heavy breath. It was too much. Living prescription to prescription, never knowing if the next batch would be the last... or if they'd reached the end of their options for care and it would just be all downhill from there. Always constant wondering—wondering about the medications, yes, but also whether the Belgae would turn up, like a monster under the bed, upsetting everything. Constantly being on the watch, poised and ready to be on the run... every once in a while it overwhelmed and exhausted him.

But this was his life. Mama's life. Any other option was indisputably worse. Most days he could deal with the stress. And on days that he couldn't—

well, on those days, he was glad he owned and operated a bar. Shaking his shoulders and rubbing his neck, he returned to the living room, trudged up the stairs, and crawled into bed. But he tossed and turned under the grating memory of Hieu's closing demand.

Don't let her compromise us.

As if it was a certainty—something that would absolutely happen, unless Julian prevented it. How could Hieu be so sure—so unfair? But Julian's conscience prodded him. His friend wasn't off the mark. He'd also sensed it in Mila. Her mouthwatering appetite for meaning—and maybe even for revenge. Hieu was right, it could pose a liability for them. But surely that was only because her sights were still set aboveground. She hadn't seen everything they could offer her yet. Once she did, surely she'd see the meaningful life—the free life—she could have with the Zetetics.

With him.

21.

"I'M GLAD WE COULD DO THIS, VICTOR," said Edmund Kent, Chief of the Domestic Terrorism Section, lifting his glass of beer in a toast. "Congratulations on your new position. You'll be a tremendous asset to my team."

Falk clinked his glass with Kent's and mimicked the sincere glint in his new boss' eye. He'd rather still be in Bay, tying up loose ends. But obligation to perform professional mimesis called him back to Erie. "The pleasure is all mine, sir."

They celebrated over beers and steaks at a favorite local tavern located not far from the Erie Bureau. Seated on the outdoor patio among university students and romantic partners, the men stood out with suit jackets hanging on the backs of their chairs, ties loosened, and white dress shirts rolled up to their elbows.

"I only wish we could've celebrated sooner. But—calendar's been full." Kent sawed off a piece of steak and shoved it into his mouth.

"Not a problem. I've been busy, too. Better late than never." A lie. He'd have preferred never. But Kent had insisted on celebrating.

Edmund's eyes widened. He swallowed. "Yes, that's right! You went to Bay."

"I did at that. There are some cases that I'm not content to farm out. Certain things need a little extra oversight, I'm sure you understand."

"I do, I do." Edmund smiled, leaned back in his chair, and pointed his fork at Falk. "That's what I like about you, Vic—can I call you Vic?"

Falk tipped his head, smiling modestly.

"That—is what I like about you. Ready and willing to get your hands dirty, no matter how high up the ranks you climb. I know we'll make great strides with you as the new special agent-in-charge."

"Such generous praise coming from someone with your impressive career is very flattering. I appreciate it. You're going to give me a big head."

"Speaking of big heads"—Edmund reached into his pocket and withdrew his wallet—"my wife had twins two weeks ago." He opened his wallet, flashing the small photo inside.

Instead of wincing at the awkward transition, Falk leaned over to inspect the photo. Two squinty-eyed, red-faced babies stared back. Falk felt nothing, but looked back at his boss with wide, admiring eyes and a big smile. "They're perfect!" he exclaimed, and the proud beam in Edmund's eyes told him he'd found just the right tone of admiration and awe. "I can see you in them. Congratulations, Edmund, there's a lot to celebrate tonight."

"There certainly is."

"Let me buy another round—I insist."

"Well, if you insist."

Falk signaled for their server and ordered another round of beers, their third. Edmund's plate screeched as he scraped the knife to cut off another bite of steak. He paused. "I can't believe I haven't asked you this. Do you have a family of your own?"

"I don't." He hoped his reply sounded pensive enough. "Someday, though."

"I know that look." Edmund's words blustered out in a guttural laugh. "Who's the lady on your mind?"

Falk focused on spearing a piece of broccoli with his fork, but sensed Edmund watching him. Irritated, he met the unrelenting, information-hungry eyes of his new boss. "A woman I knew while I worked in my previous position."

"Got a picture? Someone like you wouldn't fetch just any plain-faced dame."

Falk shook his head, but Edmund continued to stare at him expectantly. Forcing a wistful smile, he began his description. "Reddish hair—"

"Now that's what I'm talkin' about."

"One gray eye, one green—"

"Oh yeah."

"But the feelings aren't mutual." Maybe that would put a stop to this tiresome conversation.

"Persistence. That's the key. You think my lady took me and my ugly mug right away? Hell, no. I had to persevere. I think she married me out of sheer exhaustion."

The server delivered their beer, saving Falk from having to reply. He endured another half hour of grating conversation before the dinner ended. But he'd accomplished his objective: He'd completely won over Edmund Kent. With a final offer of con-gratulations and expression of enthusiasm at the opportunity to work under such excellent leadership, Falk bid Kent farewell, and they headed in opposite directions from the tavern.

As he walked, his exquisite dress shoes smacked into the puddles created by the recent rain. He'd have to shine them—again. But his crisp white dress shirt glowed the same color as the moon, and nearly shimmered next to the satin-like finish of his new, sleek black suit. Stopping on the sidewalk, he turned to gaze at the night sky. Clouds obscured the stars and slowly advanced to overtake the moon, but for the moment the waxing gibbous shined down onto the lake in the public park across the street, which was nearly empty save for some lovers nuzzling on a bench.

Living in a thriving city occupied by countless public employees—mainly within Hesperia's National Security Bureau—gave him such satisfaction. Glistening luxury magnecars, in various styles but nearly always in the classic black chosen by most public employees, whisked down the roads with important, urgent whirs. *This* was where he deserved to be—among the best and brightest, not the undesirables swarming Flint Hill like dung beetles. He deserved to be illuminated by the city lights, not hidden in the woods. Finally, his excellence was being recognized the way it always should have been.

Thump, drag. Thump, drag.

The sound came from farther down the sidewalk. Falk tore his attention from the skyline to find the source of the noise. A homeless man emerged from the alleyway ahead, wearing a tattered white T-shirt and dingy green pants, but no shoes. With long, scraggly hair and skin weathered as leather, the man appeared unfortunate enough to inspire sympathy without intimidation. He leaned against a building's brick wall and slid down to the ground, setting the metal can in his hand down with a *clink.*

Falk approached him, curious. Hesperia generally did a good job of dealing with the homeless through the Office of Worker Aid, but some stragglers remained, and he hated to come across them. They served no purpose, the homeless. A complete bane on the existences of people like him. Much better for people to be in the lower economic brackets—or even better, the poverty zone—where they're struggling but not homeless, able to provide and contribute to the economy, but still in plenty of need so as to be easily controlled. But the homeless? They had nothing to offer in return.

He stalked up to the man, who looked up at him with clouded eyes that suggested his can had been empty for a while.

"Spare any coins?" he wheezed.

"No. But we both know what you'd use them for."

The man's eyes widened. He erupted into a nervous cough.

Falk reached into the interior pocket of his suit jacket and pulled out a single white pill. "How about we get straight to the point and I just give you this instead?"

"Oh—no, sir. I don't—don't do—I..."

"Yes you do. Take it."

Falk dropped the pill into the can. The man kept his eyes trained on Falk and shook his head slowly. Falk walked past him. After a few paces, he glanced back. The man held the pill between his thumb and index finger. Popped it into his mouth.

Falk counted ten paces and arrived at a crosswalk. He looked again. The homeless man lay flat, with one hand still clutching his throat. One less straggler for the Office of Worker Aid to support. He crossed the street and entered the first building, taking the elevator to his flat on the thirtieth floor.

He strolled down the long hallway. The black lacquered door to his apartment reminded him of a coffin's lid. Striding across the high-ceilinged living area, he made a beeline for the liquor station and poured a glass of scotch. Crossing into his bed-room, he sat at the claw-footed desk situated across from his bed. A holodesk screen was embedded within the thick walnut wood of the desk. It flick-ered as he turned it on, then opened the Citizen Surveillance program. CitiSurv had helped him lo-cate, arrest, or eliminate countless Hesperians, but now he used the program purely for curiosity.

He typed in the number of the tracking device he'd injected into the back of her neck while she'd been unconscious. He'd never even activated it— not until he was certain she'd ventured far enough out of Flint Hill's reach to thwart the guards, and even then, he'd always turned the device off after he checked her location. He couldn't risk letting her get caught by anyone but himself.

The program searched for Mila Ray. Slowly, the map on the screen became patterned with red cir-cles and dotted lines, tracing her route from the Flint Hill woods to Savannah-Georgia. He waited for the program to tell him something he didn't know.

The blue circle stopped spinning, disappeared, and spit out the updated map. Her last known whereabouts: Charleston-South Carolina. It pin-pointed her location down to the street address, but he furrowed his brow. The dotted line that should have connected her location in Savannah to her whereabouts in Charleston didn't appear. He refreshed the search, but nothing. Whatever route she had taken had tripped up the tracking device—and it was certainly not just a glitch.

It had to do with Merrick. When he'd first tracked Mila to the Merrick mother and son, he thought Mila's trajectory couldn't have been more perfect. His recon on the pub proprietor revealed him to be a *former* Belgae member. But Falk suspected he still worked for the opposition, incognito. Though swatting off revolutionaries via his agents brought Falk some measure of satisfaction, Mila had handed him a swifter route through her paramour. Driven by ardor and anger, Mila would join the Belgae, follow Julian to the movement's core and—like the falcon she was—flush out Falk's prey, for him to exterminate once and for all, and reap all the accolades.

But not if he couldn't track her. He fought the anger rising in his chest. Mila didn't know about the tracking device. Something about her route was off the device's radar.

Another unconnected red circle appeared. Roanoke-Virginia.

The sharp ring of his phone interrupted his angry rumination.

"This is Falk."

"Falk, Warden Gregory." He spoke in the quiet voice of a man long run-down by his work.

"Warden. Good to hear from you. What can I do for you?"

"Nothing. I've just called to update you on our search for inmate thirty-four. We've—had no more success locating her, sir."

Falk generated a displeased growl. "That's not the kind of update I want right before I turn in for the night."

"I know, sir. I waited late because the guards were still working. I wanted to call you with some measure of good news."

"Well, we can consider that effort an utter failure, can't we?"

"I don't mean to disagree with you, sir, but I truly think she is dead. Everything about her death checks out."

"She's not dead. Tell you what, Warden. Thirty-Four will be my personal mission from now on."

The warden sputtered. "Falk—uh, sir. You have enough on your plate—"

"And I have even more when I'm worrying that your team isn't getting the job done. So how about this. You all can go back to whatever it is you do all day, which hopefully includes not letting this happen again. I'll find Mila Ray. This is my strong suit."

"Sir—"

"Enough, Warden."

"Yes, sir."

Falk ended the call, turned off the tracking device once again, and logged out of the holodesk. Making a mess of things and then playing the hero was too easy.

22.

DUST CLOUDED MILA'S VIEW through the windshield of Sidney's magnecar as they meandered down a long, winding dirt driveway. The ten-hour drive from Charleston to Roanoke should only have taken six, but the old, forgotten back roads—the kind requiring magnecars to deploy their rarely-used wheels—offered safer travel than the intensely-monitored highways and interstates. The cramped commute drained Mila. She pitied Julian for having to do it all over again in just twenty-four hours—Sidney needed her car back before her work week began again.

She squinted through the clouds of clay-red dust.

"Chet and Trudi Talbott territory," Julian said, as if reading her thoughts. "A hundred acres, passed down through Chet's family. They even live in a log cabin, hundreds of years old. Who's heard of such a thing these days?"

The car slowed and stopped, and the dust cleared. The Talbott's safe house stood surrounded by Roanoke-Virginia woods, as solitary as a lone wolf, and just as happy that way.

Mila opened the door and summer's heat blasted her cheeks. She left the car, legs aching in praise and protest. Stretching her muscles, a burden of tension she didn't know she carried released from her shoulders. The sensation of being trapped and exposed followed her, even on rural roads. Taking a deep breath, she let the uncivilized air permeate her insides, encouraging the rest of her body to relax as she leaned her head backward and focused on the sounds around her. The songs of the birds and wind reminded her that there was safety in the woods. She opened her eyes.

Julian stood close by, an amused smirk in his eyes. He apparently resisted the urge to let it travel to his mouth, too, but was losing the battle. His lips twitched.

"You're bizarre," Mila said in an effort to mask her self-consciousness.

"Watching your face is interesting. You're very expressive, especially when you're not communicating with anyone but yourself. I like trying to figure out what's running through your head."

"Oh." Mila tucked a strand of hair behind her ear. "Any luck?"

He opened his mouth but seemed to think better of it, and shook his head. "Nope."

The screened-in front door squealed open. She turned as a man and woman, appearing to be in their seventies, stepped onto the porch. A hunter-green flat cap sat atop the man's white hair, his round, pink cheeks bordered by a snow-white beard and mustache. With a couple more pounds added to his hefty frame, the plaid shirt he wore rolled up to the elbows just might need to retire in favor of a larger size.

"Julian, so good to see you!" Chet called.

Trudi elbowed him. "His friend, Chester, don't forget his friend."

"And his friend!" He hustled down the steps. "Don't tell me—Julian told me. Mmm..." He squinted one eye as he strained to recall her name. "Melinda!"

"Mila," she laughed, taking his paw-like hand. The sparkle in his eyes could have traveled miles.

"Bags? Bags? Let me get your bags." He snatched them and hefted them over each shoulder, looking like a rugged Saint Nicholas, and trudged back up the porch steps with Mila and Julian close behind. Trudi held the door open, dressed in a canary-yellow dress, a flour-dusted green gingham apron covering her hourglass figure. Mila extended a hand to greet her hostess, but the woman smiled hugely and wrapped her into a firm hug.

Trudi pulled back. "Trudi Talbott," she said. "All you need to know is one thing—I'm gonna feed you and feed you good, so you're just gonna have to let any ideas of turning down seconds or thirds slip from your little ol' mind." She led Mila into the cabin's living room and glided straight into the kitchen.

"Don't fight it," Chet called from the living room. "She's a seamstress too, so she can let the hem of your clothes out real nice. See how she did mine?" He puffed out his belly, straining the buttons on his shirt.

Julian gave a swift pat to Chet's stomach. "And that's why I can only afford to visit a few times a year."

Chet roared in laughter and wagged a finger. "No, no, no, young man. It's because your ego can't take losing at chess to an old goat like me."

"Hm. That's true, too." He cast a wink Mila's way.

"I've not even moved the pieces on the board since your last visit, so the story of your last decimation has been perfectly preserved. Wanna see?"

"I don't know if I could take it..."

"Then maybe instead you can help me carry some logs out to my burn pit. A bad storm came through a couple months back and I chopped up all the fallen trees, but Trudi didn't want me haulin' logs."

"That I can do."

Chet led the way through a sliding glass door that opened onto an expansive deck. Crossing the living room, Mila stood by the door. Potted flowers in soft and hot pinks, raspberry and ruby reds, and clementine orange brightened the deck's periphery, while the thick trunk of a tree grew up from the middle, lending its shade to the main area. Six chairs encircled the tree. Beyond the deck, Mila spotted Julian and Chet, already plunging their axes into a fallen tree by a large pond. Julian's curly locks matched the golden light of the sun and glistened as he moved to swing the axe, his angular physique bunching into sculpted, straining muscles as he worked.

A smile dallied on Mila's lips, but she suppressed it. *He's leaving tomorrow. I may never see him again.* She turned around to survey the living room.

The cabin overflowed with Trudi's touch. Whimsy whispered everywhere. It twirled in the dried flowers and herbs hanging upside down in the windows. It tinkled in the dainty wind chimes on the front porch and in the mobile of colored glass orbs hanging over the wooden dinner table. Mila guessed that the many throw blankets, strewn over the furniture and limp from years of constant use, were Trudi's creations, too.

She wandered to the dining table to take a closer look at the mobile. Five concentric spheres hung from a thin chain, each seeming to float within the next. The largest globe—made of clear glass—acted as a window to the next four, which were speckled with yellow, turquoise, royal purple, and then red. At the core of the tiniest globe, Mila could just barely see three black beads.

Dainty footsteps interrupted her wonderings. "I made that little knickknack when I got into glassblowing a decade or so back," Trudi said, chuckling lightly as she slid a casserole dish into the center of the table. "I'm always bouncing from hobby to hobby, you see. Like those crocheted blankets there, and the clay pots over there. Oh"—

she laughed—"and the oboe sittin' over in that corner."

"What's the significance?"

"Ah," she paused. "I don't know how to say it. 'Worlds' is the concept, I suppose."

"Worlds?"

"Yeah, you see 'em in there? Small to big, big to small. We live in 'em all. Those are supposed to be us, right there." She pointed to the beads rolling in the smallest orb. "We live in so many worlds. There's the biggest—the big, wide world, where everyone else is, too. Then they get more specific. Maybe the next one's Gair, then Hesperia. Then Appalachia Region and my own little town. Then there's my most personal world—my family and friends. But even though that's the one closest to me, I still live in all of the 'em." She paused and looked at Mila. "Do you follow?"

"I think so."

"I think it's like this for all of us. We live in multiple worlds. The question is, how—as one person—do we choose to relate to each one? Do we want to ignore the biggest reality or two, and focus on our smallest ones instead? If we wanted to engage in all of our domains, do we even have the time? Or would we have to sacrifice time and attention from one of our other worlds?"

Trudi's eyes took on a reflective sheen as she gazed at the mobile. Mila looked, too, wondering about the layers of her own realities. There used to be family. Career. The people. With the first two obliterated, did that leave her with only one world? Could she rebuild, in time?

"What do you think?" Mila asked.

"Oh, honey. I don't even know that I've found my answer, so how on earth could I give you yours? Or anyone else's for that matter. No one can tell you how to live in your worlds. You have to figure it out for yourself." A beeping sound came from the kitchen. Trudi jumped. "That's the cornbread!" She hurried back into the kitchen, calling over her shoulder, "Why don't you go and tell those boys to get on in here, dinner's just about ready."

A couple of hours later, Mila and Julian collapsed on the couch, bellies full of Trudi's home-cooked goodness. Trudi shuffled in behind them and lit the seven beeswax candles on the mantel above the fireplace. "Too warm for a fire, but never the wrong weather for candles," she said.

"Or for a cold beer." Chet burst through the kitchen door balancing four foaming steins on a tray. He slid the tray onto the table in the center of the rug and sat in his chair with a happy groan. "Drink up, weary travelers, and for more merriment drink fast!" He snatched his glass and raised it. Julian, Mila, and Trudi grabbed the remaining beers and clinked glasses with Chet, then each other. Chet gulped a quarter of his and wiped foam from his white beard. "My very own red ale. Never disappoints. You still brewing, Julian?"

"Still serving. Not brewing," Julian said. "I'd like to get back to it, though."

"Tell your Croatoan hub director to let you take it easy. A man's gotta have his artisanry!"

"Oh, c'mon, Chet." Trudi tilted her head in exasperation. "Don't blame Hieu. If you know anything about this young man, you know he's put too much pressure on himself."

"If the woman says it's true, it's true." With a stage whisper to Mila, he added, "It actually is true."

Mila checked the statement in Julian's eyes. He squinted in a playful glare, and she grinned. "Croatoan," she said, turning back to Chet. "What's behind that name?"

"Oh." Chet drew out the word in a dramatic, conspiratorial hiss. "Be careful when you seek *behind* things, Mila. The belly of the stone is rarely as smooth as its face."

"Good Lord, Chet," Trudi laughed. "This is why we don't have visitors."

Chet snatched a small ball of yarn from his wife's knitting basket and threw it at her. She caught it and tossed it back in the basket. "Damn. She's gotten too good at that." He cleared his throat and propped his elbows on his knees, the mantle of storyteller back in his persona and the glint of candle flames in his eyes. "Croatoan. You've not heard of The Lost Colony, then."

Mila searched her memory for any recollection of the term, but shook her head.

"Lost to wilderness, lost to time." Chet twiddled his beard. "It was fifteen eighty-four when Sir Walter Raleigh, with conquest in his heart and greed glittering in his eyes, dispatched an expedition to Roanoke, North Carolina. The stakes were high. If his colony in North America failed, he'd never get another chance.

"Perhaps the New World knew. Could nature itself have sensed the motives of its newcomers? The fate of the colonists certainly leaves this storyteller wondering if—would you knock it off?"

Trudi widened her eyes. "Hm?"

"I see the eye rolls, the sighing, the looks you're shootin' Melinda over there. I'm trying to tell a story and you're shattering the ambiance of my performance."

"Sweetie, there's no ambiance. Look at the poor girl. Her eyes are all glazed over."

"That's because of my beer."

"No it isn't."

Chet blinked at his wife slowly. He turned back to Mila. "As I was saying... the untamed wilderness wouldn't squelch the determination of the pompous Sir Richard Grenville, Raleigh's delegate. And—"

"The Roanoke colony struggled like a fly in molasses," Trudi interrupted, her speech fast and dismissive. "The colony disappeared and left nothing behind, save for the word 'Croatoan' carved into a tree. They might've been adopted by the local Croatoan tribe, but no one knows. This Zetetics' hub is named after the tribe. Mila dear"—she smirked—"you can't ask that man such questions, or you'll never see the dawn of a new day. And Chet, honey, I think I covered the story just fine without aging us another year."

"You left out all the colorful details," he grumbled into his beer.

Hours passed, and the pumpkin-orange sunset soon turned into the shadow of night, prompting Chet and Trudi to retire to bed. Julian and Mila remained on the couch, nursing the last sips of their second steins of beer.

"Have you gotten to take a good look at the pond yet?" Julian asked.

"Not yet," Mila replied.

He stood and extended his hand. "C'mon," he grinned, and she couldn't resist his invitation. He held the door to the back porch and they descended the steps to the yard below. The light of the moon percolated through the evening clouds and marbleized the ground, dancing on the pond waters that wisped in response to the night's breeze. Julian stopped underneath a tree near the pond. Mila continued a few steps ahead of him. Even without the relentless summer sun to bake her neck and shoulders, she felt sweat bead on her forehead and collarbone.

"Where's your mind at?"

Mila turned. Julian cocked his head, his turquoise eyes taking on a cornflower hue in the moonlight. "Half the time, I swear, your body's here but everything else about you is somewhere else." His lips ticked into a curious smile.

"I don't know. I guess I still feel like you're keeping me in the dark about the Zetetics." She stared at him, waiting for a response, but he remained poker-faced. "For all you've told me, there's still so much that doesn't make sense. You've told me it's an old society, rooted in history. It's apparently expansive, and I still don't even know where I'm headed tomorrow—and you're not even going with me. You've explained the theories and philosophies, but practically nothing about how they translate into action. What are the Zetetics *doing*, Julian? What are they going to do to change things in Hesperia?"

Julian leaned against the tree. "Change," he said passively, as though the concept hadn't ever occurred to him.

"Yes!" She couldn't keep the incredulity out of her voice.

"Change is important to you, isn't it? Activism."

"I—of course it is. Isn't it to you? Isn't it to the Zetetics?"

He looked away, toward the lake. "How do you think change will come to Hesperia, Mila?"

"Through truth. They *don't know*—I heard it every day when I worked at HBN. Most of them have no idea what really goes on. The truth never makes the headlines, and certainly not the top ones. If they *knew*..." She took a deep breath and released it, exasperated. "If they knew, they couldn't help but act."

He nodded, almost imperceptibly.

"What?"

"Why do you think the truth doesn't make the headlines? Why is the truth buried, or all but invisible?"

"Don't talk down to me." She stepped toward the tree. "You know as well as I do—the media chooses not to make those stories the top ones. Journalism isn't what it should be."

"Why do you think that is?"

"Julian!" she snapped.

"Seriously, Mila—I'm not trying to talk down to you. I want to know, why do *you* think that is?"

"Money. Marketing. Advertisements and advertisers. The media is—"

"A business."

"Yes."

"And that means making their bottom line is the top priority, like any other business—"

"Exactly."

"And making money happens by pleasing their—"

"Advertisers," she jumped in, "other power-holders, and—"

"Consumers."

Their gazes locked.

"A business doesn't stay in business for very long if it doesn't give its customers what they want," Julian said. "Who said the media gives the people what they *should* have, or what they *need*? They give the people what they *want*. So if the truth isn't in the top headlines... well, you tell me."

"How can they know what they want if they aren't exposed to it? They have a very limited menu from which to order."

"In this day and age? Really, Mila, the truth might not be in the top headlines, but it's out there. You look for what you want. You seek what you want."

"So what are you saying?"

"That Hesperians are like a magician's audience. They're deceived because they want to be. They're in the dark because they prefer it that way. The fact that the media isn't reporting truth—or reporting it in the top headlines—is because they know their customers, and they know what their customers want. The media is a reflection of society. So what would you be fighting for, Mila? To rescue a society that doesn't want to be rescued? To bend the ear of the people, you have to pull their fingers out first."

She whirled and walked toward the dock at the other end of the pond.

"Mila," Julian called after her. "Hey, stop." She heard his footsteps across the grass behind her, but

322 Leah Noel Sims

kept going. "I'm sorry, I should have kept my mouth shut."

She turned. "Yes, you should have." She closed the distance between them, certain her eyes radiated angry heat. "How dare you patronize me, and tell me what's worth my time. I have no family, no career—I was arrested and thrown into a government detention facility, for God's sake! And you're dense enough to ask if I want *change?* You're damn right I want change. Because after all I've seen, all I've been through—do you think I can leave the work of instigating change up to anyone but myself? That work is all I have. I'm the only one I can trust to do it. And honestly, Julian? If you want to take that away from me, you can go to hell."

She started to turn away from him again but he grasped her wrists, pulled her toward him and pressed his lips to hers, all while holding her fists against his chest. She could feel his heart pounding. She wrenched away from him. "What the hell is wrong with you?"

Breathless, his eyes widened in a mixture of confusion, embarrassment, and—of this she was fairly certain—satisfaction. "Everything, apparently," he said. One side of his mouth twitched sheepishly upward.

"At least we can agree on that." She crossed her arms and backed away from him. Her lips were raw—heated—from the insistence of his.

"I'm sorry, Mila. I am." He held his palms up. "For—this, just now. For injecting my opinion when you didn't ask for it. I'm being a cad. I just... care"—he drew out the word, testing it—"about you. I think we're similar in certain ways. Certain ways that—for me—didn't pan out so well." He shrugged. "I guess I forgot I wasn't talking to myself."

"Well, consider this your reminder."

"I will. You have to do what you have to do."

"Yes. I do."

"I just wish you didn't have to."

"Why?"

He hesitated. "Selfish reasons."

She took a step forward and leveled her gaze with his. "Then let go," she said. "You don't know what I carry with me. I'm crushed by what I know. I have information that the majority of Hesperians do not, yet no way to give it to them—except by way of this group. You don't understand—I can't live knowing what I know and not at least try to make it public. Carlo died because he told me. He hoped I could do something about it. Maybe now I can. But there is no one on this planet who I can trust to accomplish this but me. You have to get out of my way."

"Done." He stepped toward her.

Mila shook her head and sighed. "Julian, don't."

He cupped her face in his hands, forcing her to look at him. "Done," he repeated quietly, tracing her cheekbones with his thumbs.

He'd only said one word, but she struggled to find the right response to everything conveyed by his eyes. "Thank you," she managed. She stopped herself from reaching up to clasp his wrists.

He released her. "I'm going to head in. Busy day tomorrow."

"Yeah. Me too. In just a few minutes."

She watched him as he walked toward the house, until he disappeared behind the back door. Then she turned her attention back to the pond. Not even so much as a chirping cricket joined her. There she was again—in the darkness.

Alone.

~~~

Julian sat on the edge of his bed and stared at the empty one Mila would be occupying across from him. He raked his fingers through his hair. She didn't get it. Didn't understand that the Zetetics didn't plan to *do* anything to Hesperia. It was futile—history had proven that. Uprisings either failed miserably or barely lasted. The stories of long-dead countries proved it—Rome, France, Russia, The Former Nation. It was the simple law of entropy—order to disorder. Systems that started out good inevitably spoiled like meat. And ones that had already rotted were even harder to redeem, and fell even harder once they fell again.

How did she not get it?

He knew he was kidding himself. He knew why she hadn't gotten it—he hadn't explained the mission. Not clearly enough. And it was all because he knew what would happen. She'd leave. But he thought by buying some time, maybe... maybe she'd stay. For him.

For *him*? Really! How narcissistic was that notion? Sighing, he pressed the heels of his hands to his eyes. Now, he had to think of Hieu and the hub—actually, the entire organization. Mila's mindset didn't mesh with the mission, and it clearly wasn't going to change. He had hoped it would, and so he hadn't said word one to Hieu about it— about the fact that, quiet as she was, she was a loose cannon, with her fuse sparked by a noxious blend of idealism, anger, and loneliness. She couldn't stay. He owed it to Hieu to be forthright about her.

Julian went downstairs to the living room, then crossed to the basement door, where he knew Trudi and Chet's sleektop was. He opened the door, but couldn't resist glancing outside one last time. The moonlight just slightly revealed Mila's silhouette, still standing by the lake.

He'd told himself it was gone. Dead, even. But it was still there. The dam in his heart had strained against the pressure for years now, but in meeting Mila the dam had sprung a leak. His old passions, the ones he'd buried in a sea of cynicism, began to wash ashore once more. His heart swelled within his chest. What if she *could* accomplish something? What if she ignited within the rest of the Zetetics the same desire for change that he possessed so long ago? That wish whispered in all of their hearts, he knew it. It was what had led them to give up normal Hesperia life and risk everything to join the organization. Maybe Mila could make them believe again—believe in a better world that existed not underground, but in daylight, in the open air, without tunnels and safe houses and old, forgotten pathways. The Zetetics could accomplish more than the Belgae ever dreamed, but had decided it was futile to try. Like a dormant volcano, their lava swirled beneath the earth and was capable of rendering everything to rich, burnt earth—the kind from which lush new growth could spring. What if Mila could make the volcano finally erupt?

What if?

Who am I to blow out her flame? Who am I to stop her, and potentially interfere with a calling so powerful that not even Hesperia can hold it back?

His chest tightened. *Hieu—after all Hieu's done for me and Mama, can I really hold back what I know about Mila? Don't I at least owe it to the man to be honest?*

He watched Mila, and could barely see her delicate hand run through her long hair. Shutting the basement door, he returned to his room.

~~~

Mila woke to the sound of Julian's voice.

"Ready, Sunshine?" He stood at the door, barely visible in the receding moonlight, both of their bags hugged under his arms. "Gotta get an early start. We don't have time to wait for daybreak."

She pulled herself out of bed, her limbs heavy, and wrangled her tangled auburn hair into a long braid before meeting Julian in the doorframe. She expected another long drive, or rigorous hike through the Appalachia woods. But instead, Trudi held open the door to the basement.

"Let's get you on your way," she said.

Chet, Julian, Mila, and Trudi descended a narrow, dark staircase. Halfway down, Chet paused and fiddled with something on the wall. A creaking sound cued the illumination of a gas lamp, reminiscent of pre-Edison technology. Mila marveled. This portion of the house was eons older than the log cabin above it. When she reached the bottom of the stairs, her jaw dropped. Small lamps on the stone walls filled the area with a mysterious glow. They stood before a wide railway on a platform made of old brick.

"A magnerail station?" she asked.

"The Zetetics is underground in every sense of the word," Julian said.

"It was an absolute treat having you with us, Mila." Trudi pulled her into an embrace. "You'll be a surefire asset to the group, no doubt."

"Ain't that the truth." Chet took Mila's bag from Julian. "Now, c'mon. The train'll be here for us any second."

"You're going with me?" she asked.

"Darn skippy, I am! A true gentleman doesn't toss a lady onto an underground train headed to an underground secret society's lair without so much as someone to keep her company, does he? Plus, I can tell ya stories. Keep you from gettin' bored."

"Thank the Lord for that," Trudi mumbled. Chet shot her a look.

A whirring sounded from far in the distance of the tunnel. Touching her elbow, Julian led her to the edge of the platform. "Safe travels," he said. "I'll join you as soon as I can get away again."

The whirring turned into a low rumble. He looked over his shoulder in anticipation of the on-coming train, then back to Mila. His fingers lightly rubbed her elbow.

"I—" she began, but the heat in his gaze rendered her speechless. As if sensing her nervousness, Julian hastily pulled her close. Mila dropped her bag and wrapped her arms around his waist. He clutched the base of her braid in one hand and twirled the tail of it in the other.

His lips pressed to her ear. "I'll be thinking of you."

Mila pulled back. "You too," she managed, just as headlights blazed into her eyes. Squinting against the light, she focused on the advancing train until an archaic-looking trolley took shape and rolled to a stop by the platform. A final question leapt into her mind. "Where are you sending me?"

The trolley door opened to reveal a brawny silhouette, backlit by the lights of the interior. "Well, look who the dog dropped in my doorway," Ada chirped.

Julian picked up Mila's bag and handed it to her, then grasped her shoulders and gave them a squeeze. He turned her to face Ada in the doorway and answered, "Colorado. Tesla."

23.

THE TROLLEY'S STEADY JAUNT lulled Mila. Bobbing her head, she fought to keep her eyes open as Ada prattled on about her close run-ins with Hesperia, and Chet shared his own tales within the Zetetics. Their expressive faces illuminated and darkened in rhythmic flashes of light and shadow as the trolley sped past lamps within the tunnels. As they sped beneath the earth, farther and farther from Hesperia's east coast, the anxiety and dread that had plagued her since her release from Flint Hill began to thaw and slide off of her like melting snow on a tin roof. Her tracking device had been deactivated. Her paper trail led to a dead end. Falk couldn't find her here. She was deep, far, away—gone. To where, exactly?

"Tesla," she began. "As in—"

"Nikola." Chet's eyes twinkled. "How about a story while we ride?"

"Chester, you goat, you haven't changed at all." Ada sighed, but she cast a smile the man's way.

Chet fluffed his beard. "'Twasn't so far in the distant past that these chipped and crumbling bricks were bright and new, the sole witnesses to the work of a troubled genius."

"Nikola Tesla?" Mila said.

"Aye."

Ada groaned. "You're a pirate for this story?"

"I am the storyteller. I tell stories how I see fit." He cleared his throat. "The troubled genius! Shirked by society. His competitor and former boss—the one and only Edison—spurned him. Forsooth! Some say—"

"'Forsooth'?" interjected Ada.

"*Forsooth!* Some say he was spiraling into madness. He was a right tenderhearted humanitarian, that Tesla. Always wanting to better the world with his inventions. *Oft*"—he emphasized the archaic word and glared playfully at Ada—"underpaid—even unpaid—he created and created. And time and time again, he was shortchanged. From the scornful lights of New York City, he fled. From the stench and the crowds that demanded and demanded, he fled. From Edison, that rat bastard, he—"

"Fled?" Ada asked.

"I don't know why I even bother."

"He fled. Go on," she said.

Mila straightened. "So the place we're headed isn't just named after Tesla, he actually worked there?"

"Darn skippy, he did. In the open air of the area known as Knob Hill, the inventor sought freedom to create without the fear of being stolen from. And invent he did, missy. Invent, he did. More than the world ever knew. But a chill washed over him. The world had already taken too much from the Serb. He couldn't let these inventions fall into their hands, not ever. They could be used for evil, and he knew they would—even if it happened centuries and centuries after he lay cold in his grave. He needed a place to hide the inventions forever. Bury them."

"Tesla had a secret lair built and no one batted an eye?" she asked.

"One thing you have to understand is, this was later in Tesla's career. He wasn't the striking, blue-eyed genius anymore. No, ma'am. Far as the public was concerned, he'd degenerated into a madman too smart for his own good. So when Tesla picked the talented Christopher Redridge to head up the project, everyone brushed it off as the crazy man's fixation. It was built. It was forgotten."

"Until...?" she prodded.

"Until the bad times came, roughly two hundred years ago. Then, one of Redridge's descendants remembered. You see, ol' Chris Redridge wasn't just no contractor, construction worker man. He was a Jack-of-all-trades, and I do mean *all* trades. Probably neither he nor Tesla expected the arrangement to become what it did, but soon enough, Chris Red was Nik's protégé. And no one ever knew, save for his family. And his sons, and his son's sons, and so on and so forth—they heard the stories of the time their daddy, granddaddy, great-granddaddy worked for 'the lanky nutcase', as Red's wife had called him. It was all fun family tales, you see, until the hard times came. And that's when Chris Red's great-great-great—however many greats by that point—thought about those tales and the secret lair. Daniel Redridge scratched his whiskers and got it into his curly head that there might be something down there. Something he could use that no one else had. Sure enough, he found the place. More importantly, he found the inventions and all them scribbly notes and—being the descendent of Chris Red and carrying his genes through and through—Dan figured out how they all worked. So this place became the Redridge's refuge in times of trouble. Now, it's ours."

"So the Redridges were the first Zetetics?"

Ada snorted a laugh and smiled at Chet.

"You can't be getting all hung up on titles and institutions, Mila," Chet winked. "Zetetics have always been—they just haven't always called themselves that. The thing with the Zetetics is that it was the mindset that came first—the *heart*, the *desire* in the people—*then* came the group."

Ada leaned forward, propping her elbows on her knees. "Likeminded folks wanted another way. They think they're lone as a wolf without a pack, but then they meet others and it's, 'Well, let's do this thing together.'"

Chet nodded. "No one had to control it or make it happen. It was—what's that gardening word?—*organic*. The main difference between them and us is that we just ran out of space. Ain't no more frontiers left, Mila—so we had to move below the ground."

"But if everyone was so hidden, how did they all find each other?"

"True woodsmen know how to take a look at the forest and tell when someone else has been there, too. It's nothing your average layperson would notice, but the likeminded folks recognize the signs when people go off the grid. They test the waters, reach out to one another, and there you have it. Now, it's a full-blown organization."

Ada stood, stretching her burly arms above her head and yawning like a barn cat. "You two are gonna need all the rest you can get." Snatching a tattered old quilt, she tossed it at Mila. "We'll be at Tesla in another nine hours or so."

Chet saluted the woman, then sprawled on the floor. Clutching the blanket, Mila curled onto a cozy cot in the corner. Excitement trickled over her. A new beginning—here, in this fantastically unique group. What could she bring to the table? What could they accomplish together? The possibilities could be endless.

~~~

The slowing of the trolley awakened them.

"Move on out," Ada called, lumbering into the trolley car from her navigator's cabin. "Nothing to gain by dawdlin'." A lopsided smile stretched across her wrinkled face. She gave Mila's back a hearty smack that knocked the wind out of her. "Good havin' you, girl. Now go."

Mila turned just as the trolley doors slid open. The trolley station, bathed in ethereal white and golden light—from a source she couldn't see—led straight into a large, round atrium, empty save for a short man with close-cropped hair and shoulders broad as a log. Holding her head high and hoping the confidence she didn't feel would follow, she strode toward him, into the arena, with Chet by her side.

"Mila Ray?" the man asked. He held a scanner similar to the one she'd seen Ada use, but smaller and sleeker. "I'm Roejo. I've been asked to scan you for tracking devices before you advance any farther."

She glanced to Chet, then back to the man. "I was already scanned. Shortly after I—before I came to the Croatoan hub. By Ada."

Roejo nodded. "Yes. Every Squire has access to the Detracker. However, it was recently discovered that some of Hesperia's devices contain alloys that thwart devices like the Detracker, and we've only just created a tool to circumvent it. There's a slim chance—five percent, tops—that your scan rendered a false positive during the disabling process." He stepped forward and held up the instrument. "This one—the Plus model—hasn't been mass distributed yet. Come closer, please."

She obeyed. "But if I'm here, and Ada's scan didn't work, then—"

"Our tunnels and underground hubs are too far to be detected anyway." Roejo shook his head and raised the Detracker Plus, holding it near the crown of her head. The device hummed as he panned it down her body, kneeling as he got to her feet. "This scan is purely to protect you in the case that you return aboveground." Still on the floor, he looked at the tool's small screen. He furrowed his brow. "What were Ada's findings?"

"She found a device," Mila answered, "but it hadn't been turned on. Or had been turned off."

"Strange." Roejo stood, tapping on the screen. "I'm importing all data from the tracker so I can see what information—if any—Hesperia did gather on you before Ada shut it down. But as far as your time in Tesla goes, there is nothing to worry about. Chet, tell Kairos I'll brief him on what I've got in an hour or so." Roejo walked away, down a large hall on the other side of the atrium.

Chet gestured toward an amber holographic blueprint floating on the left side of the doorway. She approached it, hoping it would provide some hint—an itinerary, maybe—of where all the people were. But all it displayed was a circular room, apparently the one she stood in, with four large adjacent rooms.

"Easy way to remember your way around," Chet said. "Tesla's like a compass."

She examined the labels on the display. The two large departments to her left, Health Services and Policies. And on the right, Espionage and Technology. A green circle swirled over the Espionage Department.

"Ah." Chet pointed to the green swirl. "They're having a meeting. Come on."

He hustled across the atrium in the direction of the Espionage Department, and Mila strode after him. A large metal door barred the entrance. Chet leaned into a panel next to it for a retina scan. A beep sounded, and the door clicked its assent. He shouldered it open and held it for Mila.

She hesitated. "Are you sure I can go?"

"Kairos is expecting us. You're in the clear."

They walked down a wide hallway with doors on either side, stopping outside of a room on the left, marked Conference Room A. Voices rumbled on other side of the door.

"He's at the OWA?" Mila heard a woman ask incredulously.

"He blends in well," a man added. "Not bad for civilian intelligence."

Chet gently pulled the handle and quietly opened the door. He crossed through, and Mila followed after him.

Squinting, she tried to make sense of her surroundings, scanning the people in the room. Eleven Zetetics sat in chairs lining the walls of the bland, unadorned room. To her right, two empty seats were saved for her and Chet. But a mist filled the room from wall to wall, floor to ceiling. Within the mist, a scraggly man stood in line outdoors, under a large sign that read Office of Worker Aid. He glanced over his shoulder, his eyes darting, but Mila could only guess whether it was the Zetetics that aroused his wariness, or someone else. He turned and walked through a cement doorway that led into a large, open-aired fortress of sorts.

"Chet, Mila. Take your seats."

A man's voice tore her attention from the foggy reality. She blinked several times, watching through narrowed eyes as the two realities before her competed for dominance. The man standing at the front of the room became clear. He gestured. She and Chet sat. The group continued observing the mist.

The scraggly man lumbered through clusters of rag-clad folks, bleary-eyed and dripping with sweat. Mila crinkled her nose and held her breath against the stench. A gush of awareness surged through her. *Am I actually smelling the workers' odor?* She cast a furtive glance around at the Zetetics. Their noses wrinkled. Their lips curled. They smelled it, too—but all eyes remained locked on the one man. Mila returned her attention to him as well.

The courtyard—such a name seemed far too generous for such a dismal area, but it was all Mila could think of—was packed with individuals to the point that hardly a square foot of unoccupied area remained. A pair of sharp eyes stood out from the rest. *How have I sensed his gaze among countless others?* But she couldn't dwell on her question. The scraggly man began moving toward the sharp-eyed man, who stepped forward.

"Feck you, Pete," he spat.

"What?" the scraggly man called Pete smirked.

"You heard me. Feck. You. I said."

"'Feck'?" The smirk widened.

"Shut up. A week, you said. So I work my ass off to convince all the folks I can—I say, 'Pete's coming back when he's ready. A week, and we'll charge the country. Seven days, and things'll never be the same. Do you know what an eternity seven days is when you've lived in this rathole? They hold me to my word!" He smacked himself in the chest, then punched a firm finger into Pete's. "And *four* weeks, it's been. So I say: Feck... you."

Pete's face turned somber, traces of lines etched into his ruddy complexion. He adjusted the black flat cap on his head and brushed sweaty brown hair out of his eyes. "You're right, Benny."

"Folks're getting antsy."

"They murdered one of our guys. We had to go into hiding for a while." His voice dropped to a near-inaudible pitch. Mila leaned forward. "Took a Hesperian spy with us. Damned vermin gave us nothing to work with, so one of our guys took care of him. We're almost ready. Keep recruiting. Keep mobilizing. We need one more month."

"One more month?" Benny whisper-screamed.

Pete narrowed his eyes. "You have better things taking up your time? More than enjoying your carefully-selected government position, working the fields in Plains?"

Benny slumped.

"They *are* helpful, aren't they?" His words dripped with sarcasm. "Never have to want for employment in these parts. No, Hesperia won't let its own suffer. No one has to go without work for more than ninety days. That OWA'll fix you up..."

Pete continued talking, but Mila tuned him out. Looming, empty skyscrapers filled her thoughts.

Technological advancement hadn't turned all of those office lights off... unemployment had. And the Office of Worker Aid didn't match Hesperians to positions...

Her skin prickled.

"Internment camps," a woman next to her explained.

Was that truly the horrifying fate of Hesperia's unemployed? Hesperia's unemployment rate had always earned the territory international bragging rights as a land of opportunity. How long had the numbers been tampered with? How long had Hesperia been simply erasing the existences of those who couldn't find work, hiding them out in OWA work camps? Most importantly, what did the Zetetics plan to do about it?

"Shh," the man at the front of the room ordered.

"... worth it," Pete was saying. Benny shifted his weight back and forth, his shoulders hunched in submission. "We have to be strategic, and good strategy takes time. One month. There's someone whose help we need, and we're attempting to locate this individual."

"*One* month," Benny emphasized.

"Could be sooner."

Benny rolled his eyes.

Pete slapped him on the back. "Your time's up. So's mine. I'll be in touch." He turned and began to leave.

"Feck you," Benny cursed under his breath.

"Yep." Pete kept walking. "And if we don't do this right, feck us all."

The mist vaporized, leaving only one reality behind. Mila blinked rapidly and scanned the conference room for the reactions of the Zetetics around her.

A man stood. "Let's conclude our meeting for today. I'd like to take a few moments with our newcomer. Caide, Elzac—you both can stay."

The rest of the Zetetics gathered their belongings from underneath their seats and shuffled out of the meeting room, casting unsure glances at Mila.

When the room was empty, a scrawny man wearing a black hat—Elzac, Mila supposed—gurgled a laugh. "'Proletarians of the world unite.'" His thin mouth twitched under his hooked nose, and Mila thought of a parrot wearing a fedora.

"Their tactics couldn't be more obvious if he walked in with a hammer in one hand and a sickle in the other," the woman next to Mila snickered. She faced her. "Caide."

"Mila—"

"Ray. I know. So, let's have it."

"Have...?"

"Your takeaways. You caught the tail end, but might as well have 'em." She fixed her hazel stare onto Mila.

Mila blinked, as if the fluttering of her eyelashes were any defense against Caide's rapid-fire manner of speaking. The woman had the demeanor of an anthropomorphized steamroller. "Your technology," she said. "It's outstanding. You can't be using stationary cameras, or wireless technology, or even a spy wearing surveillance equipment. It's more than that—I was *in* Pete's reality, seeing through his eyes but without being in his body. I was in his mind, as if I was—"

"Haunting him," the fedora-donned man offered with a secretive smile. "You were."

"Don't *help* her, Elzac," Caide said with a dramatic roll of her eyes. Then, to Mila, "Quantum State Sharing. QSS. Or, as *Elzac* likes to call it, 'haunting.'" She glared at him. "Freak."

"It's catching on," Elzac smirked.

"Is it true?" Mila asked. "I mean—is that how it works? Were we actually in Pete's reality? I felt Benny's eyes on Pete, and I don't understand how, out of the crowds, I picked up on him. But if Pete was looking for him, and I was—"

"In Pete's mind?" Caide interrupted. She looked at the middle-aged man in the front of the room. "Kairos?"

Kairos stepped closer. "QSS functions efficiently thanks to the reality of M Law. The machine dissolves the boundaries between space and time, blending the two to nearly equal proportions, but maintaining an ever-so-slight imbalance that allows us to partake of another reality without being detected by those who inhabit it. And if we're fortunate enough to harbor DNA identifiers—as we are with Pete—we blend QSS with perspective-sharing technology that whisks us into a desired reality, *as well as* into the perspective of a designated point person. All of it is to say, you were. In Pete's mind, that is. *You...* were."

Elzac adjusted his fedora and winked. "Now doesn't the term 'haunting' give you the answer you were looking for, without any of our leader's babbling erudition?"

"Ignore him," Caide ordered. "We've caught him licking the QSS machine..." She trailed off and whirled one finger around her ear. Elzac laughed at her.

"Moving along." Kairos saved Mila from having to form a response. "We'll save further analysis for later"—he sent a pointed look to Caide—"so we don't drench our newest member in too much at once. Now, how do you feel?"

"A little drenched," Mila said.

Kairos laughed and his piercing black eyes twinkled. "Let's walk. I'll show you around a little and we can get something to eat."

"Oh, thank goodness," Chet exclaimed. "I'm starving as a lion trapped in an herb garden. Take the lead!"

Kairos strode ahead of them, a tall, barrel-chested man with a thick head of salt-and-pepper hair—more pepper than salt—and a wiry beard and mustache under his regal, aquiline nose. Mila couldn't decide if he would be most at home behind the lectern or in front of military ranks. He led them back through the open arena where she'd entered Tesla, then through the opposite end, under a large, hanging wooden sign. In cursive letters with little chips that indicated it was hand-carved, the sign declared The Quarters to the right and The Grounds to the left. Kairos turned left.

As they drew farther from Tesla's main entrance, the walls lining the vast, wide hallway transitioned from aged brick to pristine concrete. Two men and three women passed them in the hall. Chet and Kairos nodded in greeting. How many people lived in the Tesla hub? It didn't seem terribly crowded, though it rippled with signs of life. The halls they walked featured artwork, some that looked professional, some clearly the work of children. The lair could have easily assumed a dispassionate, technological air, but was more akin to the cozy living room of a family friend. An unbelievably intelligent friend with a mind for quantum physics and an eye for décor.

They rounded a curve in the hallway. It ended abruptly, pouring into an Eden-esque oasis that stretched as far as Mila could see. Fruit trees heavily laden, vegetable plants with such ripe pickings that the leaves could barely hide the produce, the garden burst with life. Honey bees *bzzz*-ed from stop to stop, like a floating carousel. It all flourished under the nurturing light of a sunless sky.

She stopped. "We're underground. I mean—aren't we still...?"

"We're still underground," Kairos said.

"But the sun. Where...?"

His coffee-bean eyes filled with delight. "We don't need a sun. We're beyond suns." He paused. "That could possibly be the most narcissistic thing ever to leave a man's mouth, but I don't intend it that way." He placed one hand on her elbow, guided her through the door and pointed upward. "You can't see it, but high up above, there is a ceiling.

Just beyond the clouds, although they aren't true clouds, of course. The sunny light emanates from free-floating molecules. It's a form of phosphorescence, but no glass tubes or bulbs are necessary. It's based on luciferin. Similar to releasing the juice from fireflies into the sky. And it's all perfectly safe, I assure you." He smiled. "After two hundred years, you could consider us the longest-running case study. I could explain how the rainy days work as well, but suffice it to say that Tesla recreated the atmosphere, in relatively microcosmic form."

Mila focused on the bright sky. Perhaps it was her imagination or the overwhelmingly bright light, but she thought she could see little glowing granules floating about. "Incredible," she breathed.

"It is magnificent," Kairos agreed. He turned to her. "Now, let's not delay lunch any longer. I daresay I actually heard Chet's stomach call Trudi's name."

"She'd box your ears if she knew you were starving me like this." Chet shook his head in dismay.

Kairos led them to the edge of the agricultural center, where many small paths wound through and around the gardens. Chet hustled down one path. Kairos led Mila down the center of the garden. Vines curled and scrolled in prickly curlicues, culminating in delicate white blossoms in some places and ripe, full squash and pumpkins in others. Bell pepper plants prospered, the vegetables hanging heavily in a half-rainbow of red, orange, yellow, green, and purple. Their crisp scent wafted her way, and she breathed it in. Never had she encountered produce so full of life that she could smell it from feet away. Closing her eyes, she allowed the warm, faux-sunlight to heat her cheeks and forehead. A breeze shyly brushed her face. She couldn't fathom that she wasn't truly aboveground, outside. Step after step, the honeybees and butterflies, flitting from flower to flower in the luciferin-sunlight, lured her more fully into her enchanting surroundings. Remembering that all of it was underground, Mila wondered if the creatures were, in fact, honey bees, butterflies, and birds, or if they were some related specimens, able to thrive in the luciferin-powered ecosystem. Men in dirty overalls worked the plots next to women in wide-brimmed hats that shielded their delicate shoulders, carrying woven baskets in the crooks of their arms.

She continued forward, through a maze of corn. On the other side stood a kiosk operated by a buxom young woman with a smile as wide as the Amazon. She chatted while she stirred and flipped and swayed around her small kitchen as though it were a tiny ballroom, sharing the story of how her family came to Tesla nearly a century before, contributed to the organization's seed bank, and helped to manage the gardens. She slid a steaming plate of tamales across the counter. Mila thanked her and continued through the garden with Kairos.

Her heart fluttered. The garden wasn't only lively, it *was* life and community and the beauty of hard work and charity. And this was just a small slice of the Zetetics. *The capacity of this organization, of its people—to think of all they could achieve, and how I can help!*

For the first time, all of the demands she'd rehearsed over lonely weeks at Flint Hill seemed truly within reach: Shut down citizen surveillance. Release all prisoners whose only crime is questioning their government. Now, she added another: End the OWA work camps.

She could really do something. She could *mean* something.

She could ruin Falk.

"Have a seat." Kairos stopped. She'd been so lost in thought she hadn't noticed he'd led her to a wooden picnic table underneath a generous maple tree. As they settled across from each other, Mila noticed a change—a solemnity—in Kairos' face. He sat straight, his thin mouth turned downward, his thick, angular eyebrows ever so slightly knitted.

The ease he had displayed with Chet had given way to a seriousness that caused an uncomfortable knot to form in her stomach.

"I guess Chet's been led astray by his appetite," Mila tried. "I wonder if we'll ever see him again." She cast Kairos a smile, as warm as she could muster in order to melt the frost that seemed to have formed between them.

"He's likely taken his to his quarters, to give you and I a chance to talk privately. I prefer to meet guests one-on-one. Especially in your case."

"Guest?"

"It's not often that we usher in someone new so quickly," he explained. "Most newcomers spend months on the fringes before they really join the Zetetics and see everything that you've seen in—when did you first arrive in Savannah-Georgia?"

"About ten days ago."

He nodded. "It's a painstaking vetting process that most new arrivals endure. But we know your background, and Julian vouched for you. Ardently so. And Julian is highly respected among the Zetetics. The work he has done for us, the counsel he has provided... he is an invaluable asset—an invaluable person—and he insisted that you be welcomed here."

"I'm unspeakably grateful for his kindness," she said.

"As the Tesla hub director, I decided to take it upon myself to convene with you." He leaned toward her, his obsidian gaze piercing into hers. "I know all about you, Mila. It nearly goes without saying that I know about Flint Hill, I know about Victor Falk and Forsythe Marlowe. I know about Carlo DaVanti, and Lu. Of course I know all of that. But I also know about Helen and Haley at Haven House. I know about your missionary complex and your torn dreams at HBN. I know the tragic end of your parents and what they wanted to do. I even know the titles within the Ray library. I know you are hunted. And before you catechize me about the invasion of privacy, allow me to say that because of the people I represent—the people I protect, the society I preserve—I must do so. One mistake, one error in judgment, and our entire way of life is at stake. A *fortiori*, I will conduct my due diligence with regard to your background." He studied her. "Why should I listen to Julian Merrick, Mila? Why should you be a Zetetic?"

The question caught her off guard. "Honestly, I don't know how to answer your question. You know so much about me, but do you know how much I've been told about your organization?" She shook her head. "I've been as up front as I can be in my conversations with Hieu and Julian about who I am, what I've done, and what I want. But although they've welcomed me and have promised to shield me and give me a role here, they've kept me in a fair amount of darkness about what the Zetetics is all about in a practical, literal way. How can I make you such a promise when I don't have all of the information?" It felt daring—almost disrespectful—to speak in such a candid way to this man, the Tesla hub director. Her throat grew dry as wool as she watched him, waiting for his response.

He nodded. "A fair question. As I said, most newcomers aren't rushed in like you have been. They learn in stages, whereas we've had to pull you in, yet simultaneously keep you at arms' length. Since you're considered a guest here at Tesla for now, I still can't share much with you. But I can tell you that our objectives depend on the climate aboveground. Currently, we remain in a state of monitoring, of information gathering." Tilting his chin, he raised his eyebrows as if to indicate that the information he provided should be enough, then stood. "We only have three policies. We avoid policies as much as possible, but these three preserve our freedoms and individuality. *Primum non nocere*. First, do no harm. Second, take care of you and yours. Third, share with them and theirs. These—especially that final one—are less policies than simple traits that all Zetetics possessed beforehand. The policies are the articulation of what was already in our hearts. You will observe much here during your time as a guest. I'm not threatened by that, Mila. True, you're not obligated to stay. You could leave us and disclose us to Hesperian authorities, but"—he captured her gaze—"judging by your lack of family, employment, or any other meaningful way to live outside of our group, I don't ascertain much benefit to that course of action for you. Am I correct in this presumption?"

His clinical way of listing her struggles and loss caused her to shrink inside. "You are correct," she said.

"Chet is in apartment nine hundred eight. I'm sure you and I will speak again soon." He turned, but stopped, glancing over Mila's shoulder. Footsteps rushed up behind her. She looked as Roejo approached the table. "Yes, Roejo?"

"Mila's device," he began. "The Detracker Ada used didn't disable it. Hesperia—someone—has been turning it off and on since before she arrived in Savannah-Georgia. Someone knows she was in Roanoke."

~~~

The long, dusty drive reminded Falk of the one at his isolated childhood home in Challis-Idaho—not what he had expected. This couldn't be her final destination. He grimaced. She had arrived more than twenty-four hours before. If this place wasn't her final stop, she may have already fled. But at last check, the tracking device showed no updated location. He leaned forward, squinting through the dust clouding his windshield as his magnecar advanced. What was this place?

A moment later, he pulled in front of a small log cabin, its windows glowing with yellow light—certainly a Belgae safe house of some kind. He turned the car off and stepped out. A shadow of a woman bobbled like a candle's flame in one of the windows, and he warmed in satisfaction. It didn't matter whether Mila was still at this address or not. She unwittingly led him here, and he could pry useful information from the occupant inside. No doubt.

24.

JULIAN HELD UP the brown glass bottle so the sunlight streamed through the window onto the instruction label. Mama had taken the last xianepam pill the day he'd seen Mila off to Tesla. Was that only two days ago? He'd rushed back to get the syrup from Don, but even one day with no medication left his mother significantly weaker. He read the dosage and frowned. "Two tablespoons, three times a day? Cruel and unusual punishment."

Natalie reached for the medicine from her seat at the dining table. "Just give it to me, boy. I'll mix it in my tea and gag it down."

He handed it over. "This formula's different from the pills, but it's the best Don could do with what he had. So it's... kind of an experiment."

"It's better than nothing," Natalie said tiredly as she drizzled three tablespoons' worth of algae-colored liquid into her mug. "Goodness. It smells like manure." She swirled her spoon in the cup and then brought a spoonful to her lips. "Oh, forget it," she said, and tilted the entire cup into her mouth, finishing all of it in one long gulp. She gagged, then smiled. "I feel better already."

Julian rolled his eyes. "You do not."

"Mind over matter. Thank Don for me. Really."

"I'll thank Don as soon as you can get out of bed."

"It wasn't his fault he had to retreat underground. Pour me more, tea, Julian, this aftertaste is awful."

Julian lifted the mug and poured more steaming chamomile into her cup. "I *hate* that Hesperia—"

"Some honey, too?"

"—puts us in this position." He squeezed the honey bottle into her tea. "As soon as I can figure out how, I promise—"

"That's good."

"—I'm going to make sure it never happens again. I'll insulate all the Zetetics' systems with a program that attacks and destroys any infiltrator's technology. Or—"

"Revenge doesn't bring me any peace, Julian. Just know that."

Julian sobered. "I know, Mama. I just despise how money-lust and bureaucracy have kept us from being able to get you adequate care."

"I have adequate care."

"Drinking manure-flavored syrup three times a day created by a government-hunted, rogue pharmacist is not adequate care."

"You are. More than adequate." She reached for his hand and squeezed it. "Now. You haven't told me much about your road trip with Mila." Her eyes twinkled eagerly.

"It was fine." Julian stood. He gathered their cups and dishes from lunch and walked to the sink.

"Fine..."

"Yeah. Kind of a blur." That wasn't a lie. "Can't remember much." That was. All he could do for the past few days was remember—particularly their kiss by the lake. The kiss he'd stolen at the worst possible time. He'd blown it, completely. Not a topic he wanted to discuss with his mother. "I'm glad Chet took her the rest of the way." He loaded the dishes into the dishwasher.

"You are..." Her tone was flat with disbelief.

"Yeah. He'll put her at ease. Help her get comfortable. He's a welcoming type of guy." He turned to face his mother. "Don't you think Chet is a welcoming type of guy?"

"The warmest of welcomers. Absolutely." Natalie held up both hands in a truce. "I guess I just thought that maybe Mila should've been escorted by a different type of guy."

"Hieu?" he teased.

She slammed her palms on the table. "Oh, come on, Julian! The sparks between you two are wild. Give me something."

He snatched a napkin from the counter and tossed it on the table in front of her. "Here you go, Mama. You're drooling."

She rolled her eyes and threw it back at him. "Maybe I'll ask her myself, then."

"What?"

"I thought it might be nice for us to make a visit to Tesla. I'm feeling so much better now, and Hieu wouldn't mind you taking a couple of days off. I thought I'd ask him for us tonight." She beamed and sat up a little straighter.

"You're kidding."

"Tell me."

He sighed and plunked into the chair across from her. "I kissed her."

Natalie's eyes sparkled and widened to the point of bulging.

"It wasn't good."

His mother crinkled her nose and held up a hand. "All right. No more details, please."

"Not like that. I mean—I kind of... offended her. Bad timing."

"Oh. I see. Well, give it time. I'm sure she wouldn't write you off over one ill-timed kiss. You are *my* son, after all. That makes you too wonderful to pass up." She winked.

"We'll see about that."

A hasty knock sounded at the apartment door.

"Come—" Natalie began, but the creak and crack of the door flinging open and slamming against the wall interrupted her. Julian jumped from his chair.

Hieu burst into the kitchen with blue-hot anger burning in his eyes. His tie was askew, his crisp white dress shirt rolled up at the sleeves and unbuttoned to his chest. He planted himself within inches of Julian.

"Where did you go wrong, Merrick? How did he follow you?"

Julian's pulse soared. "Who followed me?"

"Victor Falk!"

"Back up," he said through gritted teeth.

"A magnecar pulled up to the Talbott's home last night. Luckily, Trudi saw it coming and rushed underground. She watched through the SecuriCams as a man in a Hesperia Defense uniform prowled the home top to bottom." He slammed a fist into the door frame. "Damn it!" His voice dropped to a low gnarr. "How in the *hell*—"

"I don't know." He kept his voice flat, but his mind raced.

"You don't—?" Hieu began pacing the kitchen, running frazzled fingers through his hair. "I knew I shouldn't have let her in. I knew it would bite us."

"Hieu, sit down," Natalie said. "Calm down."

The man stopped at the sound of her urgent, even voice, with one hand still poised in his black locks. He turned and made his way toward the table, his movements as graceful as a primitive robot's.

"We know the prowler was Victor Falk?" Natalie asked. "It's been confirmed?"

"No," Hieu said as he sat. "But it's him. I *know* it's him."

"Where is Trudi?" Natalie's pitch rose in concern.

"She's underground with Ada for now. She's alerted Kairos." Hieu rubbed his temples and took a long, seething breath before continuing. "This is what we'll do. Julian, tell Damien that he and I will take over operating Voltaire's for now. You and Natalie must stay out of sight. Falk knows who you are, where you work, and now it's fair to assume he knows what you really do. We can't have him intercepting you. Stay in this building and out of Voltaire's during business hours."

Julian nodded.

Hieu stood and strode toward the front door. "Now. I have to get a message to Kairos about Mila."

"What about Mila?" Julian said.

"That she's more of a liability than I was led to believe. We need to decide whether she stays or goes." He yanked the door open.

Julian rushed to meet Hieu in the doorway. "What do you mean, 'stays or goes'? None of this is her fault and now that she's underground, Falk's got nothing but a dead end."

Hieu only shook his head and turned away. Julian clapped a hand over his friend's shoulder and pulled him around to face him once more. "Hieu."

Hieu stared at him, a dim expression in his dark eyes. "I'm going to do what needs to be done to keep us safe."

"What about *her* safety? She's the one whose life is in danger. We're the ones with access to more advanced technology, weaponry, and safe houses than the world knows to exist!"

"And if she reveals us," Hieu hissed, "*all* of that falls into the wrong hands. It's over. We're done." He pushed Julian's hand off of his shoulder. "Excuse me. I have an organization to protect. Stay out of sight." He descended the steps two at a time.

Julian wanted to chase him. Instead, he backed through the doorway and threw the door shut so it clattered into the frame.

~~~

Mila twisted the doorknob to apartment 908 and shoved her shoulder against the door. It had taken her a few tries to master it, but now it opened with an exasperated creak whenever she entered. The apartment was dark. She twisted the switch on the table lamp just inside the door and it filled the room with a cozy glow.

"Hi-dee ho, roomie," Chet chimed. He reclined in an overstuffed easy chair, his feet propped up on an ottoman, his flat cap over his face.

"Mid-morning nap?"

"Never!" He swung his feet down, swiped off his cap and stood. "Cornbread?"

"You made cornbread?"

He held up one finger and shook it at her. "I *make* cornbread. Best you'll ever have. Though I must warn you... it's all I know how to make. I live on the stuff when Trudi's not around."

"I'll take some."

Chet hurried from the perfectly square living room through walnut saloon doors into the adjacent kitchen straight ahead. The place was homey, like a well-loved cotton shirt, and had brick walls, an electric fireplace, dingy pine floors, and a simple, two-person wooden table and chair set. An arched doorway opened on the left and right sides of the living area, leading to each of the two bedrooms.

"Ta da." Chet shuffled back in with two saucers, each bearing a golden yellow hunk that would've caused Rumplestiltskin to abandon his fixation with straw. "Chet's legendary cornbread." He handed Mila hers and snatched his, munching into it with such gusto that crumbs sprayed into his furry beard. "Mmm—mm! You sit. Sit. It's the end of the day. It's good to sit at the end of the day. Please, take my chair," Chet insisted and plunked into the loveseat next to it.

Mila sat and tried a bite. It was moist and warm and the perfect salty-sweet taste of golden yellow corn. "Oh wow, this is good."

"Told ya." He pointed at her with his fork. "So what do you bring to the table? What'll you make me? This is a two-way street, ya know. Being room-ies." He batted crumbs from his beard.

"Banana pecan bread," she replied between bites. "How's that?"

"Nix the nuts and you've got a deal. Now, how about some hot cocoa?"

She smiled and nodded, and Chet bounced into the kitchen. She watched him go and could feel the joyful twinkle sprout in her eyes and warm up her cheeks. The old man was such a cheery fellow, like a buoy bobbing along in the water, in low tide or high, peaceful waters or choppy.

He returned to the living room with a mug in each of his brawny paws, the steam twisting and beckoning from the cups. He offered one to Mila, and reseated himself on the loveseat. For a mo-ment, she breathed in the scent of rich cocoa. Her shoulders relaxed, and she blew out some careful breaths before taking her first, dainty sip. The chocolate was thick and indulgent. She smiled and looked at her companion. "You really know how to make a cup of—"

His blue eyes squinted as he scrutinized her. He seemed concerned.

"Chet, what is it?"

"Well, I dunno how to tell you this, Mila. Um." He fluffed his beard.

"Is something wrong?"

"Kairos came by today..."

Mila's chest tightened. She held her breath. *Did he finish vetting me? Are the Zetetics rejecting me?*

"Ah, this is hard to say." He cleared his throat. "It seems that—someone you know, well, he might've almost found you. And mighta found us. Trudi and me, I mean."

Her heart hammered. The room closed in. She tried to gather her composure. "F-f-f..." she stuttered.

"That'd be the one."

"When?"

"Last night."

"Is Trudi—did he—"

"Oh, darlin', Trudi's sharp. She saw him comin' and went under. She's with Ada now and will be here later on. Don't worry!" He rushed to her side and patted—slapped—her back. "It's scary, I know, but we're thankful it wasn't worse, aren't we?"

"Yes. Very thankful." Both Chet and Trudi were out of Falk's reach. The tightness in her chest gave way a little. But her mouth went dry. "Julian and Natalie?"

"They're staying out of sight. Kairos is gonna put everyone on alert. And you're safe here, way down under. No one can watch you now." Chet gave her back a reassuring rub. "Let's put our worries away. Talk about somethin' else."

Mila's lips twitched into a pained smile. How could she think of anything other than the safety of those she cared about? How could she just forget that Falk had followed her, was still searching for her? She shook her head, forcing herself to change the subject. "How did you and Trudi find the Zetetics?"

"Our daughter." A faraway look glistened in Chet's eyes. "Dana-Marie. She was somethin'. Driven, intelligent, talented just like her mother. She wanted to make a difference." Reality jolted his gaze and he looked at Mila, "Like you. Yes. A lot like you. She worked with a human rights organization, right there on the front lines when stuff like disaster hit. Tornadoes, earthquakes. Mostly domestic. The last time we talked—gosh, that's almost two decades ago—a community member said they hadn't got their charity money. The government had collected it and was supposed to deliver it, see. But it never came. Dana-Marie set out to recover it. And, ah..." He paused for a moment. Cleared his throat. "We—we never heard from her after that."

"Oh, Chet..." Mila reached for his hand and held it tightly.

Chet gave her a pained smile. "I looked and looked. An old man like me ain't too good with the latest technology, but hell, when your little girl goes missing you get *good* at technology. And I asked everywhere. Forums, groups, organizations, virtual community meetings—even went some places in person. We never found our Dana-Marie, but we ran into Hieu. By then, we wanted peace. That was all. Just some peace. And after we healed a little, we wanted to help. So our cabin in the woods became a safe house, helping Zetetics and Hesperians like Dana-Marie stay safe when they're in trouble because they turned over a rock that they didn't know they shouldn't'a turned over."

Mila's insides ached. The sting of emptiness—of being robbed of someone dear—was all too familiar. Lost for words, she squeezed his hand.

"You're a good soul, Melinda." Chet winked as he said the name, and Mila smiled. "I know what it's like to hurt real bad." His lips turned downward. He pressed them together. "And you just gotta know—gotta know with your whole self—that you'll make it." He let go of her hand and cupped her face with both of his. "*You'll make it.*"

Everything inside her was a stormy sea, every wave an emotion crashing and colliding into another. Her entire being desired to mourn—for

Chet, for herself, for everyone hurting from the bludgeon of power corrupted. Instead, she flung her arms around her old friend's neck and held on tightly, as if he were her buoy in the tumultuous ocean of their world.

25.

A T A SMALL TABLE in the Espionage Department's kitchenette, Mila covered her face with her hands, waiting for the fresh pot of coffee to finish brewing. Errand girl—it's all she'd been for two days now, since the news of Falk's arrival at the Talbott safe house had shot throughout Tesla. Caide apparently relished the nickname, too, and hadn't referred to Mila by her first name since.

They'd said nothing was amiss at Chet and Trudi's home. Nothing missing, nothing damaged. Hieu and Damien reported no sightings of Falk—or Hesperia presence at all, for that matter. The lack of activity seemed to ease Zetetics' concerns, but a knot of nausea clutched in Mila's belly. She felt as though she, alone, stood on an eerily quiet beach, moments before a tidal wave engulfed her. After all, Falk had warned her—"Don't think you're free of me."

The beeping of the coffeemaker pulled her out of her thoughts. Lining up three mugs, she filled each one and wove their handles in her fingers, prepared to carry all at once, but Caide appeared in the doorway.

"For me?" she said.

"Yes, actually." Mila handed a mug to her.

"Thanks," she said, taking it. "C'mon. This way."

Caide led her by the elbow down the hall, past Conference Room A, and to a room at the back of the department that she'd never visited before.

Mila stopped a few steps behind her. "Are you sure I'm allowed?"

"You're on my team," Caide said. "Kairos and I think you'll be well-suited to espionage."

"But the vetting process. Falk—"

"You didn't ask him to stab you in the back of the neck, did you?"

Mila flinched.

"Thought not. You're either in, or you're out. And with all you've seen already, you're sure as hell not out, so Kairos says you're in. Now come on."

Caide dabbed a code into the security panel and opened the door.

Sleektops stood in rows on one side of the room, while Elzac sat like the captain of a ship in front of a gargantuan device. He monitored its multiple screens while also flipping switches, twisting knobs, pulling levers, and typing codes into its touchscreen keyboard. He wiped perspiration from his forehead and flicked his fedora into a jaunty angle.

"You remember Elzac," Caide said.

"Of course," Mila said.

Elzac craned his neck to flash Mila a wrinkled, lopsided smile, and then waved Caide over. "Caide? That baggie on the shelf over there, love. Marked 'Pierce'. Methinks I needs it."

Caide stepped to a wire rack lined with clear bags pinned to its rungs and waggled a finger around in search of the correct one. She snatched the last bag and tossed it to Elzac.

"Careful, love, careful!" He examined its contents. "Ah, the perfect potion for my perspicacious plan." He lifted a domed lid on the QSS, revealing a panel that glowed purple, and opened the bag. He dumped the contents—too small for Mila to see clearly, but she thought maybe they were strands of blonde hair—onto the panel and covered it again with the dome. Then, shooting the women a cagey look, he said, "Go on! Let me haunt in peace."

Caide rolled her eyes and moved over to the sleektops. Mila joined her. "How are your research skills?" the young woman asked.

"My...?"

"*Research. Skills*," Caide enunciated slowly. "Your hearing apparently leaves something to be desired."

Mila stifled a wince at Caide's bombastic manner. "They're solid. I did a lot of research in my position at the Hesperia Broadcasting Network."

"Good for you," Caide said hurriedly. "Then have a seat."

Mila sat at the sleektop and Caide flicked her fingers over the screen, pulling up tab after tab of databases Mila had never seen before. She hoped she hadn't oversold herself, but was determined to catch on quickly.

"Public records, government databases. You get it. Dive in. Give me all you've got in an hour—"

"On what?"

"I'm *getting* to it. Sheesh. You've been bored, haven't you?" Her new supervisor patted her head. "On Emory McFallon"—she snatched a piece of scrap paper and scribbled two names—"and Rigo Laslo."

"Who are they?"

Caide flashed a wry smile. "Guess you'll find out, won't ya?" She sauntered from the room.

Mila turned warily toward the sleektop. She brushed her fingers over the panel, and a jolt rushed through her fingertips. A mission. Her first one. *Tap*, she began.

Rap, tap, tap, tap, swipe. Tap tap.

The motions of her fingers hesitated at first, but quickly picked up speed. Her heart did the same, with loping, worried beats as she wondered if she'd lost her ability to *work*, to contribute, and then it sputtered and tap danced along with her fingers as the rush of purpose returned. This was her chance. She lunged for it, and in moments she played the sleektop like a concert pianist. When she finished her research, she glanced at the clock on the wall opposite her. Fifteen minutes remained. She looked to her left. Elzac was gone. She stared at her instrument.

Swipe. She opened a window. Should she do this? Did the Zetetics watch their members like Hesperia watched its citizens? Her acceptance within the group seemed so fragile. But the need rooted within her, deep and irresistible. She *had* to know.

She scattered a series of taps across her keyboard, like pebbles cast out into a pond. With one last glance to make sure she was truly alone, she looked at her search criteria.

Victor Falk.

She hit Submit.

Moments later, Caide returned. "Time's up. Amaze me."

Mila stood. "Emory McFallon, thirty-one-year-old female from New Cockaigne. Stunning level of intelligence—she finished secondary school at only thirteen, and universities practically threw full-ride scholarships her way. She earned a master's degree in engineering and then, true to her over-achieving style, finished law school and got her juris doctor, specializing in corporate law. All of this before she was twenty-one. She took a few jobs over the next six years or so—and you'd expect to see this ever-cresting arc in her achievements, but she kind of flatlines. All she's done in the last three years is work as a junior partner at a Pacifica firm. Her personal life is interesting, though. She fosters dogs on and off, and occasionally trains them for search and rescue. Lives alone in a quiet neighborhood. Semi-normal things."

"Good, good. Next?"

"Roderigo Laslo. Pomp and circumstance all the way with him. His privileged pedigree earned him a passport to study abroad, in Gair. Kind of a deadbeat, though. He lives in a house owned by his parents—not far from here, actually—and doesn't work. Just leads kayak trips down a nearby river during the summer."

Caide examined her fingertips, then bit off a hangnail and spat it out. "He's still got that gig, eh?"

"You knew all of this information already?"

"'Course. You've been here for like, three seconds. You didn't think I'd give you something *actually* important for your first assignment, did you?" She puffed out a breath. "Please. What, you think I'm gonna give you my *job,* too, Boss?"

Mila fidgeted. "So, who are these people?"

"Why don't you tell me, *jefe.*"

She cracked an accommodating smile. "Belgae."

"Bingo. Well, not exactly bingo. They're leaders. Belgae leaders. They practically started the club."

"But—"

"Wow, you really haven't been filled in, have you? Okay. Pete and Benny, remember Pete and Benny you saw through QSS a few days ago? Pete's Belgae. He's recruiting disenfranchised Hesperians at the OWA work camps, along with Benny's help. We're monitoring all of it in case the aboveground situation gets too volatile. Plus, it could put one of our guys in a tight spot"—she shook her head, as if remembering—"but I'm getting ahead of myself. You did pretty good today, Boss."

"Thanks." She hoped the sarcastic nickname wouldn't stick.

"That'll be all. See you tomorrow morning, eight sharp. Sound good?"

"Sounds good, Caide, thanks."

Caide clapped a hand on Mila's shoulder. "No. Thank *you*, Boss," she said in an emphatic, teasing tone, and grinned.

~~~

By the time Mila returned to her apartment, it was dark, save for a small table lamp in the corner. Chet and Trudi must have retired to bed early. She wished she could do the same, but her mind couldn't settle. Instead, she heated a mug of cocoa and sat in the glow of the lamplight.

Finally, she'd been accepted. Eagerness to find her place in the organization—to contribute—pulsed through her. She found the Zetetics to be truly good people, motivated by helping each other and preserving a way of life that was both altruistic and individualistic. And yet something bothered her. No one, as far as she'd witnessed, seemed concerned about the world aboveground except as it related to the Zetetics. Were they safe, or discovered? Did the Squires need to retreat underground? Could the impending revolution reveal one of their safe houses or underground railroads? In every discussion, Mila wanted to shout her questions: How were they going to help the Belgae? The Hesperian people? It bothered her that—as far as she knew—no one discussed this. She wished Chet or Trudi had been awake so she could ask them.

She thought of their daughter, Dana-Marie. As Mila had for countless others she'd crossed paths with, she'd laid hold of the Talbott's heartache, heaped it upon her own shoulders, and let it take up residence in her heart. A young woman presumably dead, or imprisoned. A family torn apart. A mother's and father's hearts broken... because of power gone wrong, and no one to stop it. Would anyone ever be able to end such atrocities? Would the Zetetics? She was determined to find out what their stance was regarding matters aboveground. Perhaps these discussions took place at another time and place, and since she was so new, she wasn't privy to such private talks. Would they just allow Falk to roam free, as long as it didn't affect them?

He had a job in the Erie Bureau of Hesperia Defense now. She'd found his trail in the databases she'd searched. He'd moved up in his career—and he'd used her as a human step stool. He was gain-ing power, and where would he stop? He wouldn't.

Fury drilled into her. Falk had to go. His veins flowed with thick, distilled evil. He was a sadist, a power-hungry psychopath. People like him shouldn't be tolerated on Earth.

He was trying to follow her. What if she led him into a trap? She could be ready for him this time—maybe even armed with some of the lightning-powerful weaponry the Zetetics possessed. She allowed herself to picture it... Falk approaching her, tall and triumphant, ready to take her prisoner or finally, permanently destroy her. She'd be fearful, her heart protesting in her ears, begging her to run. But she'd turn on him. Launch a fatal blow. Her lips twitched as she pictured the shock on his face...

But his face mutated into Forsythe Marlowe's. She dropped her mug to the floor, barely noticing as it shattered. Her hands trembled uncontrollably, even as she clamped them down over her mouth. She had been forced to destroy one evil man under orders from the other. Yet she remained tortured by the blood on her hands. Could she now take another life, purely of her own volition? Could she willingly soak her hands in human blood? Only a moment earlier, she had been delighted at the thought. She bit down on her hand to stifle a disgusted whimper. Who *was* she now?

Falk's vessel. His plaything. He'd molded her like a potter at the wheel, spinning and fashioning her into a desperate woman, then an angry one, and—finally—a vengeful one. Would murdering Falk only seal her transformation into exactly the kind of person he sought to make her?

She'd told the Zetetics that she didn't want her parents' way. That if there was a bloodless path to change, she wanted it. But she couldn't allow Falk to live. To increase in power. She took a few long breaths to slow her heart rate. Maybe she didn't have to kill him. After all, she had the Zetetics on her side. Surely they would stop Falk before he could cause more damage. And she would be only too happy to assist.

26.

JULIAN POUNDED HIS FIST into his palm over and over. He rocked on his heels, looking out his bedroom window. The moon was high and beckoning. It had only been a few days since Hieu virtually put him under house arrest, but already he itched to leave the confines of his building, to see someone other than his mother or Hieu. He clamped his palm over his face and released a hiss. Then one more deep breath, and he removed his hand, picked up the sketch pencil again and willed himself to focus on the easel in front of him. Drawing Mila usually kept his cabin fever at bay. As he flicked his pencil in light strokes around her graceful silhouette, filling in the waves of her long hair, his mind veered away from thoughts of escape and latched onto the beautiful mystery before him, one of her arms outstretched in a hopeful invitation, the other curled nonchalantly—but curiously—behind her back.

He missed her eyes, and the way they glimmered—specks of passion and reserve glinting and disappearing in a fairy-like tug of war. He missed her heart and her dedication, even if it was entangled in a web of anger and hurt. Brushing a finger onto her lips, he tenderly blended the lines he'd drawn into softer ones. He missed her lips, too. He thought of their kiss and a desperate need to see her shot through him.

The craving to get out returned. He tossed the pencil across the room onto his chest of drawers and cast a daring glare at the clock. Voltaire's would be closed in a matter of minutes. Then he'd be *allowed* downstairs into his own pub. He rolled his eyes—then bounded out of his room, out of his apartment, and down the stairs to the pub.

As Julian's footsteps resounded against the wooden floors, Damien froze in the midst of collecting the empty glasses from his remaining customer. "Dude, what the—?"

"I know, Damien, just—" but Julian's excuse stuck in his throat when the customer turned around.

"Julian." The man broke into a panther-like smile, stood, and walked to him.

"Laslo," Julian spat. "What do you want?" The memory of their last encounter flashed into his mind. The face of his friend, contorted in drunken anger as they shouted at each other. He'd hurled a beer bottle at Julian before Julian had stormed out, promising never to work alongside the hothead again.

Rigo Laslo clapped a hand on Julian's shoulder, his white teeth gleamed in faux friendliness. Julian looked at his former friend's hand and then back at Laslo. Sneering, he lifted it from his shoulder. "We're closed."

"Oh, I know that. I can read signs."

"You and me. We're closed. I thought I made that clear."

"You did!" Rigo said, his machismo in full force. "You have excellent communication skills. One of the things I liked about you." He waggled a finger at him. "I always did like that about you, Julian." He suddenly turned to Damien. "You can go on home, barman. Your work here is done." Damien looked to Julian, who nodded, and hesitantly walked past the two men and out of the front door. After it closed, Laslo continued, "We were a hell of a team—you, me, Emory, and Dale—weren't we? What say we get back together? Accomplish something big. It looks like you could use a change of pace. I mean, look at this place. It's great and all—excellent drinks, really—but honestly, Julian, a bar?" He grabbed Julian by the shoulders and shook him. "You were *going places*, man!" he mock whispered.

Julian shook free of Laslo's grasp. "Get off."

"Okay, okay. All right. The question remains: What are you *doing*, Julian?"

"None of your damned business." But the question pierced him. *What* am *I doing?*

Laslo tilted his head and stuck his bottom lip out in a pout of pity. "I already know. We found your pharmacist guy a while ago—you knew that, didn't you?—and found the Zetetics. Nice esoteric name, by the way. And I get it, I really do. Your mom needs what they've got. But what if I told you that we can offer you the xianepam too?"

"You stole Don's formula?"

"Gosh, you do use strong language. I prefer *co-opted*. We co-opted the formula. And isn't that what you really needed?"

"This isn't just about the xianepam."

Rigo took a step back. He crossed his arms and touched one finger to his mouth. "It's not? Huh. Well then I guess you can call me stumped. Because the Julian Merrick I knew didn't run and hide. He *fought*"—Rigo growled the word and clenched his fists in front of his face as if ready to throw a punch—"he fought to give Hesperia back to the people!"

Long-forgotten ardor swelled in Julian's chest, but he pressed against it. Mila's face—the passion in her eyes at the lake—flared in his mind. But all of that was behind him. "Forget it, Rigo. You shouldn't have come here." He spun and strode back toward the staircase.

"Uncle," Rigo called. His voice was loud, but weaker.

Julian turned. "What?"

"Uncle, damn it." He shrugged his shoulders and all of his confidence seemed to fall to the floor. "We're *screwed*, man. God. Emory and I, the team... we've got the numbers—ten *thousand* strong, can you believe it? Back when you were with us, what'd we have? And now we've got ten thousand Hesperians-turned-Belgae, and they're all damned straight to hell because numbers don't cut it. Hesperia Defense is smart, man, and they've got more tools than we do. I told myself we'd do fine without you, that Emory and our other recruits could cover the gaps you left and then some... but then Hesperia Defense took Dale. We're doing battle soon. *Battle.* I didn't think we'd be pushed this far. Didn't think they'd call our bluff. And then they *killed* one of our guys. Did you know that, Julian?"

He did. Sidney's team had circulated the video within minutes of its release. The bloodied, faceless man haunted Julian, daring him to fight for his cause. But the image was gone in the time it took Rigo to fill his lungs.

"Everyone's coming to me and the rest of the leadership and they're demanding retribution. My head's spinning—but for the first time, this is all becoming about lives and not just ideas, and I can't keep them under control. Their fury is insatiable. They wanna act *now.* They've wanted to act now for *months.* But Emory and I and the team have been stalling, because no ingenious strategy can compensate for the fact that we don't have anything more than civilian weaponry. But they believe in us because we've made them. God, if we were only as good at war as we are at marketing. And I have to face that I will be sending people *to their graves* if I can't pull something together *fast.* I came here..." Rigo took a deep breath and let it out in a rush of words, "to ask the Zetetics to join forces with us."

Dumbfounded, Julian whispered, "What did you say?"

"We got a whiff of what you guys have when we got into Don's system. QSS, Tesla's earthquake machine and death ray—to think they've been around all this time! Don't you all *realize* what you can accomplish with that stuff? You can change things, Julian! You *wanted* to change things. You can—" He stepped closer.

Julian could see fault lines of anxiety and fear and the burden of thousands of lives on his old friend's face. He gritted his teeth. Waves of empathy, indignation, and anger crested and swallowed each other in his chest.

"You can save us," he rasped, clasping his hands together.

Julian's heart surged. *Wasn't that my mission in the beginning, to save the people?* Memories of the Belgae's early days hammered him. The satisfaction of working alongside likeminded friends, intent on restoring true freedom—not the illusions fabricated by Hesperia. Every day was arduous work, but every night he'd lie down certain it was worth it.

No. He forced those memories away and wrenched out the ones he'd tried to forget. The days he'd watched Rigo's ego balloon with every fawning new member. He'd become high on status and power. The times when his friend had asked—no, demanded—that he complete a task that walked the line of unethical, and sometimes stomped it into the ground. The night he'd realized that the Belgae would be nothing but more of the same. It had sickened him. "Revolutions eat their young"—wasn't that how the adage went?

"Nothing can save us, Rigo," he said. "We're all pretending we're not already gone. You have to go."

Confusion and desperation flooded Rigo's face. "Julian—"

The sound of the front door flinging open and ricocheting off the wall silenced Rigo. Hieu rushed toward the men. "Get out!" he bellowed. He snatched Rigo by the collar like a stray dog and yanked him forward. "I'll say this once: Never. Come. Here. Again." His jaw was square and taut with fury, his neck muscles bulging as he flung Rigo past him and shoved him toward the front door, wrenching it open and pushing the man out of the building while he shouted and slipped down the stairs. He slammed the door behind him and smacked the lock code into the security panel as Rigo banged on the door.

Julian had never seen Hieu blaze like that before. A kernel of pity for Rigo seeded in him, but he crushed it. For the Zetetics to join forces with the Belgae? Insanity. "Hieu..."

Hieu hushed him, jabbing his finger into Julian's chest. "Don't give in to them, Julian," he thundered, then appeared to wrestle himself under control. "You'll ruin us. Now go upstairs while I figure this out."

27.

MILA GRIPPED her coffee cup and cast an anxious glance at the clock above the door of the Espionage Department's QSS center. Nine at night—eleven o'clock in Savannah.

"You're losing him, Elzac," Caide said.

"Can it, love. All respect intended, of course."

Elzac captained the QSS machine with a rigid spine and tensed shoulders. Caide hovered beside him. Mila stood behind them both. The QSS mist filled the room and all three Zetetics watched intently as a magnecar careened through the streets of Savannah.

Mila twisted a strand of her hair. "Doesn't the QSS attach us—"

"Shh," Caide snapped.

"But—"

"*Shh!* He needs to focus."

"*You* need to focus, love. Grab a tea. No, a coffee—it's a laxative that might help release that stick you've got trapped, dear." Elzac flashed Caide a menacing grin. She shot a furious glare in return, but he ignored her. "I *got* this." He flicked, spun, tapped, and typed, keeping his eyes fixed on the monitor. "Yes, Mila. The QSS can attach us to the perspective of a point person. But only if we've got their DNA. We don't have Laslo's."

The black magnecar tilted dangerously as Laslo swerved around one of the city's squares.

"What's going on that's got him driving like a madman?" Mila asked.

Elzac scooted forward in his seat, giving the chaos all of his focus.

Caide rolled her eyes. "That's Laslo for you. He always drives like this. And—I told you to hush."

Mila fought the urge to roll her eyes at Caide and instead focused on Elzac, trying to connect his movements at the machine with the results they produced in the mist. The Zetetics rounded the same corner the car had spun around. Laslo was gone. Elzac let out a low growl, smacked a code into the machine, and moved faster down the road.

Their perspective flicked left and right as he fought to catch a glimpse of the car. They flew down an alley. Laslo's black magnecar was turning right at the end of it.

"Gotcha, you—" Elzac started, but the mist disappeared. He cursed. He jumped out of his chair. "Caide—?"

Caide lunged under the desk. She restarted the machine, but it threw an error message. Mila watched as Caide rapidly plucked wires and cables from the back of the QSS, opened a panel on the side of the machine's base and began hammering out a long series of keystrokes. Mila glanced at Elzac. The same look of bewildered amazement was on his face as Caide typed and tapped and virtually disassembled and reassembled the QSS with startling fluidity and speed.

Then Caide turned it back on. It worked. Mila exhaled, relieved. She hadn't even noticed she'd been holding her breath.

"All right, Laslo," Caide mumbled, taking Elzac's seat and cueing the machine to find their target once more.

"He could be long gone by now," Mila said.

"Could be. But I can only think of one reason why he'd be in Savannah in the first place. I'm not even sure why Elzac felt he needed to follow him."

"You never know," said Elzac.

"I do." Caide parked in front of Voltaire's. In a moment, the black magnecar screeched to a halt into a parking space in front of the building. Caide stood, shut off the QSS and began to leave the room.

Elzac made to follow her. "Caide—"

"Kairos is going to want to talk about this," she called over her shoulder. "Hieu and Julian will be calling. Now that he's found him, Laslo's not going to give up before he gets his right-hand man back." She threw open the door.

"Well, I guess that's it for your work today." Elzac sighed and adjusted his fedora. "But working past nine o'clock is late enough. Caide'd probably have had you here until two in the morning if she had a mind to."

"Guess so," Mila replied. She glanced at the QSS. Could she ask...?

Elzac snatched his jacket off the back of his chair and shrugged it on. "You've caught on fast in just a few days. Get some rest. Depending on how the drama concludes"—he gestured toward the machine—"it could be a busy day tomorrow." He tipped his hat to her and passed her on his way to the door.

"Elzac, wait." Would he be suspicious?

He stopped in the doorway. "What is it, love?"

"Since we have a little time, what if—do you think you could teach me how to use the QSS?" She bit her lip as the question hung in the air.

Elzac seemed to consider, an impish smile creeping across his face. "Well, what a plucky request from our little neophyte. S'pose there's no foul in fitting another set of fingers to fiddle with it." He returned to the machine and gestured for her to sit. "Your throne, lady," he said dramatically.

She smiled at Elzac and sat. What a strange bird.

He knelt beside her. "The panel at your fingertips isn't much different from a holodesk or sleektop, no?"

She shook her head.

"Keep that in mind. This is where you'll do much of your controlling, steering, finding locations, setting speeds, taking snapshots. When you don't have a DNA identifier to occupy the perspective of a point person, you'll mostly use this panel. When you do"—he wiggled his fingers like a puppet master and moved his hand to rest on a steel-colored domed lid—"you'll place the DNA source under this." He lifted it backward so it rested on its holster, revealing a smooth, white plate. "Hair, saliva, yes—even blood. There are intricate instructions of paramount importance for maintaining the DNA dome's cleanliness when placing such matters on the plate, but you don't need to use this right now. Another day, perhaps." He cocked an eyebrow. "Ready to give it a go?"

"Yes, but... how do I turn it on?"

Elzac clapped his hands once. "Yes! Right. How brilliant you are. There's a switch at the base. Give it a flip and wait a moment."

Mila switched the machine on. A whir—startlingly quiet, given the grand capabilities of the technology—emanated from the base. The panel flared to life and the DNA dome began to glow.

Elzac lifted the lid to reveal ultraviolet electrical impulses dancing inside the white plate underneath. He waggled his eyebrows. "Like magic," he whispered conspiratorially. He guided her through using the machine—taking her back to Voltaire's, for starters—and soon the mist of an alternate reality filled the room. "It's rather intuitive once you familiarize yourself, yes?"

Mila nodded. She spun her fingers on the panel to twirl them in a circle in front of Voltaire's, taking in the building's façade, then the magnificent oaks in the square across from it, then back to the front of the pub. "That this is even possible... it's—beyond my imagination."

"Yes," Elzac agreed. "Let's practice movement, so you can float through a space as effortlessly as a spirit. Go inside."

She guided them toward the front door, then stopped and looked at her teacher. "How do I open the door?"

His choppy chortle reverberated in the room. "You don't, dear! Move through it. I call it 'haunting' for a reason. Think of yourself as a ghost."

She moved toward the door, but it flew open. Hieu shoved Rigo Laslo back onto the street— *through* Elzac and Mila, or so it seemed—and she barely caught a glimpse of Julian behind him inside the bar, a look of bewilderment freezing him in place. Her heart caught at the sight of him. Hieu slammed the door as Laslo scrambled to his feet. He ran back up the steps, yanked on the door, but it wouldn't budge. Cursing, he punched the door, ran back to his magnecar, and sped away.

Elzac abruptly shut off the machine. The mist vaporized. "I think that'll wrap up our lesson, then, love," he said as he hurried to his feet.

Mila searched the man's dark, darting gaze. "Will everyone be okay? Julian and Hieu—"

"They will be." Uncertainty lilted in his voice. "But Kairos and Caide will want to convene. I should be there." Before he'd finished the sentence, he was shutting the door behind him. Mila barely heard his muffled voice say, "Take it easy."

What did it mean for Julian, now that Laslo had located him? Were he and Natalie safe? Was the group? After days without his company, seeing Julian caused a longing for him to run ragged and raw through her. Sometimes he irked her to no end—often his diatribes and debating infuriated her—but she missed him. She refocused on the QSS.

Silence pounded, fuzzy and palpable, in her ears. A jolt of electricity flared in her fingertips. This was her moment. She flipped on the QSS again. On the panel, she keyed it in: *Erie Bureau, Hesperia Defense Department.* The machine whirred. The air around her shifted ever so slightly, just a reorganization of molecules, and the mist hissed into the room. In three heartbeats, she stood outside the bureau, its namesake lake shimmering across the road. She stood in the middle of the steps, illuminated by the glow of street lamps. One Hesperian official exited the building—relieved to be free after working so late, no doubt—pounded down the stairs and through her, without so much as a questioning glance over his shoulder. As brilliantly batty as he was, Elzac was right, it did feel like haunting. Swirling her fingers on the panel, she moved into the building, floating down hallways and scanning directories until she found his listing:

VICTOR A. FALK

SPECIAL AGENT-IN-CHARGE, DOMESTIC TERRORISM SECTION, COUNTERTERRORISM DIVISION.

Even the sight of his name sickened her. Tamping down against a wave of nausea, she flew through the building to the eleventh floor and entered the Domestic Terrorism Section. Instinctively, she held her breath, then forced herself to release it.

No one can sense me. Breathe. Move. Breathe.

Grim-faced men and women in dark-colored suits swirled around her. The Counterterrorism Division never slept, apparently. The open floor plan featured an exposed staircase leading to a walkway, lined with offices, that bordered the rectangular room. Mila floated up the walkway and scanned the doors until she found his.

Breathe. Move. I'm a ghost, remember?

But her body wouldn't listen. Dizziness threatened to envelop her as she entered the office.

There he was. Sitting at his desk. Focused. Working silently. She'd never seen Falk appear so sedate, so... normal. He typed at the holodesk in a suit and tie, like any other office worker in Hesperia. She reined in her breathing and her heart rate softened. She moved closer. His broad shoulders hunched over his task, his pine straw-colored hair raked and messy from frustrated tousling. He chewed on his lip. And he seemed so *human*. Was there a strand of humanity in Victor Falk? Could he be saved? Could he be redeemed?

Or should he be killed?

She watched his throat. His heartbeat throbbed evenly as he worked. She imagined it stopping. And then she imagined stopping it. There would be blood—or maybe there wouldn't be blood. No matter, though. Was it *right*? The man—the monster— at what point was his right to life revoked? Who could claim the right to take it? And *take* seemed such a nonchalant word...

His pulse loped, then galloped. Her gaze cut to his hands. They flickered, then clenched. Her fear climbed in tandem with his frustration. It suffocated her doubt.

"You're abominable," she whispered to him. "You're a devil in human skin." With each word, a power—long dammed up—seeped back into her veins. "You destroyed me, but count your days, Falk. I will destroy you."

His head twitched to one side as if he heard her. Mila's strength evaporated. She froze. Slowly, Falk lifted his head until his volcanic brown eyes latched onto her. Mila leapt from her seat.

"How can you see me?" she hissed, fighting the urge to scream. She clamped her hands over her mouth. Just one look and he squelched every ounce of courage from her. Hatred bludgeoned her insides.

But Falk looked down once more.

"Falk," Mila whispered and took a step closer to him. "Falk," she said louder. "If you can sense me, look at me again." She waited.

He didn't.

Instead, he stood and quietly left his office.

Mila watched him go, then considered turning off the QSS. But curiosity tickled the back of her neck and turned her head. As if possessed by something outside of herself, she walked to Falk's holodesk and examined what he had been working on.

A map, with a choppy red line tracing from Flint Hill to Savannah, then red circles... over Charleston, over Roanoke.

Her trail. In the top left corner, she noticed the search query box. Within it, Falk had typed, *Chip #7980016.*

What was she to him, an unwilling spy? A fleshly drone? A hunter's bird to flush out the rest of his prey? Surely he didn't truly need her to accomplish his missions. Was she only a toy for him to break and reassemble and break again? Fresh rage churned with rancid disgust inside of her. Deactivated or not, she could not tolerate Falk's tracking device like a parasite in her flesh. Turning off the QSS machine, she forced herself back to her apartment, step by shaky step.

~~~

"Chet?" Mila said hoarsely, entering the living room. "Trudi?"

His heavy footsteps answered her call. "Here, Mila. I's just dozing for a minute. Trudi's been asleep awhile now." He appeared in the doorway and then rushed to her. "Dear heart, what's got you ashen?"

The truth tumbled from her lips before she could second-guess it. "Elzac taught me how to use the QSS today and when I had a minute to myself, I used it to spy on Falk and—and I saw him watching me. Not me—it can't sense me anymore. But I can't have this"—she clutched the back of her neck until the skin burned—"on me. I have to get rid of it!"

Chet grasped her shoulders. "Listen up. Tesla and the Zetetics underground rail system can't be found by pesky little buggers like tracking devic-

es—they're too far underground, and they're fortified against the likes of those things. Falk's
scratchin' his noggin right now, can't figure out for
the life of him where you disappeared to. Got it?
You're safe. We's safe. That said—I understand.
And I can help you." His blue eyes darted back and
forth, searching. "But are you certain?"

"Completely."

"Stay here and I'll rustle around for what we
need." Swift as a hippopotamus, he left the apartment.

She waited on the couch for what felt like an
eternity, until Chet finally returned, holding a
small black bag in one hand and what appeared to
be a palm-sized scanner in the other.

He held up the supplies triumphantly. "I had to
do a little finaglin', but even an old goat like me can
turn on the charm enough to weasel what he wants
from a young nurse." He displayed the scanner and
motioned for Mila to scoot over. Plopping down
beside her, he held it out for her to examine. "It's a
fancy thermometer. If you did have a fever, I could
get your temperature faster than a donkey flicks his
tail. But I can also scan you—your temp'll be higher
where the tracker is. Just a touch warmer, from the
blood rushing to that spot. So I'm gonna need you
to unzip your jacket."

Mila removed the navy jacket, a piece from the basic wardrobe the Zetetics had furnished her with, exposing the black tank top she wore underneath. Chet fiddled with the thermometer and turned it on. "Tie up your hair for me, though."

Freeing the braid that ran down her back, she gathered her hair on top of her head, securing it with her hair tie. The thermometer chirped, signaling its readiness. "How do you know how to do this?"

"When you run a safe house, you gotta be prepared for a wide variety of situations. It was part of our training when we first joined the group. This kind of thing—physically removing a tracker—doesn't happen often... but sometimes it does." He slowly waved the scanner down the back of her head, pausing at the base of her skull, "Eureka."

He unzipped the black case. Mila's pulse tripped over itself.

"There ain't no easy way of doin' this next part. Best I can do is a topical numbing, but I'm gonna have to... dig a little."

She reached for the round throw pillow next to her and clutched it, shutting her eyes. "Okay."

A tinkling sound as Chet rustled in the bag, a rip as he tore open a package. "This's an antiseptic wipe."

The skin on the back of her neck prickled in response to the cool cloth. She heard a twist and the pop of a bottle's lid.

"Numbing gel."

She forced herself to breathe evenly and used all her power to ignore the sound of whatever metal instruments scraped against each other in Chet's bag... and the pressure as he pressed against her skin. The numbing gel couldn't squelch the scraping sensation as he sliced—nor the pushing and digging as he fumbled in her flesh. She clawed the throw pillow and hissed through her locked jaw.

"I got it."

"You've got it?" she squeaked.

"Yes, ma'am. Don't turn around."

He stood. She heard him exit into the bathroom and run the sink. He returned with the cleaned tweezers in hand, pinching a device too small for her to see even from only a few feet away.

A curdled mixture of revulsion and anger filled her. "What should we do with it?"

"Thought I'd let you do the honors." Chet offered the device to her.

She extended her hand and he dropped the tracker into her palm, no larger than a grain of rice. Tossing it to the floor, she slammed her heel over it and twisted, then buried her face in her hands. "I hate knowing how close he was to—how he could have"—she looked at Chet—"maybe I should leave. If he's trying to find me, I can't let him find any of you, too."

The couch rattled as Chet plunked down next to her. Taking her hands once more, he spoke gently. "Hieu and Kairos know the risks. You're not the most hunted person this place has ever sheltered— not by a long shot. The tracker couldn't'a found us down here, and it's gone now, anyway. It was a non-issue even before this"—he grimaced—"effort. And I like having you around. Don't you sneak out on me." He straightened. "And they're watching for Falk, aren't they?"

She nodded and Chet stood, a satisfied smile on his face. She forced herself to return one, then dropped her gaze. Moving her foot, she looked at the tiny spot of ground powder where the tracker had been. Conviction hammered into her. Watching for Falk would never be enough. The only solution was his total annihilation.

28.

CONNECTION LOST.

Falk re-entered the chip identification number and waited.

CONNECTION LOST.

He tried again, smacking the digits into the search bar. The swirling icon appeared again. He growled, impatient. Ever since he'd returned from Roanoke-Virginia three days before, he'd been unable to connect to the device he'd implanted in Thirty-Four's neck.

CONNECTION LOST.

This time Mila's route vanished too. His eyes burned with fury. He entered the ID one last time.

CHIP I.D. DOES NOT EXIST. PLEASE TRY AGAIN.

Falk clenched his jaw and stared at the empty map, his hands pressed down on his holodesk, bloodless and white with tension. His fingers twitched, poised to throw the holodesk and crush it into the floor.

No. He deadened himself to his anger, wrested himself under control. He was Victor Falk—he *never* lost control. All of his triumphs hinged on his inhuman capacity to remain as frozen as the Arctic. Why should losing Mila's location set him off? She was trivial. Worthless. He didn't *need* her for anything. Watching her run to the Belgae and unwittingly flush them right into his trap would've been pleasurable, but it wasn't necessary. Lording his power over her and watching her shrivel into an apoplectic mouse at his mere presence brought him satisfaction, too—but there were countless inmates at Flint Hill for that. She was expendable.

Yet the flames crackled inside him. They lapped at the glaciers, melting them, tipping his cool-headed strategizing into blinding, burning anger. Why? He had no answer, and that only fanned the flames.

Then an image of Mila appeared. A memory. She lunged forward, eyes glassy, mouth open in a tortured cry. Falk closed his eyes. He froze the picture in his mind. What was it about Thirty-Four that kept him fixated? He panned out, scanning the environment for another clue. That idiot DaVanti was there—losing his balance on the walkway as the guards forced him forward into Flint Hill. He looked back at Mila and snatched her image, yanking it closer until her memory was nose-to-nose with his icy assessment. Her pupils were dilated, her neck strained in a scream.

There. She wasn't just another radical—not another mass-market revolutionary with her hand curled into a fist for fighting and a memorized diatribe to spew. She cared. More than caring, she carried the pain of others, the pain of people like DaVanti. There was a word for it. What was the word? Empathy. That was a word that didn't enter his vocabulary often. Falk chuckled. But that was it—her uncanny, deeply human capacity for caring, standing directly opposed to his inhuman capacity for destroying. And just as relentless.

How sweet it would be to suffocate her heart, watch it throb and fight and vow to survive, even as he squeezed it until it stopped.

That was why he couldn't lose Mila. He opened his eyes. The empty map and dialog box greeted him again.

CHIP I.D. DOES NOT EXIST. PLEASE TRY AGAIN.

The words poured gasoline on the flames, sending him into a furious explosion. Toppling the holodesk, he stormed out of his office.

~~~

Nearly twelve hours since Chet had removed the device, the hole at the back of Mila's neck was at its most sensitive. It throbbed in protest against anything that touched it, even the bandage covering it, but she freed her hair from its clip on top of her head and let the tresses tumble around her shoulders anyway. She didn't want the attention.

Falk's name rang with every pang. On top of everything, the son of a bitch had injected her with a tracking device, like a dog. As if she was his property. His tool. Then again, hadn't she been? Her bones vibrated with indignation. Not anymore. Soon, she'd make him pay. For now, she focused on the idea she'd pitch to Caide and Kairos. If Rigo Laslo had located Julian and the Zetetics, perhaps instead of letting him get back to the Belgae to spread the information, they could invite Laslo into their own custody, talk with him, make *him* useful to *their* agenda instead of the other way around. A spurned revolutionary with knowledge of the Zetetics, running freely back to his radical group, couldn't be safe for them all. Perhaps some sort of merger was in order. The possibility that it could help her achieve her mission to destroy Falk was a nice perk, too.

She hoped she could raise the subject without her nerves overtaking her and without being seen as smug, since she'd only just joined them. She arrived at the Espionage Department and leaned into the retina scan. The door unlocked with a click. Mila twisted the handle and paused. Clearing her throat, she held her head high and opened the door—and all of her stored up words flew away, save one.

"Julian."

He leaned against the wall of the empty hall, arms crossed casually over his chest, his brassy curls contrasting with the black T-shirt he wore. "Hi to you, too."

She smiled. His presence thawed a part of her she didn't know was frozen, loosened something within her she hadn't known was taut. "Why are you here?"

"There's something I have to take care of." He propelled from the wall and took her hand in his. "Come with me. You should see it."

He pulled her forward toward the atrium, even as she cast a worried glance back over her shoulder at the door to the Espionage Department's conference room. What about her idea for handling Laslo?

"Caide and Kairos can wait," Julian said, as if he read her thoughts. He smiled down at her with boyish excitement. "Come on." When he threaded his fingers through hers, she decided he was right—it could wait.

He brought them to a blank space of gray stone in the center wall of the atrium. He focused on the crevices in the wall, chewing on his bottom lip and squeezing her hand in an absent-minded staccato. "It always takes me a second to see it." He pulled her in front of him, holding her left hand in his. "I'll show you."

A current flared through her as his fingers brushed up her palm and curled around one of hers. He guided her hand to a crevice in the stone. His voice sent vibrations down her spine as he murmured gently in her ear, "It always starts in the center."

A blue illumination appeared where he touched her fingertip to the stone and drew it upward into an arc, then back down, curve by curve, until they'd traced the stone's ripples into the illuminated silhouette of a five-petaled flower.

"A violet," he said. "An ancient symbol of free thought." The stone pulled backward and to the side. He stepped around her and into the darkness beyond them. She hesitated, a ripple of anxiety running over her body.

"Follow me," he said. "I promise it's not another tight crawlspace." He extended his hand and she took it, following him down a dimly-lit stairwell.

"A lair within a lair?" she asked.

He chuckled. "Redundancies are our number one line of security. It's a basic rule of thumb."

The stairwell brought them into a web of pod-like caverns, their rocky walls twinkling with the glow of multicolored lights, like electrical geodes. The air was wet with ancient moisture and the metallic scent of ore. Straight ahead of them, a large panel flicked through a marquee of headings: TESLA: SECURE. SAVANNAH: SECURE. CHARLESTON: SECURE. LYLE: SECURE. FLAGSTAFF: SECURE. The names continued to tick by, the details of their statuses written in smaller text below. To the panel's right was a switchboard dotted with levers and buttons. An incredibly large sleektop supported them both.

"It's kind of the motherboard for the organization," Julian said, crossing the space to it. "Every hub's IT security can be managed, fixed, improved, monitored, you name it. It didn't take as long as you'd think to set it up."

"You created all of this?"

"Yeah." He turned to examine the switchboard.

Her lips ticked into a half-smile. He answered her question as if developing this labyrinth were as simple as mixing a cocktail. "Business owner, artist, avid reader and intellectual, IT genius... what don't you excel at?"

"Women." He looked over his shoulder and shot her a sly smile. "Can't you see? Complete and total overcompensation, all of this."

She laughed—and doubted it. Julian had a magnetic way with her, so effortless that she hadn't begun to realize his grip until now. Warmth prickled her cheeks. She fidgeted for a distraction. "Laslo found you," she tried. Her words hung in the air.

Finally, he faced her. "They told you, huh?"

For a moment, she wondered if his casual manner matched his inner state, but the way his fingers tapped on his hips gave him away. "I saw it. I was with Elzac and Caide when they followed him to Voltaire's. I saw you"—she stopped, remembering the frozen look on his face—"I saw Hieu throw him out." She waited, but he didn't respond. "What did he want?"

"Too much."

"He wanted you back, didn't he?"

"That was the crux of it."

She sighed, exasperated. "Well, fill me in on the details." Stepping close, she scrutinized his face. "Are you really here to take care of a security issue?"

His eyes darkened to a lake-blue. "No."

She spun on her heels and threw her hands up. "Julian, we may be underground, but I'm not going to mine you for information. If you don't want to tell me, don't tell me."

"Laslo wanted the Zetetics to join the Belgae in their fight against Hesperia."

Everything within Mila went wild at the prospect. The Zetetics, with all they had to offer, and the Belgae? It was so much better than her proposition to take on Laslo, or absorb the Belgae into themselves, or even than Julian to leave and return to the group in which he'd begun. This was...

The image of Hieu throwing Laslo out squelched her excitement. "Hieu put a stop to that idea."

"Yes, he did."

"But what's going through your mind?"

He raked his fingers through his hair. "Laslo... look, you saw him in Savannah. He runs an organization like he drives. And there are so many more reasons. Hieu was right."

Maybe so. But Julian's musing tone implied he was still trying to convince himself. She watched his wavering stance, his slightly furrowed brow, the slump that had crept to his shoulders. He seemed torn in two. Fraying. And his weariness washed over her. "Julian, you don't have to hide these things from me, to keep me blind to what's happening behind the scenes. I'm not just some girl you helped and then sent on her way—"

"You're not?" He stepped closer to her.

He smelled of resin, like a pine forest on an autumn night. "No..." She lifted her chin to finish her thought, but he took her in his arms. His soft lips insisted, and she opened her mouth and kissed him deeper, wrapping her arms around him and pulling herself closer to him. His hands clasped her at the shoulder blades, then slid down to her waist. He sighed with longing—and then turned ravenous, washing her along in his wild tide, like a river after a heavy rain. Bringing her hands to his chest, she explored his muscles, then his neck, and plunged her fingers into his untamed hair. But she wanted much more than his body. She wanted his heart, his mind.

"Julian, I think I'm fall—"

"Me too." Delight blazed in his eyes before he kissed her again. His hands traveled back up her curves, his fingers twirling in her hair. He pulled her tighter to him, clasping the back of her neck.

She screamed.

Julian stepped back, his eyes wide with horror. "Mila, did I hurt you?"

She wheezed heavy breaths, willing the searing pain to subside.

He took both of her hands. "I'm so sorry—oh, God—I'm so sorry..."

"It's not—you... didn't..." she said between ragged breaths. "It's okay. I'm okay."

"Like hell you are." He placed his hands on her shoulders and turned her around.

"Don't, it's nothing—"

He twisted her hair and pulled it back from her neck. "Good God Almighty! What the hell happened to you?"

She whirled out of his reach and faced him. She grasped for the words, but was robbed of them. "I had to get rid of it," she said. "The thought of walking around like his lost dog made me sick—Chet gouged it out—"

Julian stopped the flow of her words with a tight embrace, clasping her head to his chest. She soaked in his warmth, a balm for her pain. "Don't tell me any more," he pleaded. "I can't handle it."

He held her tighter and she reveled in his care. No one had given so much concern for her well-being since her parents died. Now, she was acutely aware of how starved she'd been. How alone. She melded against his body.

"Julian? Mila?" Caide's voice echoed at the top of the stairwell. "Espionage meeting. Two minutes."

"Be right there," Julian called. "I was just checking for security gaps."

"Oh, is *that* what we're calling it?" Caide snorted. The sound of her determined footsteps signaled her exit.

He grinned. "Guess we've been found out."

She took his hand. "I don't mind if you don't."

~~~

The air in the Espionage Department crackled with tension when Mila and Julian arrived. Twelve of fourteen chairs were occupied, and Mila smiled at the sight of Natalie among them. They took their seats between Natalie and Elzac.

Kairos leaned forward at the head of the table. "Desmond, is the transcript ready?" he asked the middle-aged man beside him.

Desmond pressed a button on the small tablet he held, and nodded.

Kairos addressed the group. "I'm officially calling to order the Espionage Department daily conference. August the second." His hawkish eyes pierced the gazes of the Zetetics around him. "The aboveground climate is rife with volatility, more so than we've seen it in decades. It's likely that Hesperia and the opposition group, the Belgae, will battle each other as the Belgae continues their fight for change. The Belgae are strong in number, but that's all the strength they have and the leadership knows it. But the revolutionaries are high on the wings of fury and nothing will stop them. All of this would scarcely cause us to raise an eyebrow if it weren't for the connection of one of our own to the Belgae."

In her peripheral vision, Mila saw Julian lift his chin ever so slightly, retaining a confident posture even as he squeezed her hand under the table. The eyes around the table scrutinized him.

"Julian Merrick is not to be blamed, of course," Kairos continued. "We welcomed him into the Zetetics with complete knowledge of his former connections. He has been a phenomenal asset to our group. But Rigo Laslo is a desperate leader of a desperate people. He found Don, our Squire and pharmacist who keeps Julian's mother in medicine, and then located Julian and Hieu at Voltaire's. This has forced Julian and Natalie to relocate to Tesla, and Hieu is on watch for Laslo's reappearance. We know he won't give up."

Mila licked her lips and took a breath, preparing to present her idea about Laslo to Kairos, but he continued.

"There's another storm brewing, and it has to do with our newcomer, Mila."

Her skin prickled under the darting glances of the Espionage team.

"Victor Falk, of Hesperia's Defense Department, continues to search for her. This isn't the first time the Zetetics have sheltered a Hesperian wanted by the government and it certainly won't be the last, but Victor Falk is a ruthless, relentless investigator. His tracking device evaded the Detracker scan and was only thoroughly deactivated once Mila arrived here. This put both Voltaire's and the Talbott safe house on his radar, which is why we've pulled Chet and Trudi underground."

"What about Hieu?" asked Caide.

Julian straightened. "Falk knows nothing about Hieu. I'm the only one who interacted with him."

"Hieu is continuing to watch for any sign of Falk or Hesperia activity near Voltaire's," Kairos added.

Heads bobbed in agreement around the table, and a current of hope flushed through Mila. Were the Zetetics about to retaliate against Falk?

"Sir?" a young man raised his finger in question.

"Moltov." Kairos nodded.

"I've got Victor Falk on my radar. He's remained at the Erie Bureau ever since Trudi reported his presence at her home. I check in with Falk three times a day—"

"Via his technological activity or via QSS?"

"Mostly technological activity—where he logged in and on what device. But every morning and every evening, I find him on the QSS. Something's got him riled."

"Quantitative information, please, Moltov."

"Sorry. When I used the QSS to follow him last night, he wasn't in his office, but his holodesk was flipped over. The place was a disaster."

"What else have you learned?"

"No more than I've already told you—Falk seems to think that Mila has some type of Belgae tie, that following her will take him to an important part of the movement."

"Amp up your monitoring," Kairos ordered. "From this point on, always use the QSS. Report directly to me on what you find. Anita and Roejo are heading up Belgae watch"—an elderly woman and man nodded—"and Caide and I are optimizing the strategy for pulling everyone. But it's never come to that before. It shouldn't come to that now."

"Pulling everyone?" The question escaped her lips before she had time to think. "We're not... stopping them? Stopping Laslo? Stopping *Falk*?"

Kairos' cool gaze rested on her. "Such actions would throw us into the limelight, and at no long-term advantage to us."

"No advantage?"

"*Long-term*, Mila," Kairos said. "'The supreme art of war is to subdue the enemy without fighting.'"

"You're not subduing him at all!"

"Mila," Kairos cautioned, rising to his feet.

"No," she stopped him, pushed her chair back, and stood. "I don't believe what I'm hearing. You called us all here for a conference. You outline how dangerous the situation is, how two of your own are more compromised than any Zetetics have been in decades—and your grand plan is for us to come up with what amounts to the greatest game of hide-and-seek ever played? Is that what the Zetetics grand mission amounts to? *Hiding*?"

"There's no rescuing the world above, Mila. History supports our stance. To risk revealing ourselves as we step out to destroy a person—leaving the administration he works for in its place—gains us nothing." His voice was patient but brittle. "Everything you see down here is the product of centuries' worth of work *creating* the world, the society, we wanted for ourselves, because we watched our forebears die to try to fix something beyond repair. Such efforts are futile. It's wiser to protect what we have. In these instances, that entails circumventing trouble."

"Cowards," she said.

"Mila," Julian cautioned.

"*Excuse* me?" Caide stood and crossed her arms.

Mila lifted her chin, undeterred. "You have more advanced technology than Hesperia can fathom—in realms from weaponry to *gardening*, for God's sake! If anyone in the history of humanity is in the position to rescue the world above, *you* can. And thousands of Hesperians have the bravery to face the government with hardly anything stronger than their fists, while you hide in caves, keeping all of this to yourself. Julian came to you, improved upon your security and has been a 'phenomenal asset'—your own words—and you won't even protect him and Natalie without ferreting them all over the country. And me... I know I'm the newcomer here, but I at least had the guts to take a risk to help someone. Carlo DaVanti came to me for help and I went to Flint Hill for it. I was *tortured* for

it. And I'm being hunted by a monstrous psychopath, and your *brilliant strategy* is to find a better
hiding spot?" She stared up at Kairos.

He scarcely blinked. "We were as forthright with
you about our purpose as we could be, Mila. If you
chose to distort it and make us mean something to
you that we aren't, never were, and never have
been, that's your own unfortunate choice. Our philosophy remains, and if it weren't for our philosophy, you'd be rotting in the woods by now. Take it
or leave it."

Magma-like fury blazed within her. "How *dare*
you!"

"Get her out of here, Julian," ordered Kairos.
"She needs to cool down."

Julian stood, gently grasped Mila's arm, and led
her out of the department, her mouth agape in anger struck wordless. The rest of the Zetetics
watched their exit with expressions ranging from
modest discomfort to hot indignation.

In the hallway, Mila yanked herself away from
Julian. "How could you hang me out to dry like
that?"

"You went about it all wrong. Kairos doesn't engage on a playing field based on emotion."

"So if I hadn't lost my head, you'd have stood up
for us?"

He fidgeted. "It's more complicated than that, Mila. I have my mother to think about. The choice can be more cut and dried for you—"

"Because I have no family," she finished for him.

"I didn't mean it that way."

"I'll ask you again." She used everything within her to keep her voice even. "Look me dead in the eyes and tell me you support this plan of action."

He shook his head as if to regroup. "Let me go back in there. I'll tell you about everything we discuss. If you want to convince Kairos and the rest of the group to act against the philosophy that's guided them for two centuries, you're going to need to approach him from a different angle, with a level head."

"Tell me right now, Julian. Do you think the way the Zetetics are handling all of this is wrong?"

He pursed his lips.

"Oh my God..." Tears welled in her eyes as he walked back into the meeting and left her standing alone in the hall.

29.

HUNCHED OVER THE SINK, Mila stared at her reddened eyes in the mirror. She should have known. Julian had hinted at it in their debates. What Kairos had said was true—she *did* project her hopes onto them. But they hadn't given her anything else to go on, either.

Julian. How could he, after everything he's been through? After everything I've been through? He made her believe he cared. But he only cared as long as it didn't require him to encounter the real world anymore.

She caught sight of the hydrogen peroxide bottle on the counter—morning, noon, and night, to prevent infection. Snatching the bottle, she opened it and soaked a fresh cotton ball, planting it against the wound. The liquid fizzed and hissed and stung like a wasp. "Damn it all," she whispered. She threw the cotton ball into the trash can beside the toilet and returned to her bedroom, collapsing on the small bed.

Disappointment and anger knotted in her throat. The resources, the power, the potential of this group—selfishly underground for centuries, while people like Carlo and her parents gave their lives to change their world. In the Zetetics, she'd seen Hesperia's only legitimate hope for victory.

Now what? If I love my safety, my only choice is to hide here, at Tesla. But if I love the people... my only choice is to rise up.

A faint knock sounded outside the apartment. She waited, but it continued. Pulling herself out of bed, she plodded to the front door and opened it.

Natalie greeted her with a demure smile, leaning on her walker. "I came to see if you're alright."

The last thing Mila wanted was company. But she couldn't deny Julian's sweet mother. "That was kind of you." She held the door open.

Natalie entered the apartment—her steps more precarious than the last time they'd been together—and lowered herself to the loveseat as though she were cracked porcelain. "I've known the Belgae and the Zetetics," she began, her gaze resting softly on the fireplace. "I've watched them both through my son. The passionates and the rationals. The idealists and the skeptics. Those with hearts and those with minds. The Zetetics worship their realism, their independence, their selective altruism, their daring to set out on their own and create the world they want. The Belgae pride themselves for not giving up, for their willingness to overthrow the status quo in pursuit of change, and for fighting for people who can't or won't fight for themselves. Each believes they have the answer." She cast a placid smile at her. "And they do."

Mila took a seat in the armchair across from her.

Natalie continued, "What they don't always have is wisdom. There is a time, a place, for grit and gumption. A time and place for moving on. The world needs piercing minds, and is desperate for passionate hearts. But wisdom transcends time and place. And it eludes most all of us." She reached out, her arm as fragile as a pin-bone, and placed her hand on Mila's. "You have a gift. Your compassion, your depth of caring, your empathy. You're a burden-bearer. It's a tremendous gift."

"And look where it's gotten me," she muttered.

Natalie's warm brown stare held her own, piercing with the understanding of an ancient sage, shining with the love of a mother. She nodded. "It hurts to be tender-hearted."

Mila blinked back the moisture gathering in her eyes. Natalie saw her, heard her, felt her. But more than that... she comprehended her. Vulnerability washed over her, both burn and balm. She closed her eyes.

"To hear the irresistible call for help in every soul, and the crushing realization when you attempt a rescue only to realize it's beyond your control. And sometimes it's completely out of your control. Other times, it's not." She cupped Mila's cheek. "Wisdom."

"I can't do it alone," she said, opening her eyes. "I'm alone."

"No." Natalie cast her glance skyward briefly, then smiled. "And no."

~~~

Julian blinked hard, and forced his eyes to stay open. He sipped his coffee and glanced at the clock hanging above the door of the patient exam room in the Health Services Department. Twelve thirty in the afternoon. He'd been awake for more than twenty-four hours now. After his altercation with Laslo—was that really only the night before?—the hasty departure from Savannah, an all-night journey to Tesla, and the fiery morning meeting, everything was catching up to him. He hoped the cardiologist would arrive any minute.

"I told you, I don't need you to be with me, Julian," Natalie said. "Get some sleep."

"I couldn't if I tried. Plus, I want to hear what Doctor Mathis says." Silence hung between them. He opened his mouth, questions poised in his throat, but closed it again. He'd ask his mother later about her visit with Mila that morning.

As if on cue, the doctor returned, clipboard in hand. "Alright, Natalie." She sat on the small stool across from them and set the clipboard in her lap. "The good news is that the disease's progression seems to have stagnated. In the three years you've been on xianepam, the complications we had been anticipating before the availability of the medication have all but dissipated. If it weren't for Doctor Hamilton's drug, your prognosis would likely be much, much worse."

Julian squeezed his mother's hand.

Natalie smiled—then appeared to think better of it. "And the rest, Doctor?"

"You've developed a cardiac arrhythmia. And, unfortunately, it is a side effect of the xianepam. A rare one, but we've confirmed the connection. An arrhythmia, in normal circumstances, isn't always something to worry about. But in patients with types of muscular dystrophy, it's much more concerning."

Natalie's gaze fell to her hands.

"She needs the xianepam, though, Doctor..." Julian countered, his voice weak. "Without it, the progression will resume, she"—he swallowed, fighting the swell of emotion in his chest—"I don't know what you're recommending that we do."

Doctor Mathis nodded sympathetically. "It's a very difficult decision. Continuing the xianepam offers the benefit of slowing or halting the progression of the disease, but the arrhythmia in and of itself could cause sudden cardiac arrest, which would be fatal. Stopping the xianepam, however, means resuming the typical trajectory of the disease."

"Don doesn't have a cure on the horizon?" Julian asked.

"He was getting close before he had to abandon everything and go underground. He hopes to have it ready for human trials soon. It could be a few months, it could be much longer..."

"So we could continue the xianepam—"

"If you decide the risk is worth taking."

"—in hopes that Don's new drug would be available soon enough that we could cure her condition."

"Theoretically."

Julian looked at his mother. Would this be the decision he regretted forever? Either choice could go so wrong. What would his life be, if he lost his mother, his only family? What would he do?

"I think it's a risk we'd like to take," Natalie said.

Doctor Mathis stood. "It's decided, then. So, Natalie, you didn't report experiencing any light-headedness, dizziness, flutters in your chest—"

Natalie shook her head.

"I want you to pay attention for any of those things. Chest pain, shortness of breath, racing heartbeats or slow ones." She ticked off the list on her fingers. "That could mean the arrhythmia is getting worse. Also, sleeping issues. What we want to keep an eye out for is sleep apnea, which tells us that your heart is having trouble functioning. Any of those things would be definite cause to reconsider taking the xianepam, or at least lessening the frequency or lowering your dosage. You'll be staying in Tesla indefinitely?"

Natalie nodded and reached for Julian's arm. He stood and helped his mother to her feet, then pulled her walker to her.

"Let's go to the front, then, and get your next appointment on the books so we can keep an eye on you."

A haze enveloped Julian's mind as they left Health Services. The xianepam had been working so well. He'd truly thought his mother's quality of life would be maintained, at least. Now, he could be robbed of her instantly... but stopping the xianepam would rob her of so much more. *Will the shadow of disease lurk behind us with every step we take? Is there nothing I can do but make her as comfortable as possible?* He couldn't remember ever feeling so helpless.

"I'm thankful the medicine worked without side effects for as long as it did," said Natalie. "It has made things much better."

Julian could only offer a mechanical smile.

She patted his shoulder. "Let's go to the garden. That will lift our spirits."

As they walked through the atrium and down the hallway leading to the garden, Julian's thoughts drifted to Mila. How could he convince her not to interpret his hesitance as betrayal? That he truly knew how she was feeling, that he'd been there, too? He sighed and rubbed a growing tension in his head.

"Give her time," his mother said.

He opened his mouth to ask her about her conversation with Mila that morning, but Chet jogged up beside them, with Trudi trailing behind.

"Top o' the mornin'," he chimed.

"Well, hello!" Natalie beamed. "It's been far too long."

"You radiate from the inside out, dear Natalie," Chet said. "But Julian done looks like he *got* radiated. What's fried you, boy?"

"He's been up all night," his mother answered. "I tried to get him to sleep on the train..."

"Boy, go hit the hay before you shrivel up. Trudi and I can keep your mama company better'n you on your best day."

Julian's tired laugh sounded like a single bubble popping through swamp water.

"Please, Julian," Natalie urged.

"Listen to your mother," Trudi said.

Chet waved him away, and Julian heard their cheerful chattering as he walked back down the hall. Inside his apartment, he collapsed onto his bed.

Sleep overtook him.

He could have sworn he'd only been asleep for a few minutes when an urgent knocking began at his apartment door. Plodding out of bed, he entered the living room and rubbed his eyes, then blinked several times until the clock came into focus. Ten thirty at night? He rushed to the door and answered it.

Moltov leaned on the doorframe, his frantic breaths heaving his shoulders up and down. "We need you in the Espionage Department," he blustered. "Falk left Erie earlier this evening, after my last check-in. Caide, Elzac, and I have used every trick we can think of, but it's no use. We can't find him."

Julian tugged on his shoes and ran into the hall, with Moltov trailing behind. "Hieu needs to be alerted immediately," he called.

"We can't reach him."

30.

JULIAN HOVERED OVER ELZAC as he captained the QSS in search of Hieu. The mist of a vacant Voltaire's filled the room. Caide manned the sleektop, scanning an aerial view of Savannah for any pertinent information, her telephone pressed between her shoulder and her ear. Moltov paced and bit his fingernails. Kairos glowered into the mist.

Julian covered the mouthpiece of his phone as it rang. "Don't forget to check upstairs in our apartment. He could be there."

Elzac nodded and the mist swept toward the stairs as he navigated the team throughout the building.

Hieu was never unreachable. Never. The call patched through. "Damien? Wake up, man."

The bartender on the other end of the line groaned. "Julian? I just got in bed."

"So you don't know where Hieu is?"

"No."

"Don't turn your phone off." Julian ended the call.

"Second floor is all clear," said Elzac. "Moving up to the third."

"Answer, Samantha, damn it!" Caide yelled and tossed her phone on the sleektop.

"Caide. Calm," ordered Kairos.

"I've called her four times. Nothing!"

"Keep trying." The hub leader locked his attention on Moltov. "Did you fire the cast message?"

The young man nodded. "Minutes ago. Expect responses confirming safety any second now on my tablet. I'll call them out as I get them."

Kairos nodded.

"Don't forget the back patio, Elzac," Julian said.

"Confirming Lyle," Moltov said. "Confirming Boise."

"C'mon, Sam, c'mon," whined Caide.

"Confirming Baton Rouge."

Elzac's voice was heavy with worry as he called, "Third floor—all clear."

"Confirming Pittsfield. And Flagstaff."

"Check the streets," Kairos said. "Alleys. Every-where."

The mist swirled into a whirlwind of colors as Elzac flew out of the building. In moments, they were sweeping through the streets of Savannah.

"Confirming Charleston. Confirming Lincoln."

They swerved down street after street and around most of the city's sixteen squares before Caide finally cried, "Samantha! Oh, thank God!"

Julian locked his gaze on Caide. He held his breath.

Caide glanced to each of the men in the room, relief in her eyes. "You were just out walking. Good." Pulling the phone away from her ear, she hit a button and Samantha's voice emanated from the device.

"...didn't mean to cause so much concern, I apologize. Hieu and I both left our phones just for a minute of peace—"

"Don't do it again," said Caide.

"Confirming St. Louis."

"Is Hieu safe?" Julian asked.

"Yes, I left him at Voltaire's—"

Elzac shot a look to Caide over his shoulder, groaned, and began navigating the team back toward the pub.

"—and he locked up behind me and everything. We're safe. I deeply apologize."

"We just finished checking Voltaire's no more than fifteen minutes ago," Caide countered.

"You must've just missed us then."

Kairos planted his hands on his hips. "Falk is on the move and we don't know where he's gone, Samantha. You can understand why we became frantic when we couldn't reach you. Stay in touch with us and stay alert. Do *not* leave your phone unattended."

"I understand, sir. It won't happen again."

Caide ended the call. She looked at Julian and nodded curtly.

"Confirming Roanoke."

Julian began to dial Hieu's phone number again as they glided down Congress Street.

Ring.

Drayton Street.

Ring.

Hull Street.

Ring.

They floated up the steps to Voltaire's and flew through the front door. Falk held the barrel of a revolver in Hieu's mouth.

"Christ..." whispered Elzac.

You've reached the voicemail of Hieu Kien, certified financial planner...

Julian ended the call and dropped his phone. The blood in his veins turned to ice.

"Get Samantha back on the phone," said Kairos.

"Lock the door," Falk ordered.

Hieu flipped the lock on the door handle, keeping his eyes fixed on Falk.

"Don't insult my intelligence. Activate the entire security system."

"Samantha," began Caide in an urgent whisper, "Hieu's in danger. Get your gun and go to Voltaire's... No, take the tunnels..."

Falk backed Hieu into the main pub area, out of sight from the windows in the foyer. "Tell me where to find Mila Ray." He removed the barrel of the gun from Hieu's mouth and planted it firmly in the hollow of his throat.

"We'll guide you. Stay on the phone, Sam."

Hieu swallowed. "No."

Falk laughed. "If you don't give me what I want, I'm not going to put a bullet through your head in a fit of fury. I'm more patient than that. I'll take my time." His voice was cold and hollow as an empty casket. "Where is she?"

Hieu swung his arm and catapulted the gun from Falk's grasp, then launched a kick into his abdomen. Falk doubled over and staggered back. The gun clattered and skidded across the wooden floor.

"Shit!" Moltov shouted.

Julian clutched the back of Elzac's chair.

Hieu dove for the gun, barely sliding far enough to snatch it with the very tips of his fingers. He fumbled and twirled it as Falk ran toward him. Spinning onto his back, he pulled the trigger.

Nothing happened. Falk laughed.

Hieu scrambled to his feet.

Falk snatched a nearby barstool without breaking his stride and swung it at Hieu. It clattered against his torso, sending him sprawling to the floor. The Hesperian knelt beside him and clasped his large hand around Hieu's throat. Pulling a knife from his belt, he plunged it into Hieu's shoulder.

Hieu screamed. A river of blood dulled the shimmering cloth of his silver shirt.

"Hurry, Sam," Caide urged. "We're running out of time."

Julian closed his eyes, tightened his jaw. Rage ripped through him. He looked at Caide.

"She's climbing the ladder to Voltaire's underground. From there, she can use the staircase to get into the pub from underneath the fireplace, right?"

He could only manage to nod.

"Tell me where to find Mila," Falk demanded.

Hieu's chest rose and fell like a boat on a choppy sea. He gasped. "She's with Laslo—at Belgae headquarters."

"Move fast, Sam. Stay quiet." Caide's voice was a husky whisper.

Kairos held out his hand. Caide placed the phone into it. "When you open the fireplace entrance, aim left. You've got a clean shot... Locked?" He looked to Julian.

Julian took the phone, but couldn't tear his eyes from the vision of his friend struggling for breath in an ever-growing pool of blood. "You can disarm the security panel from underneath the door. The black box to your right. Open it. Unplug the wires..." His voice trailed off as Falk spoke again.

"Where is the Belgae headquarters?"

"I—don't—know," Hieu gasped.

Falk twisted the knife. Hieu roared in pain. "I know you work for them," he growled.

Hieu's head shook violently. He spoke in ragged, urgent breaths. "No—not Belgae. That's why she—couldn't stay. She's a—liability. I—sent—her—*away.*"

"Don't lie to me," Falk warned. "If you're not Belgae, why wouldn't you give her up to me when I asked you first?"

Hieu closed his eyes. When he opened them, his coal-black gaze fixed on Falk in a disgusted glare. Drawing one long, battered breath, he slammed his fist into the hardwood floor as if to launch the words from his lungs. "Belgae—aren't our friends, but—we share—the same—enemy."

Falk punched him in the mouth.

Blood trickled from his lip. He hocked a mouthful and spat it into Falk's face.

"Now, Samantha!" Julian yelled. He could hear the rattling as Sam struggled to pull the fireplace's false bottom down and out of her way. His heart thrashed inside his chest.

Falk yanked the knife from Hieu's shoulder and poised it above his neck.

"It's jammed!" Her voice quaked with panic. "Oh God, it's jammed!"

Falk drove the blade into Hieu's throat. Leaving the knife lodged, he stood and strode out of the building.

Elzac buried his face in his hands. Caide spun away from the scene and stifled a cry behind her palms as Kairos hung his head. Julian collapsed to the floor, dropping Caide's phone. But he could still hear Sam's keening question, "Is Hieu dead?"

His friend's desperate gurgles continued for a moment.

But only for a moment.

~~~

Hunched over the small hotel holodesk, Falk plugged in his encryption stick, rendering every keystroke he performed secure. When he removed the two-inch device, all evidence of his work on the holodesk would go with him.

"Laslo and the Belgae," Hieu had said. The Domestic Terrorism Section's own investigations had yielded a profile for the hypothetical extremist leader. A male, somewhere between his mid-twenties and mid-thirties, who either had access to vast wealth or had received gifts-in-kind from his recruits or supporters. By choosing the name Belgae for his group—a nod to the ancient Gallic tribe of *the people who swell with fury*—he likely possessed a prestigious education outside of Hesperia's borders.

A rich, smart guy. That didn't narrow down much. To top it all off, the lack of a money trail gave DTS no breadcrumbs to follow, and the Belgae's random appearances throughout the country kept them from narrowing down the group's base of operations even to a region. The group sorely lacked military experience of any kind—the fact that they disappeared after the July murder of one of their men supported that hypothesis—but they knew how to do one thing well: Keep quiet.

Falk huffed. He could've found them faster, if he hadn't been banished to Flint Hill and then preoccupied with snatching Marlowe's position. Though truly, playing puppeteer to Mila's marionette had proved quite satisfying. He'd nearly wrung her for all she was worth.

He dug through Hesperia databases, scouring individuals named Laslo for ones meeting the DTS profile. Finally, there he was. Roderigo Laslo, the wild son of the prestigious banker, Thornton Laslo, floating on a path to nowhere down the Arkansas River in Colorado Springs-Colorado. Decent cover.

Just as he'd suspected, Mila was flying like a falcon to the Belgae's core. Now, the circles—Mila's and Rigo's—overlapped. Soon they'd completely close in, forming a perfect bullseye.

31.

THE VOICES IN THE FOLLOWING DAYS ran together like smeared ink. Julian struggled to focus on the expressions of grief and anger, wielded like weapons no one quite knew how to use in those aftershock hours. He struggled to make sense of it all, but the haze pulled him back under.

"Hieu is dead." His own words to Sam, and yet he couldn't believe them. Even though his friend fought and fell before his eyes, the fact floated in his mind unhinged, unanchored. It couldn't possibly be true.

Samantha had cleared the crime scene immediately, and Ada had arrived in the middle of the night to help remove important items and documents from the building and load it onto her underground train.

Then they set the place ablaze. Kairos' orders.

The fog in Julian's mind insulated him from the loss of his home, his business and, most of all, his friend. He operated on autopilot, caring for his mother and scarcely seeing anyone for two days. Now, as he stood with Kairos on the Tesla train station platform, the static finally began to retreat. The doors to one of Ada's train cars slid open, revealing stacks of boxes. Their hastily-scrawled, barely-readable labels nearly overwhelmed him: Zetetics - Security. Zetetics - Docs. Julian - Clothes. Julian - Notebooks.

"Shall we?" Kairos stepped into the car and hoisted the first box.

Julian followed suit. He grabbed one labeled J - Art and peeked inside. One of Mila's pencil-sketched eyes peered back at him. He hadn't spoken to her in almost three days. If he was truly honest with himself, he'd avoided her. It was too much. Hieu's death, his mother's health, the loss of the business he'd built himself—all of it was too much. He set the box on the platform and returned for more. The two men emptied the car within an hour.

Kairos placed his hand on Julian's shoulder. "This is difficult for us all, but perhaps it's harder for you than anyone else here," he said. "If you just want to take the boxes you need right away, I will get the rest for you."

"Thanks. It's actually not bad to be occupied."

"I can help." Mila stood in the archway. "If you want."

Julian's clouded mind left him speechless, but Kairos spoke for him. "It's good to see you're well, Mila. It seems no one has heard from you in a couple of days."

She dipped her chin, stepping toward them. "I know. I needed to process some things. I want to apologize. The way I acted and spoke to you the other day was inappropriate and uncalled for. I should have expressed my concerns diplomatically and respectfully, but instead my past trauma... took over. I am truly sorry."

"It's understandable," replied Kairos.

Mila's eyes darted anxiously between them, and Julian knew she had come with more to offer than an apology. "May I ask," she began gently, "how the Zetetics plan to respond to—Hieu's death?"

Kairos barely concealed a sigh. "We've had to shut down Voltaire's as a Squire location and clear everything out. As far as the community knows, some old electrical wiring caused a fire that ruined everything. But I suppose what you really want to know is how we'll handle Falk."

The name cut through Julian like a lancet.

Mila nodded.

Kairos spoke in patient—but no less assured—tones. "Hieu was one of the most honorable men I know. He was a pillar of morality, as focused and steady as the finest archer, and he was my friend. His murder didn't only leave a glaring hole in our organization, but tore my heart. I would love nothing more than to assure the destruction of Victor Falk."

Julian straightened, watching Kairos intently.

"But that is my personal motivation," Kairos continued. "I need—I *must*—act, as the leader of the Zetetics, only for the good of my entire organization. My personal vendettas cannot color my leadership. So allow me to turn the question over to you, Mila. Why is hunting Falk a mission that works in favor of the Zetetics in its entirety?"

With each heartbeat that Julian waited for Mila's response, an uncomfortable awareness trickled over him: He wasn't only curious about what she'd say. He wanted her to win Kairos over.

She took a breath. "In our last conversation—"

"A generous term."

"—you stressed the importance of long-term advantages. Avoiding confrontations with Falk or Hesperia may serve us now. It may even serve us for years. But, eventually, Falk and Hesperia will turn their attentions on us. It's an inevitable confrontation. We *could* get it over with now—maybe even increasing our strength in numbers if we found an ally in the Belgae."

Julian pursed his lips. There was no way Kairos would accept a partnership with the Belgae.

"Or we can leave it for later. Maybe even for the next generation to handle. Is that really what we want, what we stand for? To run from a problem we have the capacity to solve now, so our *children* can handle it later? Waiting until a battle is unavoidable isn't always wise. And besides, is avenging the death of our friend such an unfair motivation? Falk and Hesperia haven't only murdered *our* friend. They've murdered, wrongfully imprisoned, and committed so many other injustices against countless people. We may be spurred to act because of Hieu, but that doesn't mean it only benefits us."

The faces of the small girls and boys in the gardens at Tesla flashed through Julian's mind. When he and Kairos and the rest of the Zetetics leadership were old and gray, how would those children feel about being forced to react to a situation that their parents and grandparents had avoided, and avoided, and avoided? And would there be any allies left to back them up, or would they face Hesperia alone?

"Mila, I can appreciate your thought processes and will allow that you make valid points," Kairos said. "But for now, my stance still holds. The Zetetics weren't founded upon the notion of changing the world, of saving society. They were born from failed revolutions, overturned idealism, and the painful truth that entropy is an inevitability within every society. Order to disorder. There is nothing inherently wrong with any political philosophy, except that they depend upon humans to carry them out. And in our humanity lies our downfall, every society's downfall."

"Even your own?"

"Even our own. All the Zetetics are concerned with—all we've ever been concerned with—is preserving what we've created for ourselves. We've opted out of the mess above. We've blazed our own path. Our intention isn't to be cold or merciless— indeed, we have been a refuge for anyone who seeks us out, as you did. But even if we did go against Hesperia and we succeeded in the short-term, if we prevailed against Hesperia and dismantled the unjust system, we cannot leave a vacuum. Yet we also will not fill it. To try to rescue a people who are complicit in their own oppression will do nothing but pull us back along into their tide. And once the world of the Zetetics is gone, it's gone forever."

He walked toward her and placed his hands on her shoulders. When he spoke, his voice was tender, yet firm. "I loathe Victor Falk. I mourn Hieu's murder, more deeply than you can fathom. But I must stand true to these people, the Zetetics, who have *chosen* to leave Hesperia and the Gair Empire because *they didn't want it anymore*, they saw no hope there, and wanted another life. To force them back from where they came, to force them into a fight they never wanted in the first place, is betrayal. We cannot do it. I will not do it." He released his grip on her and stepped back. "If that's unacceptable to you, Ada can return you aboveground at your own risk."

Julian watched as Mila eyed Kairos. Then her eyes shifted to him. In the presence of his love and his leader existed the personification of his struggle. It spun like a whirlpool within him, and in his pain and exhaustion, no words would come. He grasped for them, but could manage nothing before Mila spoke again.

"Understood. Now, how can I help you both?"

Kairos smiled. "Thank you for this open and professional discussion, and thank you for your offer, but I think Julian and I have it handled."

Mila nodded. She flashed one more look to Julian, then turned and left.

With every fading footstep, his desperation grew. He turned to Kairos. "Do you mind if I...?"

Kairos waved him away. "Go on. I'll take care of this."

Julian ran into the atrium. "Mila, wait." She stopped and he caught up with her. "I could use some fresh air." He laughed nervously, remembering where they were. "Would you like to go to the garden with me?"

"Okay."

They crossed the atrium in palpable silence. In his mind, he started their conversation hundreds of different ways. When they stood in the bright morning sunlight together, he finally said, "I'm sorry I've avoided you lately."

"It's okay. I understand. I haven't exactly sought you out either."

"Oh." He hadn't realized. He shifted uncomfortably, then walked farther into the garden, leading her to a large white elm. He sat and leaned against its trunk, and she joined him. "I thought I'd found it," he spoke into the cerulean sky. "I thought I'd found my stance. My answer. But everything—Hieu, Laslo's reappearance, my mother's changing condition—has shaken me. I'm confused. I don't know which way is the right way anymore. And because of all of this, I'm frozen." He looked at her, and a plea that could not be hinged to words welled within him. "I've never been frozen before, Mila."

Her marvelous eyes implored him, piercing into his spirit and searching for understanding in a way no one else ever had. Lost in the intensity of her gaze—one half the color of a gray day, the other as fresh a green as the elm leaves fluttering above them—he almost missed it when she asked, "Are you frozen by love or by fear? And are you prompted to move by love or by fear?"

Love for his mother kept him still. Love for the people moved him. Fear for his mother kept him still. Fear for the people moved him. Fear for himself calcified his stance. Love for others rocked him. "I don't know anymore. Both can be at work at once, can't they?"

"I think so."

He clutched both of her hands.

"I can't tell you what your answer is, Julian. I'm sorry I tried before."

"Stop." Reaching up, he brushed her cheek with his thumb. "You have upended my world and capsized it with questions. Whatever journeys we have ahead, isn't it a tragic illusion always to be assured of ourselves?"

~~~

Mila watched Julian retreat into the atrium. Leaning against the elm tree, she stared up at the complex tangle of branches, with delicate, uncertain leaves shivering at their tips and blue skies filling in the spaces. She was thankful for its shroud around her, so she could steep in her confusion privately.

Her thoughts reeled. Did the Zetetics act in cowardice, or pragmatism? Selfishness or rational altruism? And how was it possible to confuse any of those qualities with the other? Were the Belgae on a fool's errand, or brave? If David had lost his fight against Goliath, how would the telling of his story have changed? What about the Pilgrims or the Palatines—cowards for running away, or wise for recognizing a futile fight?

Was the answer only found in how their stories ended?

Aside from the histories, the morals of the stories, the Zetetics and the Belgae, Hesperians and

Hesperia... where did that leave her? Where did she stand? And should stances ever change?

She plumbed the depths within her, combing mind and memory for all the wisdom she'd ever witnessed, but came up empty. Like Sisyphus and his rock, would she forever be lowering her bucket of questions into a bone-dry well?

One thing was now clear: She couldn't agree with the Zetetics.

She stood. Her feet moved before her mind could catch up. In moments, she stood on the train platform. "Ada?" she called.

The husky woman appeared in the doorway of the conductor's cabin, a half-eaten sandwich in one hand, and one cheek puffed out, mid-bite. "What can I do ya for, darlin'?"

"Where are you going after this?"

Ada swallowed. "Don't rightly know, myself. Just dropped all them boxes off. Can't go back to Savannah for a while. Might go West."

"Will you be here for a while longer?"

"Another hour or two."

"Wait for me, please."

Ada saluted her with her sandwich and returned to her cabin. Mila walked back toward the apartments. Just one more thing.

~~~

460 Leah Noel Sims

Hours later, old leaves crunched under Mila's boots as she trekked through the Colorado woods, shielded by towering spruce trees. The raucous rushing of the nearby river drowned out all other noise, and Mila reveled in it. When was the last time a Zetetic heard the sound of a river?

She'd kept nothing on her that could implicate them in the event that she was discovered. But she'd memorized the address and the rough path to her destination. When she arrived, he was closing up the souvenir shop. He spotted her in the parking lot as he was flipping the sign on the door from Open to Closed.

"Sorry," he called. "Day's done. River tours start again at eight tomorrow morning."

"I'm not here for a river tour," she said.

He shook water out of his dark hair and scratched his head. "Huh. Well, call me confused."

Walking toward him, she asked, "Can I call you Rigo instead?"

32.

RIGO'S MAGNECAR PITCHED as he swerved around the twists and turns of the road. Clutching the door handle, Mila breathed deeply to stay the undulating in her stomach and squinted into the darkness. "We're not going far, you said?"

"Nope." Rigo tugged the steering wheel. The car fishtailed.

She thought she might get sick.

"So you escaped from Flint Hill almost three weeks ago, huh? Whatcha been up to since then?"

"Trying to get to you." She pursed her lips and released another breath. "A difficult thing to do after you've faked your own death. Not many traditional avenues for travel and lodging are open to me." She bit her lip and prayed she'd succeed in keeping the Zetetics—especially Julian—off Rigo's radar.

"I see. You must be quite the woodswoman."

"Desperate times, and all that."

"Don't I know it. So—fun fact—Hesperia doesn't know who I am. They know of the Belgae, but we've managed to keep the names of the leaders secret. How'd you find me?"

"The source I told you about. Carlo DaVanti," she lied.

Rigo's eyes widened. "God. Carlo told us about the data facility, did some stuff for us, then he disappeared. What happened to him?"

"He died at Flint Hill."

He slammed his palm on the steering wheel. "God. No matter how many times the government screws one of us over... I shouldn't be thrown by now, but I always am." He pressed a button on his steering wheel and the ringing of a phone call sounded in the car's speakers. "Pardon me," he said. "Due diligence."

"Rigo," a female voice answered. "She checks out."

"Really?" He sounded mildly surprised.

Mila's shoulders relaxed.

"From my crude analysis. You gave me no warning she was coming. I can do more."

"Sure. Thanks, Emory. We'll see you in a minute."

"We—?"

But Rigo hung up. He slowed as they approached a gravel drive. Smacking a button on the dash, he lowered the wheels of the magnecar and turned onto the road. A wrought iron gate with a cursive L on each door blocked their way a few hundred yards later. Pulling up to a security box, Rigo rolled down his window. He leaned out and peered into the box. It beeped once and the doors glided open. For several more minutes, Rigo led them down the gravel driveway, flanked in forest cover on either side, until it turned into pavement and brought them to a grand stone mansion. The car rolled around the circular drive, pulling in between the front steps and a crescent-shaped fountain spurting water in graceful plumes.

Rigo turned off the car. "Okay, then. Lez go." He exited the car and waited for her by the steps.

She followed, maintaining her focus on her host and not the magnificence of their surroundings.

"Place makes you curious about my river tours, huh? Must be a pretty popular experience, to afford me all this."

"I wasn't going to ask," she said.

"I'll save you the trouble. It's my dad's. He's a banker."

One of the primary financial backers for the Belgae, too. I know.

At the top of the steps, Rigo completed an additional retina scan to unlock the front doors. When they automatically swept open, Mila's eyes widened at the opulence before her. Pearly white marble floors glistened in the expansive living area, which had to be at least twice as tall as it was wide. The evening summer sun blazed through four arched windows, which revealed a balcony and the tips of trees manicured into perfect spirals, hinting at a pristine courtyard beyond. To Mila's right and left, staircases coiled flirtatiously to the upper level, each leading to a hallway. She looked up. A delicate chandelier—fashioned of crystals spun so thin, they could've been woven by spiders—hung in a masterful tangle of illuminated ringlets and curlicues.

Sorely conscious of her sweaty T-shirt, dirt-caked zip jacket and jeans, and muddy shoes, Mila stopped as Rigo—in his dried bathing suit and T-shirt—walked ahead of her and collapsed on one of two gold-colored, velvet wingback couches.

"Don't be shy," he said. "The place looks pretentious, but I'm not. Everything will clean."

Still, Mila removed her shoes. She took delicate steps to the other couch, but couldn't bring herself to sit down. She looked around uncomfortably, but the echoing sound of footsteps prompted Rigo to stand again, rescuing her from further awkwardness.

A willowy woman, with hair as blonde as moonlight and a pensive countenance to match, entered the room, dressed smartly in all black. Emory McFallon, Mila remembered. But wasn't she based in Pacifica?

She joined Rigo at the couch but remained standing. Her glacial blue eyes assessed Mila with cool, but not unfriendly, detachment.

Mila blinked under the scrutiny.

"She's in," said her host.

"Impulsivity, Rigo," warned Emory. "I can do more reconnaissance." When she spoke, her lips barely moved. Her voice was quiet, but assured, like the humming wings of a dragonfly.

"This isn't an impulsive decision, this is a gut decision. My gut says she's in the clear."

"I want to do more."

Rigo stood. "Fine. But I want her to help sway Hawthorne when we meet with him tomorrow."

Emory raised her eyebrows.

"He's leaving Hesperia in a matter of days. This is our only shot with him, and her story could tip the scales just enough. The timing couldn't be better."

Emory nodded and faced Mila. "Normally, we're more careful than this. Time is tight. I'll vet you as we go."

An image of Falk prowling the forest outside gripped her. Falk couldn't track her anymore. In his rabid anger, he'd murdered Hieu. Julian said Hieu hadn't provided any hint of Mila's whereabouts, but she knew better than to allow that to lull her into a false sense of safety.

"Wait," said Mila. "An agent of Hesperia—Victor Falk—is after me. He's been at my heels at every turn. I need to know how you've kept Hesperian officials off your trail, or I can't stay here—it won't be safe for any of us if I do. How have you managed to keep them from identifying you?"

"It's been a multi-pronged approach," Rigo began. "Of course, I'm the no-good, mooching son with a go-nowhere job as a river tour guide, so there's that. But the team is constantly casting out red herrings for Hesperia to chase after. And as a prestigious banker who works closely with Hesperia, Dad manages to wine and dine their officials regularly, keeping our enemies close and whatnot. During those times, we move all of our equipment but the essentials to the cellar, and make ourselves scarce. And Emory is a formidable investigator, hacker, and skip tracer."

Mila cocked her head. "Skip tracer?"

"She finds people who have disappeared on purpose. Things, too. But mostly people. And since she's a professional follower, she knows what signs to look at to see if we're being followed or watched." He shrugged. "Her legal background is a plus, too."

Mila looked at Emory. The quiet, waif-like woman sure packed a punch. "You'll watch for Falk?"

She nodded. "You can stay with me. I'm having dinner sent up soon. Have you eaten?"

Mila's stomach growled. "It's been a while."

"Come with me, then. Rigo, have Anna clean Mila's shoes and bring them up later."

Mila followed Emory. If the Belgae were a bracelet, Emory would be the chain and Rigo the charm. Her sparse pattern of speech caused Mila to think her new roommate was most at home behind the scenes, rather than swaying the crowds as her partner had done.

Emory led her up the spiral staircase on the left and down a wide hallway with three arched, wooden doors on either side. The hall ended in a circular sitting room with floor-to-ceiling windows, lavender furniture, and a grand piano, but Emory stopped at the first door on the right, withdrew a key from her pocket, unlocked the door, and held it for Mila.

Two twin beds—both meticulously made—gave the room an inn-like quality, but the comparison stopped there. A holodesk sat under six wall-mounted monitors, five of which currently read, ENTER PASSCODE TO ACCESS FEEDS. Lines and lines of white text skittered over the sixth monitor, as the screen scrolled continuously to keep up. Orderly stacks of papers and notebooks adorned both nightstands, the window seat directly across from the door, and the breakfast nook in the opposite corner.

Mila's eyes widened. "All of this is your sole responsibility?"

"I've got it down to a system now." Emory pointed to the sixth monitor. "That one's been my labyrinth. Carlo's data dump. I've been going through it for over a month and still haven't hit bottom."

Emory opened a door to their immediate right, revealing her closet. "I'll have what you're wearing washed. In the meantime, my clothes should fit."

She picked up a neatly folded set of pajamas and offered them to Mila. "Shower's that way." She cocked her head in the direction around the corner.

"Thank you."

Taking the clothing, Mila walked into the bathroom and flicked on the light, squinting against the bright glare. White tile floors collided into white walls, and the white tiled shower even had a sensible white shower curtain. The white porcelain counter was spotless, holding nothing except a simple white vase containing a bouquet of makeup brushes. If Emory's housekeeping habits were any indication of her leadership skills, the Belgae were in more than capable hands. She looked at her feet and winced. Crusted dirt from her clothes had crumbled around her. With more care than a museum curator, she removed her clothing and stashed them in the trash. Maybe she could wipe up the mess she made with—she glanced around— the *white* towels? She rolled her eyes. Sighing, she turned on the shower.

When she came out of the bathroom, a tray table with a thick sandwich and steaming bowl of soup stood beside her bed. Emory perched atop her own.

Mila sat on the bed. "This looks excellent, thank you."

They ate in silence, with Emory occasionally glancing over at Mila with unshared questions in her eyes. Finally, her hostess asked, "Why now?"

"I'm sorry?"

"The Belgae have been organized and active for a few years. I know from my research who your family was. Rigo even tried to recruit your parents. Why us, and why now?"

Mila bit her lip and paused to think. "We— Hesperians, I mean—were always taught that because of the infrastructure of our government, accountability was inherent in the way our country operated. If there was corruption, if there was wrongdoing, if the balance of power tipped too far in one way or another, there were checks. Things would right themselves, because that's how the *system* was designed." She cast a knowing glance at Emory. "My parents knew better. They taught me that once corruption passes a certain level, there's nothing that can be done except beat it at its own game. I argued with them for many reasons, one of them being that I still believed in the role of journalism in keeping systems honest. But as I worked, and as I watched and listened and questioned, my trust developed fissures, and then cracks.

"The rulebook—the system—is all well and good. But it means nothing if people don't play by it. And our leaders and representatives have an affinity for loopholes, for technicalities, that allow them to play outside the system in actuality without playing outside the system in technicalities. Still, I thought"—she swirled her spoon in her bowl and sighed—"I thought where every other aspect of the system hadn't, journalism could provide accountability. It's the watchdog, the messenger to the people. But so much of journalism revolves around stories that serve the lowest common denominator. And that lowest common denominator eats up budgets and manpower, energy and attention, so there's hardly anything left for the real stories—the important stories. And those stories often don't get told. Too expensive, too time consuming, 'lack of editorial interest'"—even now, Alyson Vernon's words were difficult to utter—"but the people still need to know."

Images from her time at HBN flashed through her mind. It seemed eons ago. An entirely different existence that might've happened to an entirely different person. She reached for her glass of water and took a sip, then stared into it as if it contained her words. "Even when I began to understand my parents' will to fight, I couldn't embrace their perspective. In my mind, to drag the people down a path they didn't choose is the same kind of betrayal, of tyranny, my parents hated so ardently.

"Awareness is the key. I landed in Flint Hill because I intended to tell the people the truth. The rulebook should've protected me. But it didn't, because they don't play by it." She met Emory's solemn blue gaze and said, "I don't have faith in Hesperia, and my faith in journalism has been wounded, critically. But I still have faith in the people, Emory, and I still believe that awareness is the key. If they only *knew*... I really think we could change things for the better."

Emory's face didn't move, but the light of a smile traveled across her eyes. "So do we," she said. "Let's get some rest. Big day tomorrow." Reaching for the lamp on the table between them, she turned off the light. "Mila?"

"Yes?"

"I pulled up your obituary. You faked your death in Bay, in Savannah."

"Yes."

"Did you ever frequent an establishment called Voltaire's?"

Her insides somersaulted. "No."

"It burned down the other day. No one was hurt. The owner was a friend of Rigo's. If you knew him, maybe you could put us in touch."

"Sorry."

Loss twisted inside of her. Julian, Natalie, Chet and Trudi had almost become her family—even her home. Yet she'd chosen her love for the people—and her need to bring Falk to justice—instead of them. Should she have abandoned the people and her convictions in favor of her own love and security? How unfair it was, that she couldn't keep both. Had she made the right choice? Or would only the results of her efforts, the end of it all, provide the answer?

~~~

When Julian returned to his apartment, a mountain of stacked boxes greeted him outside the door. Still mulling over his conversation with Mila several hours before, he rubbed the back of his neck and groaned—then stepped around the heap and entered his apartment. After he'd cooked and shared dinner with his mother, cleaned the kitchen, and found solace in some sketching, he finally mustered his waning energy to unpack—or, at least, move the boxes inside. By midnight, just two boxes remained. He hoisted one but the sound of footsteps rushing up behind him stopped him before he carried it inside.

"Have you seen Mila?" Chet asked, breathless. He clutched his round belly. Kairos approached behind him.

"We were talking in the garden around lunchtime. I left her under the elm tree. She never came home?" He walked into his apartment and set the box in the hall.

Chet shook his head and gulped. "No," he said, leaning on the doorframe.

"She hasn't trained with Elzac on the QSS, either," Kairos added. "I thought she was with you. I'll get that box."

"I got it—"

Kairos lifted the box and an envelope, stuck to its bottom, fluttered to the floor.

Julian stooped to pick it up. Scrawled on the front, in hasty cursive, was his name. His pulse halted. He tore it open.

"From her?" asked Chet. Kairos set the box down.

He nodded, his focus locked on the letter in his hands.

Julian,

I needed to tell you goodbye this afternoon, but the words wouldn't come out when I was with you. But even then, it hadn't become clear that it was my time to leave. Now I know it is.

It is a deeply serious matter to leave the Zetetics, especially without an official announcement, I understand. Please believe me—I promise I will tell no one about my time here.

I care so deeply for you and will never forget you. As much as I wish that our answers in life were the same, now I can respect that they aren't. No matter what, I'm grateful for the wisdom I've gleaned from you and Natalie.

Julian, we'll forever be searchers, won't we? Though I am moving, don't let that cause you to think that I've found what I'm looking for. Because maybe this mysterious pull we call purpose isn't a grand, overarching philosophy. Maybe it's amorphous. Maybe it's like the weather, it changes all of the time.

I hope it's true, because then maybe you and I will meet again.

Mila.

Understanding knocked the wind out of his lungs. He looked at Chet and Kairos, his eyes wide and unblinking. "You have to let me go to the Belgae."

"What?" Chet asked.

Julian spun and rushed into his apartment with the two men trailing behind him. His mother struggled to her feet from her rocking chair in the living room.

"Julian," Kairos began, "you mustn't pursue someone who doesn't want to be here in the first place. You have to let her—"

"Die?" Julian shouted. The word bayonetted him as he uttered it. He yanked a backpack off his dresser, throwing open the drawers and shoving clothes in by the handful. "Hieu lied to Falk to keep her safe, don't you remember? He sent Falk on a rabbit trail, but now Mila is heading right for him." Every muscle in his body trembled at the thought of losing her.

"How are you certain she's gone to the Belgae?"

"I know her. She wants to destroy Falk, but more than anything, she believes the world can be saved—and that she can help save it. She and the Belgae are perfect for each other."

"You can't leave. It's dangerous for you, for your mother, for all of us. It's far too risky, and the chances that you'll succeed in convincing this woman—"

Julian whirled and stepped toe-to-toe with Kairos. "You will *not* tell me I'll fail," he spat. "I'll be damned if I let Mila die without so much as trying to save her." Slinging the backpack over his shoulder, Julian pushed around the men and strode into the living room.

Kairos rushed behind him. "You will jeopard-ize—"

"*Kairos.*" Natalie's strong voice froze all three men. Leaning on her walker, she lifted her chin and fixed a gentle, authoritative look on the Tesla direc-tor. "You are a skilled leader. You have a sharp mind, and you're loyal to your people. But hear me now—you are wrong." She inched closer to him until her walker nearly pressed to his abdomen. "You will not speak failure onto Julian, Mila, or our group. You will not declare this battle lost when it hasn't even been fought. Love calls us to defy logic and to defy the odds. It is not your place to dis-suade someone from acting in love. Julian will go." Natalie smiled as Kairos stood statue-still, his mouth agape. Finally, he nodded.

Julian rushed into the kitchen. "The Laslo man-sion is only a few hours from here," he called as he stuffed food into his bag. "If I move fast, I might even beat her there."

"It's midnight, son—"

"You don't need to be traipsing around the woods at midnight," Chet interrupted. "You'll waste more time stumbling around."

He shifted anxiously. "You don't understand—if I didn't have to bring food or water, I'd already be out the door. I can't sit still. Falk could already be there."

"Come with me," said Kairos, walking to the door. "We'll use the time to ensure you're prepared."

Julian followed him into the hall, but then turned and hurried to his mother. Clasping her shoulders, he looked into her eyes. "Mama, are you sure you'll—?"

"I'll be fine," Natalie said.

"I got her, boy," Chet said. "Now go!"

In the Espionage Department, Kairos outfitted Julian. He clasped a delicate pair of tweezers and hovered over a metal tray containing rows of thread-thin coils ranging in color from platinum to black. He lifted a brassy gold one for Julian to see.

"A communication coil," Julian said. "Last time I saw one, they were much thicker."

"Elzac and Moltov refined the ComCoil. Now, it will fit snugly around one of your ears and no one will think it's anything other than a strand of hair. This one will match your color. And now it's waterproof." He offered the ComCoil.

Julian took it and curled it tightly around his right ear. "How'd you get around the buttons that it used to have?"

"We can always speak to you—we'll show discretion of course. All you have to do is tap it once to turn yourself on, then tap again to turn it off. All it takes is a simple scratch of the ear, or tucking hair out of the way. Nonchalant movements and no one will suspect."

"And if it falls out?"

"Don't let it fall out. We'll increase our monitoring of both Falk and the Belgae—which may prove a challenge, with only one QSS machine, but we'll streamline who to watch, when. Now, let's test your ComCoil." He walked to a sleektop and turned it on. "No one's used this one, so I need to identify it and connect it with all of Tesla's communication devices."

"More than just the sleektops now?"

"Everything. The QSS can sense it, as can the tablets and the handheld ComWands."

They established the connection, tested it, and tweaked the volume levels. Finally, Kairos said, "Sunrise is around the corner. I'll walk you up."

In moments, Julian and Kairos stood next to Tesla's secret cave entrance, deep in the Colorado woods. The night sky weakened, relinquishing its grip on the sun. A cautionary wind whipped around them as if to hurry Julian on his way.

Lifting his face to the sky, Kairos closed his eyes, just for a moment. "No matter what we do below, the wind and sky are never as beautiful as above."

"Do you ever miss it?" Julian asked.

"It's the sacrifice I chose." Kairos pursed his lips. "Your mother was right. While I focused on remaining loyal to our people, I would have been disloyal to you—and to Hieu. He died protecting Mila. We cannot let it be in vain. Be safe."

Kairos retreated into the cave. Steeling his gaze on the shady forest before him, Julian trudged ahead into the world he'd left years before. He only hoped he wasn't too late.

33.

A KNOCK SOUNDED AT THE DOOR—Rigo had arrived. Mila anxiously twisted the fabric of Emory's navy business suit and gave herself one last inspection in the full-length mirror. The clothing almost fit, but the taller woman's arms were slightly longer. She smoothed her hair, which fell in carefully-styled curls down her back, dabbed on a modest layer of rosy lip color, and slipped into the conservative pair of black heels Emory had set out for her. She hadn't put this much effort into her appearance since she'd worked at HBN. The sensation of professionalism—normalcy—wrapped around her like a blanket that wasn't hers to keep. Nervously, she smoothed her slacks, saying a silent prayer that she'd shine in the meeting with Hawthorne. She left the bathroom and opened the door.

Rigo, his wavy black hair and chestnut eyes pairing nicely with his black suit, cut a dashing figure. He smiled, his teeth gleaming white. "Let's head to the East Wing." He waved for her to follow him as he strode toward the other side of the mansion. "Hawthorne will be checking in with us soon. There's just enough time to let you meet some of the group."

In sharp contrast to the West Wing, the short hallway in the East Wing opened into a ballroom with richly-colored, medallion-patterned carpet and dramatic velvet curtains, drawn closed. But in lieu of elegant dining tables and a grand piano, rows upon rows of holodesks lined the ballroom floor. The Belgae—Mila estimated close to two hundred—tapped away on the devices, so focused that no one noticed their leader enter the room.

"What is everyone working on?" she asked Rigo.

"Public image. We've got decent numbers—though we could always use more—but what we really need is public support and sympathy. So they're writing editorials, starting and participating in conversations around the web, et cetera. *You* will be a great help with that." He clapped her on the back and she nearly stumbled in Emory's high heels. As she watched the group in front of her, she imagined herself seated among them, crafting persuasive messages and leading discussions, guiding the Hesperian people to awareness, truth and, finally, change. A small smile crept to her lips as she considered her new role, but she stifled it. After her time at the Zetetics, she'd learned better than to let herself get swept up into a movement before fully understanding who they were. And yet, what other choice remained?

Rigo marched ahead of her to the front of the room. Unsure if she should follow, Mila stayed by the ballroom doors.

"Good morning, everyone," he called. The sounds of tapping subsided as the Belgae returned his greeting. "Every day, you all *move* me, in my core." He thumped his fist on his chest. "We all remember what it was like to feel hopeless and out of control. To feel like we could never—*never!*—stand up to the entrenched, gargantuan force of Hesperia. That nothing could change. But now? Oh, friends!" He smiled widely. "Now we know better!"

Some Belgae clapped, while others called, "Hell, yeah!"

Rigo held up his hands and the room quieted. "Change is coming. We've got numbers, we've got strategy. Most importantly, we've got each other. But there's one thing we need." He paused dramatically and looked around at his team. "A dynamic, irresistibly positive public image."

The Belgae scanned each other's faces for reaction. Confused looks shot at Rigo. Mila bit her lip. She'd witnessed the media's treatment of the Belgae from the inside. Building the type of public image Rigo desired would be a more formidable task than he could fathom.

"You all are working on that right now, and have been for months. Years, really, but the media keeps their eyes averted. Friends, starting now, the journalists won't be able to ignore us. We are going to give them a face. We're going to give the people a heart to beat for, because we all know that numbers and facts can help, but it's *stories* that move people. *People* move people. *You* move people. And finally, we have a story—a woman —who isn't afraid to stand up, to speak. She doesn't hide behind anonymity. Her name is Mila Ray."

He stretched out one arm in her direction, and every neck craned to look at Mila. Her stomach shivered like a bird in a birdbath. Rigo motioned, and she walked to the front of the room to join him, her steps teetering in Emory's heels.

"Mila's story encapsulates our struggle. She spent her entire childhood being groomed by her parents—revolutionaries themselves—until Hesperia killed them. Alone, Mila fought to get the people's stories heard through her work at the Hesperia Broadcasting Network. She fought to get Theo Wilkes'—our friend and brother, slain in cold blood by Hesperia—story heard. But she was shut down. Displaying intense bravery, she met with a source—we all remember Carlo DaVanti and how he helped us"—heads shook and dropped sullenly at the mention of Carlo's name—"and Mila was determined to get the information he shared out there. Then she was arrested, and held—tortured—in Flint Hill Detention Facility before she escaped.

"Until now, Mila has been in hiding. But after everything—every horrific event she's been through—she is *still* determined to speak to the people and to fight for something new. The people will know us now. The *real* us, not the backwoods terrorists the media talks about, *if* they even talk about us. We are going to *grab* the face of the media and *turn* it to our cause—we will *make. Them. Help. Us. Win!*"

The Belgae jumped to their feet. The room erupted in cheers and applause.

"We're ready for you, Hesperia!" Rigo shouted. He grabbed Mila's hand and thrust it upward in victory.

Mila smiled and squinted against the dazzling ballroom lights as she looked at Rigo, at his chiseled face, gleaming white teeth, and sparkling dark eyes. Charisma cascaded from him. He possessed the looks of Apollo, and projected the confidence of Narcissus, the bravery of Achilles, the passion of Hector, the guile of Odysseus. It was no wonder he had a following. Looking away from the leader, she met the gazes of many Belgae. She doubted anyone could detect her reserve as she remembered Rigo desperately careening through Savannah in search of Julian. The Belgae had an enrapturing leader, great numbers, strategy, and a face for the cause, but they lacked tools—namely technology sufficient for standing up to Hesperia. But no one seemed concerned. How could they, under the blinding guiding light of Rigo, their sun?

The room began to quiet as Rigo spoke again. "Soon, Roger Hawthorne of Hawthorne Defense Industries will conference in. We know he's supported us in mind. We know he's privately held concerns about Hesperia—about the very work of his own defense contracting company. Today, I think we will convince him to take the leap, to take meaningful action when our day comes."

At that moment, a ringing sound emanated over the speakers in the ballroom. A call patched through, and a grim-faced, middle-aged man appeared on the large screen hanging behind Rigo.

"Mister Laslo?" the man said.

"Mister Thompson, we're connected, sir. Thank you for facilitating this conversation for us."

"Yes... about that. I'm afraid Mister Hawthorne will have to reschedule. He has—company."

Dread sprouted like a vine in Mila's gut. *Hesperia showed up, I know it.*

Rigo didn't skip a beat. "Understood. I'll be in touch to discuss a better time with you."

"Please do." The man ended the call.

"Well," Rigo clapped his hands once, "let's talk PR." He jaunted to a seat at one of the holodesks at the front of the room and plopped into it. Mila followed him. He pulled a chair out for her with his foot. A couple dozen Belgae members shared the row of holodesks with them, and several more wandered over.

"I've already started on a piece that will rely heavily on Mila's story in order to garner sympathies," one woman said, handing Rigo a sheet of paper.

Rigo's eyes flickered over the document. "Excellent." He handed it back to her. "Writing while I was talking, huh?"

She shrugged and smiled sheepishly. "For a good cause. I'm a multitasker."

"Only kidding. Hey, James," he addressed a tall, lanky man standing close by, "I loved the way you found a podium in the neighborhood forums. *Smart* choice, man. The chatter going well?"

"Without a doubt. Fact is, it's going so well that I've got a score of people helping me maintain and guide the conversation. We've got public support building, Rigo, and her story"—he flicked his gaze on Mila—"is gonna help so much."

Rigo placed his hand on Mila's back. "I think so, too."

"I could do some live, two-way conversations," Mila added, "so the people can ask me questions and learn more about what really goes on in Hesperia's justice system, at least as it pertains to those in similar situations as mine. Maybe it could help us build the relationship and add a personal touch. As long as it's a secured connection—"

"Absolutely encrypted," said Rigo. "Fantastic suggestion."

Her stomach knotted. How confident would Rigo be about his group's security if he'd known how the Zetetics had followed him in Savannah, and watched Pete at the OWA? *Before I do anything on their systems, I have to make certain I'm covered.*

"Mila," said a young woman as she took Mila's hand, "I never want to hear of another person going through what you have. We're going to work tirelessly together to make sure of it."

"Yes, we will," she said.

"I think it's so admirable for you to stand up like this. I can't imagine—"

"I'm sick of this, Rigo!" A man barged into the ballroom. Everyone fell silent. Mila recognized Pete, the man the Zetetics had spied on as he visited the OWA camps.

Rigo stood. "What's up, Pete?"

Pete closed the distance between them, his neck and arms tense, fists clenched. "Stop stalling, man! The Hesperians running the OWA suspect Benny and his crew are up to something. Until they come out with it, they've cut their food and drink allotments in *half!* Do you know how many people have collapsed by the end of the day from dehydration? Fucking too many, man! I swear to God, Rigo, if you don't start putting your words to action, I'm going to fight Hesperia on my own."

He held up his arms. They shook in anger. She looked around the room. Many of the Belgae cast each other sidelong glances, nodding at Pete's words. *Is Rigo's hold on the group as strong as he thinks? What have I truly walked into?*

"I hear you, Pete." Rigo placed one hand on the man's shoulder. Pete tilted his head to the side and pursed his lips into a tight line, as though he were about to fling Rigo's hand—maybe even Rigo himself. "And I feel the same way. But we've got to fight smart."

"Tell me Julian and his group are on board."

Mila's heart skipped a beat, then sank. Rigo had blabbed to the entire headquarters about the Zetetics and his mission to get them on board.

"I can't tell you that."

"Tell me *Hawthorne's* on board, then!"

"Hawthorne had to reschedule. Hesperia showed up at his office when we were supposed to talk."

"We're gonna *lose* them if *you* don't act! And then we'll lose everything. The OWA accounts for almost half of our numbers! You don't have much time before they say 'screw this' and give up on you."

"I understand—"

Pete jabbed a finger into Rigo's shoulder. Rigo winced. "I'm going back in a week," he growled, "and you better give me some fucking good news for them by then." With that, he stormed out of the ballroom. One person started to clap, and was quickly elbowed into silence.

Mila zeroed in on Rigo. His jaw ticked as he watched the door Pete had walked through, his eyes simmering. The Belgae's sun had a dark side.

He took a breath. His gaze locked on hers. He smiled like nothing had happened. "Pete's right, but I can only do what I can do. Let's get some fresh air, and I can fill you in."

As she followed him out of the ballroom and down the staircase, words Julian used to describe the group scrolled through her mind. "Volatile," he had said. The same reason her parents had eyed the Belgae with wariness. If they'd lived longer, they may have joined in the end, seeing it as the only option in their lifetime. But with numbers and strategy—even if they got the tools they needed—would they be able to change Hesperia without turning on each other?

Rigo led her to the balcony, the bright morning sun illuminating the landscape she'd barely been able to discern the night before. Evergreens, sculpted into spirals that reached for the brilliant blue sky, stood in a symmetrical guard around the balcony. On the grounds below, stone pathways lined with colorful flowers led to a pond. To the far left stood a small gardening cottage and an old, broken-down fence behind it.

"That thing's an eyesore," Rigo sighed. "It *was* a garden. Grandfather's favorite place. He never paid anyone to manage the garden. It was his domain. His place of peace. He died a decade ago, and my dad's never been able to bring himself to change a thing with it. I say it's time to move on, but what can ya do?" He shrugged. "Don't let Pete's outburst throw you. I've—we've got things under control. I'll get Hawthorne on board, and then we'll open the floodgates on Hesperia."

"What does Hawthorne bring to the table that no one else can?" Mila asked.

He turned to face her and leaned against the railing. "Hawthorne owns and operates a defense contracting company that performs maintenance and repairs on much of Hesperia Defense's machinery—particularly on the transportation side of things. He even has the ability to disable the magnetism in the roads for the entire country. We know that, privately, his views toward Hesperia have greatly disintegrated. If I can get him to issue an immediate recall of all of the magnecars for Hesperia Defense in the capitol city's area, and maybe even disable the magneroads, we can unleash the battle with a *huge* head start."

"Battle?" Mila repeated. "I've been under the impression that the Belgae wanted a hearing—that they wanted to bend the ear of the people and start a dialogue for change."

"We did. Do." He straightened and paced around the balcony. "That's how we started. Then, we pursued secession, but thought—what the hell are we doing? We aren't just going to *hand* the people and the country to the government and walk away. We don't give up. We fight for change. But we're running out of time. We have to act fast—meaning that even though many of our guys are in there working on a brilliant PR strategy, we might not be able to afford lengthy conversations with the people. They might just have to pick a side." He crossed his arms. "Does that bother you?"

"Blindsiding the people with a bloody revolution bothers me, yes."

He scratched the back of his neck. "Mila, revolutions are not a new thing. Think of all of the uprisings throughout history. Yeah, some of them failed, but many of them succeeded. It was painful—it came at a huge cost—but weren't they worth it? Weren't they celebrated? Weren't those people hailed as heroes in history?"

"But if we steal the country, rob the people of the choice in their own fate... if we acquire leadership by immoral means, aren't we destined to cave to the same fate in the future?"

"Sometimes the ends justify the means."

"Or sometimes the means *are* the ends."

"'You do what you can with what you have and clothe it in moral garments.' Didn't you read Alinsky? Come look at Grandfather's garden." Grabbing her hand, he pulled her to the railing. "It's covered in weeds, completely overgrown. There are even young trees growing there now. You can barely *enter* the place, much less grow anything useful in it. What can you do? You can't work around the weeds. You can't reason with them and ask them to make room for the good stuff, or say, 'Hey, would you consider not sucking the life out of things and produce a tomato instead?' You can't even ask the soil to stop feeding the weeds and put its energy toward nourishing only the produce. Yeah, there's a fence around it, and yeah, it's called a garden because—for a long time—it *was* a garden and a hell of a good one. But now look at it, Mila." He stabbed an accusatory finger in its direction. "*That* is *not* a garden. Not anymore. And there's nothing you can do to make it a garden again but bulldoze the hell out of it. Clean slate. It's not anyone's favorite option. It wasn't even our first option. But now? Now it's our *only* option."

For a moment, Mila thought Rigo might say more. Instead, he abruptly walked back toward the home. Then, he stopped. "Look," he said, without glancing back at her. "I'm going to meet with Hawthorne. I'm *going* to get his support, one way or another. You could really, really help me out in this, and I hope you will. This is how we do things, Mila. We don't equivocate. If you're with us, neither can you." He opened the door and went inside.

She watched Rigo through the glass doors, striding across the mansion floor and greeting those he encountered with hypnotic congeniality. Split between a desire to reflect on his words and a desire to punch him, she spun and walked down the balcony steps and to the fence surrounding the former garden.

Were her ideas unrealistic? Was it so naive to envision a transformation brought about by peaceful means? If she couldn't agree with Hesperia, the Zetetics, *or* the Belgae, maybe the problem didn't reside in the two revolutionary groups—but within herself. If she couldn't relinquish her white-knuckle grip on her utopian ideals, perhaps she'd be destined to wander alone forever. The hopes she carried pulled, strained like a veil on the brink of tearing.

She focused on the garden. The tangled weeds and brush filled her with helplessness. *If it belonged to me, what would I do?*

~~~

Julian half-trudged, half-raced through the last stretch of brush-tangled woods before the Laslo mansion. Every breath stabbed in his side. He reached the courtyard just in time to see Rigo stride back into the home, leaving Mila on the balcony. He raced to the garden, gravel under his pounding footsteps announcing his arrival.

She turned and opened her mouth as if to shout, but stopped when she saw him. "What are you doing here?" she whispered.

He grasped her shoulders. "Mila, you have to come with me," he panted.

She backed away. "I'm not leaving, Julian—"

"If I'd known you were leaving I would've warned you—"

"I'm not—"

"Falk is coming!"

Terror flared in her eyes. "How does he—"

"Hieu lied to keep you safe. He threw Falk off your trail by telling him you were going to the Belgae. Please, Mila"—he gulped in air—"we don't have much time."

"I'm *not* leaving."

"Mila! Do you hear me—?" The opening of the balcony door silenced him. Julian looked up to see Rigo and Emory running down the stairs.

"Julian goddamned Merrick!" Rigo exclaimed. "What the—how do you two know each other? Did the Zetetics change their minds?"

"The Zetetics did not change their minds. Mila and I were just leaving." He took her hand.

"Leaving?" Rigo's voice was incredulous.

Mila pulled her hand from Julian's. "I'm not leaving. I'm not going to run from Falk to save myself, only to leave everyone else here as his prey."

"Falk is coming?" Rigo shot an accusing look at Emory. "How did you not know this?"

Emory's eyes went saucer-wide. She floundered but didn't respond.

Julian ran his hands through his hair and spun away from the group. "I can't believe what I'm hearing."

The ComCoil clicked. The voices around him faded as Kairos' filled his ear. "Falk isn't in Savannah or Erie, but he's not in Colorado yet either. Hesperia knows everything. A double agent turned them over. If the Belgae fights now, they're ruined."

He turned, watching his former best friends and the woman he loved, their voices warbling in his ears. Everything seemed to move in slow motion. They'd all be destroyed. Imminently.

"Julian?" Kairos asked. "Do you hear me?"

"I hear you." He could barely murmur his response. "The Belgae is ruined."

Mila and Emory silenced. Rigo shoved him. "What the *hell* did you just say?"

"Hesperia... knows everything. About you. Someone gave you away."

"Hawthorne," Emory whispered.

"You're going to lose." His voice nearly broke. His shoulders slumped.

Rigo staggered backward. "No," he choked. He shook his head. "No! Our plan will still work. If we can put it into action immediately, the element of surprise—"

"It won't work, Rigo," Emory stopped him. "We have to think of something else."

He turned on Julian, his lips curled into a snarl. "Well, then. Does your *dear leader* plan to do anything to help us?"

"No. He sent me to get Mila—that's all." The Zetetics' non-interventionist credo had seemed entirely acceptable—until he looked into his friend's angry, pleading eyes and told him they'd provide no help, no protection. A pit formed in his stomach.

"Unbelievable," Emory said.

"Un-*fucking*-believable," spat Rigo. He rushed up the stairs. "I'm going for a drive."

"Rigo!" Emory chased after him.

The balcony doors smacked into the frame. Mila took Julian's hands. "Mila, please—"

"I won't go. Living with the knowledge that I surrendered to injustice is worse than not living at all. Deep down, I think you agree."

Her words knifed him. "Mila." He spoke her name as a plea.

"I don't want to be without you," she said. "*Join* me here. Didn't you want to change the movement when you were here? *Now*, we can—together. We can see Hawthorne's move as our defeat, or we can see it as our opportunity to stand up for the people in a way that is unprecedented in recent history. We can finally deliver the truth and win freedom with peace, Julian, can't you see it?"

His thoughts knotted around themselves. He shut his eyes, unable to stand the fantastic hope shining in hers.

"Don't give up on the people without giving them a chance first."

Meeting her gaze once more, he relented. "I won't give up without giving *you* a chance first."

~~~

When Mila and Julian entered the ballroom, they found the Belgae scrambling like ants in a crushed mound. Mila located Emory in a corner. "Did Rigo really leave?"

"If you knew Rigo, you wouldn't be surprised," she responded flatly. "He can handle himself."

Distaste burned like acid at the back of Mila's throat. What kind of leader bailed in an emergency?

"You told them Hesperia discovered your plans?" Julian asked Emory.

"Took everything I had to get in front of them, but yes." She held out a trembling hand. "You know how much I hate stages and microphones."

Mila scanned the room. Some people jerked plugs out of the walls and floors, wrapping cords and disassembling holodesks. Others rolled out round ballroom tables and carried folded stacks of white tablecloths. "What are we doing now?"

"*We* are dismantling our headquarters and taking it to the cellar. I don't know what *you* both plan to do."

"We're with you," Mila said. Without waiting for Emory's response, she snatched a folded up table leaning against the wall and rolled it into the ballroom. Julian grabbed another. With every passing minute, her skin crawled. Falk was closing in.

In an hour, the ballroom was transformed. By mid-afternoon, the Belgae headquarters functioned fully in the cellar, located under a secret door that blended seamlessly into the tile floor of the foyer. Though they tapped away tirelessly on the holodesks, Mila noticed wary gazes cast around the room with increasing frequency.

She turned to Emory, seated at her holodesk and surrounded by monitors. "Where is Rigo?" she hissed. "Everyone can sense something isn't right. We can't just stay on pause until he deigns to come back."

Emory's shoulders tensed. "I don't know. I'll give him one more hour. I've been monitoring everything. We can afford to give him—"

Julian returned, a case of water bottles under his arm. "Where's—"

"*One* more hour," she repeated.

"And if he's not back then?"

Keeping her eyes on the monitors, she said, "I'll keep doing what I do. Julian, you will resume your leadership role—"

"I've been gone three years, Emory."

"And Mila, you'll become what Rigo intended you to be. The face of the movement." She flashed Mila a pointed look.

"Truth before battle, Emory," she said, willing her manner to stay strong even as her nerves grew brittle. "I refuse to be the face of a bombastic, violent movement."

Emory clasped Mila's forearm, pulling her down to eye level. "You've been here not twenty-four hours. What makes you think you're so important that we'd change our entire operation?"

"I'm not asking you to change it because of me. I'm asking you to change it because it won't work." She shook her head. "My ancestors pursued revolution Rigo's way for two centuries, and they *all* failed. Look behind you, Emory, and there's a graveyard of revolutionaries who already walked the path you're on. We still have time to turn around and choose another one. We bring the people the truth, and we keep everyone under control. Can we agree on that course of action? We only do battle only if we have no other shot at victory."

She hesitated. "Agreed."

Mila's throat ran dry. She turned away and took a deep breath.

Julian bent and spoke into her ear. "It's the opportunity you've always talked about. The messenger to the people. Is it still what you want?"

"Yes," she said. And she knew exactly what she'd tell them.

Suddenly, the cellar door flung open with a crack. Screams ricocheted off the walls. Some Belgae jumped to their feet. Others dove under their desks. Julian blocked Mila's body with his own, obscuring her view. She shoved him out of the way in time to see Pete leap from a rung in the ladder.

He bellowed above the din, "That bastard got himself arrested!"

34.

THE CELLAR ERUPTED in furious clamor at Pete's news. Mila watched Emory push her way through the crowd like a tiny missile until she stood in front of Pete.

"Everyone quiet!" she screamed, and Mila could have sworn she saw the young woman quake like an old barn door. The Belgae hushed instantly, shocked by the shy young woman's outburst. "How do you know this, Pete?"

Pete scanned the room as he spoke. "I saw him stomp out of here like a petulant toddler."

Emory shot him a look.

"Sorry. So I thought I'd follow him, but he drives so damn fast, I couldn't keep up. By the time

I finally find him, he's in Fitz's Bar, one of the only guys in there at lunchtime, and he's so drunk he's singin' at the top of his lungs. I try to get him to come with me, but he tries to start a fight—tells me to leave. So I go stand in the corner and watch. But then, some Amity officers come in—"

Groans rolled across the room.

"—and Rigo sees 'em and just goes berserk. Starts shouting about the Belgae." Pete shook his head as if to refocus his thoughts. "They cuffed him. God, where do you think they'll take him?"

"They'll take him to Flint Hill." Mila's voice rose above the cacophony as she crossed the room to Pete and Emory. "They'll take him to Flint Hill."

As silence swept across the room, she continued, "They'll do to Rigo what they did to me, to Carlo, and to countless others whose names you've never heard. They'll make and mold him into whatever they need him to be. The terrorist, to scare the people into submission. The extremist, to get them to dismiss this movement and all of the ideas it stands for. The example, to quiet anyone who has ever dared to question their power and demand they relinquish even a sliver of it. Rigo will further Hesperia's cause and cement their power. He'll have no choice about it."

Voices climbed, but Mila spoke again, and they quieted. "I know I'm new here. You may not trust me yet. But we need a new plan now, and in order to stand against Hesperia with barely even a fighting chance, we have to have the people on our side. If you'll let me, I'd like to try a new way."

Every face looked to Emory. "I know what we can do," she whispered.

~~~

Fresh from the airport, Falk ambled between Colorado Springs-Colorado's skyscrapers, lit by an angry, setting summer sun. Damn the tracking device—he didn't need it to find Mila, especially since the fool at Voltaire's gave away the Belgae leader Laslo through blood-choked gurgles. Once he'd nailed down Laslo's location, all he had to do was go to Colorado Springs. He'd find Mila among Laslo's anthill of revolutionaries. Anticipation fired through his veins as he pictured the moment he'd intercept her—the horror on her face, the clamminess of her skin.

His earpiece rang.

"Victor, it's Edmund Kent. I just learned Roderigo Laslo was arrested yesterday and will be booked into Flint Hill any minute now—thanks to your investigation. You're quite the one-man show."

"I'm not done yet, sir. As soon as Flint Hill extracts the rest of the information from him, we'll stamp out the Belgae before they cause any more trouble."

"Your men haven't located their base?"

He turned down a wide, busy street, flanked on both sides by tall buildings and dotted with enormous screens displaying news broadcasts from the major network. All networks harped on about tomorrow's Hesperia Games, the country's most televised annual event. He stopped underneath them, plugging one of his ears to deafen himself to the sound of honking magnecars and cacophonous voices. "The Laslo mansion was nothing but normal when our agents arrived to investigate shortly after Laslo's arrest," he said. "Thornton Laslo himself said he'd have shown them around, if he'd been home. Looks like Rigo did his dirty work away from Daddy's house."

"I have to say, Vic, I hoped you'd give me better news than that."

"Have I ever let you down, sir?" He raised his voice. "Trust me when I say this—the Belgae will come to us."

Suddenly, every screen blackened. Kent kept talking, but Falk didn't listen. "Sir, turn on your TV."

"What? Okay... wait, it's malfunctioning."

Falk peered into the windows of the bar nearby. All screens were dark. "It's not malfunctioning. It's the Belgae." But what were they about to do? For the first time in years, he couldn't anticipate the next move of his target. He stiffened.

The screens flickered several times. Bar patrons exited their booths and stood, enraptured at the mystery unfolding in front of them. When an unknown face took the place of the blackness, doors flew open as people hurried onto the sidewalks to watch and listen.

"People of Hesperia, I come to you from the Belgae headquarters."

She stood, dimly lit, against a background of old brick. Shadows all but enveloped her, so that only a dark outline revealed the contours of her neck and her close-cropped hair.

Falk could feel his pupils dilate hungrily. *You don't fool me, Thirty-Four.*

"We're not the terrorists you think we are—if you think of us at all. We're a group devoted to freedom and truth, both of which Hesperia has stolen from you. If you doubt our claims, allow me to show you proof of our devotion and proof of your leaders' deception. Earlier this year, while the news fed you petty stories, Hesperia murdered one of our men."

A brief warning of explicit content replaced Mila, followed by the video of Theo Wilkes' shattered face in the grass. Hesperians groaned, cringed, and clutched themselves—but they watched.

She returned to the screen once more. "You never learned Theo Wilkes' name, did you? Hesperia never wanted you to."

Falk listened, his lips curling into a contemptuous smirk as she shared another name and another story—not her own, but Carlo DaVanti's. Falk glanced around. Hesperians cast wary, fearful looks at each other. Strangers clutched hands. He heard them ask, "Do you think she's trouble? Do you think she's telling the truth?"

If they doubted her, they didn't leave. And she continued to speak.

"Hesperians, what is it to be free? Is it really possible, or is it another plane of living altogether? Is our fullness of life so dependent on our circumstances and our politicians? Are they so powerful that they can watch our every move, chill our every word—even abduct our hope and pilfer our peace? No. We can have hope in a hopeless world. We can have peace in chaos. But the most crucial point to understand is this: We can *be* hope in a hopeless world. We can *bring* peace to the chaos. That is why we, the Belgae, are here. To pursue a better tomorrow in a way our children will be proud of.

"Tomorrow, I will stand outside the Walden Data Facility. Some of the Belgae will be with me. Others will gather around Flint Hill Detention Facility in Kanawha-West Virginia, as well as the Office of Worker Aid, where your fellow Hesperians are not matched to jobs, but are instead enslaved in work camps. There, from our positions, we will make our demands.

"We will demand an end to government surveillance. We will demand an end to work camps. We will demand the release of prisoners whose only crime was questioning their government. We will do it all while modeling the peace that we desire in our country. And we won't stop until we get it.

"Will you be there?"

She disappeared. The screen blackened. Then, the HBN broadcast returned, with the anchor struck wordless.

"Like I said, Ed," continued Falk, "the Belgae will come to us."

"We have to shut it down."

"And stamp out their right to peaceful protest and free speech?" Falk scoffed. "We'll only look like the monsters they say we are. Give them time, Kent. Let them look like a gaggle of fools and liars. Let them tie their own noose."

~~~

The lights went out. The cameras turned off. Without their electrical hums, fear-filled silence hung in the cellar.

In Julian's ear, Kairos sighed. "Her faith in the people is inexhaustible."

"It is," he agreed, keeping his voice low to avoid drawing attention to himself. "That's why they need her."

"They'll let her down."

"I don't think they're what holds her up."

He watched as the Belgae embraced each other, their fists clutching each other's shirts in unspoken desperation. A few approached Mila as she stepped from the stool on the makeshift set. They reached out with shaky hands to grasp hers. Julian tuned in to the chatter happening around him.

"So now our plan is to convince a tyrannical government to do an about-face by *asking nicely?*" one man huffed. "Who's buying that idea?"

"If you have a better one that won't end in our massacre, speak now," Emory said.

The man looked away.

"Rigo's ideas did make me nervous," admitted one person.

"But this one doesn't?" responded another. "We're essentially lying down and exposing our throats to the lion."

"Do you think you'll leave the group?"

"And go where? Back to the way it was before? There's nowhere to go now but forward."

Julian nudged his way through the crowd, toward Mila. She looked even tinier without her long, red hair—the shorter, mouse-brown locks stuck out haphazardly, highlighting her slender neck and thin shoulders. "So," he said. "It's happening. Tomorrow."

"Tomorrow." The glint in her eyes was nearly as solemn as their new brown hue.

"You think it will work?"

"Peace has changed the world before," she said.

"Never in Hesperia."

"No, never in Hesperia. But there are times and seasons for everything. Now is the time."

"And Falk? Do you think peace will take care of Falk?"

Darkness pooled in her gaze like an oil spill. "I will take care of Falk."

~~~

The hours swirled, wild as a sandstorm, so Mila could hardly make sense of the vignettes rapidly unfolding around her. Before she knew it, Emory was ushering Julian, Pete, and her up the cellar ladder, through the mansion foyer and into one of Thornton Laslo's shiny black magnecars.

Emory craned her neck to peer into the car's open window. "Remember—wear your earpieces at all times."

"How long do you think you all will be trapped in the cellar?" Mila asked, worried.

"As long as it takes. It's our official center of operations now. Julian, Mila—stay safe. Pete—behave."

Pete sniffed. "Please. My people at the OWA are just glad we're not stuck anymore. That keeps me happy. You can count on me with all your fingers and toes."

"Fine. Do you have the camera?"

Pete patted the black backpack on his lap.

Emory straightened and tapped the car twice. "Richard, thank Mister Laslo for us."

The chauffeur waved. "Of course, madame. Mister Laslo wishes me to remind you that after I drop these three at the bus station, he cannot in any capacity be involved in the Belgae's doings."

"Yes, Richard, I know," Emory said flatly. "Drive safe." With that, she strode back inside the mansion and the driver guided the car down the non-magnetized drive.

"So, uh, good Mister Laslo ditched his son," said Pete. "Is that it, Dick?"

Richard kept his eyes locked on the road. "No, sir."

"Just us then."

Richard flicked his gaze at Pete, then back to the street.

"We're screwed."

"No," Julian said. "We just have no choice but to succeed."

"*We?* You abandoned ship a long time ago. Far as I'm concerned, you're a spectator."

Mila took a breath to stifle the heat flaring in her chest at Pete's comment. But even she couldn't help but question Julian's commitment.

35.

THE FIRST RAINDROPS FELL around four in the morning, as Mila, Julian, and Pete stepped off the empty bus that took them from Colorado to the lonely stop about five miles from the Walden in Jordan-Utah. The rust-red, sandy soil gritted under Mila's thick-soled boots even while wet with rain. Hoisting the large pack she carried over her shoulder, she placed a hand on Julian's arm to steady herself, then looked out. A few straggling stars managed to escape the clouds. The August landscape stretched endlessly before them, but far in the distance blazed lights of an unheavenly kind.

Walden.

Julian unzipped his backpack and handed out bottles of water. "Hope everyone's legs rested up on the way over here."

Mila clutched the bottle and walked forward, with the men flanking her either side. She kept her pace brisk even as the straps of her backpack dug grooves into her shoulders and each step sent thuds of fear through her. In a matter of hours, she'd be in front of a camera, speaking once more to Hesperia—if she made it that far. She squinted, examining the distant Walden as best she could and saw no sign or silhouette of Amity officers, but that did little to allay her growing anxiety.

"Could Hesperia be waiting for us?" she asked. "Certainly they see us coming."

"It'd give us too much validation," Pete said. "If you look back at how they handled any other demonstrations in the past—the few that there were—they try to ignore until they can't anymore."

Julian snorted.

Mila looked at Julian, then Pete. They kept their eyes far ahead on the Walden, their mouths set in thin, determined lines. *This could be my end—the end of all of us. Is it worth it? How simple it could have been, long ago, to turn away and pray that someone else carry the torch for truth. And yet here we are putting country above all—and to what end? Will our lives only matter if we triumph?*

Within a couple of hours, sizzling electrical fences, barbed wire, and warning signs demanding that trespassers KEEP OUT stopped their advancement miles ahead of the facility itself.

Trespassers will be shot without warning beyond this point.

Danger: Military property.

Far ahead, almost in the vanishing point of the scene before them, Mila discerned the building—a rectangular block, ghastly gray under the harsh glare of stadium lights.

Pete stepped ahead of them, wiped the rain from his face and brought a pair of binoculars to his eyes. He laughed.

"What?" asked Mila.

Handing her the binoculars, he said, "Look."

She did. Carved into a concrete slab sign were the words, WELCOME TO THE WALDEN DATA FACILITY. And underneath, IF YOU HAVE NOTHING TO HIDE, YOU HAVE NOTHING TO FEAR. Seething, she shoved the binoculars back to Pete.

"You still think peaceful protests will unseat these guys, huh?" he gibed.

Mila ignored his tone. "I think they got this power because of our passive, implicit consent. They don't have our consent anymore."

Pete shrugged. He looked up at the lightening, gray sky. "Daylight's arriving. Is this where we set up shop?"

"It's our only choice," Julian said. "Need help?"

"No," Pete snipped, unzipping his backpack and removing a skinny tripod and small camera. "It'll stay poised on us. Making the feed accessible to the public is the trickiest part, but that's a one-guy job. Well, and Emory. Can't do it without her." After several moments, he pressed a finger to his earpiece. "Emory? Pete. You can connect now. Let me know when you see us... Good. We'll be ready, then." He ended the call and pointed at Mila. "Stand by the 'Trespassers will be shot' sign. Hesperia opens the Games with the country's anthem at seven o'clock sharp. At three minutes past seven, you'll go live and tell Hesperia specifically what to do if they ally themselves with us."

A final burst of nervousness flailed in her stomach. "We're certain they won't arrest me on the spot?"

"And give us a martyr for the cause? Hell no. They'd have a much bigger mess on their hands if they did that. Just remember—focus on Carlo and Theo. You're the nameless messenger."

It's only a matter of time. Falk will know me, no matter what. Mila's heart loped, but she took her place. Pete tweaked the camera's position. Julian watched her gravely. She closed her eyes and focused on the sound of the rain. The hiss as the drops hit the electric fence. The lukewarm trickles down her cheeks and neck.

"Sixty seconds," Pete called.

Thunder clapped, and the rain launched a full-scale assault.

"Fantastic," griped Pete.

Mila adjusted her earpiece. "As long as they can hear me."

"Speak loud—in five, four, three, two, one..."

"Hesperians," her voice resounded in the cascading rain, "today begins the Belgae's Insistence. I stand outside the Walden—electric fences and threats of death prevent me from going any farther, as the government seeks complete and total privacy as they invade ours. We insist on shutting this place down. Outside of the OWA, my compatriots stand with those forced into under-compensated, overworked positions that artificially boost Hesperia's unemployment statistics. And at Flint Hill Detention Facility, we are the face of Hesperians separated from their families and held for years without charge—many, like me, being innocent of any wrongdoing other than seriously examining our leaders. We insist on the end of these evil practices.

"We insist. How? By peacefully refusing to partake. Those inside the OWA will not work—even as Hesperia has punished them by cutting their rations in half. Those who are supposed to report after ninety days of unemployment—under the false promise of a good-paying job—should not check in. Those inside Flint Hill are shut off from all of this, but anyone arrested without charges should repeatedly and tirelessly demand to know them. And here at the Walden, we will not leave until Hesperia agrees to stop spying on its own citizens without just cause. Join us here.

"I know many of your hearts beat with mine. I can sense it. But you have families—small arms and warm cheeks that need your hugs and kisses in bed in the morning. They need you to arrive home at night—not to be flung onto a cold cot in Flint Hill. They need you to abide by the law, even if the laws are immoral and authoritarian and chilling. Your family comes first. However, you can still give us your support in small ways. You can drop off food. You can point others to us. You can spread the word—and when the going gets tough for us, maybe you can speak out. Loudly.

"Every three hours, I'll communicate with you, giving you an update on our progress. In the event that Hesperia shuts us down, you will know the lies.

"I don't know what Hesperia will do to us, its own people. But against their force, we will stand firm. Against their brutality, we will remain gentle. To their cruelty, we'll be kind. We will not stoop to their level—but we will insist.

"Will you?"

Pete signaled. "That does it," he said, disconnecting the camera and putting it into his large backpack. He tapped his ear, conferencing in with Emory. "Emory, how'd it go on your end? Did Carlo's codes work? Our transmission's stable?"

"Hesperia hammered me—almost shut us down once, but I'm beating them at the game so far."

"You're the best," Pete said, ending the call. He retrieved a black monitor and attached it to the tripod. "And this is how we'll see the media's reaction to us."

Mila nodded. "And now?"

Julian turned his backpack upside down and shook it, dumping out its contents. "We set up camp and wait to see who joins us."

Searching his somber eyes, she offered a reserved smile. "I'm truly glad you're with me."

"Me too," he said, spreading out a large, brown ground cloth.

"And your mother? Is she—?"

"Supportive of you and I, and well taken care of by Chet."

"Any word from Kairos since we left the Laslo mansion?"

He stopped his work to meet her gaze. "We shouldn't expect much from him as far as this effort is concerned."

She disguised the wince that creased her brow by looking over her shoulder at the landscape. The desert, marred by one towering butte, filled her with a sense of smallness that parched her spirit. Kairos' lack of faith—his refusal to lend support in the most microscopic way—left her feeling as inconsequential as the grit under her boots. Did she stand a chance against Hesperia? Did any of them?

Shoving her questions aside, she bent to help Julian pitch their shelter, but the crunching sound of wet dirt and rocks under tires startled her. She turned to witness the arrival of a black magnecar, Hesperia's insignia emblazoned on its side. The engine died, the two front doors opened, and two Amity officers exited the vehicle. Standing straight and tall, hands resting on the weapons on their hips, their faces were as expressionless as the dead land around them.

A cavalcade of Hesperia law enforcement followed.

~~~

Mila pressed her earpiece deeper into her ear, straining to hear Emory's quiet voice as the rain roared around her.

"Fifteen minutes until your first briefing, and no one?"

"No," Mila said. Amity officers, armed and poised, stood hundreds of feet away but she still turned her back to them as she spoke. "Probably a hundred of *them*, but no Hesperians have joined us."

Emory sighed. "Some Belgae are trying to get to you, but it will still be several hours. Don't give any indication you're alone. Focus on encouragement for the cause. Emphasize the standoff at the OWA—that's momentum, even if we'd like to see more support from—"

"Wait, Emory, wait. Civilian vehicles are coming."

A modest caravan—no more than five magnecars—wound down the road and parked far beyond the line of Amity cars. Doors opened, and plain-clothes Hesperians exited, hauling bags and back-packs and coolers with them.

"Are they—?" Pete began.

"Here for us, I'd say so," Julian said.

Mila estimated around twenty Hesperians. They walked stiffly, their brows creased with fear and streaked with rain. Touching Pete's shoulder, she said, "I can't let them walk alone."

"What?"

She ran toward them. The Amity officers jumped with anticipation, but she met their eyes and sent them a modest smile. They cast confused glances at each other. When she reached the first Hesperian—a middle-aged woman—she clasped her in an embrace. "Thank you," she said.

The woman nodded once. Her gaze flew around at the Amity officers, as erratic as a hunted bird.

"Let me walk with you," Mila said. "It will be okay."

"What if they arrest us?"

"They won't." Mila spoke loud. "Hesperia's power hinges on the illusion of freedom. If they arrest peaceful protesters, the people will see them for what they are."

Taking the woman's arm, she led her to Pete—who lifted his camera, apparently recording the entire exchange—and Julian. The rest of the people followed shortly behind them. "I'm Mila. These are my friends, Julian and Pete."

"Tasha," the woman said. "We brought as much food and drink as we could manage."

Mila watched as the group unloaded their bags and took their places in front of the Walden. In her earpiece, Emory said, "Mila, I got the footage from Pete. It will be great to show after your update. Be ready in five minutes."

She delivered her message with Tasha and a few of the newcomers standing next to her. The rain slowed as she spoke, halting completely by the time her briefing ended.

Pete switched the camera for the monitor. He tweaked a couple of knobs, dividing its eight-by-ten screen four ways. In each one, he pulled up a major network broadcast, but selected HBN's as a silver-haired man reported the news, then he increased the volume.

"The first day of what the extremist Belgae group call their Insistence began this morning, with a nameless spokeswoman calling upon the public to join her cause from her position outside the Walden Data Facility in Jordan-Utah in the Rocky Mountains Region," the man reported as B-roll footage showed Mila running. But they cut it—skipping the moment of the women's tender embrace, and resuming with footage of Mila walking back to Pete and Julian with Tasha by her side.

Tasha and the newcomers cast confused glances at Mila, Pete and Julian.

Mila shook her head. "This is only the beginning."

"And it's exactly why we will provide our own updates, with all of the footage," Julian added.

The anchor's serious face filled the screen once more. "HBN was able to confirm with Hesperia Defense that the Belgae's efforts have remained in concentrated areas, with few participants. Amity officers remain present at all protest locations in order to protect from outbreaks of violence.

"Also today, singer sensation Durango stands by his shocking new music video, featuring a flamingo suspended upside down from a rafter. Animal rights activists swarmed the singer's mansion this week." The camera cut to a wide shot, showing two men and a woman sitting around the table with the anchor. "Joining me today is lawyer Jonathan Jones, award-winning producer David Mitford, and HBN entertainment analyst Danielle Gomez. Let's talk about—"

Pete muted the monitor. "An entire panel for a music video. Anyone care if I vomit?"

"You aren't really surprised, are you?" Julian asked.

"Of course not." Pete walked to a cooler and retrieved a home-baked muffin and another bottle of water and handed it to one of the newcomers. The rest of the protesters began spreading out tarps, pitching tents, and passing out food and drinks.

Mila bit into a dry, crumbly sandwich, taking the interim between briefings to steal a glance at the Amity officers. They stood statue-still—except one, who shifted his weight around as he watched the Belgae eat. Nipped by sympathy, she pulled a water bottle and a sandwich from one of the coolers and walked slowly to the officer.

His eyes grew wide. He looked uncomfortably at the officers on either side of him.

"Officer Redmond," Mila said, reading his badge. "Have this, please."

He averted his eyes.

"We have no ill-will toward you all. You're here to follow orders, that's all."

"It's unlawful to take goods or services from you," Redmond stated.

"I understand." She backed away. "But it's here if you want it, and we won't tell your superiors if you won't."

When she rejoined the group, the newcomers eyed her with wary stares. Pete rushed to her. "What the hell was that?"

"We don't know how many of them are here solely because they have to be, and how many of them really despise us. No matter why they're here, though—I think it can only strengthen us to extend kindness and civility."

"I guess I can see your point."

~~~

With the passing of each Belgae briefing, more Hesperians arrived. By the end of the first day, Julian guessed more than two hundred civilians had arrived to stand at the Walden, and each group brought goods—food, drink, simple shelter, first aid, and extra clothing and shoes—with them. Belgae, perhaps fifty, arrived, too. By the end of the second day, the total number at the Walden hovered near seven hundred—with Emory reporting just as many at each of the other twenty protest locations around the country. Ten thousand in all—with the Amity officers' presence matching their growth.

In just two days, Julian witnessed strangers become acquaintances, then friends, until the Belgae camp thrived with community. They commiserated, trading stories about their journeys and what had attracted them to the movement—particularly after media coverage over the last few years portrayed the group as an unstable one. More than once, Julian overheard Mila's name mentioned. As he ambled under the clear dark sky, with Amity officers standing guard on one side and Belgae sitting in clusters around lanterns on the other, he tuned into the conversation around him.

"When I heard her," one man said, "I just thought... something's different, here. This isn't the group I've been told about. Maybe they changed, or maybe it was all a lie from the get-go. But if this tiny woman can see hope on the other side of all those terrible injustices... if she believes in me, even when I'm sittin' on my ass watching that Durango fool"—he laughed—"maybe I can believe in her. And me, too." The group laughed and nodded.

Mila remained wholly unaware of her magnetic pull. He marveled at her ability to encourage, to understand, to bring unity. And yet a part of him held back. The people had corroded long ago. Was Mila—was anyone—enough to restore their shine? And how long until society succumbed again? Julian scanned the camp for her. He spotted her sitting in the dirt with two women at the edge of the camp, engrossed in conversation. Quietly, he walked closer.

"I don't know," one woman said. "I'm here, so on some level I must believe. But I also, just... doubt."

Mila leaned in. "I understand," she said. "I doubted, too. It's normal, especially when you're constantly barraged with evidence of selfishness, power-lust, trivialities, and petty fights. But what we've done is forget who we are." Her voice grew bold with conviction. "We have to peel back all of the distractions, the worries we live with, and our base tendencies that lead us to engage on those levels, and remember our true identities. Because look around... right now, you and I are *surrounded* by people—very different people—taking serious risks to help others. Watch them listen to one another. See them share belongings. In front of us right now is evidence of true community—the community we want to bring alive all throughout Hesperia. There is so much reason to doubt, Rhonda—there *really* is—but we are the people who sift through all of that and instead latch onto these moments"—she clasped her hands—"hold them tight, hold them sacred, and guard them—but most of all, perpetuate them. And we do that by living in belief, not doubt."

Suddenly, Mila's face snapped up, and she saw him. He heard her quietly ask Rhonda, "Do you mind if I step away?" The women nodded and Mila trotted toward him, a sheepish smile on her face. She must've known he'd been listening.

"You..." he trailed off, his heart warming. "This is you. It's—it's something else."

"This is working," she said. "For so long, everyone believed the only way to win against Hesperia was to beat them at their own evil game—they never even considered trying to rise above it. I can't believe what I'm witnessing. And yet, I believe it entirely. Ten thousand people, and I think even some of the Amity officers are beginning to wonder why they even need to be here." Her eyes drifted to the officers and lost their spark. An anxious glaze took its place.

"Wondering where he is in all of this?" asked Julian, his voice dark.

"The worst part is knowing it's all a matter of time." She folded her arms. "He may not be here, but he's not giving up."

Placing his hand at her elbow, Julian led her farther from the group. He sensed the eyes of the Amity officers following them.

"He's out there," she said. "He's coming for me. My worst fear is that he'll make it grotesquely public—" her voice broke. She stopped talking.

"Mila. He will not lay a hand on you."

Her face contorted in disgust. "You don't know F—"

"He will not lay a hand on you." He cupped her face and searched her eyes. Leaning in, he brushed her nose with his.

She pulled back, and he searched her face. Longing and loss swirled in her eyes. "What is it?" he asked.

"I can't let myself get lost in you if our paths aren't the same. I care for you so much, Julian, but—are we on the same path?"

He took both of her hands in his. "I'm here now, aren't I?"

She closed her eyes for a moment, gave his hands a squeeze, and walked away.

36.

FALK'S PHONE RANG—again. Snatching it off his bedside table in his Utah hotel room, he peered at it, then took the call. "Hello, Ed."

"Your suggestion to encourage news coverage of the Insistence was well-received after all, Vic. I shouldn't have bristled at it."

"The Belgae's public support has skyrocketed and it's only been two days. The media has no choice but to cover the story and capitalize on it. We only need to veer the conversation."

"I couldn't agree more. Especially since the Belgae have given Amity officers nothing—not a single count—for which they can arrest. Ten thousand protesters—no lawlessness. It's unbelievable. We've managed to schedule someone on several HBN shows, beginning with Alyson Vernon this afternoon."

"A woman?"

"It just so happens... why do you ask?"

"If a man criticizes the Belgae spokeswoman, it will look sexist. Best to make it a woman—and a likable one at that."

Ed huffed. "We need to I.D. her to be truly effective. You're lagging on that effort, Falk."

"I'm stirring the pot," Falk assured his boss. "Just you wait. Make sure the Amity squadrons know not to make any arrests for now. Wait awhile longer, and the people will be begging you to step in."

~~~

The sweltering heat of the August afternoon sun baked Mila's bare shoulders. Her black tank top—one of two she had to switch out and hand wash—clung to her dirty, sweat-beaded skin. Without taking a breath, she gulped down two-thirds of her water bottle, and patted the remainder on her cheeks, neck, and shoulders. She looked behind her at the Belgae campground. On the fringes, Rhonda stood with a group of about twelve protesters. Their crossed arms, tensed shoulders and jerky motions sent a spear of worry through her. Then, Rhonda made eye contact.

Trudging up to her, the woman said, "It's day three. Hesperia has not backed down. Is all of this a waste of time?"

"They can't budge on anything so soon," Mila said. "If they did, they'd look weak. We have to be patient"—as she spoke, her body threatened to collapse with exhaustion—"and persist."

Rhonda bit her lip. Without a word, the woman spun and strode away.

Mila fought the urge to fall to the dusty, hot ground. It would appear to the Belgae that she was beginning to cave. Instead, she walked farther away and stared up at the cloudless, cerulean sky.

Three days in, and they were getting restless—this society so accustomed to instant gratification. In her effort to be encouraging and inspiring, had she not adequately stressed the amount of time, commitment, and work everyone would have to contribute? If a dozen Belgae at the Walden felt this way, no doubt more did—such sentiments bred like viruses. She held down a button on the rim of her earpiece. A dial tone signaled the device's readiness.

"Call Emory McFallon," she ordered. The call rang.

Emory answered almost immediately. "Hi."

"What's morale like at the other protest sites?"

She didn't hesitate. "They could use a boost."

"I'll work it into my briefing," she said. "What time is it?"

"Quarter till."

"Already?"

"Are you watching—?"

"Gotta go."

"But—"

"I need to think, Emory. Gather my thoughts." She ended the call. Squaring her shoulders, she rushed back to the camp.

Pete met her at the edge. "Get over here." Taking her by the arm, he pulled her to the briefing station.

"Is something wrong?"

He hurried ahead of her to the monitor, which displayed the HBN broadcast. He turned the volume to full blast.

Alyson Vernon anchored the segment. A beautiful blonde woman with an intelligent smile sat by her side. The slugline in the lower third read, HESPERIA DEFENSE ON BELGAE LEADER: PROCEED WITH CAUTION.

"...with me is Dana Ericsson, spokesperson for Hesperia Defense. Miss Ericsson, is it true that Hesperia has identified the Belgae spokeswoman?"

"It is, Alyson. Our investigation is ongoing, but we believe her to be Mila Ray, an ex-Flint Hill detainee."

Vernon's eyes widened. "Tell me about Hesperia's position on Mila Ray."

The woman smiled politely. "Hesperia has no position regarding Miss Ray or the Belgae movement. Hesperians are allowed and encouraged to speak freely and protest peacefully, it's one of the most incredible freedoms of our country. But it's important to be educated on the leaders of a movement, and we believe Miss Ray's story has been intentionally left out of her narrative, for whatever reason."

"What has Hesperia Defense confirmed so far, if anything?" Vernon asked.

Horror filled Mila. She sensed the eyes of the protesters train on her for her reaction. Wrestling every ounce of her strength, she maintained an unshaken expression, but she couldn't control the color that drained from her face.

"Well, we know Mila Ray was a former employee of HBN, in an entry-level news gathering position." She placed both of her hands delicately on top of a file sitting in front of her. "We know she was arrested and booked into Flint Hill Detention Facility after investigating a tip. What she unfortunately didn't share was that her research fell flagrantly outside the bounds of her job description—and the tipster she made contact with was a dangerous ex-government official who leaked classified information."

"The tipster Carlo DaVanti?"

"Correct. And HBN stresses that it had no knowledge of, nor would it have condoned, Miss Ray's actions," Alyson added. "In fact, she was fired because she stepped outside her job responsibilities."

Ericsson nodded. "Completely understandable. And while in Flint Hill, she was escalated very quickly through the wards—once because she attacked a guard. Following her escalation to Ward C, which is reserved for the most dangerous criminals, Miss Ray escaped and was believed to have killed herself."

Alyson emitted an, "Mmm," that almost sounded heartfelt.

"Look, Mila Ray is an only child of parents who died in a gas explosion—the cause of which was never discovered. She isn't known to have had a roommate or any close friends." Dana Ericsson's voice rose to a sympathetic pitch. "What we are seeing here may be the desperate grasping of a young woman—with no family, no friends, no career—to find a purpose for her life. And *if* that is what powers her... it could lend a certain degree of instability to the entire Belgae movement." She shrugged. "And for those considering joining—"

"People are risking *everything* because they believe in this cause—this woman," Vernon opined.

"It's certainly important information to consider," Ericsson said.

"Dana Ericsson, thank you for joining me. We'll be back after the break."

Pete muted the broadcast.

Mila scanned those around her. Expressions of confusion, concern, and anger—whether at her or at Hesperia and HBN, she didn't know—littered their faces. Looking at Pete, she said, "I think it's time for my briefing."

"Have at it."

She took her place. He signaled.

"Good evening, Hesperians," she began. "You should be proud. In just three days, you have come together in a display of strength, vigor, faith, and courage that rivals the annals of history. Yet, our government has not budged. I know you're exhausted, and your hope threatens to wane—but has anything that possessed true, abiding worth ever come easily? This—true freedom—is worth the fight, and it's worth the wait. Keep standing. Stand with me, and stand together." She paused. Several people pushed their way through the crowd—leaving the camp. Panic writhed within her, but she tamped down against it. "Tonight, some information was shared about me for which I believe I must provide clarification. While the core facts are true"—groans rolled across the group like thunder—"the sentiment and implications behind them are not."

More people abandoned the group. In her ear, Emory said, "Stop, Mila. The more you defend yourself, the more you'll need to defend yourself. Just close it out. Now."

"You all are here because of what you believe in. The *causes* you believe in, the *rights* you believe in—to speech and thought, privacy and true, untainted justice—not because of me. I only happen to be on the camera."

She walked out of the frame with her heart pounding so loudly in her ears, she could barely hear the questions shouted at her by the people.

Julian shouldered his way to her side. "Give her a minute, guys. Just a minute, okay?"

She looked at him. "Shatter my credibility. Utterly predictable, and damn it if it isn't always effective."

"I think your response was a good one."

Suddenly, Alyson Vernon's voice filled the air when Pete unmuted the broadcast.

"...confirm information from an anonymous source who says Mila Ray made her escape from Flint Hill Detention Facility on the same night that Forsythe Marlowe, a high-ranking official with Hesperia Defense, was found dead in the prison yard. Flint Hill's warden, James Gregory, spoke with HBN a moment ago—"

Pete blackened the monitor. He glared at her.

Forsythe Marlowe's bloodied, empty face seized her mind, even with her eyes wide open. Her legs trembled. She gripped Julian's arm and fought to keep her stance firm.

The report was factual. But the truth was even worse. It bared its teeth like a vicious animal, rabid in its aim to eviscerate her. She had murdered a man. If the Belgae learned—and soon they would—any small print about Falk forcing her to do so would fall to the wayside in light of the blood on her hands.

The faces around her implored, judged, accused. Her mouth fell agape, empty of words.

"Consider the source," Julian said, his voice loud with authority. "The media-government hailstorm was inevitable. It's crucial that you consider the source." He turned to her. "Mila, Pete and I need to speak with you. Come with me, please."

Pete cocked his head in confusion, but followed them as they made their way through the masses. Mila glanced around. The crowd was already noticeably thinner.

"I just wanted to get you out of there," Julian confessed when they got to the camp's fringe.

Her head ached and pulsed. "Water?"

He handed her one. She chugged it dry without stopping for air. A clicking sounded in her earbud.

"Emory, you here?" Pete asked, apparently experiencing the same sound.

"I am," she answered.

"Well?" Pete challenged Mila. "Is it true?"

"Yes," Mila said.

"Victor Falk—the agent following her—threatened to kill another innocent inmate if she didn't kill Marlowe," Julian clarified. "She had no choice."

"Fuck if that matters!" Pete shouted.

"Stay composed, Peter," Emory said. "Okay. Okay. Okay, I—God, I can't even think straight."

Mila had never heard Emory sound so rattled. She steeled against her own sense of rising panic. "Someone else needs to be the face," Mila said. "The people can't separate me from the Belgae—we're inextricably linked in their minds. We have to undo that, and give them someone else to latch onto."

"But who?" Emory asked. "Pete's not exactly stable. No offense, Pete."

Pete held his middle finger to the sky.

"Emory," Mila said. "It has to be you."

"It can't be me."

"You're the only one."

"I don't do speeches—and I definitely don't do cameras," she argued. "Plus, it'll take too long before I could get there, and—"

"I'll do it," Julian offered over Emory's excuses. "Some of them know me. Remember me."

"What'd he say?" Emory asked.

"He said he'll do it," Mila said, perplexed.

"I didn't know he was really one of us." Pete crossed his arms.

"Are you really one of us?" Mila asked.

"Yes," Julian said. "But you can't walk away, Mila."

"But how can I—?"

"If you walk away and I replace you, it looks like an implicit admission of guilt. We'll do it together."

Mila paused, considering. "Emory, Julian says he and I will work together. I'll still be on camera, so as not to appear guilty. Do you have any reservations with that plan?"

"I'll see you both during your next briefing."

~~~

Julian stayed behind for a minute as Mila and Pete walked back to the camp. He called Kairos and updated him so he wouldn't be surprised to see Julian on camera in a couple of hours.

"So you're Belgae now?" the Zetetics leader asked.

"I'm trying to do what's right, regardless of whose label is on the cause. Hesperia was shredding Mila. I couldn't let that happen. Being here—doing this—it's the best way I can make sure she's safe."

"There's still a place for you here, when all of this falls apart."

"Thanks," Julian said through a locked jaw. He wanted to buck against Kairos' faithlessness, but the thinning crowd in front of him only supported everything he and the Zetetics had claimed all along. Mila guided the people like the North Star—and after one cloudy night, they stopped following her. Together, maybe they could unite everyone once again.

When he returned to the group, he expected to find Mila dutifully answering questions flung at her by the protesters, but she stood awkwardly by the camera, ignored even by people only an arm's length away.

He joined her. "You okay?"

She looked at him, her eyes wide with disbelief. "This is absurd," she said, keeping her voice low. "I'm right here—they could get the full story—and yet they'd prefer to speculate among themselves. What am I supposed to do, go tap them on their shoulders?"

"We'll broach the subject on camera. At least, then, we'll take care of it all at once. You could spend hours explaining everything if they were bombarding you right now."

She shrugged. "I'd find it preferable to whatever stories HBN and Hesperia have conjured in their imaginations." She folded her arms, then returned them to her side, as though realizing her posture appeared too defensive.

All too soon, Pete trained the camera on them once again. Julian's breathing accelerated. He focused on the sunset straight ahead. Was there anything they could say that would uproot the weed Hesperia had planted?

The red light on the camera lit up. Pete pointed.

Julian allowed a small, confident smile to play at the edges of his lips. "Would you look at that, friends? It looks like our strength isn't just all in our own heads—Hesperia's seen it, too. If we weren't worth their time, they'd still be ignoring us. Instead, they released their hounds to attack the credibility of one woman, seeking to destroy her— and then destroy us. But I have news." He tilted his chin and cast a daring glare at the camera. "It's. Not. Happening. Be bold, friends. Be empowered. They're scared of you."

After a couple seconds of silence, he turned to look at Mila, cueing her.

She smiled widely. "We are standing on the brink of a better life," she said. "I see hope in the stones that have been cast our way. They tell me that if we can hold tight for a while longer, we will see victory. Take a look at what you've accomplished."

Pete sliced the air with his hand and Emory filled the remaining minutes of the briefing with footage and reports from other protest locations. The red light darkened. Mila walked into the center of the crowd, and relief trickled over Julian when several Belgae approached her with smiles on their faces—even if concern glittered in their eyes. He trailed behind her, just close enough to overhear her explain the events at Flint Hill.

"That's grotesque," a woman said. "What kind of horrible person makes someone do such a thing?"

"The kind you'll hopefully never meet," Mila answered.

"What else do they have on you, that they can attack us with?" demanded a gruff-looking man.

"I think they emptied their cartridge on me, for better or worse. If we can get through this and still be strong and growing, we'll be well on our way to getting our demands met." Placing her hand on the man's shoulder, Mila said, "The past few hours have taken a lot out of me. Would you all mind if I took a few minutes of quiet, to watch the rest of the sunset? I promise I'll answer all of your questions as soon as I get back."

The group responded gracefully. Julian watched Mila retreat to the far edge of the camp. He circled around the opposite side and found her sitting in the dirt. He joined her, gazing out into the distance at the endless desert and its lone butte, like a deformity in the landscape. Golden clouds spattered the vermillion sky, and Julian couldn't tell if it was red with passion, humiliation, anger, or injury.

He turned his attention on her. Her eyes, fixed on the clouds, appeared hollow—her mind somewhere else. "The response to our message seemed encouraging enough," he tried. "With time, I think—"

"Is this real?" she interrupted, looking at him. "You. Being here. Doing this. Tell me if it's real."

He took her hand. "It's real. I'm doing this. I'm doing it for you."

She bit her lip, as though that wasn't enough.

"Why do I have to do it for the people, Mila? Why can't I do it for you—only you—and if it betters the people, it's a fringe benefit?"

She released his hand, returning her focus to the sky. He looked away, irritated. Why did she think they needed perfect alignment in everything in order to be together? Why wasn't his devotion to her enough? He studied the grace of her pensive profile, the way her cheekbones glistened with beads of sweat, and he considered pulling her to him in the dirt and kissing her, but decided against it.

"Shh," she said, shaking her head.

He waited.

"Don't you hear it? Listen to them."

Voices rose, fell, then gushed, like the first rushes of lava spewing from a volcano.

"They're arguing."

He opened his mouth to offer some semblance of encouragement, but the HBN news van speeding toward the Walden silenced him.

37.

MILA SCRAMBLED TO HER FEET. Julian jumped up beside her. "Oh no," she said. "Go back to the camp—I'll run to meet the reporters while you get everyone to calm down."

Julian rushed back.

About a mile ahead of her, the magnevan—white with HBN in royal blue letters on each side—pulled in front of the Amity officers, its wheels deployed. She raced toward it, her feet pounding the dirt, kicking it up in clouds behind her. With her heartbeat clobbering her chest and desperate breaths drowning out all noise, she didn't hear the man until he sacked her to the ground.

She writhed, face down in the dirt. Her earpiece flew out of her ear. She gasped to recapture her breath—inhaling a mouthful of sandy soil. Pinned down, she coughed and hacked while her arms were wrestled behind her—and though she hadn't glimpsed his face, she didn't need to.

Cold metal encircled her wrists and *click-click-clicked* until they trapped her. She kicked and thrashed. He grabbed her by the arm, bruising-tight, and yanked her to her feet, then wrangled her against him. She spat out the soil, wheezed in air to power her voice, but he smacked his palm over her face.

"Scream," he said, "and all you'll do is give HBN a live shot of your arrest."

She sensed him rustle for something in his pocket with his free hand. He held the hooked, metal object in front of her face. The sight of her old murder weapon sent a cold sweat over her body. He pressed it hard against her temple. Terror radiated from the spot he touched, down her face and spine. It hammered inside her chest as she anticipated Falk plunging it into her brain.

"Walk," he ordered.

They marched ahead and to the left, far out of the vision of the HBN news crew scurrying with their sights set solely on the Belgae camp. Over the sound of her stumbling, scraping footsteps and Falk's hot breath in her ear, she couldn't hear if the Belgae still argued. Did Julian pacify them? Would she live to know? What would happen once they realized she was gone—or worse, dead?

They passed the van. Nearby, a small group of Amity officers gathered away from the rest. As their trajectory aligned with them, Falk removed his hand from her face and his arm from her waist, resuming a standard escort posture as he clutched her by the cuffs and pushed her forward. The Amity officers took notice. In her peripheral vision, Falk flashed his badge.

Ahead, the jagged butte towered like a turncoat centurion. Falk marched her to it, then around the back. He shoved her to the ground. The side of her head clattered against the butte's rocky base, lacerating her face. She shouted in pain as blood trickled down her face and neck. She struggled to bend her knees underneath her and get into a sitting position, but he yanked her by the ankles and wrestled a rope around them into a vicious knot, then flipped her so she lay on her back. She whimpered as her head smacked the rock.

The red sky purpled, ushering in darkness and appearing as a massive bruise in the heavens. Falk towered over her, rusted hook in one hand and gun in the other. He wore plain clothes—a thin gray T-shirt that clung to him in sweat, and dark denim pants, all covered in rust-red dirt from their struggle. His dark eyes narrowed into slits, shining hungrily, boring into her as he knelt over her.

"You planned this all along," she said. "Marlowe. My escape. You knew I'd eventually come to the Belgae"—she inhaled desperately—"that it was all a matter of time. You captured me and freed me, just to capture me again. You destroyed me and reconstructed me so you could destroy me again. So now, kill me. What's going on out there can live without me—it's bigger than me. So I dare you to kill me."

Falk smiled. Lifting the old murder weapon to her temple, he dragged it down the curve of her face in a caress. "Do you hate me, Mila?" he whispered tenderly, then cocked his head like a vulture studying a carcass from its perch. "Do your hands tingle with heat at night, as they remember the way the skull chisel"—he twirled the object menacingly—"felt in them? The resistance of a man's neck for just a little while? When you imagine how your friend's blood washed Voltaire's wooden floors for you while you hid in safety, does your spirit want to vomit you out? Reject you? Tell me, Thirty-Four. Do you hate?"

Her heart stopped, flailed, and tightened until it drilled and contorted within her chest. It screwed—the furious sensation that had assaulted her at Flint Hill and reared its ugly, malformed head since her escape.

Hate, the seed. Falk, the gardener.

How much of her passion had been fueled—controlled—by him? How much of her devotion was pseudonymous vengeance? His eyes devoured her, awaiting her answer—but horror clogged her throat.

He leaned close to her, so close every grotesque fleck in his irises became visible. His laugh gurgled, low and mucous, like oil from a barrel. "Kill you? No," he whispered. "Ruin you." Reaching into his back pocket, he pulled out a wad of discolored cloth. He grabbed her face so hard she feared her cheeks would break, forced her mouth open, and shoved it into her mouth. She gagged—it smelled like sweat.

Standing, Falk slipped behind the butte for a moment. When he returned, he carried a black bag and pulled from it a tripod and a wireless monitor. He mounted the monitor to the tripod. "Your people," he said, pulling her to a sitting position, "the ones you believe in, the ones you've risked life and love for, are going to eat each other." He lowered the monitor to her eye level, tuned into the HBN broadcast and turned up the volume. "And you will watch."

From his other pocket, he pulled out a wadded up, black cap. Shaking it out, he tugged it onto his head, tossed her a reptilian smile, and strode away.

When he was out of sight, Mila struggled against the rope around her ankles, attempting to twist and separate her feet to loosen its grip. She fought and writhed until her raw skin broke against the prickly hemp and she couldn't bear the pain—then she tried to spit out the cloth in her mouth. But Falk had stuffed her so full, she couldn't even move her tongue. She screamed. The muffled sound didn't make it past her own toes.

Sobs shook her, drowning out the sound of the HBN reporter emanating from the monitor. Between her cries, she gasped for air—gagging on the nasty cloth.

Under the ink blue, new moon night, no one would find her. Exhaustion filled her head with fuzziness. She let her chin drop to her chest. The broadcast faded in.

"...go to Rebecca Watson, live in front of the Walden Data Facility, where the peaceful protests have turned ugly. Rebecca?"

Mila's head snapped up.

"Thank you, Alyson. After three days of unproductive peaceful protests, violence among the group's own members threatens to stop the movement in its tracks. Just a moment ago, the argument blew up when"—B-roll of the Belgae filled the screen—"the first punch was thrown."

Mila froze as she watched a man in a black cap and a gray T-shirt plow his fist into another man's face. As the match escalated, Falk slipped out of the frame.

"The crew and I stepped far away once the altercation began," Rebecca Watson continued, "and while many of the Belgae are trying to quell the outbreak, I've gotta tell you—things are not looking good."

The camera showed a handful of injured protesters kneeling on the ground while others cleaned wounds, applied bandages, and sobbed. Two men—with Falk nowhere in sight—shoved and shouted, with protesters on either side floundering to stop the match. Mila squinted, scanning the monitor for any sign of Julian or Pete, but the screen split down the middle, showing Alyson on one side and Rebecca on the other.

"Have the Amity officers stepped in?" Alyson asked.

"I talked to one officer a moment ago, who said they're monitoring the situation and will step in once it's clear the Belgae are not solving the problem themselves."

Alyson chimed in, "Now, I have to ask what I'm sure everyone is wondering, Rebecca, and that is— where is Mila Ray in all of this?"

"That's an excellent question. I've kept a sharp eye out since we arrived half an hour ago, and no one reports seeing Miss Ray since shortly after her last briefing, when she responded to accusations that she murdered a Hesperian official before escaping Flint Hill."

"Perhaps many are thinking that her disappearance answers more questions than her briefing did," Alyson said. "Is that what they're fighting about now?"

"It's hard to say, Alyson. But with the arrest of their longtime leader, Rigo Laslo, and these shocking revelations about Miss Ray—whom many hailed as the hope of their cause—there seems to be no shortage of gasoline to pour on the flames."

"Rebecca Watson, stay safe. Thanks."

Tears stung Mila's eyes. Hopelessness crashed over her. *Is this it—hope and freedom doomed to failure, while I watch and waste away in the desert?*

She hung her head, praying desperately for a rebellious breeze to topple and break the monitor, drowning out the torturous sound of the headlines.

38.

WHERE WAS MILA?

Julian raked his fingers through his hair, casting his glance around the camp, but the darkness obscured his vision despite the Belgae's lamps and the dissolving glow of the Walden's stadium lights. He'd raced to the group and he and Pete had managed to corral and quell the Belgae for a while, as the HBN news team approached—without Mila. But he'd scarcely had time to wonder where she was.

An arm's length away—shouts. Shoves. And then a loud *sock* to the face. What fool had done that?

He looked around the camp, mentally tallying the remaining crowd. Only about one hundred protesters now—a quarter of the amount present two days ago, but still too many to contain if things continued to get out of hand.

"What have any of the Belgae's ideas got us so far?" one man boomed. "Nothing! I spent two years waiting for that bastard Laslo to make good on his promise and I'm done waiting." Several around him cheered their assent.

Near Julian, a woman sneered. "All this time, Mila spews out hope and peace with her fingers crossed behind her back. God, I should have known."

"I don't care if she is a woman," the man next to her said. "As soon as I catch a glimpse of her, I'll tear her up and down for wasting my time with her lies."

The woman hushed him and jerked her head in Julian's direction.

Julian kept walking. In all the turmoil, he hadn't had a chance to check in. He tapped his ComCoil. "Weren't you watching her?" he asked, his voice rife with accusation.

"We were monitoring the crowd," Kairos answered.

"Get Elzac to sail the QSS everywhere. She can't have gone far."

He hurried toward sounds of grunts and scrambling feet. Far ahead, two men grappled. He rushed forward with no plan—and Pete plowed into him. Julian stumbled several steps, grabbing Pete around the middle to steady them both. Onlookers gasped at the possibility of yet another scuffle.

An older man shoved between them, pushing them apart. "Settle, you two! We've got enough trouble as it is. What, do you want the Amity officers to be the ones who stop all of this? Damn!"

Julian raised his hands in the air. "It was an accident." He crossed to Pete. "What the hell were you doing?" Julian demanded.

"I was going to stop them!"

"You'll make it worse if you get in the middle."

Pete's eyes ricocheted around the camp. "What do we do? Where the hell is Mila?"

"I don't know—I don't know," he said. What could have happened to her? "Did you see who started all this? Where'd he go?"

"Someone said some guy in a black cap. Have no idea where."

In his ear, Kairos clicked in. "There's nothing you can do, Julian. Hesperia will intervene at any minute. Get out of there—now."

"I can't leave without Mila," Julian said.

Pete huffed and stepped back. Contempt gnarled his face. "Who the hell are you talking to? The jackass group you abandoned us for—the one that won't do *shit* to help us right now—telling them you'd *leave* again if you could? Fuck you!" He lurched forward and shoved Julian.

Julian staggered into a cluster of protesters. They caught him, shouting expletives. "Pete!" he barked. "I'm not the one you should be fighting right now! Back off, man!"

Pete held his hands up in surrender, but spat on the ground in front of Julian's feet.

Julian turned to apologize to the group, but froze. His blood turned to venom. Falk stared back, his dirt-brown eyes swirling with sadistic satisfaction. He clutched a crumpled black cap in his hands.

"Where'd you take her?" Julian demanded.

Falk smiled, bent his head in a slow nod, then spun and rushed through the crowd, tugging on his cap as he went.

"Where'd you take her?" he bellowed. He pushed ahead, but Falk shoved confused protesters behind him, blocking his path. "Falk!"

Pete stumbled to his side. "Him?" He stabbed his finger in Falk's direction. "That's Victor Falk?" his voice rose to a shriek. "Hesperia!"

"Pete, don't—!"

But Pete couldn't be stopped. "Hesperia!" He fought through the crowd, shouting, "The man in the black cap is Hesperia—he started everything and he's getting away!"

"Get out, Julian!" Kairos ordered.

"Pete—!"

The crowd roared, erupting in chaos.

~~~

The blood, caked on her forehead and cheeks, crunched and itched when she so much as blinked. Her ankles fizzed with lack of blood flow and stung as the rope ground into ripped skin. She couldn't take it anymore. HBN stopped all other coverage in favor of breaking news—the disintegrating Belgae Insistence. She closed her eyes, hummed, and wept as loudly as she could to cover the sounds of the voices until exhaustion drained her. Finally, she let the stories wash over her like vinegar on her broken skin.

Her mother's voice filled her mind. "You can't fight an immoral opponent on a battlefield of morality, Mila."

I failed. I'm a fool—fool for believing that peace could ever win the war against evil. Fool for my faith in the people. Fool for rejecting the Zetetics. They were right. No hope lives in the world above anymore. None.

Footsteps crunched nearby. Lifting her boulder-heavy head, she blinked until the man came into focus.

Officer Redmond approached and knelt beside her. His dull blue eyes filled with pain as he reached up and gently pulled out the wad of cloth. Her cheeks ached as she closed her cotton-dry mouth and swallowed. He pulled a key from his uniform and unlocked the handcuffs that had bruised her wrists, then sawed through the rope with a pocketknife.

Blood rushed to her feet. Her legs creaked as she bent them. The officer clasped her hands and pulled her up.

"Thank you." Her raspy voice cracked.

"This is all I can do for you," he said. Helplessness wrinkled his forehead. "You should go as far away as you can—we're about to put a stop to everything down there."

"I can't abandon them," she said, taking her first steps toward the Belgae camp. The cuts encircling her ankles screamed and stung, but she kept walking.

"You were right," Officer Redmond called.

Mila turned.

"Not all of us are the same."

She nodded. Turning, she ran against the pain flaring in her ankles, against Hesperia, against Falk. Half a mile ahead, the Belgae thrashed as a mob while the media swarmed around them. Desperation pushed her forward—but Amity officers rushed the camp.

She skidded to a stop. The officers wrestled, beat, and cuffed protesters. They led them away, forcing them to bend at the waist as they had her at Flint Hill, shoving them forward as they screamed. What could she ever do now? She was too late.

Something floundered at the edges of her vision. She turned. Far from the crowd, a man staggered and stumbled in the direction of the butte. Jogging closer, Mila recognized Falk. Fear and fury fired within her—but a protester charging toward him pulled her attention.

"Pete!" she called.

He lunged, tackling the wounded Falk to the ground. He raised the folded-up tripod over his head and bludgeoned the Hesperian in the face— over and over and over, every brutal blow turning

Mila's panic to horror, then dread, then despair—until Falk lay still.

Her legs pumped as she closed in on Pete, nearly ramming into him. Grabbing him by the shoulders, she shrieked and shook him. "What have you done? What have you done?"

Pete shoved her.

She collapsed to the ground—next to Falk. She wheezed.

"If I'm going to get arrested anyway..." He left the rest unsaid, and walked in the direction of the Belgae.

Mila scrambled to her feet. She looked at Falk, not sure if she truly wanted to see the state of him.

Crimson flowed from his face and head. What skin wasn't covered in blood had already colored into an eggplant-purple bruise. One eye already swelled shut. His lips puffed three times their normal size. Her eyes traveled down his body. The center of his abdomen was stained thick, saturated red. Had someone stabbed him?

As his chest rose and fell in hacking, choppy breaths, her pulse fluttered, sending white-hot vindication through her veins. At his waist, the skull chisel protruded from his belt. She bent and grabbed the object, savoring its roughness. Its power.

There she stood, far from the fray. Poised. Ready to strike the final, fatal blow. No one would know she had ended his life. She'd carry the knowledge—the pride—with her, in secret satisfaction. For seconds, she considered the idea. To plunge this rusted old piece of metal—his own weapon—into his chest. He'd writhe, horror and submission on his face as he died at her hand, the fate he always deserved.

The cool metal chilled her skin, clotting her resolve. She knelt beside him, raising the weapon. *If I have to beat evil at its own game, fine.*

One eye lolled about in Falk's head—then fixated on her. "Your eyes," he said.

She froze, barely able to interpret the gurgles that came from his swollen, blood-filled mouth.

"Like mine." One side of his lips curled out into a nasty smile. "Empty."

Clarity hit her like a cold wind. Everything Falk had done since her arrest—the torture, deceit, the relentless obsession with her—collided together like magnetic dust. She vibrated with awareness.

"Kill you?" His words echoed in her memory. "No. Ruin you."

Shaking, she dropped the weapon into the dust, rising to her feet on wobbly legs. Steeling her gaze, she bent over him. "You're wrong," she said. "You wasted yourself."

He watched her, his one eye flickering in and out of awareness like a candle under a bowl, fighting to stay alive, to watch her watch him die. But she spun toward the Belgae camp, depriving him in his last moments.

The vibration rang through her once again. She shook her head, determined to ignore it, and ran toward the tumult ahead of her. The lights illuminated a dusty-looking cloud hovering over the camp. As she neared it, she saw protesters crying and holding their faces. Mass pepper spray. She squinted and kept running, even as the sting grew in her own eyes. A figure separated from the group—rushing toward her.

"Mila!"

"Julian?" Relieved, she ran to him, clutching him in an embrace. Another vibration—this one definitely outside of her. Pulling away, she looked up at Julian, then to the Walden. Smoke billowed from the building in raging plumes. "What's happening?"

"We have to go—now!"

"I can't abandon them!" Fighting her way out of his grip, she raced toward the Belgae. Arriving at the fringes of the hemorrhaging group, she hardly had a moment to collect her thoughts when a protester charged up to her.

"Please," she blustered, breathless. "How can I help—"

He plunged a knife into her abdomen.

She froze in shock. Everything around her halted and faded. Then—the pain. It seared before growing, radiating, and finally, overtaking her. She stumbled, hanging in infinity. Her eyes rolled upward as the lights, the smoke, the rush of the people swirled into a nauseating pinwheel, spinning, spinning, spinning until her head and body smashed into the ground and it all turned to—

39.

MILA FOUGHT TO OPEN HER EYELIDS, but they wouldn't budge. Lifting one iron-heavy hand, she patted around—what was clipped to her forefinger?—feeling cloth, then her hips, then her stomach. Sore. Padded. A bandage, on her upper right abdomen. The crooks of her arms pulsated from the vinelike tubes coming out of them. She whimpered. The noise scraped in her throat.

A warm hand encased hers. "Mila?" His voice was patient. Or was it tired?

"Mmm," she groaned.

"Squeeze if you understand me."

She squeezed.

"Oh, thank God," he sighed, his breath brushing her cheeks.

She swallowed. Her throat might as well have been silt. Her lips felt like old pottery. For a moment, they fluttered helplessly, but she finally managed, "Water?"

The cold rim of a glass touched her lips. Wetness followed. Drinking eagerly, she welcomed its cool freshness as it puddled over her tongue and washed down her throat. "Where?"

"Tesla," he answered. "In the hospital. It's been twelve hours."

Twelve hours. Since what? Since... Everything flooded back to memory. "News?"

"What?" Julian asked.

"Put on—news."

"Mila, no—"

"News. Please."

He sighed. She heard the high-pitched ringing when the television came on. A female voice filled the room.

"After Belgae members assaulted and murdered an undercover Hesperian official, Victor Falk, Amity officers were in the process of putting a stop to the so-called Insistence—arresting nearly five hundred protesters—when Mother Nature intervened. It's the first time an earthquake has ever been experienced in the Rocky Mountains Region in recent history, and seismologists nationwide are scratching their heads. Here today is Doctor—"

"Off."

The set clicked off.

"Pete?" she asked.

"Arrested."

"Emory?"

"Not sure, but Hesperia found the cellar and raided it several hours ago."

Fresh tears bit her still-closed eyes. "Others?"

"Many had already abandoned ship. Many were arrested. Some peacefully agreed to leave—others bargained for their freedom by giving up their friends."

The hospital bed creaked and swayed along with her cries. Finally, she opened her eyes.

Julian sat beside her on a meager chair. He leaned close, his brow knit in worry, his gaze lifeless with defeat. Brushing her cheek with his thumb, he whispered, "I thought I was too late for you."

"What happened?"

"I chased you when you ran from me, but by the time I got to you, you were"—he swallowed, closed his eyes—"bleeding so badly. Limp. The doctors said if the knife had been any longer, anywhere else." He clenched his jaw. "I carried you as far away as possible. Hesperia spotted me and started after me. Then, the earthquake hit, full-force. Kairos had sent Caide and Elzac hours before, but didn't tell me. They smuggled us back to Colorado and into Tesla. Hesperia believes you're dead."

"Earthquake?"

"I told you Tesla's machine was real." The slightest of smiles ticked in one cheek.

Her mind whirred. She closed her eyes, striving to remember more. Clouds—gray. Smoke. Fire. "The Walden?"

"Burned to the ground."

She searched his face. "How?"

"Tesla's death ray."

"But Kairos—" She stopped as the room began to spin. Her eyelids weighed tons. She had to ask one more question. "Falk?"

"Dead." His voice was full with finality. "Unrecognizably so. Vultures swarmed him before Hesperia could even gather the body."

She grimaced, fighting away the images assaulting her mind. Something welled deep within her, rising, burning, and cleansing as it grew. Lifting her hands, she covered her face and released a deep, guttural wail.

"Mila..." Julian's voice twirled through the air in a mix of sadness and confusion. "I don't understand."

"Sleep," she rasped. "Please."

The chair creaked. His footsteps receded. When she heard the door click shut, she succumbed to the heavy rest of the mourning.

~~~

The people chased her, even in sleep. Their tortured screams, their expressions twisted in anger, the disfigured face of hopes forever dashed. They shook their cuffed fists at her, hurling words like daggers.

"You promised. You lied. You fool! You failed."

Behind the mob, Falk—what remained of him—towered. Even in death, the Victor.

A barn owl flew over the crowds, growing rapidly in size as the crowd shrunk below it.

"Wisdom turned inward," her own voice rang like a knell, "or turned blind."

Suddenly, Trudi floated in, carrying her centerpiece of concentric glass orbs. The barn owl shrank and glided, perching on her shoulder. "Worlds, worlds," she sang. "We live in so many worlds. What do you choose, Mila? What do you choose?" She thrust the centerpiece forward. "Choose."

The orbs encased her—but instead of glass under her feet, they were like bubbles. She scrambled and slipped, falling from the smallest bubble-orb to the largest, and fighting her way back again. Then—they popped.

She fell, screaming, flailing, and landed in the woods.

Natalie appeared. Next to her, Julian. Falk. Chet. Kairos. Worlds collided and words collided, whirling around her in a clanging, confusing shivaree.

"A magician's audience, deceived because they want to be."

"We are born of failed revolutions."

"You are a burden-bearer. A tremendous gift."

"Empty. Like mine."

"To bend the ear of the people, you have to pull their fingers out first."

Finally, her voice echoed louder than all the others, with Natalie's whispering underneath it.

"I can't abandon the people."

"Wisdom."

Everyone melted together like water spilled on a painting. Then came the black.

~~~

A week after her injury, she left the hospital in fresh clothes from Natalie, a shimmering lavender top and sleek black pants. With each hesitant step, the sore spot in her side throbbed as she made her way to the Espionage Department. Voices rumbled behind the conference room door. She entered anyway.

Kairos, standing before the group, stopped in the middle of a sentence. Every head—Elzac, Caide, Moltov, Desmond, Roejo, Anita, Julian, Chet, and Trudi—turned to look at her.

"I came to thank you," she said. "All of you."

Kairos tipped his chin.

"You saved my life, even though I wasn't a part of you. You watched out for the Belgae, and told us when Hesperia knew their plans. You caused the earthquake in order to end the madness. And... you *destroyed* the Walden Data Facility."

"It seemed," the Tesla leader hesitated, "the right thing to do."

"It's against everything you told me," she pressed, a small smile breaking across her face.

He remained silent.

She looked at her feet. Taking a breath, she met the eyes of everyone in the room, saving Julian for last. "I came to say goodbye." Pain and loss pricked her heart. The brokenness in his eyes could not be ignored.

"Forgive me, Mila, but I am confused," said Kairos.

Breaking her gaze from Julian's, she looked at Kairos once more. "Life—the people, the powers, the world—doesn't truly follow the principle of entropy. Order to disorder. It's not so simple as that. To box it all into such a clear-cut concept robs us, because time and history, society, and you and me... we swirl, we ebb and flow, we twist and turn, we fall and we get up again. We hurt each other." Her hand unconsciously went to her wound. "It's not a trajectory, but a tug-of-war. The world above lives in a dark time of history. But they're not hopeless. They're not hopeless because of people like Emory McFallon—because of people like Rigo Laslo, who is flawed, but fighting. They're not hopeless because of people like Helen, the woman I met who runs a shelter for abused women, even though so many of them run back to their abusers. And they're not hopeless because of me." Her voice quieted and cracked. "We have to stand in truth, in peace, even if it means defeat in the short term, and loss in the now. We have to trust that those virtues will win in the end, even if we don't see them triumph in our lifetime." She took a step forward. "I promised the people, Kairos. If the world is a battle of tug-of-war... there is only hope as long as we hold onto the rope. I won't let go."

Not a blink, not a breath. Not a movement flitted across the faces of the Zetetics when she finished. Her stomach sank. She trained her eyes on Julian. "I won't forget you," she promised.

She left the Espionage Department and crossed the atrium. With every step, her heart cracked a little. She loved Julian, but her love flowed like saltwater over her sore soul. The spaces between her fingers seemed ocean-wide without his to fill them. And her spirit, though convinced of her life's direction, felt lost. They occupied the same space at the same time for a while, but they lived in two different worlds. He refused to leave his. She refused to leave hers.

Not even love transcended that.

Mechanical humming filled the air when she arrived at the Tesla train station. Ada's magnetrain zoomed forward, its circular light beaming like the full moon. Mila stepped to the edge. It slowed, stopped. A hiss puffed from its engine as it settled.

Ada leaned out of her conductor's cab. "Didn't I leave you just outside'a Denver?"

"I came back."

"Oh."

"But I have to leave again."

"Oh..."

"It'll be the last time, I assure you."

"Well, I'm certainly sorry to hear that." She slammed something with her fist. The doors of the first train car slid open.

With nothing but the clothes she wore, Mila boarded Ada's train. Turning, she took one last look at Tesla, the Zetetics' headquarters, wishing she could indulge in one more conversation with Julian under the elm tree.

"Goodbye," she mouthed. Goodbye to this unseen world—of shattered dreams made real, of history's downtrodden, of advancement that leapt into the realm of the fantastic, of true freedom. Of isolation.

Maybe she wasn't the one who was truly alone, after all.

The doors slid closed. Ada's voice rang over the intercom. "Where to, m'girl?"

"Can you take me back to New Cockaigne?" She thought of winding dirt roads and broken, forgotten fences—and the old, large Haven House, tucked far away to keep bruised souls safe. "I need to regather myself. Then"—she took a breath—"I think I'll go to Gair."

"Okey doke. I can only help you with the first part." The train whirred. Then, it stopped.

"Is everything okay, Ada?" Mila called.

"I'm sure you'll think so," she answered cryptically. The doors flew open again.

Chet peered in.

Mila struggled to her feet. "Chet?"

He grinned, appearing like a mischievous old gnome with his rosy cheeks and puffy white beard. He held out a thick folder. "Thought you might need a fresh start."

She took the folder and opened it, her eyes scanning the documents containing her new identity. Looking at Chet, she smiled. "Thank Kairos for me."

"Oh, we're not going anywhere. We thought it's high time for change."

"We?"

Trudi joined him in the doorway. Together, the elderly couple shuffled aboard. "Our purpose with the Zetetics is done. It's"—Trudi's voice wobbled—"it's what Dana-Marie would have wanted."

Mila hugged Trudi, then threw her arms around Chet. He patted her back. "I'm so glad I met you, Melinda," he whispered in her ear. Pulling back, he winked. "We'll have such stories to tell!"

Laughter erupted from deep within her belly. Tears blurred her vision. Stepping away from Chet, she rubbed the wetness away, blinked—and froze.

Julian stood in the doorway. Natalie leaned on her walker next to him.

"You came," she said. It's all she allowed herself to say, for fear she'd crumble with joy. Natalie smiled knowingly.

Julian walked to her, his eyes flickering from side to side as he implored hers. Taking her hands in his, he raised them and held them against his chest.

"I spent years running from darkness," he said. "Little did I know, I carried it with me. But you"—his face broke into a wide smile and he laughed, almost nervously—"you are my twin flame. And you lit me up again."

Reaching up, she cupped his face and pulled him close. When their lips met, her countenance burned with the brightness of an entire candelabra.

The doors closed. The magnetrain thrummed with life, with direction. It throttled forward into the night.

Back to the world above.

ACKNOWLEDGMENTS

A few brief thanks...
To my editor, Caroline Smailes.
To my critique group—Linda, Melissa, and Leigh—
for teaching me, encouraging me, and sharpening
me.
To Connie—for your detailed, honest feedback, for
your advice and perspective, and your generosity
with your time.
To my beta readers—Tiffany, Lauren, Ashley, Isaac,
Herb, and Tracy—for not holding back, for
challenging me, and for chiming in far beyond the
beta reader's call of duty as I sent you question
after question while I worked through hurdles.
To Heather—for your creative assistance.
To my husband, Andy—for reading, re-reading,
brainstorming, watching babies, giving me naps,
giving me writing time. For your honesty. For your
endless and complete support. For being my love
and partner, in the deepest, most profound sense
possible. I adore you.

ABOUT THE AUTHOR

Leah Noel Sims lives south of Atlanta with her husband, two children, and German Shepherd. This is her first novel.

FOLLOW THE AUTHOR

@LeahNoelSims
on Facebook, Twitter and Instagram

Website: LeahNoelSims.com

Goodreads.com/LeahNoelSims

61045714R00328

Made in the USA
Lexington, KY
27 February 2017